BROTHERLESS NIGHT

BY V. V. GANESHANANTHAN

Love Marriage

Brotherless Night

BROTHERLESS NIGHT

V. V. GANESHANANTHAN

VIKING
an imprint of
PENGUIN BOOKS

VIKING

UK | USA | Canada | Ireland | Australia
India | New Zealand | South Africa

Viking is part of the Penguin Random House group of companies
whose addresses can be found at global.penguinrandomhouse.com.

First published in the United States of America by Random House, an imprint
and division of Penguin Random House LLC, New York 2023
First published in Great Britain by Viking 2023

001

Printed and bound in Great Britain by Clays Ltd, Elcograf S.p.A.

The authorized representative in the EEA is Penguin Random House Ireland,
Morrison Chambers, 32 Nassau Street, Dublin D02 YH68

A CIP catalogue record for this book is available from the British Library

HARDBACK ISBN: 978-0-241-61104-3
TRADE PAPERBACK ISBN: 978-0-241-61108-1

This project is supported in part by an award from the
National Endowment for the Arts.

www.greenpenguin.co.uk

Penguin Random House is committed to a
sustainable future for our business, our readers
and our planet. This book is made from Forest
Stewardship Council® certified paper.

for my family

THERE IS NO LIFE FOR ME APART FROM MY PEOPLE.

—*Rajani Thiranagama*

HISTORY IS ALSO A CASUALTY OF TERROR.

—*Rajan Hoole*

CONTENTS

PART IV: THE END OF HUNGER

PART V: THE PALACE OF HISTORY

BROTHERLESS NIGHT

PROLOGUE

I RECENTLY SENT A LETTER TO A TERRORIST I USED TO KNOW. He lives near me, here in New York City, and when I opened the envelope and slid in the note that said *I would like to come and see you,* I thought of how much he had always required of me and how little I had ever asked of him. Even when I was growing up in Sri Lanka, before I had ever heard the word *terrorist,* I knew that if a certain kind of person wanted something done, I should comply without asking too many questions. I met a lot of these sorts of people when I was younger because I used to be what you would call a terrorist myself.

We were civilians first. You must understand: that word, *terrorist,* is too simple for the history we have lived—too simple for me, too simple even for this man. How could one word be enough? But I am going to say it anyway, because it is the language you know, and it will help you to understand who we were, what we were called, and who we have truly become.

We begin with this word. But I promise that you will come to see that it cannot contain everything that has happened. Someday the story will begin with the word *civilian,* the word *home.* And while I am no longer the version of myself who met with terrorists every day, I also want you to understand that when I was that woman, when two terrorists encountered each other in my world, what they said first was simply hello. Like any two people you might know or love.

PART I
A NEAR-INVISIBLE SCAR

1.

The Boys with the Jaffna Eyes

———

JAFFNA, 1981

MET THE FIRST TERRORIST I KNEW WHEN HE WAS DECIDING TO become one. K and his family lived down the road from me and mine, in one village of the Tamil town called Jaffna, in Sri Lanka. The Jaffna peninsula is the northernmost part of the country. Many people have died there: some killed by the Sri Lankan Army and the state, some by the Indian Peace Keeping Force, and some by the Tamil separatists, whom you know as the terrorists. Many people, of course, have also lived.

In early 1981, I was almost sixteen years old. I already wanted to become a doctor like my grandfather, and I had recently begun attending my brothers' school, where girls my age were accepted for Advanced Level studies. In those days, I thought mostly about the university entrance exams. K, too, dreamed of medical school. And this was what made us alike, long before K chose the movement, long before I treated patients in a New York City emergency room. Long before we became so different.

K had the upper hand from the first, not because he was one year older, or a boy, but because I was his patient. Our meeting was both gruesome and fortunate for me. On the day that we met, I was boiling water for tea. I had to use a piece of cloth to hold the pot's metal handle. But that morning the cloth slipped, the handle slipped, and the pot slipped, pouring scalding water all over me. I screamed and screamed for my mother—*Amma!* My shrill voice carried out onto the road, where K was passing. Letting his bicycle fall in the dirt at our gate, he ran inside.

By the time he reached me in the kitchen at the back of the house, Amma had already found me. As bubbles rose and popped on my skin, I shut my eyes, but I could hear her sobbing, and the sounds of pots and pans clattering to the floor. With every clang, heat flared around and inside me. Under my skin, another skin burned. I cried and called for Murugan, Pillaiyar, Shiva.

"Sashi!" he said, and I opened my eyes to his face without recognising it. "Sit!" he said, and pointed to a chair. When I kept screaming but did not move, he grabbed my hands, pushed me down into the chair, and peeled my blouse up, baring my scorched stomach. I heard Amma's *aiyo!* beside me as though she were speaking from a great distance. Snatching a bowl of eggs off the table, K began cracking them onto the wounds.

"I have to fetch water—" Amma said. Clutching a pan, she tried to move past him.

But he put his shoulders between her and the doorway. "This will cool the burn," he said.

She stood there uselessly. I stared at him, trying to focus on anything but the pain, and saw only his thumbs working in and out of the eggshells, scraping the slime of the whites cleanly onto the swelling rawness. He did it very swiftly, as though he had had a lot of practise, as though every scrap of egg was precious. My skin was so hot that even now, when I remember those quick and clever hands and the slippery shock of relief, I cannot quite believe that the eggs did not just cook on my flesh.

When the last one was cracked and steaming on my skin, K looked up at Amma. "Are there more?" She did not respond, still stunned. "More eggs?" he said. She blinked, then nodded. "Good—keep covering the burn. I'll go for the doctor—"

When K returned with the physician half an hour later, the older man looked over the makeshift dressing with approval. "It should heal," he said. "You may not even have a scar. My own mother used to crack eggs onto burns. This is not the kind of medicine they teach in school. Whose idea was it?"

K glanced at me without saying anything. I crackled inside still.

"I didn't know what to do," Amma said softly.

"His idea," I said.

So I began as K's patient, though he ended as mine.

SO MANY FOODS REMIND me of K now.

When he came to visit me a few days after the accident, his aunt Neelo came with him, bearing my favourite maampazham—mangoes—and vaazhaipazham, the special small, sweet bananas that grew in their yard. My mother must have mentioned that I liked them. The fruit pleased me, but for once, I felt more interested in the boy, who until this moment had belonged more to my brothers than to me. I tried to examine him without being too obvious. His shirt was tucked unevenly into his trousers, which were too large. He looked sturdy, but not skinny, and had a rim of hair on his upper lip that was not quite a moustache. It barely showed—he was dark from the sun. Thick, black-framed spectacles dominated his thin, sensitive face. He wiped them carefully with a handkerchief so worn it was nearly transparent. I did not know then that it had belonged to his late mother.

He replaced his spectacles, and when I realised that he was studying me with equal intensity I looked away. Everyone always spoke about how clever K was and what an excellent physician he would be. But those people were only speculating. I knew absolutely, with an indebtedness that ran through my body, and I felt both envy and something else that confused me. The thick lenses distorted his eyes, but it was too late; I already knew they were lovely and old, full of a certainty that appealed to me. I wanted that certainty for myself, to be someone who could look at burned flesh and then touch it.

K looked over at my mother and his aunt, who were deep in conversation, and then back at me.

"How are you feeling?" he asked.

"I feel better. But it itches," I said, plucking at my blouse. My mother had given me the oldest, most worn dress she had, and still, every time the fabric touched my skin, I hurt. "I also want to do medicine. How did you know what to do?"

He shrugged. "It made sense, even though it wasn't modern. The protein and fat soothe the burn."

Out of habit, I rubbed at the wound. "Had you ever treated some—"

He leaned forward abruptly and put his hand over mine. "Don't scratch it—you'll scar," he said. After a moment, he let his fingers fall away. I looked over at my mother and his aunt, who were still talking. I moved my hand from my stomach, and we sat in silence.

"Are your brothers here?" he asked finally.

They weren't, and we sat quietly until Neelo Aunty came to collect him. He bid me goodbye with a formal face. "Good luck with your studies," he said impersonally, as though his hands had never touched me.

So we were not friends at first, although he had already been more intimate with me than any other boy I had known.

When I was well enough to return to school, I walked stiffly through the green of our campus, looking for him. My torso was bandaged and schoolgirl-uniformed, the pain appropriately dressed and private again. As I walked, I laid my hand gently over the hurt to make sure it was still there. The burn matched my pulse in its throbbing, already on its way to becoming a near-invisible scar. He was the only other person there who had seen my injury—even my brothers had not—and I felt that he knew some indecent, vital secret that I needed to confirm. But although I looked for him in the sea of faces, he was nowhere to be found.

When we did meet again, some time later at the temple in our village, his moustache appeared slightly more successful. He glanced at my belly, where one of my mother's old sari blouses covered smaller bandages. I lowered my arm across my body and looked away. Standing with my brothers in the line of men waiting to be blessed, K did not seem unusual. You would have thought him just one of many dark men with white smiles. And, you know, you would have been wrong.

LET ME TELL YOU about dark men with white smiles, these Tamil men I loved and who belonged with me. In my house there were four of them. Each of my brothers resembled my father in a different way. All of them had what some people call Jaffna eyes—dark and piercing. If you have seen such eyes, you will know what I mean.

Niranjan, my steady, sturdy oldest brother, had Appa's clear, straightforward smile, hooked nose, and thick hair. That year, Periannai, as he was called because he was the eldest brother, turned twenty-five. He had almost finished studying medicine at the University of Peradeniya, a too-long train ride away from us. Quiet, pleasant Dayalan, who was nineteen and the tallest among us, worked at the Jaffna Public Library and took classes while he waited to matriculate. He was mathematically minded but, unusually for someone pursuing engineering, also loved to read. He always carried a novel with him; as he finished each one, he passed it to me, in the same fashion Niranjan had given me his science textbooks. When he was not studying or reading, Dayalan spent hours tinkering with his bicycle, which he had assembled himself, from spare parts gathered around town. He might have been my father's shadow, so closely did his tall and solid build resemble Appa's. When Dayalan came home from work or class and stood in the doorway, Amma always looked at him a moment too long, and I wondered what she was thinking. Seelan, my hot-tempered, popular, bright third brother, was one year ahead of me, and in K's class. Like my father, he loved music and, in a good mood, could charm anyone. He was in his second year of preparing for Advanced Levels, the university entrance exams. And my youngest brother, Aran, the only one younger than me, was a skinny, precocious thirteen. He talked like

Appa, very reasonably, so that he seemed far older than he was, although he was only preparing for his Ordinary Levels.

If my brothers walked down our lane with K, as they often did, they were just five Tamil boys, capable of anything—wily pranks, endearing sweetness. But if you were not one of us, if you did not care to look closely, the five men who robbed a bank in March of the same year that I met K might have looked like any of them. Perhaps the five robbers, too, seemed capable of anything; they were the beginning of the Liberation Tigers of Tamil Eelam, the Tamil Tigers, and among them was the Tiger leader, Prabhakaran, who had already murdered the mayor of Jaffna, although he had not yet claimed responsibility.

Appa, who was a surveyor for the government, travelled around the country to different postings, and came home only when he was given leave, so when he heard about the robbery he wrote and told Amma to take all of her jewellery out of the bank and hide it at home. When she got his letter, I could hear her crying from my room all the way down the hall. I got out of bed to talk to her, thought better of it, and lay back down.

"But why does Appa want her to hide the jewellery?" I asked Seelan, who was trying to sleep in the bed across from me.

"What?" he asked, his voice muffled by his pillow. Periannai had come home from university on weekend holiday and taken a bed. After a flurry of rearranging, Seelan had come to bunk with me. The close quarters made us short with each other.

"Why does he want her to take the jewellery from the bank?" I asked.

"These fellows are stealing. Of course Appa doesn't want to leave it there."

"What about the money in the bank?"

"The jewellery is harder to replace. And he has some money here in the house too. But Amma wants to think everything is all right."

"Do you think it's going to be all right?"

Seelan rolled over again without answering, and, feeling foolish, I did not press him. A few minutes passed before I could hear him snoring. Niranjan had gone to an international conference on Tamil language and culture in Jaffna proper several years earlier. Policemen had fired into the audience, and some of his friends had gotten hurt. Niranjan had come home stained bloody and silent and thoughtful. Days later, I saw him pull *Emergency '58,* the old bestseller about the 1958 anti-Tamil riots, from the shelf in Appa's study. When I wanted to take the next turn reading, Periannai shook his head. "Not yet," he said. "When?" I asked. He had already turned away. Whatever he was thinking about, he didn't plan to share it with his nine-year-old sister. But Seelan, only one year older than me, didn't wait for permission, or even for Niranjan to be done—he took the book from Periannai's desk. When my father realised what Seelan was reading, he tried to reclaim it, but Seelan would neither relinquish *Emergency '58* nor talk about its contents. When he was finished, he glowered as he handed it back to Niranjan. Periannai, who had not attempted to stop Seelan, gave him a long, measured look. "Did you learn what you wanted to learn, thaambi?" he asked. "Enough, Periannai," Seelan said. "More than enough about the government."

At sixteen, I still hadn't touched *Emergency '58,* but I knew it was a brutal testimony to Sri Lanka's willingness to slaughter its own Tamil citizens. My father's slim, battered copy of the book had taken on the aura of something forbidden and terrifying. Did I need to read it to know that because we were ethnic minorities, Tamils were considered expendable? I didn't know how old one needed to be to read the whole of a violent story. I didn't know if the whole of any violent story could be told. I did faithfully read the newspapers, which quoted Tamil political leaders saying that any move for a separate homeland in the northern part of the country would not be violent. The party my father supported had adopted a resolution saying exactly that the previous year—Tamils would work for a separate state in the north and east of the country peacefully, like the Gandhians, whom we admired. But we could no longer bear the discrimination of a government dominated by the majority Sinhalese, the Tamil politicians declared: no more second-class status for our language, double standards and quotas for Tamil students, government-run Sinhala colonization schemes in traditionally Tamil areas, no more government-fomented anti-Tamil violence. The 1958 riots had taken place ten years after the British left, and the riots of my childhood, well into the years of independence, had also been vicious. But I knew that when Appa listened to Tamil politicians argue about the right path to self-determination, their incompetence and inconsistency worried him. When he went to postings in other parts of the country, he kept his own counsel, but at home, he often vented his feelings to Niranjan, Dayalan, or my mother. "These fellows would say anything to help themselves," he said darkly. I was never sure whether my mother was listening to him or not; she silently went on with her daily tasks: chopping vegetables, washing dishes, and sweeping up the cigarette ash he dropped as he pounded his fists.

Other empires had reached for Sri Lanka: the Dutch, the Portuguese, and the British had seized and relinquished it in succession, leaving in their wake peoples divided by colonial powers, ancestral angers, and bullheaded pride. Long before I was born, Sri-Lanka-then-Ceylon stumbled once more into a lazy, self-indulgent independence: the majority Sinhalese, smarting at slights perceived and actual, discovered ways for the country to promote their Buddha, their language, and their histories—a comeuppance for us, for Tamils, who were a minority, and who had flourished in English. Learn Sinhalese, or leave your job, Tamil civil servants were told—my father among them. I still haven't forgotten the look on his face when he told us.

Appa was lucky—unlike us, when he had gone to school in Jaffna, he had studied Sinhala and had several Sinhalese friends, and he still spoke the language fluently. But when Sinhala had become the only official government language, several years after the British left and well before I was born, the schools in Jaffna had stopped teaching Sinhala in protest. Now the language of instruction was Tamil; although I spoke excellent English, I could not say a word in Sinhala. My future depended on a language I did not know, no one wanted to teach me, and, on principle, I did not want to learn.

None of us, of course, liked to be told what to do. But we had also seen enough to know the costs of that. When I was ten, some of Niranjan's friends had disappeared after protesting the changes in national university admissions that restricted the number of Tamils that could enter. I knew they had been putting up posters—Amma had forbidden Periannai to join them. They were imprisoned for two years with no explanation. Three years ago, when they were released, crowds turned out to see them return. But as far as I could see, their status as heroes had not gotten them much. They had not gone to university. They were clerks now, or unemployed.

They were not the only ones caught in the sights of the authorities. The police had begun to stop my older brothers and their friends on their bicycles, which were known to be the preferred method of transportation for Tamil militants and their supporters. But bicycles were the preferred method of transportation for almost all the boys in Jaffna—and most of the girls too. Since no one thought that girls were joining the movement, I could ride mine to and from school and sometimes to the market, where I did errands for my mother. But after that first bank robbery, after my mother retrieved her jewellery from the bank, Appa decreed that my brothers were to put their bicycles away.

THAT YEAR, SEELAN AND K studied for Advanced Levels together. On weekend mornings, they went to tuition classes for students in their year; then they came home and had lunch, at K's house or at ours, and went to the Jaffna Public Library to continue. I wanted to go with them in the afternoons, but could not bring myself to ask. K and I were studying the same four subjects—botany, zoology, chemistry, and physics—and I, too, needed to prepare if I was to have any hope of entering medicine. Proud and shy, I sat on the veranda and watched them leave rather than saying anything. On the first day, Amma saw me observing them and laughed gently. After they left, she set me up at Appa's desk, and I studied alone, drinking the cups of sugary tea she brought me. "Here, kunju," she said to me, setting a fresh one down. "You'll do as well as them."

By the third weekend, I was buried in my notes and resigned to my exclusion. But something had changed for my brother. "Well, come on," Seelan said impatiently from the front steps that Saturday morning, as I lingered on the veranda.

I stared at him, confused.

"Are you ready?" K asked.

He had come to the gate and was waiting, I realised, for both of us. K grinned up at Seelan, and then, at an angle, at me. The glare of the sun hid his eyes behind his spectacles. He took them off and wiped them. Good luck with your studies, he had said. Perhaps he meant it.

I was careful to keep Seelan between me and K.

The walk was a hot, dusty three-quarters of an hour—long, without bicycles, but they had vowed to walk, and they kept their word. I found I didn't mind too much. The weekend commute to and from the library gave us a chance to stop and talk with people we knew, to talk to each other, to think over the questions that were beginning to form in our minds. At first I just listened to the two of them talk and banter— Did you hear that record? Can you believe what happened in Muttiah Master's class? Did you know the captain of the other school's cricket team? Thank goodness we get a fresh frog for each dissection—but then I began to ask questions. What were the tuition classes like? They talked about their teacher, a slightly older man who had just graduated from the university. They imitated him, laughing, gesturing at each other wildly and lowering their brows as though they were giving great speeches, and I laughed too, but it was clear how much they respected and liked him. Whoever he was, he talked to them about politics in a way they wished their fathers and teachers would. They wanted to be taken seriously. Oh, how seriously I took K. I almost told him so. What kind of medicine did he want to do? Cardiology, he explained. His slim, elegant fingers sketched the shape of a heart in the air, and mine leapt with interest. And you? he asked. I want to be like my grandfather, I said, helping anyone who needs it. *First do no harm,* I quoted. I said nothing about the ways in which my Paata had bent and broken rules to aid his patients. Who knew what K would think of such a thing? He turned then to my brother. What did Seelan want to do as an engineer? My brother spoke of bridges, how they were constructed to keep us safe, how precarious they could be, the physics of keeping them aloft. K made him explain and explain again and finally shook his head. "Some people think I'm clever, but I don't have a maths brain like yours, machan," he said. Mathematics was not my brother's only talent; one morning, Seelan began to sing under his breath, and that was when I learned he had been listening to music at the house of another classmate. He hummed the same melody—Bob Marley's "Redemption Song"—so often I learned it too and sang it back at him. Once, as I did, I turned to see K's eyes trained on me. He smiled and shrugged slightly. "You have a beautiful voice," he admitted, sounding surprised.

Everything felt like music in that month of beautiful walks. During that time, I realised how little I had known my brother, and how much I wanted to know his friend. When we arrived at the library, I separated from them and took to my own nearby desk, where I could hear them talking over their work, which was slightly more advanced than mine. Although sometimes I wondered if K was purposely discussing his lesson loudly enough for me to overhear, again, I did not dare to ask. And when we returned to the lane, K went his way, and my brother and I retreated to our house, where we fell back into our usual relationship. Seelan's brief congeniality evaporated; I was once again just an inconvenient sister. My disappointment at these moments washed over me like a familiar cold wind. The walks existed in a separate world, a world between the Jaffna Public Library and our house— a place K had somehow brought into being.

These days, I wish I had told Seelan how much I loved those interludes, how much I longed to bring their feeling into our house. Back then, I did not want him to realise the time was something he had given me, because then he could take it away. I had never gotten along as well with Seelan as I had with my other brothers, perhaps because of the closeness in our ages, or perhaps because I resented how masculinity and charm kept him from being accountable for the things he said and did. Of the five of us, he was the most jealous, the most possessive. He had the sharpest temper, at least at home. But he was also the wittiest,.the one who knew the news from far away, the one, who had heard the newest music and whose friends swarmed wherever he went. He was popular with his batchmates because of his public charm and athleticism, but another part of his appeal was his wild cleverness. And as he was reckless with his intelligence, I guarded mine. We were nearly twins, but our temperaments were so different. Seelan and I had never had that much to talk about, or so I had thought. On those walks, I discovered that I liked my brother. Seelan was quick to anger, but how could I not love him when that anger was so frequently over our imperilled futures? Still, while my other brothers and I were easy with our affection, Seelan and I were not. Now I found myself shy around him for another reason: he was—and I had made him—the person between me and K.

I distracted myself with the textbooks I had inherited from Niranjan and the classes required to enter medical school. In each subject, we braced ourselves to be tested twice, with theoretical and practical exams. On paper, I felt safe and ready, but we considered the practical exams dangerous, as they were dependent on the whims of mercurial examiners. For physics, you might have to prove Boyle's law, or Charles's law, or Dalton's law. For chemistry, you were given a substance and asked to identify or make it: How do you mix hydrogen peroxide or prepare hydrochloric acid? Biology was divided in two: botany and zoology. For botany, we were asked to use a microscope to name a plant specimen on a slide. While I respected the students who— like my brother—excelled at physics, I found it dull. Chemistry and botany struck me as more useful and interesting. I liked the idea of being able to heal with some plants and substances and protect myself from others; I liked to walk through familiar spaces and recite the Latin names of their flowers. And zoology I loved.

I feared the practical exams, but the zoology test excited me too. Give me a knife, I thought; give me a pattern I can trace and memorise and adapt to different bodies. We all quietly idolised the stern, balding zoology teacher, who trained us in the required dissections. He had gone to school with my father, and his name was Rajan Master. We called him Sir.

Sir was famous for sending students on to medical school. He spoke often and with fondness about those he had taught, many of whom had gone on to become prominent physicians. Some had even emigrated. The doctor he talked about most often and most admiringly, however, was not only a former student but also his niece, and the only woman on the medical faculty at the University of Jaffna. I had dreamed of going there since it had opened when I was nine, and listened to his stories hungrily. Anjali Premachandran taught anatomy, and, he warned, she was far stricter than him. She loved dissections, he claimed. Ours was a small town, and many of us already knew Dr. Premachandran from a distance. It seemed impossible that she had ever studied in our classroom, but we liked imagining her at our age. If we wanted to impress her, we understood, we would have to impress him first.

Sir handed us diagrams and made us memorise them well enough to redraw them without looking. Only when we knew them cold did he bestow blades. Eager and quick with my scalpel, I caught his attention and he warned me, bemused, that I was not a surgeon yet and, if I did not learn patience, might never be. "Take your time with the body, young lady," Sir advised. "Look how artful the mechanisms of living." Even after decades of teaching, he still sounded awed. Guided by his eye, I, too, marvelled at the lacework of veins and the soft, fragile balloons of tiny mammalian lungs.

During the final practical exam, Sir informed us, we would receive a frog, a cockroach, a rat, or the head of a small shark to dissect. We would practise with the same. If the frog, then you would have to open its chest cavity and show its major organs; if the rat, then you would need to display the heart and cardiovascular system. The cockroach, inconveniently small, required not only mounting on wax but also washing; if you opened the lab tap too forcefully, you might wash away your entire carefully separated insect, and Sir would show you no mercy. You were permitted unlimited cockroaches, and even the indulgence of a fresh frog every time, but the heads of small sharks were precious and rationed one to a student, to be kept pristine in formalin when not in use. We were competitive enough that when the girl next to me found her shark head missing one day, I had no idea who to suspect; any of my classmates might have done it. "If I had spent more time practising, I would be able to identify mine," Tharini wailed. "I ought to recognise it."

I hated the formaldehyde smell, which nauseated me and followed me home, but on principle, I refused to complain or ask for any kind of indulgence during these lessons. Becoming accustomed to the medicinal scents was part of the training, I realised only later. And of the required specimens, the shark, of course, was the most difficult; you had to separate and display its intricate nervous system. If you fouled up, you had to practise with the dainty, ruined head, its malevolent eye staring at you balefully for the rest of the term. If you failed to bathe it in the formalin solution every time, its flesh might cross the precipitous border into decay.

The level of attention required was exhausting and exhilarating. When—giddy with new knowledge and equally horrified by the very real possibility of eventual failure—I occasionally lamented my situation, Amma reminded me of family legend: Paata. In my grandfather's time as a student, she told me, university entrance had required not only theoretical and practical exams but also interviews; the interviewers could ask you anything they liked and were known to be capricious and cruel. ("Yet another habit inherited from the British," my father would have said ruefully.) Paata—then only young Thanabalasingham—had had to travel all the way to Colombo for his appointment. There, the interviewer, a Tamil professor, asked him only one question: to describe the shape of a dagoba, a Buddhist temple. Startled, Bala, a Jaffna boy who had never been to a dagoba, fumbled his answer. He returned to Jaffna despondent and almost missed the cutoff to enter medicine. "These exams used to be difficult," Amma said encouragingly. "But they have never been easier than they will be for you." This might have been true, but I did not find it reassuring.

I had more than a year left before my exams, but in one of his letters home Appa had advised me not to delay preparing. *If you want to become a doctor,* he wrote, *studying is now and always.* A choir of ancestors rose behind him, urging me on with fear, guilt, and ambition: Think of what your grandfather would have said, what your late aunt would have advised, remember your uncle who never got the chance to go to university! How many Tamil fathers had said such things to their daughters? Appa's letter came, as his notes always did, on the mail train, and Amma read it out to me, slowing down at *now and always.*

And so, in the mornings, K and Seelan went to tuition classes, and I went to practise my dissections; in the afternoons, all three of us went to the library to review notes for the theoretical exams. There, in the room across from us, where he had been shelving books since the very early morning, Dayalan observed the three of us and said nothing.

EVERYTHING WAS QUIET AND happy. Then, one weekend late in May, my father came home for a holiday between postings. We were all so eager to spend time with him that we lingered around the house rather than going about our usual routines. I was disappointed to miss the library walk, but content in my father's proximity. Appa was popular locally, though, and kept leaving for brief cups of tea with the neighbour, this relation and that relation. That Sunday afternoon he was visiting Saras Aunty and Jega Uncle, who lived four doors down, when Seelan and Aran came and found me reading in his study. They beckoned me over. I got up from the desk, which I had borrowed and spread with my papers.

I looked at their faces, their folded mouths turned envelopes of worry. "Tell me," I said.

Aran lifted a finger to his lips, then bent his head and murmured to me. "We've just heard on the radio—two men on bicycles, and one of them shot a politician in Jaffna town. And they rode off."

"Dayalan's bicycle is gone," Seelan said.

Panic rushed into me. Wetness pooled under my arms and at my neck.

"If he's cycling around, they could even be just arresting anyone on a bicycle," Aran said.

"Do Amma and Appa know?"

"No," Seelan said. "And don't tell them."

After they slipped back out, I tried to return to studying, but I could not concentrate. In the courtyard the breeze moved gently; I could hear the plants rustling and the neighbourhood dog snoring peacefully. I felt hotter than I usually did in Appa's study, the coolest room of the house. I got up to get a glass of water and realised that Amma was standing in the doorway.

"Are you feeling ill?" she asked me, reaching out to put her hand on my forehand. "You look flushed."

I slipped under her hand and into the corridor behind her. She turned to look at me, surprised.

"I'm fine, Amma," I said. I forced a small laugh. "What a lot of pages I have left to read. It's awfully hot in there. I'll just drink some water."

"All right," she said. "Food is ready. Is Dayalan back yet?"

"I don't think so," I said. "He probably had to work late at the library." New to the habit of lying to my mother, I found my tongue stuck thick and dry in my mouth.

Dayalan did not come. Amma kept the food covered on the back veranda for hours. She read the newspaper, waiting patiently. When it was nine o'clock, Seelan went to ask if she wanted to eat.

She looked up absently at the question. "I'll wait for Dayalan and for your Appa," Amma said. "You go ahead."

In my worry for my brother I had failed to notice that Appa had not returned either. I was not the only one growing more nervous. When Amma urged us to eat, Aran shook his head uncomfortably.

Amma put the newspaper down then and looked at him sharply. "Aran," Amma said. "Do you know where Dayalan is?"

"No," Seelan answered for him, too quickly.

My mother looked at the three of us, arrayed there before her with our perfect, masked faces. She got up from the veranda and went into her bedroom. She brought the radio out and turned it on. We stood there, listening with her for a few minutes until the newscast began. Just as the voice on the radio was saying, "—policeman was attacked today in Jaffna town. A young man on a bicycle, believed to be part of the Tamil—" my father came in.

Appa looked around at all of us. "You've heard," he said. "Someone just rang Jega's house."

Amma motioned for him to be quiet.

"—man and two others—police are in pur—" the voice continued.

Appa reached out and turned the radio off. Amma looked at him.

"What is it?" she asked.

Aran glanced at Seelan for permission. Seelan nodded at him, but Appa spoke first.

"Dayalan's bicycle is gone."

Amma blanched. "He couldn't have ridden the bicycle. We told him. Some thief must have come and taken it."

"The bicycles are by the back gate. Nobody would have stolen it," Appa said. "He must have been late this morning and taken it. Did any of you see him leave on the bicycle?"

"Appa, it's all right," Seelan said. "He can just leave the bicycle at the library and walk. Or take the bus."

"He'll have been working all day," I said. "He won't have been listening to the radio. He won't know."

Seelan gave me a hard look. Amma and Appa did not need my help to worry.

"I'm sure he's fine, Amma," Aran said.

"He's never been so late," Amma said. "Can you go back and find out what's happened to him?" Jega Uncle and Saras Aunty were the only ones on the lane with a phone.

"He must be on the way home. We have to wait and see," Appa said.

"I think we should eat," Seelan said. "I'm hungry."

"I'm not," Amma said.

She went to Saras Aunty's and called the library, but there was no answer. When she came back, she took the radio into Appa's study. As the rest of us had dinner without her on the back veranda, we could hear the voice of the newscaster over the whir of the fan. I filled my mouth with rice and fried fish and made myself swallow. Appa and Aran traced their fingers around their plates. Only Seelan ate with his usual appetite. I wished Niranjan were at home rather than at university; he would have known what to say.

Later I took Amma a cup of tea, but she would not drink it.

"Thank you, kunju." Her eyes, which were fixed on the ceiling, refocused on me for a moment. "When Dayalan comes home——" she said.

"When he comes home, he's really going to hear it," Appa said from behind me. He frowned, pushed a button on the turntable, and then lifted the needle into the groove of a record. "Don't worry," he said to my mother as the scratchy arpeggio of the music unfurled itself. She lifted her head to meet his eyes, which were full of reassurance for her. It was a look so private and intense I wondered if they had forgotten I was there. "Don't worry," he said again, and then: "I promise you he's safe."

Even then, I recognised that he couldn't have known that. But I forgave him, because it was such an authoritative, fatherly declaration: he was hoping, even if he was also lying.

AMMA, WHO BY THEN was resting in my parents' bedroom with the radio on and the fan turning above her, heard the noise at the door first, although she was the farthest away from it. Mothers, with their ears like cats. I heard her quick bare feet padding on the floor and swung my own legs out of bed.

When I went out into the hall, Seelan and Aran were standing there too. Amma squatted next to Dayalan, who sat with his long back propped up against the inside of our front door. My father stood over them both. My mother made a sound like desperate gasping for air and I realised she was crying.

"Thank God," she said, touching Dayalan's dusty face. "Thank God. Thank God."

My father did not or could not say anything. Dayalan looked so much like him, with his stooped shoulders and long legs.

"Lock the door," Dayalan said.

I reached out and locked it and then I knelt on the floor next to Amma, next to him. I laid my hand on his shoulder and pressed my face into his neck, and his shirt felt gritty with dirt. It was not the sort of dirt a boy got from riding a bicycle. He was damp with sweat and mud and he smelled like the dogs that wandered along the roadsides. I wanted Dayalan to put his arm around me, but he could not, so I put my arms around him instead. Even his eyelashes were dusty.

"What happened?" Seelan asked from behind me.

"It wasn't me," Dayalan said, and my father sighed.

"Of course it wasn't you," Appa said. "But that doesn't matter to them." He wiped his face with his handkerchief.

"I didn't even know about what had happened until I was halfway home," Dayalan said. "Then I saw K running home from his tuition class."

"Running," Seelan repeated. He passed Dayalan water.

Pushing me away gently, Dayalan took the tumbler and drank. He trickled some of the water over his hands and wiped his fingertips over his eyes. "Yes, he's so well known as a good student, his father must have thought—he only rides it to and from class. He must have thought that no one was going to stop him."

"That was foolish," Appa said, his voice harsh.

"So they stopped him," Amma prompted. "And?"

"He was just outside his tutor's house when some policemen came up to him and asked to see his identity card," Dayalan said. "And he didn't know why, and they shouted at him and told him that a cyclist had shot someone. They kept him for almost an hour and threatened him with all sorts of things. The tutor came out to defend him and got beaten, and then K got beaten as well. Finally the policemen let them both go. K left the bicycle at his tutor's house and started to walk home.

"I ran into him partway, and he yelled at me and waved his hands for me to stop. I didn't recognise him at first, his face was so—but then I realised it was him, and I got down. He told me what the policemen had said. He wanted me to leave the bicycle right then and there. I didn't want to do it—I need that bicycle! for someday, Appa, when they stop being suspicious of every boy on a bicycle. But he convinced me that it would be worse to be stopped.

"I was going to remove one of the wheels to prevent anyone taking it, but there wasn't time," Dayalan said. "So I left it."

My father was silent.

"I should have listened to you," Dayalan said. He put his head into his hands. "What is going to happen to us?"

Appa bent and put his hand on Dayalan's other shoulder. "It's just a bicycle," he said gently. "A bicycle we can afford."

It's you, my brother: you we can't lose.

THE NEXT MORNING, WHILE I washed Dayalan's grimy clothes, he came out of the house and watched me. Soapy, muddy water flowed between my fingers as I worked. "I hid in a ditch," he said at last. "I could hear the police talking above me. I had to wait a long time for them to go."

I rinsed. "What happened?" I addressed the wet fabric I was holding, and then draped it over the line strung across the garden.

"After a while I was able to get up and keep moving," he said. "But then a kilometre later it happened again."

He told me how he had made his way in this fashion, by fits and starts, occasionally catching a glimpse of a fellow traveller in the nearby shadows. At one point, he said, he dove into a roadside trench next to a field, only to find it already occupied by another boy who wanted no company. "I had to insist," Dayalan said, looking down and away, and I could not help but speculate about how the biggest and gentlest of my brothers had insisted.

By the time he and his reluctant companion left their sodden hide-out, it was almost dark. The other boy was gone before disoriented Dayalan had even figured out which way was north. For the first time, he said, he felt lost in Jaffna. He took off his shirt and wrung out the mud and put back on. He searched the vanishing horizon, looking for anything familiar.

"What led you in the right direction?" I asked. I hung his trousers on the line.

"Nothing," he said. "Finally I thought that I would never move again unless I guessed the way home. So that was what I did."

THAT AFTERNOON, AS HIS clean clothes drip-dried, Dayalan re-turned to the place where he had left the bicycle. It was gone. Once he told us, none of us mentioned it again, but even Seelan went out of his way to share things. The two of them took polite, cautious turns rid-ing Seelan's bicycle in circles glumly on the road in front of our house. They never went farther, as though the whole world had shrunk to the boundaries of our small lane. Worried about Dayalan, Appa managed to delay his return to work, but his presence in the house was no longer comforting. Even he seemed uncertain.

The day after that, K came over. He walked tentatively, picking his way down the road. Now I realise he was walking that way because every step hurt. It was probably the first time he had been injured like that, and he wore a look of faint, violated surprise. His thin, sensitive face looked naked without his spectacles and I wondered if they had been broken. A string of dark bruises ran along his left cheekbone and temple, both of which were swollen; his ear was bandaged, and he held his arms stiffly, as though his shoulders and back ached. When he came into the house, he avoided my eyes and went into Appa's study with Dayalan and Seelan. I flinched at the sound of the door closing against me. When I turned around, I saw Aran behind me, watching too. When his eyes caught mine, he inclined his head as if to say, Yes, I also want to know.

Dayalan missed work that Monday and Tuesday, but by Wednesday he insisted on returning to his tuition classes and to the library. Although he went about his usual routine, he moved absentmindedly and he was even quieter than usual; he carried a novel with him, but the bookmark did not advance. Amma's eyes said: Sashi, make Dayalan a cup of tea; pass him a piece of cake; cook his favourite curries; love him harder in his disappointment, which is not his fault. So I did. When I borrowed a book from a friend and enjoyed it, I left it on his bed. Amma invited his batchmates to lunch. K came over and sat by him quietly while Seelan and Aran played carom.

"This is all going to get worse," Aran predicted, his eyes owlish over the newspaper.

He was right, I suspected. The United National Party, the president's party, had sent Sinhalese police to Jaffna. The official reason was election security, but everyone knew they were there to make sure that the District Development Council elections, to be held in early June, favoured them. Who knew what they would do? Stuff the ballot boxes, probably, or try to prevent people from voting. Appa thought the councils were a farce, but still, we had the right to vote. I swallowed my useless anger. Every day the week after Dayalan lost his bicycle, I went to school, and every day that week the girls walked home in clusters, the thickening police presence making us cautious. The shops and roads slowed subtly; people thought they were being watched, and behaved accordingly. Neelo Aunty had debated whether or not to let K go to school, given that he could not hide his damaged face. They had come over to our house and argued about it, with my father mediating like a judge. "It will be like announcing that they should question you," Neelo Aunty had told K. "You should go to the doctor," she said. "I don't go to the doctor," he had replied. "I am the doctor." The declaration was so nearly a prayer that she had given in.

And so the whole town held its breath. When it was announced that the Tamil United Liberation Front was going to hold a party rally the following Sunday, Amma sighed. "No need for this," she said grumpily. "Politics this, politics that—all the time. Politics politics, enough politics. Everyone stay home and mind your business."

"Politics is my business, Amma," Seelan said. "If it's not our business, our lives, whose is it?"

"Yes," Dayalan said quietly. "I also want to go."

"We can go," my father said, but his voice tilted upward into doubt. I think it was hard for him to say no to anything that made my brother's face brighten. But as the days passed and things became more and more tense in town, I could see Appa also tensing, anticipating, worrying. Normally he kept his preoccupations to himself, but because he was at home, I could see him pacing up and down the hall long after Amma had said her prayers and gone to sleep. At night, when I usually heard music through his study door, there was only silence.

On Saturday morning, Niranjan turned up, having taken the overnight mail train journey from Peradeniya for the weekend. One of his old friends from our village had called him about the bicycle incident, and he had come to see Dayalan.

"You're not supposed to be here," Amma said, delighted. Even Appa looked slightly relieved. Niranjan had a way of putting everyone at ease.

"You don't look too much the worse for wear, thaambi," Niranjan said genially, looking up at Dayalan.

"You stink of the train," Dayalan said, smiling for the first time in days.

"Well, let a fellow have a wash and some food before commenting on his smell," Niranjan said, kissing Amma on one cheek. "Other side," he said, and tipped her face the other way, smacking his lips on her skin like a child. He was not much taller than her. He kissed the other cheek and the other cheek and the other cheek again, turning her face back and forth in his hands until she, too, finally laughed.

She wrinkled her nose. "Silly boy!" she said fondly. "Take a bath and go to the temple quickly and come," she advised. "I'll make a nice lunch."

"Yes, Amma," he said, and kissed her once more. "Of course, Amma." He looked at me. "A good thanggachi comes with her periannai to the temple," he suggested. I laughed and agreed.

After he finished bathing, I went to the well for my turn. He was already drawing the water for me—something my other brothers had long ago stopped doing. I smiled, happy to be taken care of for a moment.

"You look tired," he said, setting the heavy bucket down. "Too much studying?"

"Too much excitement," I said. I was exhausted, although I had not known that until he had said it. "It was scary," I said honestly.

"Well," he said, and passed me the bucket. "Have a wash and we'll walk, and you can tell me about it."

Niranjan had not tried to get any of the others to come with us. Appa was in his study, looking at the newspaper and listening to records; Seelan was poring over his textbooks, and Dayalan had a new novel—the first I'd seen him look at with interest in a week. Aran had gotten a jackfruit out of the front yard tree and was oiling his hands in preparation to peel it. I laughed—Aran looked the same way Seelan did when he was preparing to run school races. "Oh, I see," said Niranjan, peering around the corner of the back veranda and catching a glimpse. "Let's go before we're asked to help him with that. We can come back in time to eat it if we're lucky."

We set off together. To get to our temple, there were two routes: the regular path on the main road, and another path that cut through several fields and back lanes. Niranjan chose the irregular route, and we walked in silence for a bit. We passed a paddy field. It was early and not many people were out. Neelo Aunty waved to us across one crossroads.

"I miss the bicycles," Niranjan said after a while.

"Yes," I said briefly. Walking to the temple took a quarter of an hour. On bicycles, it would have taken us just a few minutes.

"Do you still ride yours?" he asked.

My father had not forbidden me to ride, as he had my brothers. But I had left my own bicycle locked to the back gate in solidarity.

"No," I said.

Niranjan nodded. We rounded the corner to the Pillaiyar kovil, the main temple of our village, and passed the red-and-white-striped walls marking the grounds. Inside the temple, the two priests recited morning prayers. Niranjan stood to one side, with the other men, and I stood opposite, with the other women. A few of our neighbours were already there, and several of the men nodded at Niranjan and asked him how his studies were going. He was a favourite among these people; even elders known for their sternness smiled at him. They mostly ignored me, which was fine. One of my batchmates, standing with her mother, did catch my eye and nodded. Villagers went to the temple to see people, to watch each other, and to gossip. ("You would think gossip, too, was a form of prayer," my father said wryly.) I preferred to be left alone at the temple, but going with just Niranjan was a rare joy. Although I was not religious, there was much in this space to comfort me: the rituals, the sounds, the fragrances, the familiar gods, the familiar faces of the worshippers and priests. Just past the bells of the threshold, a friendly, impish Pillaiyar waited. You might know him as Ganesha but that was not what we called him.

The priest came around with the kungumum, the vibhuthi, the water, the prasatham. We touched our foreheads with ash and with the bright red kungumum and held our hands out for food. Niranjan looked like he was praying very earnestly. Really, I knew, he was thinking. Perhaps there is no difference between those two things for some people. I wished I were standing with my brother instead of opposite him. The priest, who had known us since we were small, smiled at Niranjan especially and handed us a bunch of sweet bananas to take home. We circumnavigated the nine gods of the planets and the rest of the temple idols quickly—Say what needs saying and be done, Aran would have counselled—and then Niranjan said, Come.

In a corner of the temple's main hall, we sat cross-legged on the floor, a little bit away from the other worshippers. Periannai pulled a banana from the cluster and handed it to me. "Tell me," he said.

I told him. When I got to the part about K and his tutor being beaten, Niranjan stopped me. "Did Dayalan see that?" he asked, dismayed.

"He didn't get hurt," I said.

"I'm sure he got affected, seeing that, even if he wasn't beaten himself," Niranjan said. "None of this should have happened to him—to any of them. I should look in on K also, while I'm home." He paused. "How is he?"

Remembering K's swollen face, I suddenly couldn't go on.

"I see," Niranjan said softly. "You all got affected, then. I'm sorry, thanggachi. That's too much. Did you see the police as we were walking here?"

I had. We had passed several men who were obviously not from here. Only some had been in police uniforms. To Niranjan, who had been away, this all looked even worse; the last time he had been home, just a month ago, there hadn't been nearly so many of them. How generous it was of the United National Party to send police to help, Niranjan said, his even voice leaning on the last word ever so slightly. How generous it was for them to watch everything. "We're being observed everywhere," he said. At the Peradeniya medical campus, where several of the students were from Jaffna, his classmates traded stories of what had happened after the shooting the previous week.

"And you also want to go to this rally tomorrow?" he asked.

"I did," I said cautiously.

"You know that at the tuition classes—like the ones that K and Seelan are going to—some of the students are being recruited," Niranjan said.

He meant to the Tigers, but also some of the other Tamil militant groups that had begun to sprout up. To me, such recruitment was still a rumour. "How?" I asked. I had thought of the tuition classes as just that, classes.

"The teachers," Niranjan said simply. "I know because some of my old batchmates run the tuition classes, and fellows from the Tigers or PLOTE or TELO come to speak to the boys there. Or the teachers do it themselves. At least, that's what I hear."

"Are they recruiting at the medical campus?"

"Not yet," Niranjan said. "Not at mine, as far as I know. But it's a matter of time. Here." He took the half of the banana I still had in my hand, peeled it, and popped it into his mouth. "We should go back. Amma will be wondering if we've become much more pious. And that will be suspicious." He grinned at me, but then sobered. "We're probably being watched at the temple also. I've never liked this place. I just come here to please Amma. I shouldn't do even that."

"I didn't know you didn't like it," I said, startled.

He curled the banana peel up into his palm. "Think sometime about the people who can't come here, Sashi," he said. "And it isn't only the temple where they aren't welcome. You can't just stay in the house studying. You have to see the world yourself—don't let others tell you what it looks like."

WHEN WE REACHED HOME, Amma was making the promised elaborate lunch. Appa, Seelan, and Aran were sitting in the courtyard, talking about the rally. Everyone had a cup of tea except Dayalan, who was focused on drawing. Peering over his shoulder, I observed that he was sketching our house. The fine pencil style of his picture resembled that of an engineering diagram.

"I don't know if we should go to this rally tomorrow," Niranjan said as we came in.

Dayalan looked up from his paper. "It's our town," he said. "Our election."

"When was anything worthwhile ever said at a TULF rally?" Seelan asked, creasing his part of the newspaper.

Dayalan laughed bitterly. "There you might have a point."

"I want to go," I said, and Aran also looked up from the partially peeled jackfruit to which he was still applying himself.

"Do you all want to go?" Appa asked us.

"Of course," Aran said cheerfully. "How will I decide who to vote for without going? And it's my birthday. I can't think of a better present than a TULF rally." He held up his oily, dripping hands in a mock cheer.

Appa laughed. "God help the politicians," he said. Aran wouldn't be able to vote for another three years.

"Stay and help me with the cooking, Sashi," Amma said to me. She caught my eye meaningfully and looked at Aran. He would turn fourteen on Sunday, and before we had known about the rally or Niranjan's spontaneous visit, we had decided to throw him a surprise birthday. She had planned an even more elaborate menu of Aran's favourite things, and I had promised to assist her. I sighed.

"Political rallies are men's business anyway," Seelan said, winking at me. Niranjan chuckled at his baiting me.

"No wonder they're so ineffective," I said, and my brothers hooted. I got up from the newspaper and went into the kitchen with Amma, where a pile of red Jaffna onions awaited me.

Appa and my brothers set out for the rally shortly before noon the next day. Niranjan bid us a calm goodbye, but his mouth tightened as he looked over Dayalan, Seelan, and Aran. Despite that, or perhaps because of it, I wanted to go. From my place on the veranda, I saw K leave his house to join them. I opened my mouth to call after them, but they didn't hear me, and none of them looked back.

THE HALL, WHICH WAS almost in Jaffna town proper, barely contained the people who had come; old men and young men and a few young women spilled out onto the edges of each hallway and entrance, craning their necks to see the TULF speakers. Just beyond them, at the edge of the crowd and also at the edge of the stage, stood several policemen. Just beyond that, a gunman from one of the Tamil militant groups lurked. Perhaps there was more than one; because my brothers went without me, I can only tell you what I heard over the years. He was from the LTTE or TELO or PLOTE. The groups had not yet begun to murder each other, so the person telling me the story did not mention which one, only that the militants wanted to make clear their dominance over the politicians. The gunman stood and waited as the first speaker offered a long and tiresome introduction, and the crowd fidgeted, shifting from foot to foot, looking at their watches, muttering to each other and trading judgements on his performance. The speaker, sweating profusely and wiping his forehead with a handkerchief, introduced another man, who introduced another man, who introduced the chief guest. No one in my family who tells this story remembers who this prominent politician was either. As this so-important person began speaking, the gunman lifted his weapon, considered his life, and fired. At least that is how I imagine it, as I have imagined so much violence in the years since I lived inside it. Am I imagining or am I remembering? I no longer know. But I want to imagine that the gunman considered his life, as I have considered mine.

Before it found its target, his bullet whizzed close to the ear of the woman standing next to him. She clutched her fingers to the side of her head and fell to the floor. Her scream, like a stone thrown into the ocean, rippled forward and outward. For years after this her hearing would trouble her. Beside the stage, the bullet struck a policeman. Another shot flew, and a second policeman dropped. The one beside him stepped forward and raised his own pistol, but then knelt abruptly, holding a bloodied shoulder with a pale, shocked face. He yelled at his colleagues at the back of the crowd. Catch him! That one! Panic spread in expanding circles.

The gunman had joined one of the Tamil militant groups with the dream of firing a shot like this at a moment like this. He had promised his superiors that he could do the job. He had aspirations. He was Dayalan's age and they had once played a cricket match against each other. He replaced the gun at his waist and disappeared, one of history's rumours.

My father warned my brothers to stay together, but as the mass of people swayed back and forth, shouting, anticipating and ducking gunfire real and dreamed, Aran lost hold of Niranjan's shoulder. Dayalan pushed forward, trying to see what was happening, and Seelan went with him, surging between the sway of bodies. My father called for his sons, but in the crowd, they could not hear him for long, terrible minutes. "Niranjan," my father called. "Niranjan!" Appa was tall, but he could not see his eldest son, who was the shortest among them.

Finally, Niranjan reappeared at Appa's elbow. He had Seelan by one shoulder and Dayalan by the other. "Just a minute—stay here," he said firmly, and ducked back into the ocean of people to find Aran, who was drowning in the rising tide of the rally's panic.

When Niranjan emerged some moments later, he had Aran by the arm. "Let's get out of here," Niranjan said. "Now. Move quickly." Still startled, his brothers and his father obeyed.

They had taken the bus there, but now the crowd spilled out of the building all at once. The buses that were passing that way rocked, overfull with people, and stalled among rally attendees trying to get rides away. Niranjan looked up and saw that they would not reach any of the vehicles. More shots echoed behind them, and it was not clear who was shooting or from where. Hurry, hurry, Niranjan said, and headed down a side lane, away from the building. He was almost running. Stay with Appa, he said over his shoulder to Dayalan, and Dayalan nodded. My father, who was getting older, couldn't move as fast as them anymore. Dayalan took Appa's arm.

"Where is K?" Aran said.

"What?" Dayalan said.

"Where is K? Where is he?" Seelan said more urgently, and then they realised that none of them knew.

"I'll have to—I'll go back," Niranjan said. "Wait here for me."

"No," said Seelan, about to volunteer.

"You wait here for me," Niranjan said, his face a stone. "There isn't time to argue. Just listen for once, will you?" Then he turned to Dayalan and my father.

"I'll go back in and find K," Niranjan said, "but if I am not back in ten minutes and if this spot becomes overrun with people, you leave. I will come."

Seelan started to protest again but then stopped.

My father nodded. "Be careful," he said, his voice low. He held Niranjan's arm and then released him.

"I promise, Appa," Niranjan said. "I'll come. Don't worry."

My father nodded and Niranjan ran back towards the building.

In the days after this, when Appa told me and Amma about those minutes of Niranjan disappearing and returning, first with Dayalan and Seelan and then again with Aran, and then leaving again to get K, his mouth trembled, and he had to stop several times because he was shaking too much to talk. When he regained himself, he said: What to do? What to do? As a boy, in a time of earlier communal trouble, my father had lived through his own brother disappearing. In his study there was a garlanded picture of my uncle, who was neither the first nor the last boy to be lost this way.

I should have gone myself, Appa said. Nobody would have thought I was a militant. They are young men. I am old compared to these boys, with their guns. I should never have let Niranjan go back into that building.

We were not safe, Appa meant; he could not protect us. But I did not need him to tell me. I had known from the moment Dayalan returned to our house without his bicycle.

EVERYONE WAS GOING IN the other direction, Niranjan told me later. I was trying to swim against a tide.

He found his way back into the building. The dark made it harder to see people's faces. Some people held torches, but mostly, the remaining few faces were dimly lit. The policemen were questioning

witnesses. Across the room, Niranjan saw K talking to someone. Later
Dayalan would tell Niranjan that this was the tutor, the same man who
had been beaten for trying to protect K from the police, but at the
time, he seemed to be merely a stranger. He was tall and stocky and had
thick, dark eyebrows and thick-framed spectacles. What were they still
doing here? K wore his most serious, listening face. Look at me, Niranjan said to himself very softly. And miraculously, K did. Then his expression turned guilty, as though he had been caught at something.
But what? Niranjan had no time to wonder about this; K said goodbye
to the man and cut across the room to Niranjan swiftly, like a ship with
the wind at its back.

"I'm sorry," he said to Niranjan. "Let's go."

"Who is that?"

"Your father will be waiting," K said.

But K glanced back at the other man, whose Jaffna eyes were trained
on them.

BECAUSE TWO POLICEMEN DIED at that rally, the police at large
went on a rampage. They were angry, the government said later, unrolling its infinite list of excuses and apologies. Surely and understand-
ably, this was true: with two men slain and two more wounded, the
remaining police went to take their revenge and their pleasure. The
knife of their anger pointed at Jaffna town, where they lit up Tamil
shops, houses, and other institutions. Community centres ignited, and
bewildered shop owners fled roadside kades, not knowing why their
lives were being torched but realising that the police were too many to
resist. When it took Niranjan too long to return, my father ushered his
three remaining sons away from town as he had promised he would,
seeing the line of flame that would hunt them if they were not fast
enough. "Come," he said, and they obeyed reluctantly, all three trained
by younger-brother habit and duty to wait for Niranjan's word.

The stories that the government chose to tell about such violent nights described them as though they were not deliberate, like no one was choosing, but in fact, every target had been chosen as carefully as a flower in the best bouquet: the TULF office, which the unremarkable, speech-giving politician called his headquarters; the ancestral home of a young member of Parliament who also belonged to the party; the office of a Tamil newspaper; a Hindu temple; the Jaffna market, where I had done errands for my mother since my childhood.

I was not there, and for that I did my penance imagining it. I had company in the dreaming, too: all of us left behind spent the days that followed reconstructing the events obsessively, until we felt so certain of some details it was as though we had lived them. Eventually the six men of our lane, now two parties, found buses back to our village. Out the windows they could see a parade of people and animals, commingled in their respective businesses. My father's bus passed three dour working elephants in their chains, four men beating a boy, and a swarm of policemen—Sinhalese men carrying sticks. Dayalan looked away. The boy being beaten was about his age. Through the open windows he could hear the vicious, biting sound of flesh stinging flesh. Underneath that, there was the chaotic and uncanny noise of a place emptying of one set of people and filling with another. Those who could manage it had fled the roads overrun by the so-called authorities bringing so-called order, while others pressed on in the other direction: Jaffna proper.

In that direction, beyond the six of them coming home to my mother and me and Aran's forgotten birthday dinner, the dark scent of burnt wood clogged the air at Jaffna market. I loved the market, and often chose to help my mother by going there. I could have drawn a map of it as it stood before it burned. I knew where to find everything: the tidy packets of fragrant curry leaves; the sinuous heaps of yellow-green snake gourds, burnished eggplants, long green beans, and hot chillies; toasted cashews; the ground pockmarked with remnants of betel leaf; the betel itself; the king coconuts halved and ready with spoons carved from their shells; the neat rows of uncracked eggs; the dark canisters of gingelly and coconut oil; the bloody halal meats; the barrels of brown rice, red rice, white rice, lentils, curry powder, and flour; the men yelling, "Vadai-vadai-vadai-vadai-vadai-vadai-vadai," as they hawked snacks; the beggar who collected coins and scraps of food by a well in a filched metal cup.

As my mother baked Aran's birthday cake in a kitchen filled with food from the market, the bright blossoms of its vendor awnings wilted under clouds of smoke. Police brandished sticks and guns. Entire rows of stalls had already been abandoned. Old women ran with baskets in their arms. Chickens and dogs screamed. Later, one vendor my father knew swore he had stepped on the loose eye of a fish and felt it searing between his toes. Blackened Jaffna mangoes and jackfruit lay scattered in the dirt, encrusted with the rime of carbon, the air choking with their sweetness and another sweetness: the unknowably worse stench of the scorched animals.

The rioting and rampaging by the police lasted for days. After the first hectic hours, as the news spread, Tamil people stayed indoors. No, my mother said firmly when my brothers looked at the windows. Four people were yanked from their houses and slain for no reason, and news of their deaths leapt fences to our ears. From my bed, I could hear my father pacing in his study. Grimly, my mother served us birthday cake. When we tried to sing to Aran, my youngest brother, old too soon, he held up his hand for us to stop.

The Sinhalese policemen burned our library last. Mercifully, we did not see it; we did not see the white walls blacken and fall into each other like so many dominoes. When K snuck out of his house and down the road to tell us what he had heard—from whom and how we were too stunned to ask—Dayalan went into his room and shut the door and did not come out for many hours. I sat in our courtyard, staring up into its cup of sunlight. They had torched the elegant palace of white rooms where Seelan and K and I had studied, its clean and well-lit shelves, the rare book section with the beautifully lettered palm leaf manuscripts. Dayalan had shown some to me when he had first begun working there. Ninety thousand volumes gone, some of them original and single copies. Our past, but also—oh, the beautiful wooden tables where I had turned the pages of my textbooks, and my brothers' textbooks!—the future. And it was gone.

Imagine the places you grew up, the places you studied, places that belonged to your people, burned. But I should stop pretending that I know you. Perhaps you do not have to imagine. Perhaps your library, too, went up in smoke.

WE WERE EATING LISTLESSLY the night after K told us when Dayalan said, "Tomorrow I'm going to go see the library."

Niranjan looked thoughtful, but Seelan and Aran stared into their plates. Appa took another idiappam and ladled sothi generously over it. None of them said anything. Amma glanced at Dayalan and then me.

"I'll go with you," I said immediately. I did not want to see it, but he needed to go, and not alone.

The next morning, Dayalan and I took turns washing at the well, and dressed almost as nicely as if we were going to a temple or a formal school function. I chose the clean white blouse of my school uniform and a long skirt; my colourful saris felt wrong. This was a funeral, and for those, we wore white. "Are you also coming?" I asked Periannai, who was already dressed and sitting on the back veranda.

Niranjan hesitated and glanced over at Dayalan, who was combing his hair by the well. "I wish I could go with you, but Appa and I have to catch the train," he said. Of course—he looked school-tidy, in a newly ironed shirt. He was already several days overdue in Peradeniya. For this I could forgive him. A second later, my father appeared in the doorway behind us, similarly turned out; he was already late to his next outstation posting, in Batticaloa.

"We'll be all right," I said.

"Take good care of everyone, eh, kunju?" Appa said, patting my cheek.

I nodded.

"And yourself," Niranjan said, and before goodbye could turn too terrible I kissed their dear, cologne-scented, clean-shaven faces.

After Amma had sent Appa and Niranjan off to the station with lunch parcels and murukku packets for their respective journeys, Dayalan and I set out for the library. But we were only at the end of the lane when I heard Aran call, "Acca, wait!" I turned and saw Aran, Seelan, and K running to catch up with us. Dayalan and I stopped, and then the five of us stood in an awkward circle, the three of them panting a little. Dayalan looked around at all of us strangely, like we were not quite real. Perhaps he would have preferred to be alone.

"We thought we would join," K said.

"Come then," Dayalan said brusquely. I reached for his hand, as I had not in years, like a little girl, and he let me take it. Most of the time, he had a firm grip on anything he held, but that morning his fingers felt like they might slip from my grasp if I did not pay attention.

Horror made our walk seem twice as long. The day was hot, and the closer we got to the library, the more the air smelled like char. The people we passed murmured to each other in small groups. It was as though the entire town had had a death in the family. I suppose we had. No one raised their voices or sang or laughed. Even the street dogs seemed to have disappeared. We passed other burnt buildings and closed shops. Aran whistled when we passed a smashed tea stall, its awning a slumped shoulder.

When we came to the library gate, I released Dayalan's hand and the four of us let him go ahead of us. "Aiyo, Muruga," he whispered, and bent in half, his head at his knees.

Burned paper littered the ground. A breeze hummed gaily through the building's grey shell, as though nothing had happened. Others gathered wept openly. Some men standing towards the west side of the building spoke quietly and seriously with each other in a way that made me wonder what they were saying. Would the place be rebuilt? Was it even possible? Were they plotting reconstruction or revenge? Certainly the library had contained precious and irreplaceable items.

Dayalan must have known exactly what had been lost. Aran slipped into the space between us and took the hand I had released.

"Someone will have to pay for this," Seelan said, his face distant.

"What do you mean?" Aran asked.

"To rebuild it," K said.

"No," said Dayalan. "It can't be rebuilt."

It wasn't just the market and the library. A newspaper, too, had been torched. In the decades to come, parents would tell their children how some of the most prominent officials in the country had watched the library burn and done nothing. Anger made it easy to memorise their names. Later we learned that one old scholar dropped dead upon hearing the news.

EXAMS STILL AWAITED US. With the library gone, we studied at home. No walks; no laughing exchanges on the lane. To work we went—dutiful, grave, the joy drained from our days. We sat at fresh desks in separate rooms and tried to concentrate. Exams, Amma said, instead of good morning; exams, she reminded us, bringing us tea. "Promise me you'll study," Appa said when he called home. I went back to the temple of learning I still had: Sir's classroom. "You have to go on," he told me.

None of us argued. How could we? We heard what they all meant, the other half that they weren't saying. We understood the lesson. Carry on, students. Open your books, read while you can, and remember: there are people in our country who would burn what we love and laugh at the flames.

2.

A Good Sister

WHEN SEELAN AND K'S MARKS CAME OUT, OUR VILLAGE WAS jubilant: not only had K gotten four As in his required subjects of botany, zoology, chemistry, and physics, but he had also come first in the whole island. The ranking, though unofficial, was widely known. Even his quiet eyes smiled behind his glasses; even his sober mouth turned up under his still-tentative moustache. K would go to the University of Jaffna medical faculty, which had a good reputation and was, almost as importantly, close to home. Seelan, who had aimed to attend the engineering faculty at the University of Colombo, would have to try again; like most people, he had not passed with marks high enough to follow the course he wanted. Although it put him in a foul mood, this was no terrible or unexpected failure; only very clever people got what they wanted immediately, and it was nearly unheard of for someone to come first on the island on their first try. With his Advanced Level marks, K passed into Jaffna schoolboy legend. His aunt cooked an elaborate feast to celebrate him; from all over our neighbourhood people brought different kinds of seafood to their house. When she had enough, she made odiyal kool, the rich soup I loved and that we usually had only on holidays. At the party, Seelan ate well and congratulated K too heartily, which was a sign of how upset he was.

K was given a space at the university immediately; he did not have to wait as some did. Perhaps the authorities were afraid of someone so bright being recruited abroad. After he matriculated, he took a bed in a hostel closer to the university and came to visit his aunt and father only on the weekends, so I did not see him as much. As the sting faded, Seelan sometimes still studied with him, but he generally went to the hostel, and the impromptu cricket games between our houses slowed to a standstill. Unwilling to give up on playing, Aran tried to teach me; I fared decently, but neither of us really had time to continue. Aran's Ordinary Levels loomed; my first Advanced Levels were coming up. I had been on the chess team and the track team at my old girls' school, but with the exams approaching, Appa had advised me to quit and to spend the time on my books. I knew he was right. I wasn't a particular talent at either chess or running, although I had worked hard; but, I thought, when it came to science, I belonged.

WHEN HIS SECOND TRY at the Advanced Levels came a year later, in late 1982, Seelan got into school. His relief was visible; his eyes lost some of their restlessness. But as usual, fate—or circumstance—kept us just a notch apart.

I took the theoretical exams confidently. But on the morning of the practical exam for zoology, I quailed, my insides uneasy in the terrifying, familiar way I had discovered all the way back at the beginning of the subject. Only a shark, only a frog, only a rat, only a cockroach, I told myself. Only a smell, only a feeling, only a stilled body, nothing that could hurt me. I had rehearsed; I was prepared. Yet somehow, inside the room with the examiners, I trembled. They assigned me the shark, and when the specimen emerged from its pool of formalin onto the table, my stomach dropped. I swallowed roughly and concentrated on keeping my food down; I moved the scalpel hesitantly, with an erratic motion rather than smooth cuts. I tried and failed to summon the diagrams with which Sir had drilled us. Sick and blank, I felt rather than heard the disapproval when I presented my work. The resulting marks kept me just outside the ranks of those accepted to medical school.

My family said little about my performance, other than assuming that I would try again, but I dreaded seeing Sir. While I had always believed that there was no great embarrassment in failing to enter on the first try, having it happen to me was different. Too late, I sympathised with Seelan. I was appalled to have come so close only to fumble in zoology, a subject I loved and in which I revered my teacher. On the day that I returned to Sir's classroom, I focused on my notebook as I listened to him congratulate the two students who had earned places in the medical faculty: well done, well deserved, claps on the back and handshakes all around. My own hands felt damp. At the end of class, my face hot, I got up to leave only to have him stop me. Stay for a word, Sashikala, he said. I assented, my eyes fixed somewhere above his bald head. When the others were gone, he sat down in the chair in front of mine and gestured at my seat. "Tell me what happened," he said.

Humiliatingly, my vision blurred with tears. He pulled a handkerchief from his shirt pocket. "I felt ill at the formaldehyde smell," I admitted. "As though all of the practise I had with you never happened and I was at the beginning again."

He smiled at me, his eyes crinkling at their corners behind his spectacles. "You know," he said, "a great many people who go on to become excellent physicians do not enter on their first attempt."

"And some people enter on the first try!" I blurted. Listening to him congratulate my successful batchmates, I had envied not only them and not only my brother, but also my personal classroom ghost, K, the recipient of the previous year's backslaps and handshakes. The competition in my head was strong. Worse, I wondered if I had been wrong about myself. What if I was too cowardly to be a doctor?

"You are brave enough," Sir said. Had I confessed my uncertainty aloud? "You know," he continued, "I told you that my niece Anjali loves dissections. But that wasn't always true. She also received poor marks in zoology on her first attempt."

This was news. I had always imagined Anjali at my age like K, giving the impression of immediate, effortless achievement. The stories people told about her did not include any failures. "What did she get wrong?" I asked, curious.

Sir shrugged. "Bad at cutting," he said succinctly.

I wanted more details, the gory innards of her mistakes, but sensed that he would go no further. "What did she do when she failed?" I said instead.

He leaned back in his chair and crossed his arms over his chest. "She worked harder and tried again. What to do? Like you, she was worried. Angry, unsure. So the next time she set out to defeat not the exam, but her own fear." He spread his arms wide, as if offering something. "I tutored her, of course. But even without that, without me—she would have been fine. All she needed was a bit of time. Professor Premachandran was good enough, Sashikala. And so are you."

LATER THAT AFTERNOON, I sat in the open courtyard of our house, my face up to the sunlight, thinking about what Sir had said. Some subconscious part of me had aimed to replicate K's success, to catch up to him. I needed a moment to reconcile myself to the distance between what I wanted and what had actually taken place.

"It happens to most people," Niranjan said when he found me. He held our new puppy, Henry, in one hand and a glass of fresh lime juice in the other. He passed the glass to me. "Come, don't pout, thanggachi. No one will admit it, but failing, too, is a Jaffna tradition. I sat my exams three times to go to Peradeniya, and even then, I had to wait to enter. Here, this fellow will make you feel better." He set Henry in the crook of my free arm, and the dog sank his soft face into my blouse.

"K didn't fail," I said, still sullen. I thought of the eggs and his steady hands. And then I remembered that the younger Anjali had also raged at herself.

Niranjan laughed. "I know you think of K as some clever god, and he is smart. But he's also just a student like anyone else, and he studied with some of the best teachers in Jaffna. You have those teachers too. And we aren't all good students in exactly the same way. Nor should we be. Try again," Niranjan said calmly. "That's what I did. What See-lan did."

I couldn't tell Niranjan my secret, lingering fear: that like K, Niran-jan and Seelan were smarter than me. What if everyone was smarter than me? I wished Periannai would leave. I did not want to talk, not even to him; I wanted to be alone with what Sir had said, to try to believe in the story he had told me about myself, that someday I would pass.

But Periannai sat down in the chair across from me. The puppy tumbled from my arm—nearly toppling the lime juice—to beg at my brother's feet. Grumpy, I steadied the glass and sipped. "I haven't got anything for you, little chap," he told the dog seriously. "Speaking of excellent teachers, there are some students who want to go to medical school and never make it. I would bet there's no real chance of that happening to you. You're bright, brighter than I was. But even if you never passed, you would be all right."

I stared at him. "How would that be all right? What do you mean?" The dog, switching tacks, snuffled at my feet, and I rubbed his head.

Niranjan sighed. "He doesn't talk about it, but Sir wanted to go to medical school," he said quietly.

Niranjan's information floored me. "How do you know?" I de-manded. "That Sir failed?"

My brother shrugged. "He told me," he said simply. Of course. Sir had been his teacher too, and people always told Niranjan the truth. To be fair, it was because he always asked the right questions, but he also had a clear-eyed, guileless face that made everyone want to give him an honest accounting. So Sir had told my brother about failing the en-trance exam three times.

"I have never repeated that story. Of course, the people of his gen-eration know. Appa knows. That's why he sent us to Sir's school. Sir is so thorough," Niranjan said. "Such an excellent teacher. Our people talk as if your life is over if you are not a doctor, or an engineer, or an accountant. So much pressure to be the same things! But look at him—or look at Appa. There are plenty of other ways to live."

If there were so many other ways to live, I wanted to hear about a few more of them. It did not seem like anyone spoke of them here. To be a doctor was every good student's ambition, or so it appeared to me. I had considered my aspirations my own, but perhaps I was mistaken; Jaffna was a cage of expectations. What could I expect of myself? "Sir is a great teacher, but—I wish I didn't have to study here. I wish I could go to Colombo with you," I blurted. After graduating from medical school, doctors were required to work for the government for five years. Periannai had landed a coveted posting in Colombo. Seelan was flat-out envious; although he had been promised a seat at the University of Colombo's engineering faculty, where Dayalan was also supposed to go, they would both have to wait at least another year in Jaffna. In recent weeks, I had been dreading Niranjan's imminent departure. With another year of work ahead of me, I thought, going with him was not an option.

But—Niranjan's dark eyes narrowed with interest. "Perhaps you could."

I sat up, astonished anew. "Really?" I had travelled within the country, but I had never lived outside of Jaffna. I had been so certain this was impossible that I hadn't closely examined the question of whether I would really want to do it. "Where would we stay?" I asked.

He held his hand out for the glass and I passed it back to him. He drained it and set it down. "I'm going to live with Ammammah for a while," Niranjan said. "We can ask Amma and Appa, and Ammammah of course, and you can come with me. We'll find you a tuition class, and you can prepare again. Would you like that? A fresh start?"

I had never been apart from both my parents at once. And we had visited Ammammah in Colombo only occasionally; on holidays she generally came on the train to see us, not the other way around. I loved her, but had never seriously thought about what it would be like to stay there for an extended stretch. The idea of a city adventure with Periannai scared and thrilled me.

"It will be fun," he said. "The two of us in Colombo with Ammammah?"

"All right," I said hesitantly. "Let's ask them."

Amma's face fell a little bit when Niranjan mentioned his idea over lunch the next day, but Appa, who was home for the weekend, nodded. "A good idea," he said.

"I don't want Acca to go also," Aran said, and guilt flickered through me.

"And should she really be rewarded for getting poor marks?" Seelan said cruelly. "I stayed here and studied." Startled, I kicked at him under the table, but missed.

"It will be good for her," Appa said. "Go and learn how to live in Colombo, Sashi, and spend some time with Ammammah, and study hard. Then you can come back here for medical school, or go to Peradeniya like Niranjan did."

"Will you be all right on your own?" Amma said, looking fretful.

"I won't be alone, I'll be with Periannai," I pointed out.

"And with your mother," Appa said gently to Amma.

"I'll take good care of her, Amma," Niranjan said at last, and because everyone believed that, because he was the eldest son, it was settled.

PERIANNAI AND I PACKED for Colombo at the beginning of the next school year, in mid-August. Although I tried to seem nonchalant, I was nervous. The capital was 350 kilometres away from home, in the Western Province. I had last travelled there four years earlier, when I was thirteen. I remembered, dimly, the sound of Sinhala being spoken on the streets, and the feeling of being both constantly observed and entirely invisible. The city was a loud, busy place. Whether moving south would be terrifying or exciting I did not know. But when I looked over at my brother, he smiled reassuringly, and I knew I had the answer.

All my good clothes fit into one small suitcase. We were taken for haircuts and given presents. Even Seelan and Aran snuck me packets of sweets for the train like they were going to miss me. To my surprise, Seelan also handed me a map of Colombo and a list of sights to see. "Study hard and have fun, in that order," he instructed. Then he frowned, winked, and told me not to do anything he wouldn't do. ("A good bit of leeway there, Acca," Aran noted dryly.) Dayalan reminded Niranjan to pack his old medical school textbooks so I could keep looking at them, and gave me a novel as a parting gift—the Tamil translation of Maxim Gorky's *Mother,* which was titled *Thai.* When I opened the book on the train, a folded bit of paper slipped to the floor. I retrieved it to find an elegant sketch of my family in front of our house, with good likenesses of each of us in our most characteristic mood. Dayalan's pencil made us look somehow warm and alive— Appa, heavy-browed and stern; Niranjan with his steady, quietly content gaze; Seelan smiling a slightly angry smile; Aran clutching a newspaper; Amma happy and worried; Dayalan himself at one edge, with a too-serious expression. He had put me in the center, a stethoscope around my neck. I laughed at the vote of confidence. In the small, formal photographs I had brought with me, my family looked like some other blank, emotionless set of people. I preferred the honesty of the sketch. "What's that?" Niranjan asked through a mouthful of lunch parcel. When I held it up, he whistled. "He's got us," he admitted. When I went to stow it away, I discovered a tiny, breathtaking picture of K in one corner of the opposite side—a handsome, detailed profile in an oval circle, like an old-style cameo. My hand hovered over it, blocking Niranjan's view, before I pressed the drawing inside a heavy textbook for safekeeping.

When we arrived at Colombo Fort Station, Ammammah was waiting for us, along with a short, friendly man who it turned out was the taxi driver. That day, for the first time, I realised Ammammah looked young for a grandmother. She wore her jet-black hair in a long, thick braid, and wrinkles had not yet found her. Her features did not seem

acquainted with each other, and a long, skinny black birthmark travelled across the left half of her face. She embraced me warmly, and I let
her. She smelled like jasmine, as usual. She was wearing enormous diamond earrings, also as usual. We kissed each other on both cheeks and
then she turned and did the same with my brother, who was grinning.
We adored her.

In the car on the way to her house, as Niranjan told her how everyone in Jaffna was doing, I stared hungrily at the city, trying to understand how Colombo was laid out. On previous visits, we had been
taken to the homes of friends and distant relatives. I did not know how
to get around myself, and the idea of having to do so overwhelmed me.
The air felt bad, and I sneezed. "Nooru," Ammammah said, and smiled
at me. May you live to be a hundred, that blessing meant. Although
Amma was beautiful and Ammammah was not, they looked alike, and
like Amma, Ammammah had a clear, bright torch of a smile, full of
genuine pleasure in seeing us.

Ammammah's house in Wellawatte was the only one on the street
with a white roof. It was the same welcoming space I remembered; she
kept a shrine full of small brass vilakku, and by the front door, she had
the two same big, grand ones she had had since I was a child. I had forgotten the piano, somehow, although playing it had been one of the
treats of past visits. I cast a longing glance at it, and she nodded. "Of
course," she said, "it's too late today, but play it tomorrow." She normally put me and Aran in the same room when we came, but this time,
she showed me to Paata's old library, where she had made me a small,
soft, low bed and placed an old and dainty lady's writing desk near a
shelf full of medical texts. I felt gloriously adult. I scanned the titles
eagerly, and even Niranjan looked interested. We had never had time
to read his books before.

"Where will I put my clothes, Ammammah?" I asked.

She pointed to the gorgeous old-fashioned wooden almirah in the
hall. "I cleared half for you," she told me. The almirah had been in
Paata's family for generations, and as a child, I had hidden in it during

many games of hide-and-seek. Inside, I knew, was the carved bone and ivory chess set he had brought back from India when he was young, in which each piece was from the pantheon of Hindu gods. We had never been permitted to touch it.

She took us down the corridor, where, I saw, she had given Niranjan a room in the front, a large, well-appointed space with pin-striped linen curtains and another big desk. I felt envious—why were men always given everything bigger?—and then glad for him.

"That was Paata's," Ammammah said. "I had it moved in here for you—it doesn't fit in the library, Sashi. I thought one of you could have his desk and the other the books, but really, you ought to share both. He would have been very happy to have you here."

I remembered my grandfather only dimly but worshipped him. An elegant man, he had died when I was five of a heart attack. He had been a very well-respected physician in Colombo, a gynaecologist who had delivered, my grandmother claimed, fully half of the babies in Wella-watte, nearby Bambalapitiya, and even wealthy Cinnamon Gardens, including my mother. Tamil mothers, Sinhalese mothers—everyone called my grandfather, she said. More unusually, those who did not want to be mothers had called him, too. He ran a discreet abortion clinic, where he treated anyone who needed it. Women in trouble ex-plained their appointments by saying they were going to have their wombs cleaned, Ammammah told me, and this bit of code and Paata's part in it astonished me. My grandmother, who had told me this secret on her first visit to Jaffna after I came of age, always spoke of him with such great love that it embarrassed other people. Paata had always been my hero, too, and it was the revelation of his underground work—in my grandmother's passionate voice—that had cemented my desire to be a doctor. His desk, now Niranjan's, was a handsome carved ma-hogany, of a style that had been common during the British colonial era and was considered an heirloom now. Niranjan stood over it, trac-ing its lines. He tapped the inkwell gently and looked at my grand-mother. "Thanks, Ammammah," he said sincerely.

"A family house is for family, your grandfather would have said," she said, her eyes twinkling. "Thanking your family is not necessary. Come, Dr. Niranjan, and eat."

IN COLOMBO I WAS a stranger, a fate from which even my grandmother's welcome and warmth could not save me. I was my Colombo-raised mother's daughter, but the other girls at my Tamil medium tuition class wore smarter clothes than me and sometimes mocked my Jaffna vocabulary; at home I had been considered quick, but my classmates in Colombo seemed determined to declare me awkward and provincial. My tuition classmates walled me away from them with a growing pile of small but effective humiliations. Only one girl, Hasna, was kind to me from the first day. She was plump and pretty, with a wide face and fair skin, small, arched brows over round wire glasses, and a tiny, rosy mouth. When she moved I smelled jasmine. She was also the only Muslim student in the class. "Come along," she said at the tea break, when I stood apart. "We get tea over here."

I followed her to a roadside shop just outside our building and ordered some mutton rolls with my tea.

"Aren't you veg?" said a girl behind me. I turned around and she was sneering at me.

"No," I said, and then wondered if she was just trying to find another way to make me feel uncomfortable. Were the fancy girls of this tuition class all vegetarian?

"I like the rolls also," Hasna said encouragingly. I followed her to a table in the building courtyard and then realised that no one else was coming with us.

"There are some nicer people in the other class that meet at this time," Hasna said. "I'll introduce you later. The ones in our class are . . . not kind."

I bit into a limp mutton roll. "I can tell," I muttered. At my school in Jaffna, we had had hot lunch. I had never thought of myself as fussy or pampered and was dismayed to realise I might have been.

"When did you come to Colombo, and where are you staying?" she asked. I told her, and when I described it, she knew where my grandmother's house was, and also the hospital where Periannai worked. Inwardly, I cheered. "Were your parents angry that you did not do well on the exam?" she asked. "My parents were."

My parents had understood, actually, and helped me find this tuition class in Colombo. Niranjan and Seelan and Dayalan had all had to try more than once to enter the courses they wanted; everyone loved Periannai in particular and thought he was bright, and I was his favourite, so they would not have dared to apply a different standard to me. But I hadn't anticipated how isolated I might feel here. No matter, I had decided; all I needed were my specimens and my books and improved marks. Now, unexpectedly, I had Hasna.

"What happened in your exam?" she asked. "I did terribly on the theory exam in chemistry. My mother says I'll poison someone as a doctor." She laughed.

I laughed too. "I'm not sure," I admitted. "My weak point was the practical exam in zoology. It was my favourite when we were studying—I loved the dissections, and I knew them backwards and forwards. And still when the exam came I was nervous. I don't know why."

"Next time we'll do better," she assured me. I hoped she was right. She smiled brightly. "Come over after class tomorrow and we can study," she said. I accepted the invitation with a cautious sense of relief. When I went home and told my grandmother, she was pleased. "I know that family," she said. "I taught that girl when she was younger, and her mother was your mother's friend when they were children." When I asked Hasna about it, she admitted that she had known.

"My mother told me to look for you," she said to me as we were eating tea and biscuits at her house. Her mother came in just then and smiled at us.

"When I was new at school, your mother was kind to me," she said. "I was the only Muslim student at that school, like Hasna is now. I have never forgotten. You look just like her."

I do not look like my mother, and I never have; it was a kindness to say I did. I thought of Amma in Colombo, a little girl meeting another little girl in a classroom, in the park or on a playground. In my small dream my mother threaded her fingers through the other girl's fingers. I looked at Hasna's mother, whose kind eyes and rosy mouth were like her daughter's. I felt homesick for Jaffna, but I was in my mother's city. The watchful ghosts of her childhood walked beside me.

WHEN MY BROTHER'S FIRST cheque for his new posting at the government hospital came, he divided it into three parts. One he sent to Amma along with a telegram: FROM MY FIRST CHEQUE STOP WITH GRATITUDE STOP YOUR LOVING SON NIRANJAN. A second portion he used to buy Ammammah a beautiful sari. "You don't thank your family," she told him again. Pleased nonetheless, she fingered the rich embroidery of the royal blue pallu. I thought all the money was gone, but to my surprise, the third portion he used for me.

"What would you like to do?" he asked. "I thought we could go out for a day, on a Sunday. See a film, take a sea bath."

"Can Hasna come?" I asked, delighted.

"Of course."

We were a strange foursome: Niranjan, Hasna, my grandmother, and me. Instead of a film, we went to the Galle Face and walked on the beach; Niranjan bought us all ice creams and we strolled into the beginnings of waves with our skirts held above our ankles, my brother with his trouser bottoms rolled up so that he looked like a boy. "What an undignified physician," my grandmother teased, and he smiled, unembarrassed. We ate fresh fried fish for lunch at a small restaurant by the beach and then dropped my grandmother and Hasna at home. "I have one more errand to run, and you might as well come with me," Niranjan said. When we headed for the Pettah, I was surprised. He bade the driver stop in the jewellers' district, and we got down in front of a small shop. He rang the bell and we went inside.

"I'm a friend of Dr. Paramsothy's," he told the clerk. "I was told to come to this shop and ask for Ramesh."

Ramesh came out quickly and shook my brother's hand. "You must be Dr. Niranjan's sister," he said to me.

"Yes," I said, confused.

Niranjan laughed. "Ramesh, I wanted to get my sister some earrings, a good luck present for her exams this year."

"You shouldn't spend your cheque on me!" I exclaimed. "I haven't passed yet."

"It's my cheque," he said. "And besides, it's your birthday soon."

Ramesh brought over a few pairs of earrings. Niranjan pointed to a pair that were made of garnet. They were heavy and in the old, burnished style. Ramesh unfastened them and I tenderly inserted them into my ears. I had never had a set this fancy.

"Do you like them?"

"I do," I said, and hesitated. Such a lot of money. I wondered what my parents would have said about it. "Are you sure?"

"You only turn eighteen once," he said.

"For luck," I said, and when we walked out with the box, foolishly, I did feel lucky.

AS THE DAYS ROLLED on and I burrowed myself further and further into my cave of studying, my parents began fielding proposals for Periannai. He detested the process but spoke little to me about it; it was his habit to endure without complaint, and this was no exception, apparently. I observed and occasionally aided as Ammammah, at my parents' request, hosted a series of awkward teas for demure young women accompanied by their inquisitive parents. Ammammah used the good china, with its delicate pattern of blue flowers, which Paata's parents had given them as a wedding gift; since my childhood, those cups had been a sign that something important was happening. Sometimes Hasna, too, was there when these teas occurred, and then we cloistered ourselves in the library and whispered about it. In the women came, a parade of propriety: tall, short, fair, dark, wheatish, plump, slender, all of them educated but only quiet and quieter. Most of them barely spoke while their parents sat there and talked. I could see the neighbours watching their entrances and exits curiously from the adjacent garden. At night, after I had closed myself up in my grandfather's library to study, I could sometimes hear Ammammah and Niranjan discussing them, the steady volume of her persuasive voice interrupted only occasionally by his. In the mornings, he rose before me and was often at work before I had a chance to ask him how he felt about it. It wasn't my place to enquire, but he had never expected me to stay in my place, so I waited for a good moment.

None came before November, when a young woman with whom he had gone to medical school visited. She was not quiet but conversed easily with my grandmother. Seeing this from a hallway, I came into the parlour to meet her. She had a plain, soft oval face with a sharp widow's peak and a braid woven into a knot at the nape of her long neck. Her sari was a pretty, light, lemon yellow, better suited to the daily business of an office than a proposal call, and she wore a simple chain that was likewise badly chosen for the occasion. She drank plain tea; she indelicately took two biscuits and just as indelicately smiled at me. She looked at me right in the eyes, and so did her parents. It turned out she was a younger sister herself. Her name was Malathy, and like Amma, she had been raised in Colombo. A paediatrician, she worked at another nearby hospital.

The morning after she visited, Niranjan waited for me at breakfast.

"What did you think?" he asked me. We were eating idlis and sambar.

"The whole business is strange," I said, through a mouthful. "I never saw it up close like this before."

"I mean about the one who came yesterday," he said. "Malathy."

"I liked her," I said cautiously, and swallowed.

"I wanted to ask you first," he said.

"First," I said, serving myself a big spoon of coconut sambol and then putting another on his plate. "First, before what?"

"Thank you. I was going to tell Amma and Appa that I would agree to be engaged to her," Niranjan said, and concentrated on his plate.

I had never seen him embarrassed before, so it took a second to figure out that that was what it was.

"Oh, that's wonderful!" I said. "She'll make a good Anni."

"I think so," he said, taking two more idlis. "We met in an anti-caste reading group at Peradeniya," he added. His ears reddened and because it was clear he never wanted to talk about it again if we could avoid it, with the possible exception of the actual day he was married, we busied ourselves with eating. A few minutes later, when my grandmother came in and found us eating in uncharacteristic silence, her eyes went from Niranjan to me, and she smiled.

I wore the garnet earrings for the first time at the Christmas holiday, when my parents and Malathy's parents formalised the engagement at our Jaffna house with the usual ceremonies. I shrank against the wall whenever I could; I wasn't used to so many strangers and so much wedding-related religious pomp. My fancy sari rustled. My mother had promised it would grow softer with use, but that day it moved around me like a suit of sunset-coloured silk armour. I would have preferred to hide, but the sari made me unmissable. "Come on," Aran said to me reprovingly, "you can't just vanish. They're practically our relatives now." Still, I stood back, until my mother came and found me in a lull.

"You look very nice," she said. "Where did the earrings come from?" When I explained, she raised her eyebrows. "That boy has always spoiled you," she said, but she smiled, too. "As an older brother should. Malathy will be lucky." Looking over at my quiet, constant brother and his fiancée, I too thought she had found good fortune.

PERIANNAI WORE HIS NEW status as an engaged man lightly, and not much changed in the subsequent months, except that we seemed to fall into a peaceful, happy routine with my grandmother. I grew used to hearing Ammammah praying early in the morning; her prayers, different than those of my parents, were no longer strange to me, but became their own kind of music. I rose earlier and earlier myself, anx-

iety setting my alarm at dawn or sometimes while it was still dark, and
so occasionally I found Niranjan reading at his desk or writing a letter
home. We became accustomed to Malathy coming by to see my brother
once or twice a week. Sometimes her mother joined her and then the
two of them would discuss the wedding with my grandmother, my
brother gracefully excusing himself partway through. I, too, wanted
to avoid those conversations, but once Malathy caught me passing by
and invited me to join. Seeing my face, she laughed; all right, thanggachi, she winked, you should go and study. For that, I liked her even
more.

As June approached, the weather grew hotter and hotter; Hasna
and I had been studying at her house, but we moved our preparations
to Ammammah's house, which was both cooler and less crowded. Although I had played Ammammah's upright piano earlier in the year, by
summer I had given it up, and on some days, we spread our notes over
its top and stand and bench as we tested each other's memories. On
other days, under the fan at the dining table, we read and took notes
and swapped papers and read each other's notes and worried. Exams
are coming, we chanted at each other: exams, exams, exams. Even the
bullies became too anxious for unkindnesses. The class was more or
less united in its chorus of daily work and worry. My brothers and
parents sent a steady stream of good luck notes and parcels: odiyal,
which you couldn't easily get in Colombo, and that Ammammah
promptly commandeered to make odiyal kool ("good for the brain,
full of iron," she reminded me); three new novels from Dayalan (re-
wards for after the exams, he advised sternly, and not before); a short,
cranky letter from Seelan; and a parcel of butter cake from Amma,
with just a brief admonition to study well and be good to Ammammah. Aran wrote me nothing at all but slipped a trick pen into Amma's
cake box. When I tried to use it, black ink bled everywhere. I shook
my fist at him across the distance, laughed, and tore the ruined pages
from my notebook.

Normally, then, my family in Jaffna wrote—they didn't call, because although Ammammah had a telephone, my parents did not, and it was often too much trouble or an imposition to ask Saras Aunty to use hers. Then, one Saturday in late July, the phone rang. It was Seelan and Amma, ringing from Saras Aunty's house. They were calling with news, and a warning: some Tamil militants in Jaffna had attacked and killed thirteen soldiers, and the bodies were, they had heard, coming back to Colombo for burial. There was sure to be—

"—trouble," Amma said, her voice bristling with static and uncertainty. Niranjan was holding the phone, but it was loud enough that I could hear every third or fourth word she said. "Careful," she finished emphatically, and Niranjan said goodbye to her and carefully set the phone back in its cradle. His usual calm had shifted in a way I could not measure.

"What do you think?" Ammammah asked him. "And what were those boys doing? What were they thinking?" She shook her head in dismay.

"We'll have to wait and see," he said.

"Wait for what?" I asked.

"Just wait, thanggachi," he said, and put his hand on my shoulder. "Just wait."

AMMAMMAH'S WELLAWATTE HOUSE WAS tucked away at the bottom of a hill, so that you almost couldn't see it from the top of the lane. I was used to walking a short distance to hail Rajendran, the short and cheerful moustachioed taxi driver, who usually stood at the top of the lane, smoking. But the next morning, when I walked partway up the slope to wave at him, he was not there. "Sunday," Niranjan said, when I told him. "The fellow must be busy."

By that night, we had heard, because a colleague of my brother's rang the house: the bodies of the dead soldiers had finally arrived, very late, and the crowd that had been waiting for them had grown angry. They were rampaging; Tamil shops in Borella were burning. Niranjan's colleague Paramsothy, who lived in Borella, arrived at our house. Tall and bushy-haired, with spectacles that reminded me of K's, he gave me barely a glance before turning to my brother with a guarded look of alarm. Niranjan ushered Param into his room and shut the door; I heard the two of them talking, and then my grandmother pacing around the parlour, her footsteps grown heavy.

"We should leave," she said to me when I went in to encourage her to sleep.

"Ammammah," I said. "It's late."

"They'll come here," she said, already certain. "I know they'll come here. I remember what happened before."

She went on, talking to me and to herself, worrying. Was she talking about 1958, when she had lived through the anti-Tamil violence with my grandfather? Or 1977, when she had survived riots without him? Some other time I didn't know and couldn't understand? We often spoke in English, but Ammammah was speaking in Tamil then, as though what she was telling me could only be known in Tamil. She spoke faster and faster, her voice rising in horror, and I had never heard her sound so afraid. I want you to understand: I can't even tell you the words she used. The unholy, untranslatable fear. You tell yourself that you are prepared, but then the terror rises inside you. There is no real way to know what you will be able to do until the moment you are required to do it.

MONDAY MORNING USUALLY BROUGHT the beginning of the workweek but that day, the phone rang. It was Niranjan's senior from the hospital. Periannai hung up the phone, shaken.

"I said I would come to work," he said. "But they rang back and said not to go out. There are men on the street."

Looking for Tamils, I understood, although he did not say it.

We tried to eat, but after a while it became clear that none of us could. Ammammah, who had solicitously made four cups of tea, just as solicitously collected them, still full, and began to wash. She was not wearing her usual diamond earrings and as she rinsed the china her face looked somehow defenceless without them. Four soft-boiled eggs grew cold in their egg cups. Niranjan telephoned Malathy and spoke to her and to her parents and hung up with a look of relief on his face. But then, beyond the windows, I heard a bus at the top of the lane, and then another bus, and another noise, something indistinct, almost like the sea was rising. On the piano, Paata's old clock said it was not yet noon. Outside a dog barked. The smell of the sea, too, seemed near. We could hear shouting outside, the wash of sound drawing closer and closer.

"I'll talk to them," Niranjan suggested to Param, who was absently tearing a piece of bread into shreds. "Whoever comes."

"I don't think you should open the door," Param said. He raked a hand through his bushy hair, leaving it dishevelled, and removed his spectacles, polishing them anxiously. "Do you think they'll knock politely? They're only coming for one thing. I already saw them in Borella, machan."

"Perhaps if we just speak to them reasonably," Ammammah said.

"Aunty," Param said. "There is no reasoning with these people. We should hide."

"Go to the library and block the door with your desk," Niranjan said to me. "Take Ammammah with you."

I would have obeyed, but by then we could hear talking outside our front door, and I remained still. What if they heard me? A group of insistent voices clamoured and then a lower one interjected. I closed my eyes and did not move. Someone entered our front garden. There was nothing between us and those people, that sound, but the front door. The lower voice returned, sounding official but indistinct, and then, after a rustling, the roar moved away. I braced myself, and for long minutes the four of us stayed in silence. The phone rang once and I started as if to pick it up, but then it stopped again. At last we heard a rapping at the door. Steadily the person knocked and knocked. The sound grew more and more horrifying.

Niranjan got up.

"Shall I come with you," Param said. Niranjan nodded. The two of them went to the front door. Niranjan opened the door slightly, and then wider, and someone slipped inside.

"I told them there were no Tamils in this house," Rajendran, the taxi driver, said.

"How——" my brother started.

"I have always spoken Sinhala," Rajendran said quietly. "Since I was a child. My first jobs in Colombo were for Sinhalese families. So I told them I was Sinhalese."

Ammammah murmured the names of several gods. Rajendran was from the Hill Country.

"They're gone," Rajendran said. He bowed his head. "But they might come back." He crossed his arms across his chest, and I saw that he was not adopting a posture of defiance but rather trying to hold himself together. He shuddered and exhaled and shuddered again.

WE GATHERED AROUND THE dining table in an impromptu conference of fears.

"They will certainly come back," Niranjan said. "It's just a matter of when."

Rajendran had brought us several parcels of groceries. "I knew you couldn't go out," he explained. "I told them I lived here."

"And they believed you?" Param asked.

"They believed me," he said. "I think so. At least for now, they believe me. Or they pretended to. Do you want me to take you somewhere else? I think they are setting up some shelters for displaced persons. Other neighbourhoods might also be safer. I would have to go and get another vehicle. The one I have here is not large enough to hide you. Many places are burning. They have gone to Maradana and Kotahena and Narahenpita also. Lots of other places. Tamil shops, restaurants, hotels. Factories also, some other drivers said. My wife came and told me that even some buildings across from the President's House are on fire."

Ammammah shut her eyes and opened them again slowly. I grasped her arm. Niranjan looked at her carefully.

"Thank you for offering," my brother said. "I have to think."

"You should call me if you need," Rajendran said. He pulled a piece of newspaper from his pocket and tore a strip from it. He wrote something and handed it to Niranjan. "My number," he said. "Call if you need," he repeated.

"Ammammah," Niranjan said. "This is your house. What would you like to do?"

My grandmother put her hand to her temple. "We should leave," she said. "Together. We should go. We should not be separated."

"I should try to get to Dehiwala," Param said. "My sister is there and my mother lives with her. They didn't answer their telephone. That was why I stopped here instead."

I did not know him well, but Param looked to me like a steady and reliable person. Most of my brother's friends were. Now he looked fearful.

"Ammammah, why don't I go with Param and see what there is to see?" Niranjan said. "Then we will know if it is bad. If Rajendran is willing to take the two of us. I can go and see and come back and then we can decide if we have to pack up properly. If you are sure, Rajendran," Niranjan said to him.

"Yes, if that is what you wish to do," Rajendran said. "The car I will fetch has a flat tyre but it should be enough to get there. I can take you to Dehiwala and bring you back again. But," he said, and nodded at me, "you should block the door."

"You don't think it's better for us just all to go together?" I said to Niranjan uncertainly.

"I need to see where we might shift," he said. "We haven't anyone else in this city, no other relations. I rang some of my colleagues, but now they aren't picking up the phone either. I have no sense of where we can go or how freely we can move. Wouldn't it be worse to go out and have nowhere to go and be unable to get back? Here at least we are in Ammammah's house. We have food and beds."

"I don't know," I said.

"I would suggest my sister's but I don't know what has happened there," Param said, worry thickening his voice.

"Already one friend is staying in my flat," Rajendran said. He inclined his head in apology. "The other neighbours are suspicious. I do not think I can bring more people there—and I do not think we can stay long there ourselves."

"I'll go to Dehiwala with you," Niranjan said to Param, "and find out what we can. I'll come back for you," he said to me and my grandmother, and seeing my face, repeated, "Sashi, Ammammah, I promise. I'll come back for you."

NIRANJAN TOOK HIS LEAVE of us as he had done everything: kindly but efficiently. Curfew would start at six, we had heard. So by half past two that afternoon Rajendran went and got the other car and the three of them left. "I will try to come back before the curfew, thanggachi," Niranjan said. "And if it can't be managed this evening, then tomorrow. I'll try to ring from Param's house, also." He kissed my grandmother and kissed me and put his hand briefly on my cheek. "Be careful, please," he said, "and take good care of Ammammah, and don't open the door to any unknown persons. And if I don't call, try not to worry. It may be simply that the line is cut."

"You be careful," I said back to him fiercely, and he nodded. "Go and come back to me," I said. "I'll go and come back," he said in return, and when his shadow had disappeared into Rajendran's car, my grandmother went back into the house and directly to the armoire. From under a pile of old saris she excavated the bone and ivory chess set. A small and ornately carved Pillaiyar winked at me: a knight piece.

"We'll go into his library and shut the door," she said. "I wish he were here."

I thought she meant Niranjan. She meant my grandfather, his impenetrable castle of books.

THE AFTERNOON CREPT ON. We blocked the door to the library with my small desk and I realised just how insubstantial the elegant piece of furniture was. We played chess, and in between turns, I packed the garnet earrings and Ammammah's jewellery and a change of clothes for each of us in a small satchel, in case Niranjan returned ready to take us away with him. I leafed through my books idly, wondering what my brother was seeing outside. Which of the places I had come to know this year were burning now? "Checkmate," my grandmother said again and again; I lost several games of chess in a row without caring. My grandmother was ruthless in her concentration, perhaps as a stay against other things to which her mind could have wandered. Where was my brother? The phone rang: Hasna, calling to check on us.

"When did Niranjan say he would be back?" she said urgently.

Paata's clock said half past six. Curfew had begun half an hour ago.

"It might be tomorrow," I said dully.

"Where did he go?"

"Dehiwala," I said.

"But Dehiwala is burning, Sashi," Hasna said.

"He is with his colleague. And Rajendran," I explained. Perhaps if I repeated it enough, like a poosai, it would protect them.

"He must be coming tomorrow," Hasna said at last, too late.

"But Dehiwala—is—burning—" I said, gasping into the receiver.

"But there is a curfew," Hasna said, too reasonably.

And then she said, slowly, as though she almost did not believe it herself: "Sashi, in our neighbourhood, the houses that do not belong to Tamils are untouched. I can see the Tamil houses burning, and there is nothing I can do."

WHEN I WOKE UP on the floor, confused, lost in my own room, it was only nine o'clock. Still Monday evening. Why would this brotherless night not pass? We had played chess, keeping watch on the house and each other. Finally, I had given Ammammah my bed, despite her trying to insist that we share. She slept on, curled up, her face anxious. I got up and moved the desk and went to our small washroom, where I rinsed my face and looked at it in the smeared old glass. In the dark distance, something roared again, but this time it sounded different. In the parlour I knelt on the piano bench and squinted out the high window. It was not yet completely dark, and I could make out that a group of men had gathered in the garden of our neighbor's house. My throat seized and I clapped my hand over my mouth before I could scream. Not known persons, as my grandmother would have said. Persons to whom a curfew did not apply.

In the dim light, I could see the father of the house, a man I had met only in passing, kneeling in front of his own door, trying and failing to cover his head with his hands. Before him, the man at the head of the mob brandished a machete. Behind that man, twenty more, each carrying a knife or stick of some kind. Some wielded rough kitchen knives. Were these the same men who had banged on our door yesterday? The men who, thanks to Rajendran, thought Sinhalese people occupied Ammammah's house? It would only be a matter of time before they realised they had been deceived. We would not be able to wait for my brother.

Niranjan—oldest, dearest, gone—had given me no instructions for this scenario, and I had not asked for any. Neither of us had imagined such a thing. But at that moment, newly in charge, I burned with anger at myself for not having foreseen, for not having prepared. I turned away from the sound of the screaming and protesting and our neighbour being beaten. His wife shouting behind him and him telling her to go. Their dogs barking and then suddenly stopping. If I went outside, to the side of our house, could I help her and her small son into our garden? Would she be able to escape?

I ran back to the library and woke Ammammah.

"We have to go," I told her.

She got up swiftly and began dressing. "Yes," she said. A tin fell on the floor but she did not bother to pick it up. The smell of Yardley lavender powder, which my grandmother and my mother both used, wafted into the air.

"Can you hear them?"

"No."

"Next door," I said. "They are beating Mr. Chelliah. About twenty men. Hurry, Ammammah."

She looked at me sharply. "Can we help him?"

"No," I said. "But Mrs. Chelliah, I can try. More than that we can't do. They will come for us next."

"Rajendran told them this was a Sinhalese house," Ammammah said.

"That will give us only time," I said. "Hurry. Here, take the satchel and go out to the garden and then call to the Jayasinghes and see if they will help you. I'll help Mrs. Chelliah and then come." To escape, my grandmother would have to get over the high wall between us and the house on the other side, which belonged to the Jayasinghes, who were Sinhalese and presumably safe. If they did not help her she would not be able to do it herself. And we could not dare to go out to the main road now. Others would be waiting for us.

We went down the hall towards the kitchen and Ammammah went right and I went left; she went in the direction of the Jayasinghes and I went in the direction of the Chelliahs. We had not been anything beyond cordial with the Jayasinghes; now we might find out what kind of people they were. What would they do with an old Tamil woman on the other side of their wall? I went out and around to the narrow strip of lawn before the Chelliah-side fence and peered through the gap in the slats so that I had a different angle on the same violent scene I had watched from the parlour. The crowd of men dragged Mr. Chelliah across the tender grass, into their house, Mrs. Chelliah following and screaming and flailing at them with her fists. One of them whirled and struck her and she went down without a sound. On the other side of the fence, I covered my mouth again to stop my horror from betraying me. Her little boy, Jegan, pulled on her arm, weeping. How long did I have before the throng of men had had their fill of looting the house and remembered the woman they had left on the ground? I found a cinder block and waited until the men had gone inside. Then I stepped up onto it and heaved myself over, into the Chelliahs' destroyed garden.

I ran to Jegan. "Jegan, darling," I said, "can you come here to Acca?" He screamed but let me pick him up. "Good boy," I said automatically. His small soft weight was heavy in my arms and his face wet in my neck. His mother lay at my feet with one of her legs bent. Her right cheek had a bright mark where the man had struck her. From here I could see what I had missed from the parlour: their two dogs lay to her left, their bellies slit. I looked away quickly. "Nanthini," I said, bending down as far as I could without letting go of her child. She did not respond. "Nanthini," I said again, and then, looking up, I made a quick calculation. I shifted Jegan left in my arms, then used my right hand to drag a stone back to the fence. I do not know quite how I managed to get up and over once more, this time with him. As I landed, I fell slightly onto my left hip, but Jegan tumbled out of my arms and landed squarely on his feet. "Good—boy," I said again, out of breath. I took his hand, and we went across our back green, and then over to the Jayasinghes. "It's me," I called over their wall, "Sashikala." How I hoped nobody had seen me. How I hoped the Chelliah house was so full of treasure that they would not notice one escaped girl, one escaped child, one escaped grandmother.

Lasitha Jayasinghe's head emerged above the wall, his eyes wide and focused. He held his arms out for the child, and then I went up and over once more. Ammammah stood behind him, holding one of her wrists, which was now bandaged. In the other hand she clutched the satchel. I took in the sight of her hungrily; she was whole and safe. I felt dizzy with relief. Perhaps Lasitha would help her again and onward if I could not. "Come, Sashi," she said to me hurriedly, and took my arm to bring me inside the house with them. "I am sorry, Ammammah," I said. "I have to go back. Jegan's mother is still over there." She blanched. Then, after a pause: "I'll go with you," Lasitha said. "It will be safer." He passed Jegan to his wife. We could hear a sound, shouting, and I wondered if they were pouring petrol on the Chelliah house. "Quickly, go," Lasitha's wife said to us.

Up and over again, but this time Lasitha helped me, and fear made my feet quick. I led him back through our yard and to the edge of the Chelliahs'. Both of us put our hands over our noses and mouths. My eyes watered at the smell of the petrol and the growing fire. Up and over, up and over, and I was glad for Lasitha behind me, for another witness. I had not dreamed it. Mrs. Chelliah still lay heavy in the garden, not yet violated, not yet physically any worse than unconscious. "I can do it," he said like he was trying to convince himself, and he bent over her and picked her up and slung her over his shoulder. If I had come without him, I realised, I would not have been able to carry her. "Where is Mr. Chelliah?" he asked. "In the house," I said, and he understood and for a second his eyes flashed. Then he turned around and said, "There's no time." And with Mrs. Chelliah in our arms and Mr. Chelliah behind us in the burning house, we went.

LASITHA JAYASINGHE'S FACE WAS grey, and he appeared suddenly old, though he could not have been past his mid-thirties. Before I had thought him shy and retiring. "Our neighbours on the other side are the ones who told those men that you are Tamil," he said. "Your house can't even be seen from the top of the road, Mrs. Thanabalasingham. Those men were going to go on, and those neighbours, the Waduges, they stopped them. They pointed you out. Mr. Waduge has always been, I don't know what to say. We cannot stay here for very long. Sushila said we can take you to Hindu College. There is a shelter in place there. Come, Sashi, Aunty, get in the car. Come, come."

I had forgotten that Lasitha's wife, Sushila, was Tamil. Normally she wore a pottu but she had wiped her brow clear. She spoke to Jegan in Tamil, calming him, and hearing her, I closed my eyes and wanted my own mother. But I was not the child here; I had made choices for people who were here and people who were not. I tried not to think of Suresh Chelliah being dragged into his own house, the Chelliahs' furniture become kindling. Sushila tucked Jegan into the back seat, in my arms, before she got into the front and spoke to Lasitha in Sinhala. Nanthini and my grandmother climbed in next and bent themselves around us. Nanthini had come to about half an hour after we had brought her to the Jayasinghes', and after crying her husband's name once, she had been entirely silent. My grandmother gripped her shoulder and Jegan clung to her hand, and together the four of us hunkered down, our heads lowered as far as they could go. Above Lasitha's head, the rearview mirror reflected flames. The Chelliahs' house, I thought at first, at the end of its burning. Then the roof crashed in, and I saw the colour. No, I realised, looking up, leaning back. It was the beginning of ours.

3.

Displacement

COLOMBO TO JAFFNA,
1983

WHAT CAN I TELL YOU ABOUT MY BROTHER NIRANJAN? I ALWAYS listened to him, every second of every minute of every hour since I had been born. Periannai was the first person to take me to live beyond Jaffna, and the first person to tell me to question its traditions and boundaries. His was the first face I knew and trusted—not Amma's, not Appa's, but his, with its earnest brow and thick hair and my father's hooked nose. We had the same smile. I still have it—his is the face I see in my mirror. He said he would come back. I have never forgiven myself for letting him go. Could you?

In the years since those days, people have asked me not only to remember the riots but also to explain them. How can I explain? I want you to understand: leaving my grandmother's house was the first choice I made without my brother, the first choice I made alone. I decided how to proceed, but how little I remember, how little I know for certain. I have tried to retrace my own steps, to find where I made mistakes, to repair them. What could I have done differently to travel once more with my brother, to see Rajendran smoking at the top of the lane, to keep Nanthini Chelliah from becoming a widow? You must understand—or someday, I must understand: there was nothing I could have done.

Later I learned that the violence against Tamils during Black July marked the beginning of the war, but then, I could not have counted how many people were sheltering at Colombo Hindu College, where Lasitha Jayasinghe took us. It did not occur to me to count or prove, to measure our losses for history or for other people to understand or believe. I did not collect the evidence of my own destroyed life; I did not know people would ask me for it. I did not know that the gangs of Sinhalese men who had gone down the streets seeking Tamil houses and businesses had voter rolls, to identify us by ethnicity. I did not yet understand that it was organised. I did not know how long it had taken the government to declare a curfew, to pretend to protect us. I did not yet understand how many of my people, marked by language and mukkuthis and pottus, by a thousand other tiny inheritances, never made it to any shelter and instead were slain in their homes, on the streets, even on trains running through Colombo Fort Station. They died in places I had shopped and walked and visited; they died in places I had never imagined people dying. They died in places beyond Colombo when the violence spread. They died privately and publicly, with their families and separated from them. I did not know. In the wake of what had happened at our house, in the early days at Colombo Hindu College, I could not comprehend the scale of the cataclysm.

Thousands of displaced Tamils must have gone to stay in the refugee camps. Later, when someone asked me how I had felt there, I realised I had felt safe. So it must have been guarded in some way. It was unclear to me who was in charge. When we arrived, a British man asked me my name in a loud voice, and someone told me he worked for an international charity, which was a way of saying that he might not be helpful. "The poor Tamils," he kept saying in a plaintive, plummy voice. Another man with a clipboard asked me questions, which I must have answered for myself and for my grandmother. His name was Mr. Shanmugam and he had a kind, dark, unwrinkled face and yellowed white hair. I must have given him our family names and told him who in our household was missing. I must have asked if anyone in the camp had seen my brother. He must have written Niranjan's name down on his clipboard, along with mine. It must have been the first record that my brother was missing: Sashikala Kulenthiren, with her grandmother, Mrs. Revathy Thanabalasingham, and without her elder brother, Niranjan.

I do not know how long we were there. I think it must have been more than a week. It may have been less. At some point, Nanthini Chelliah separated from us, as some relatives of hers came to take her and Jegan with them, and then it was just me and my grandmother and the dull nightly memory of carrying Jegan's warm weight over the barriers between our houses. No matter the hour when I woke up drenched with fear, she was always awake and watching me. Like Nanthini, Ammammah had stopped talking very much. She carried the Pillaiyar chess piece with her—had she hidden it in her blouse as we fled?—and when I sat up in the dark, I saw her turning it over and over in her hand, murmuring to herself in a way that made me wonder about the state of her mind. When I first saw her holding it, I realised that in my own haste I had left my books. If circumstances had been different, I could have spent the long hours in the camp reading. I wanted my exam notes, but more than that, I wished for Niranjan's medical textbooks, and the copy of *Thai* Dayalan had given me—pages my brothers had turned. A book could have removed me from that world.

There were other missing things, too. In the College there was no privacy and not enough toilets; the day after we arrived, I got my period and looked dumbly at my soiled clothes until a woman my mother's age came over and gave me an old sari to tear into rags. I was fleetingly and illogically glad that we had not been taken to the shelter in the temple; menstruating women were not supposed to be in temples. Perhaps nobody would have cared then. Many people were injured and in shock. My grandmother's bandaged hand swelled around the wound she had sustained; she had cut her wrist deeply on the wall as she had lowered herself into the Jayasinghes' garden. I kept my worries about her mostly to myself, because everyone seemed to be a stranger.

I saw many people I knew casually—tuition schoolmates, neighbours, some of the other women who had visited our house with proposals for my disappeared brother—but though I hunted through the blank-faced and exhausted rows of Tamil people for Malathy and her parents, I did not see them. Nor did I find Niranjan, Rajendran, and Param, though daily I studied new arrivals and asked if any had met a young pair of doctors and a Hill Country Tamil driver in Dehiwala. Nobody I spoke to had seen them, although everyone answered me patiently. Perhaps they hoped for the same kindness when they enquired after their own missing people. I wished I could enquire after Rajendran's wife, or Param's family, but I did not know where they lived or their names. If they were alive, I thought, they must be wondering and wait-ing and searching, like me.

And as I searched for my brother, others searched for me. After some lonely days, Hasna came to know where we were. She must have gone to every camp to locate us. She and her father, who I called Ibra-him Uncle, took us out every morning so that we could bathe and eat at their house, rather than eating the terrible, scant camp food. Hasna did not make me talk too much, for which mercy I was grateful; she talked to me instead. No matter how much I shook, she spoke to me steadily, as though I was not doing anything out of the ordinary. On the first day we went there, as I ate the fresh pittu and fish curry her mother had made, Hasna told me what I already knew: our house had burned. Her father had gone to find us and found the house ransacked and in flames. It had burned all night, our beloved things the fuel. Now, Hasna told me regretfully, there was nothing. "I'm so sorry," she said, watching me over her glasses to see how I took the news. I thought of my small library bedroom, my grandfather's shelves and irreplaceable photographs, the inkwell and broad desk into which my brother had dipped his pen, the chess set that my grandmother and I had used at last, after years of thinking it an heirloom too precious to touch. The piano, which had been her piano. Oh, I can tell you: as I heard what Hasna said, I wanted nothing more than a house—my house. If I could not return to my grandmother's home in Colombo, I wanted the four clean walls of my Jaffna childhood, the courtyard with its cup of sunlight, the small and dear lane where I had grown up. Give me a house that hasn't burned, I thought: an upright home full of people who consider me precious.

Hasna had three sisters and two brothers, so despite the generosity of her family, there was no room to stay at her place, and every afternoon Ammammah and I came back and lay down in a hall at the school, where almost a hundred women slept together. Every time Hasna and her father came to get us, Ibrahim Uncle escorted my grandmother very gently to and from their car, as though she were a piece of china that might break. She walked gingerly, as though the world had become foreign to her. I worried about her, but in comparison to others, we were lucky to have friends to help us. Still, I longed to see my parents and my brothers—and feared seeing them, too, since they would ask me what had happened to Niranjan, a question to which I had no answer. Hasna, kindly, did not ask, but I knew that her father was trying to find out.

After some blurry days, we were notified that we were among the next to be sent to Jaffna. The departure was too swift for me to bid Hasna goodbye. We would be safe in a Tamil place, the government had decided. Most of us had family or friends there, but of course, for me, it was home. I do not know how they chose who was to go when; we went on the second or third ship. We were bused to the harbour and walked to a pier and then they directed us into the belly of a small cargo ship, in which we sat too close to each other, the ripe scents of each other's pain unavoidable. From the open centre where we waited you could only look up. All you could see was the sky. Colombo receded invisibly into the distance, but others whispered about which neighbourhoods behind us were gone. I am from Borella, I am from Dehiwala, I am from Wellawatte, people confessed to each other. I will never go back, some claimed; I will go back immediately, others insisted. Give me a biscuit for my child, one woman asked; give me some water for my mother, another said. Having almost nothing, we traded the smallest favours and mercies. The trip took, like everything did during that time, immeasurable and interminable hours; the clock stretched its arms generously to enfold us. Later someone told me our trip had lasted four days, but I recalled only one long, starred, cold night on the ocean, during which I held on to the small satchel and my silent grandmother's uninjured hand like they were what would keep me alive.

When we disembarked, some passengers were collected by people they knew in Jaffna. Others were made to wait in a hall. I had thought I would be relieved when we arrived, but I did not recognise where we were, and my family had not come. Who was in charge? Impossibly tired, I tried to speak to a man next to me, but could not make sense of his words or my own. Perhaps we were in a school or a community centre near the harbour. It was no place I recognised, and no place to which I have since returned. How was I not at home yet? I told anyone who would listen that I was from Jaffna, but the men checking our papers and organising transport and making lists of us paid no attention. I must have looked to them such a wrecked, unimportant slip of a girl. Why hadn't my parents come for us? Did they know where we were?

"Sashi," I heard behind me, and then there, at one of the makeshift volunteer desks, was K. Time snapped back into place as though it obeyed him. I blinked—he wasn't wearing spectacles, but behind his thicker moustache, it was his slim, sensitive face. Of course K was here, at the centre of things, organising. I should have expected him.

He and several of his medical school batchmates were helping, he explained. "Let's get this sorted," he said in a businesslike fashion. "Come. Where is Niranjan? Your grandmother?"

My grandmother was huddled on the floor in a corner behind the desk, watching us. "There," I said, and stretched my arm towards her.

He searched her face and then mine. "Unwell," he suggested.

"Yes," I said. I was choking, I thought.

"Here," he said. "Sit." He pushed me gently into a chair and extracted a handkerchief from his pocket. "Here. Sashi—Sashi, take a breath. Can you tell me what happened?"

I stumbled through, wiping my face at intervals. I apologised for sweating although we both knew I was crying. So much violence, I could hardly believe it, even as it came out of my own mouth. I did not want to tell him. Even as I tell you, I know you must find it unbelievable. But he was prepared to listen. And he would believe me, I saw; I would tell him the whole thing until I learned how to come as close as I could to describing it. I started and stopped and began again and still I could not reach the end, which I had to tell him and he needed to know. He crouched in front of the chair in which he had put me. He was wearing a plaid cotton shirt of the sort that was in fashion then, and I leaned forward in my exhaustion and laid my mouth against the cloth on his chest and said what had happened to Niranjan.

K pulled me up.

"Sashi, I am so sorry," he said. "I need you to say it again. I want to make sure I'm hearing you right."

Still aflame with my own horror, I told K clearly that my brother was missing, my brother was gone, I did not know where my brother was. Once I started saying it, I could not stop, the rush of words growing stranger and stranger by the second. At last, ashamed, I stopped and gasped. "I let him go," I said, and sobbed. K put his hand over his face for a second, and when he lifted it again his eyes were like the ocean when the sky has no colour to it. I did not see it then, but with every piece of information I gave him he was becoming someone else.

"I'm so sorry," he said again, but this time his words were slower. He paused for a long minute. "And you, Sashi?"

I understood what K was asking. "Nothing happened to me," I said.

He studied me. "You can tell me," he offered.

I believed that. I could have told him. But I had escaped. Unlike most of the people who had come on the ship with me, I still had a home, although I had seen another burn.

"Nothing happened, I promise," I said.

"And your grandmother?" he asked.

I looked away. "Perhaps she can talk to you," I muttered.

K came around the desk and stood next to Ammammah. She gazed up at him and said nothing. He slid down, down, down, until he was sitting beside her, as tender as I ever saw him. Their backs against the same wall, you see. I thought of bedside manner, the bedside manner he would have someday, this boy who had cracked eggs onto my body. "Thana Paati," he said. He was addressing her as he would have addressed his own grandmother. "Mrs. Thanabalasingham. I don't know if you remember me. I'm K. I live down the lane from your daughter and her family.

"I've come to take you home," he said.

SOMEHOW—A DOER OF IMPROBABLE things in improbable times—K procured a car and took us back to our village, our lane. He was a bad driver, or the roads were bad; as we hurtled along my heart climbed into my throat. When we arrived Amma and Appa were on the veranda with Seelan and Dayalan and Aran. My mother called my name, and I ran to open the gate. I stumbled up the steps into her strong, clean arms. She caught me, and everything about her smelled fresh and sweet and safe and impossible. The next words out of my mouth would ruin her.

"But where is Niranjan?" my father asked.

Ammammah met that sentence with eyes of such misery that I had to look away. "It's my fault," she cried out. "It's my fault." She clasped her bandaged wrist in her other hand. I turned to her, startled; she had barely spoken in days.

"It is not your fault, Thana Paati," K said, and then he told my parents so that neither my grandmother nor I would have to do it. Appa sat down on the steps and put his head in his hands, and suddenly each of my brothers seemed younger and smaller, standing in a row without Periannai. In my arms, Amma wilted: I held her up.

"I am so sorry, sir," K said to my father.

"He must be dead," Appa said wonderingly. "Niranjan must be dead. But, my God, my God, how will we know?"

OUR HOUSE FELT PERIANNAI'S absence. I had longed for home, but what I found there, after what had happened, did not bring me the comfort I sought. My brothers, new to the knowledge that had drowned me for days, did not know what to do with their anger and grief. Seelan chopped down a tree in the garden without asking anyone's permission and, when asked why, replied that it was in the wrong place. Dayalan vanished for long hours; none of us knew or asked where he went. Aran assumed the duties that had belonged to our three older brothers; he helped Amma around the house with heavy tasks and ran errands for her. I sympathised with the part of Aran that seemed to be wondering, if he worked hard enough, would Niranjan return to us? I, too, bargained silently.

And the house offered reminders of Niranjan in every corner. Everywhere I went, I saw things Periannai had left behind when he had last been there with us. In cabinets and on shelves I found things he had put away, or things Amma had secreted away against his return, a mother's small treasures. In a drawer, I touched some of his shirts; his old cricket bat; the political histories he had loved to read; photographs of batchmates; his shaving kit. It smelled like him. Under one bed I found a favourite pair of chappals. My own sisterly talismans were mostly gone: on the bookshelf where he had kept old medical textbooks, there was only painful bare space. He had taken those books to Colombo for me to study, and now they were ashes. One exception: the garnet earrings glistened in the dark, hidden in a secret compartment of my dresser. I did not dare to wear them anywhere. I did not go anywhere, even to the temple. When one of us arrived home after a long trip, my mother usually required us to visit the kovil immediately. This time she said nothing. When someone in the family dies, we do not enter the temple or others' homes for a year. In this case, however, we did not know what space we were allowed. What had happened to him? There were days when I found myself just beyond the temple's striped walls, remembering my brother's words about who could enter and who could not.

Then, some days after we had returned, Seelan came and found me in Appa's study where I was staring at books without reading them. He said, "Sashi. Someone is at the gate. Some unknown person. I think he must have come for you."

I went to the veranda. Ibrahim Uncle, Hasna's father, stood on the other side of the gate, in the red dirt of our small Jaffna lane.

"Come in, come in," I urged, dread rising inside me. In Colombo, Ibrahim Uncle was a figure of comfort and safety, but his presence in Jaffna unsettled me. I made myself smile at him; he was our friend, after all. My parents had come out behind me and my father also smiled emptily.

"Amma, Appa, this is Ibrahim Uncle," I said. "His daughter Hasna studied with me at the tuition class in Colombo. Her mother is your friend, Amma—Rizana. Rizana Aunty. When Ammammah and I were waiting in the school, after being displaced, they came and helped us."

My father immediately stepped forward to shake Ibrahim Uncle's hand. "Thank you for helping my daughter and my mother," Appa said very formally.

"Please, sit," Amma said. "It's an honor to meet you. What can I offer you?"

Ibrahim Uncle sat, uncertainly, and accepted a tumbler of lime juice. As he sipped, he asked after my grandmother, who was sleeping, as she had been for days. My brothers slowly came out to the veranda to join us; I asked how Rizana Aunty and Hasna were. Hasna had not come with him? No, she was still in Colombo, but she had sent me a parcel. He lifted a bag from over his shoulder. She had given me a set of schoolbooks for the A/L exam. Looking more closely, I saw that they were her personal copies, with her dog-eared pages and markings. I hadn't told her mine had burned in the house, but she had guessed or known.

"I can't accept these, Ibrahim Uncle," I said.

"She said she would share with others," he said.

"She needs these," I said. "They belong to her. They have her notes."

"Please," Ibrahim Uncle said. "Please. This is what my daughter asked of me and I gave her my word that I would give them to you. She said they were from you studying together, so they are your notes too, Sashikala. The exams in Colombo are in September. We are all right. She can find another way."

I opened one of the textbooks to find a letter addressed to me, in Hasna's handwriting. I suddenly remembered: I had saved Dayalan's sketch of our family between the pages of one of Niranjan's books in just this fashion. So it, too, had burned, with K's face still a secret on the other side.

"Thank you, Ibrahim Uncle," I said. The letter had slipped to the floor. Seelan picked the paper up and handed it to me. It smelled like Hasna, like some faint flower. If only she had come with him.

"I think you knew while you were at Hindu College, after you were displaced, that I was trying to find out about Dr. Niranjan," Ibrahim Uncle said. "His whereabouts."

"Yes," I said.

"I can tell you," he said, and my mother's mouth twisted painfully. "Do you want to fetch your Ammammah?"

"Amma can sleep," my mother said. "Tell us."

Ibrahim Uncle took a breath and put his hands together as if in prayer.

"Dr. Niranjan went to Dehiwala with the driver, Rajendran, and with his colleague, Dr. Paramsothy. After several enquiries, I did meet someone who saw what happened to them. I am so sorry to bring this news. But I am a father also, and I would want to know.

"They were killed in Dehiwala," he said.

I must have been crying. I am not sure. But it does not matter what I did. Whatever it was, Ibrahim Uncle did what Hasna would have done. He reached out and took my hand and held it.

"What happened to my brother?" I whispered. "Please go on."

"I am lucky—if one can say that—to have found the information I was looking for. A Sinhalese friend of mine was sheltering some people in Dehiwala," Ibrahim Uncle said. "The friend described a car that matched the description you gave me, Sashikala. I told him about the flat. He said yes. He said a mob set upon a car like that, a black car with three Tamil men inside of it. A flat tyre."

"Say it," my mother said urgently.

"They set the car on fire," Ibrahim Uncle said.

IN OUR FAMILY, as in many Tamil families, after death, there is ceremony. On the third day, on the thirty-first day—the timing and shape of the rituals depend on your caste, on your village and history, the state and presence of the body, and when mourners can come. Our family was among Jaffna's caste-privileged; Niranjan would have hated everything about what we did. My mother, if pressed, would have said that such formalities make a path for grief. I only know that with or without these customs, you mark time, and you learn that the days march on, even though you would prefer for them to stop. Ask the clock for mercy; I promise, there is none—only a day on which your loved one is dead, and another, and another, and another after that. A day, at last, when you cook meat for the first time; a day when you make all the favourite meals of the departed person and serve it to their photograph or empty clothes, so that they might exit our world and enter the world of spirits in peace, well-fed and loved and let go.

Most people would not perform these rituals without the body, but my mother was not most people, and so she did them. The neighbourhood thought her mad. Amma, who was beside herself with a strange and stoic grief, insisted on following the path she would have followed if she could have laid hands on her boy. Who could blame her? My brother's body had been part of her body. And so on the appropriate day, she made all his favourite curries: eggplant, mutton, chicken, murungakkai. She sang to herself, under her breath, the lullabies she had sung to him when he was a little child. She plated the food and laid the plates, heaped with rice, in front of a chair on which she had draped an old pair of his trousers, a crisp collared shirt and a tie. But she did not finish there. When I went out into the courtyard that day, I saw what she had done.

"Malathy came," Amma said, her gaze slippery and vague. "Malathy gave me Niranjan's white coat. He left it one time when he went to see her."

Amma draped the coat, too, over the back of the chair. I thought of Ophelia going mad.

"Malathy," I said wonderingly. "She came? When did she come?"

"This morning," Amma said.

As Amma wandered around the chair, adjusting things, I went to ask my father if it was true. Had Malathy come, or had my mother lost her hold on what was real? Appa confirmed: Malathy had come very early in the morning, directly from a visit to the Nallur Temple, and had gone again, unable to bear staying. She was also with her family in Jaffna, having been displaced from Colombo. She had asked my parents to hold a celebration of Niranjan's life, and they had agreed to do so. She had left my mother the coat, and a stethoscope that Niranjan had given her. He had joked with her, she said, that it was a placeholder for her wedding thali.

The following week, when my parents held prayers and the promised celebration in our home, I saw her, my almost sister, in the back of the crowd of neighbours and friends and relatives who came to honour my brother. Her parents flanked her. I sat beside Ammammah, and when I rose to bring them to be with our family, Malathy lifted her hand to stop me. She was not part of our family, I understood. The riots had prevented that from happening. Their time as a couple had been intensely private and outside the sphere of this world; the last time most of these people had seen her had been at the engagement. So she was alone, and she wanted to be as alone as she could be in that crowd, for as long as she could.

But after a while, when people were done singing thevaram and

giving speeches about Periannai and were eating the food my mother
and her friends had made, Malathy did come forward, and people
looked up from their plates to watch her in gossipy sympathy. She
wore a white sari and my brother's ring and a thin, shining gold necklace around her throat. Had he given her that too? They would have
had clever, sensitive children, with his hooked nose and her direct
smile. How much about him I would never see or know, and how
much about her. To this day I do not know what happened to her during the riots. Her plain, soft oval face had slimmed since I had seen her
last, and her widow's peak aimed like a pointed arrow at the top of her
brow, with her braid woven as usual into a glossy knot at the nape of
her elegant neck. I thought she would look at me as she walked towards
us, but she had eyes for no one but Periannai in the photograph at the
front of the room. Why had I let Niranjan leave? I cursed myself. My
mother had never asked me, and neither, I realised, would Malathy.
There she goes, the almost bride, the people around me murmured to
each other. Did you know she is also a doctor? Like him. What a beautiful girl. What a shame.

ALTHOUGH SO MANY PEOPLE in Jaffna and all over the country
were mourning and gathering themselves, exams still approached. Of
course, Appa said. "You have to study when you can," he told me.
"Every moment is precious." And every moment was haunted. At
night I found myself awake more often than not, and to blot out the
images of Ammammah's crashing white roof and Mr. Chelliah's kneeling form and a burning black car that I had not seen but which I could
and did imagine, the pictures that would come no matter what, I lit a
lamp and turned the pages of the textbooks Hasna had given me. In
some places my friend had written me notes and underlined parts of
the texts, reminding me to study my weak points. Knowing my mind
better than anyone else, she offered merciless advice, paired with
knowing jokes and clever memory tricks; I read over and over again
her words of encouragement. Her letter, even dearer, offered some-

thing else: blunt sympathy and a brief, funny description of what it had been like to observe me with my brother. "The big, stubborn goat loved the little, stubborn goat," she wrote. I laughed until I cried over that letter, and the memory of the three of us, with my grandmother, walking into the sea together on the beautiful Saturday Niranjan had given us with his first cheque.

When it was time to take the exams, I had nothing left to fear. I wonder if you know this, the still feeling past your first real sorrow, watching your own pen move across paper as though you are not the one holding it. I want you to understand: the riots made a planet on which I did not wish to live, a planet without my brother. The examiners gave me the body of a creature that had been living and I cut into it coolly. I was not afraid. Later, when the results came, I gave Amma and Appa the paper with the news and went into the courtyard where so often I had sat with Periannai. I could hear my mother sobbing with pained happiness in the other room; she had not wept since Ibrahim Uncle had brought the news of Niranjan's death, and if anything I had done had cracked her open from the vague stoicism of her mourning, I was glad. Henry the dog came and pressed his small head into my calf consolingly, as though he, too, wished my brother were there to pass him from person to grieving, celebrating person. I had gotten near-perfect marks; I could go to the medical school at the University of Jaffna if I wished—the only thing I had ever known I wanted. The possibility seemed hollow and unreal. For my achievement, my father gave me my first stethoscope, the same one Malathy had brought back to us, the same one Niranjan had given to her. "Do you want a new one?" Appa asked. I did not. I wanted nothing new. I wanted anything I could have that had belonged to my brother, anything he had seen or touched or chosen. The metal pressed against my neck, and for the first time in my life, even having done what I had promised myself I would do, I could not imagine the future.

I want you to understand: it does not matter if you cannot imagine the future. Still, relentless, it comes.

4.

Recruitment

JAFFNA, 1983–1984

ON THE MORNING AFTER THE CELEBRATION OF NIRANJAN'S LIFE, Ammammah began, at last, to speak again. By then white was creeping into her hair; she gave no sign of noticing or caring. Instead, "my hand," she murmured, "my hand, my hand." She talked to herself, at first, and then she talked to us. "My hand," she informed us, and we took her to a doctor, who said we were too late. I blamed myself for not taking action earlier. After some time, the injury, which had been swollen with infection, healed, but imperfectly; Ammammah's grip and fingers remained weak, and she kept a deep and narrow scar that bent like a cuff around the underside of her slender wrist. She protected the hand when she walked, bending her body on the right, and began to do more and more with her left side, even though some people in Sri Lanka thought that to be left-handed was bad luck. "No," my grandmother said when people asked her about this: "I make my own luck." They thought she was just being proud, but she held herself responsible for her bad luck, too. She thought Periannai's death was her fault, and I thought it was my fault, and when our paths crossed in the Jaffna house, she averted her eyes and neither of us spoke of it. My bright and blazing young grandmother became old.

Only days after the riots, after a debate in Parliament, it became illegal to advocate separatism in Sri Lanka, as the Tamil politicians had been doing. The Tamil MPs resigned their seats in protest. The government denied responsibility for the violence, laying blame at the feet of Sinhalese Marxist rebels. These people were out of control, officials said heavily. But this, like so much of what the government had always said about communal violence, was obviously preposterous. Even in Jaffna, we knew how the government had brutally killed so many members of that southern insurrection. The bodies of young Sinhalese men had floated down rivers. The state controlled what it wanted to control. Seelan, telling me about this bureaucratic fabulism, laughed incredulously. In our house, in our village, in all of Jaffna, in all the Tamil communities I knew, we were watching reality remake itself.

Still, some people struggled to return to what they knew. When Amma asked Ammammah to stay in Jaffna instead of returning home, my grandmother refused. I could not bear to think about what it would be like now to walk the streets of Colombo. But perhaps she could not bear to look at my mother's face any longer. Amma and Appa asked her if she wanted to try to emigrate to Canada or the U.K., where they were taking refugees, but she refused that also. "Emigration is for the young," she said. "I have lived in Colombo and I will die in Colombo." And so as soon as she could go back, she did, against our wishes and with our love, to a small, shabby flat that had been rented for her there, in Wellawatte, not far from where her house had been. She took the train, declining all company, and when she boarded, she carried only the small satchel I had packed when we fled her house. "Tell that boy I said thank you," she said to me when she kissed me goodbye. She meant K. To my surprise, he had not been among the parade of those bidding her farewell, but when I turned back after settling her in her seat, I saw that he was watching us from the station platform. She leaned out the window and raised her altered right hand in his direction.

When she arrived back in Colombo, she telephoned Saras Aunty and had her inform us, and then we did not hear from her for many months. I wrote her letters on Sundays, and Amma wrote her too, but neither of us received replies, and after some time, we did not even ask each other about it. I often thought of my grandmother re-entering Colombo, the very neighbourhood where her home and her life had been destroyed. In my sleep, I went with her into the burned house and cradled her torn hand. In daylight, I sat on the veranda, turning over and over in my palm the Pillaiyar chess piece she had left behind.

AFTER THE RIOTS, RUMOURS BEGAN to move through the group of young people who lived in the world between the Jaffna schools, the university entrance exams, and the university itself. So many of us occupied a strange, grey space of waiting. Which rules and procedures and schedules would be followed, and which abandoned, amidst what kind of political trouble? We did not know, and so we waited for political trouble as we waited for exam results. And some of us waited to return to our studies.

The boys I knew grew restless. I grew restless. I should have gone to university that year, at eighteen, but there would not be a seat for me until I was twenty. Once you were accepted to university, you matriculated based on space, and in those days, there were sometimes not enough spaces for how diligent we were. We, the dutiful children, made ourselves busy, with our families, with jobs, with other kinds of classes, and with gatherings of friends. Some people who had come from Colombo went back, or abroad; others stayed and became a part of our lives. The Jaffna students sometimes mocked those from Colombo. "Poor refugees, city people come with no clothes," they jeered. "Do you think you wouldn't have been one of them?" I asked once, reprimanding a group of boys calling insults at another. "What do they expect, living in that place," was the reply. Remembering Hasna, thinking of my grandmother, I turned on my heel and stomped off.

In our restlessness, we near-students circled the life of the university like expectant vultures. My friend is at the university, and he told me what is going on there, we said importantly to each other. And so the rumours about the movement travelled like a dangerous infection, slowly but persistently between different groups, and without much clarity regarding their source. Before you fully realised it, someone close to you was already involved. I heard from Seelan, who by then knew that he would definitely be offered a space in the next engineering batch at the University of Colombo.

"How is K?" I asked him one day. We did our daily chores together. Seelan was deepening the irrigation furrows in our garden with a rake. I swept the steps of the back veranda. This was my task now that Amma complained so often of fatigue.

"I haven't spoken with him in a while," Seelan said. He brushed rust from his hands. "We need a new rake."

I stopped sweeping. "Why?"

He swatted at a chicken wandering between yards. "It's rusty."

I waited.

"He's busy," Seelan said.

"Studying, of course," I said, but my brother did not smile. He regarded me soberly. "Well, what is he doing?"

"T— keeps him busy."

That gave me pause. I had never met T—, K's former tuition instructor, although I had heard my brothers speak about his influence. As Niranjan had told me long ago, boys studying in such classes sometimes returned clutching unopened textbooks and well-thumbed pamphlets about Tamil militancy and political rights. T— had been in shadowy conversation with K on the night of the TULF rally shooting, before the library was burned. Now, the Tamil militant groups that had existed before the riots were gaining real strength, and among people our age, there was more open talk of recruitment.

"He's going to leave medical school? Is he thinking of—"

Seelan gave me a look and I fell silent. The neighbours could probably hear us. Amma could probably hear us if we weren't careful.

"You wouldn't go with him," I said quietly. "Appa would—"

Seelan gestured aimlessly, angrily. "I don't have to wait for Appa to be angry or tell me what to do. The government will go ahead and do it for him. Should I sit around and wait? Every week one of my batchmates goes."

I did not know the names of all the new armed groups myself, but it was true that the boys craving action had no shortage of choices. "Think about what you're saying, Seelan," I said. I tried to sound reasonable, like Appa or Aran. "You've spent years studying to go to university."

In saying that, I wanted to remind him of the walks to the library, and perhaps I did; he leaned on the rake for a moment and frowned, and then walked towards the well. In the distance, one of the goats bleated, and Seelan paused and lifted his face to the air, listening.

"Seelan," I said.

He continued on to the well and turned the crank to lower the bucket into it. He brought the full bucket back to the end of the irrigation system. Tipping the pail, he watched the water flow into the maze of small channels he had made. The water touched the mango tree, the jackfruit tree, the murungakkai. After a while, Seelan went into the middle of the yard and diverted the water with a small board so that the rivulets trickled in the opposite direction, towards the flowers and some other, smaller trees.

"Thanggachi," he said, keeping his eyes on the board. "Do you think I will go to university in Colombo now? Ammammah's house burned. Periannai is dead. How can we act as though that did not happen? The library burned. All of this and more has happened. You want to go on in some sort of peaceful life, but there was never a peaceful life. That was a myth. Are you so surprised that people want to join the movement?"

To tell you the truth, I was not. And you can be honest: you are not surprised either. You are thinking, as anyone would, as everyone has, at least in passing, about what you would have done. If I were in his shoes, I would never, you might have said to yourself; or perhaps you are sure you would have done exactly the same. There is no way to know, truly, without standing where we did.

"Where are they going?" I asked. I thought I knew, but I wanted Seelan to say it.

"Training," he said. "India."

As I had suspected. Some people had gone to India as refugees too, and I had a vague sense of it as a place where we might find sympathy. Still, sympathy was one thing, and politics another—even I was not so naive as to doubt that. "Why would India help with training?"

He shrugged, and I could see that he was mostly past caring. "In Tamil Nadu they also think of a homeland. Perhaps they just understand our cause."

I did not want him to go, and I did not want K to go, and I wished I could go too. I was as angry as them. Niranjan's death had devastated all of us. After my grandmother left, we became unable to talk to each other, perhaps because we had nothing to say except to blame each other and ourselves for what had happened. On some mornings, I woke up wanting to shriek at my father for sending us to Colombo. But now, Appa stayed at his outstation post on days when he would have normally come home. My mother strayed towards the borders of madness, speaking not to us but to herself. Aran turned contemplative, Dayalan drew and redrew the library, and Seelan was simply, quietly, constantly enraged. He did very little to express this, but even the smallest motions he made—pouring a cup of tea, turning a page— gave the impression of barely contained tremors. I missed the days of his casual temper. Our anger, which had nowhere to go, filled the space where Niranjan had been.

I did not want Seelan to go, because I could not bear the thought of losing another brother. I did not want him to go, because I needed his anger beside mine. I wanted him to go, because if I could not have revenge, I thought he should.

"If you are going to go," I said, and then stopped. "I don't need you to stay. Do what you want. You always have. But if you are going to go, tell me before you leave."

It took the government and the Tigers together to make our lives so small. I remember how my three remaining brothers, who loved music and art and libraries and school, became quieter as the call of militancy grew louder. Their jokes dried up, as though politics had sapped all their humour. As siblings, we had cupped our hands around those tiny flames of shared laughter: the intimacies of family habits and histories. But then the lights winked out across the peninsula, as boy after boy I had known and loved was extinguished or gone.

A DESPERATE OR PRACTISED man can swim from the northern lip of Sri Lanka's Jaffna peninsula, where my brothers and I grew up, to the southern tip of India's thin breast: twenty-five miles across the Palk Strait to Tamil Nadu. Look across the water and you will see the route they took when I was young. In the early 1980s, many of the Sri Lankan Tamil boys who joined militant groups went to India. The boys with the Jaffna eyes slipped out of their beds or classrooms, turned their faces from their mothers, fathers, sisters, and teachers, and walked to the sea. They crossed the water quietly, in small boats guided by their elder brothers, teachers, and schoolmates, and pressed their feet into the sands of India, which trained them, gave them guns, and sent them back to wage war.

They wanted an independent state for Sri Lankan Tamils, or so they said. They called it Eelam; on a map it looked like a mantle spread over the shoulders of the northern coastline, a generous arm slung around the east. In fact, it was not so welcoming, although I was then too young to see it. The embrace would not include those who were not Tamil. It made no room for Tamils who refused to fall in line. It did not count the Hill Country in the Central Province, where Malaiyaha Tamils plucked tea. It made no particular provision for Wellawatte, my grandmother's neighborhood in Colombo, or the other Tamil sections of the capital. What Eelam held—or so I thought, despite what I had said to Seelan—was the promise of freedom, however imperfect. The militants said homeland, and fortified by generations of inherited anger and our own new riot-fueled rage, we listened.

It had been a long time coming, that storm of Tamil-speaking boys across the water, lifting weapons. They became Tigers. That's all most of us talk about now; people have forgotten how many militant groups there were, that at first our boys were not all Liberation Tigers of Tamil Eelam, but also other brands of gun-toter. Boys joined slowly, in a trickle, one here, another there, one brother to the LTTE and another to another acronym. They made an alphabet stew of rebellion: EROS, PLOTE, EPRLF, TELO. Each group announced itself with a different set of politics, a different set of ideas about change. They had different ways, too, of treating those who were not aligned with them. Some of those who fought had no politics at all. By the mid-1980s, the Tigers had destroyed almost all the others—just eaten them alive. Civilians whispered to each other about how the militants had massacred each other at the junctions of our villages. A boy you studied with murdered other Tamil people, I was told. I heard it again and again. Red earth grown redder. Come with us, or die, the Tigers said. Mothers also became militant, but to different purpose: they grew watchful over their sons' beds and bicycles, waiting for the one to be empty and the other gone.

After the riots and Niranjan's death, my mother, too, feared the departure of her sons. I am sure that in those early days, when I was still dutiful, she never imagined that her daughter would be the one to invent new ways to leave her.

BY EARLY 1984, SEVERAL MONTHS after Black July, the ranks of boys in Jaffna town were beginning to thin. Walking down the street, I could see it. All around me, boys I had known were vanishing, but the people I knew would not talk about where they had gone. Only my mother, her gaze still slippery and vague, would sometimes remark on the change. "I haven't seen that boy in some time," Amma would say absently about one of my brothers' batchmates. "Nor that one." I watched Amma carefully, waiting for her to recover from her grief. But her observations were not madness; they were the only thing that made me feel sane. At least one other person saw it too and would name it, this epidemic of disappearing boys. In the first part of the year, it became more and more pronounced.

Around that time, too, we reeled from news of several more bank robberies in the north and east. When that news floated into my world as part of the kuzhambu of political gossip, it came attached to rumour: the thieves were militants, probably the Tigers. They needed money, everyone knew, and their brazenness was growing; their connection to the burglaries was an open secret. It seemed like they could do almost anything they wanted. I didn't give much thought to what that had to do with me, but then one day, walking home from town with a small group of my former batchmates, we passed through a central junction and, from a distance, saw someone leaning against an electrical pole. He was standing strangely.

"What is that," my friend Tharini whispered to me as we drew closer to him. It was not a question, but still I answered it.

"It's a man," I said. He was standing strangely because he was tied to the pole.

The other girls, four or five of them, were hurrying along and trying not to look because they already knew what it was, somehow, but Tharini and I were new to this and not smart enough to save ourselves from the sight. They called back to us to keep walking, but the two of us had stopped cold. I stood squarely across from him, perhaps two metres away. The man's brown face, which had once been the colour of my own, or near to it, was blanched with death.

"The police should have taken him down already," I said. "Or is it the police who have left him like this? We should call someone to remove the body. We can't leave him like this. Look at him, Tharini!"

"Come, Sashi, let's go," Tharini said, pulling on my hand. "I don't want to see this. And we don't want to be seen stopping to look at him either. We can't do anything, Sashi—let's go, it's not safe."

Studying his face, I revised myself; he was not really a man, but a boy. When I had imagined the cadavers of medical school training, I had never thought of this: a boy about my age tied to a lamppost. His wrists were bound behind the electrical pole; rope wrapped his ankles, too. His feet were still in his chappals, his chappals still touching the ground, as if he could just walk away. His wiry body resembled See-lan's, or K's. His head had fallen forward, but I could see his stunned mouth still open with surprise, his half-closed eyes. His glasses were snapped across the bridge of his nose. A forelock of black hair cur-tained his forehead, in which there was a single bullet wound. I saw the pile of paper next to his chappals and darted forward.

"Sashi," Tharini said desperately.

"Let's go," I said, the pamphlet in my hand, and we hurried away. We walked so fast we were almost running. As I flipped a page, Tharini went ahead of me. "Wait," I called after her. "I want to read it."

After a minute she stopped, out of breath. She looked around. The other girls were gone, and we were well away from what we had seen. The few people on the street were moving normally. Nothing ap-peared out of place here. Nothing unusual had happened. We were still ourselves. "Go ahead," she said.

"This man and a number of others have been punished for misusing the name of the Liberation Tigers of Tamil Eelam," I read.

"Traitors, then," Tharini said. "Perhaps they were the bank rob-bers, and the Tigers are warning about what will happen to others who pretend to be Tigers."

"My God," I said. "Can that be it? How long has his body been there? And there are others?" I dropped the pamphlet like it was a live coal. I had known Tharini all my life, but still I did not know her well enough to be sure that I could say what I really thought in front of her. I wanted a bath, to wash my body clean of having seen that body. I also wanted to go back and cut him away from that pole. Let him rest, at least in death. Did he have a sister somewhere? A mother? But I knew Tharini was right; there was nothing I could do. I closed my hands into fists and opened them again. "Let's go home," I said to her.

That night, I waited until Amma had gone to sleep to tell my broth-ers what I had seen. Seelan and Dayalan traded looks.

Aran frowned. "I've heard about this. The movement says they won't observe caste," Aran said, "but the lamppost killings, they're Dalit people. Is that how they try not to observe caste?"

"How do you know that?" Seelan asked. "And did they steal and pretend they were from the movement?"

"The Tigers kill them, and you think that's fine?" Aran cried.

"If they stole—" Seelan started, and then stopped. "Certain measures might be necessary," he said finally.

Aran stormed out. I left with less fanfare, but the calm tone of Seelan's voice made me furious. I thought—but did not say—that someday someone might say the same thing when the body belonged to one of us.

ONE SATURDAY MORNING, a few months into 1984, I woke up and our house was quieter than usual. Somehow it was also colder. I shivered. Sun filtered through the windows of my room, but my limbs felt stiff. I ached. When I looked in Amma's room, she was still sleeping, splayed across the bed as if to take up all of her space and also Appa's. He had left two nights earlier for his latest posting. Her long, thick braid lay across her pillow, and she looked so tired I couldn't bear to wake her up. It was late. If I let her rest, I would have to get breakfast for Seelan and Dayalan and Aran before they went about their respective days. Forcing myself to move past my own fatigue, I hurried down the hall to start the kitchen stove and, once I had put the tea on, went to get them.

In the time since Niranjan's death, Dayalan and Seelan had slept and eaten and studied together, one of them quiet and one of them loud, one of them full of doubts and one of them surer and surer of himself. Aran stayed apart from them; he lay in the courtyard most nights, on a reed mat. He liked the cool air on his skin, he said when we protested, but we knew he did not want to continue to occupy the bedroom that had once belonged to Niranjan. That morning, he appeared younger in his slumber, sweeter and less irritable, less suspicious, more his little-boy self. I could not bring myself to wake him either. I went on to Dayalan and Seelan's door and opened it to find their beds empty and made—strange. I went down the back steps and out into the green to see if they were in the garden, but the yard was empty and quiet until one of the neighbour's roosters meandered past me and crowed bru-tally.

A feeling of airlessness rose in me, as though I were on a shaky train. I closed my eyes, but I could not get off that train, could not get enough air. I tried to slow my breathing. Don't go, I had said, but also: if you are going to go, tell me before you leave. Surely this was not so much to ask. My father had locked the bicycles at the side of the house when he had told my brothers to stop riding them. I walked out to see: the bicycles were gone.

As I poured the ruined tea into the garden, bitter steam rose from the dry ground. The space behind the back veranda was filled with the glad arms of trees my brothers and I had grown and watered together, fruit we had planned to harvest and eat. After that one conversation with Seelan, my older brothers had spoken to me as though the future was always in front of us, collectively. Was it not? Do not wake Amma, I thought; leave her alone, do it yourself. I went back inside, forgotten teapot still warm in one hand. She has had enough, I told myself, more than enough with one son already gone. Just look for them. And so I followed my own instructions, leading myself on, sentence by sen-tence, with the voice in my head that belonged half to Niranjan and half to me. Here, Sashi, look here, take your time, be methodical and thorough. The next room, the next, the hallway, the front veranda and the back. Henry came with me and sniffed obligingly along. How much time had passed? The insolent clock marched on, a quarter of an hour, then a half, long enough for them to have come back from any reasonable errand. They had not gone to the market or to visit a friend or neighbour; they had not gone to borrow a book or to find a cricket game on the next lane. Have you looked or waited so fruitlessly for your loved ones? I went back to their room, searching for a note or a letter or a trinket. Those made beds. I sat on one and opened and shook each book on Dayalan's shelf in case he had left a scrap of paper for me. Nothing in *Veedu,* nothing in *Kanal,* nothing in *Naanayam,* nothing in *Ponniyin Selvan.* These were the books he had checked out from the Jaffna Public Library when it burned, books we would never have to return. He had not taken a single one with him. I tried to imagine Dayalan without a paperback in his pocket. I picked up the framed picture of Niranjan they kept on their small, shared desk; it looked the same as it always did, as though he were about to speak. I had asked them to tell me if they were going to leave. But perhaps, from their point of view, they had.

"Where are they?" Amma said urgently when I woke her and tried to explain to her that Seelan and Dayalan were nowhere to be found.

Aran came in, rubbing his eyes. "What?"

"Seelan and Dayalan are gone," I said.

He sat down on Amma's bed suddenly. "They went." I wondered if he had it too, the sense that something inside my body had been removed. Henry came and put his small, wet nose under my hand.

"What do you mean?" Amma said.

"Amma," I said. She was holding her arms in front of her face now and I tried to insert myself into her embrace, but she had left no space for anyone else. She wrapped her arms around her own shoulders and tucked her head down, as though she were trying to make herself a room in which two—no, three—of her sons had not left her. She rocked back and forth, not yet weeping.

"They must have walked right out past me while I was asleep," Aran said softly. I thought he was going to cry, but his face stiffened, the little boy expression erased. "They just left me there."

"I told them that they couldn't go," Amma said into the cradle of her own arms. "And they told me, they told me, they told me—they were not even thinking about leaving. I cannot believe it," she said, and again, and again, until she had said she could not believe it so many times that we knew she finally understood that they were gone.

———

LATE THAT AFTERNOON, I sat at my father's desk, where I had studied for my exams, and wrote him a letter, telling him in veiled words what had happened. I did not dare to put it in its plainest terms. Who knew who was reading the mail? I missed Appa; would this have happened if he had been there? But he hadn't been there, not that night and not that morning, and we would never know. What could you have done? I asked myself again, and the well of that question was bottomless. "Promise me you will keep them here," he had said to us before he left, clasping my mother's wrist in one hand and mine in the other. The letter to him was the first code I ever wrote. Dear Appa, anbu Appa, dear Appa, my brothers have gone to visit our uncle in Anuradhapura for some time. My father would understand. We had no uncle in Anuradhapura.

I was getting ready to go to the main station to catch the night mail train to post the letter full of nothing when Aran came to the door of my father's study. Neelo Aunty had come, he said. I took my glasses off and got up, automatically smoothing my dress.

K's aunt waited on the front veranda. At the sight of her I stopped cold.

"K left," she said. Her face, like Amma's, flushed with emotion, as though she, too, had spent all her efforts damming up her tears. When I stepped towards her, she put her hands up.

"Please don't," she said. She had just come to tell us, she said. K had come home the previous night as usual, to spend the weekend with them, she thought. But she had awoken to find his bed undisturbed, as though he had never slept. On his desk he had left a note for her and for his father. "He didn't even stay for the exams for the second MBBS," she said. "They would have been next week." K, like the rest of his batch, had spent his first five terms in medical school studying the basics: anatomy, physiology, and biochemistry. Without the record of having passed the first major exam, that time was erased; he would never even be able to transfer the credits elsewhere. He had made his intentions plain: he was gone, truly gone. But even K had thought to tell his family where he was going and what he was doing, to say good-bye, as my brothers had not done. I was surprised, and then surprised again by a rush of hurt and longing to see his handwriting: the square, firm hand I knew from our study sessions in the Jaffna Public Library.

I asked her if K had said anything about Dayalan and Seelan.

"He said they went together, the three of them." Neelo Aunty lifted her face. "I'm so sorry," she said, but the statement was not directed at me. Amma stood behind me.

"It's not your fault," Amma said, with some difficulty. "My sons make their own choices."

"K would have convinced them," Neelo Aunty said, and reddened more.

"They wouldn't have needed much convincing, Aunty," Aran said. "I think they had decided."

"What?" Amma turned on him. "Did you know?"

"They didn't tell me anything, Amma," he said. "It's just a feeling I have."

"Can I see the note?" I asked. Neelo Aunty passed me the piece of paper reluctantly.

K had written it on some old exam notes. On one side, questions that would have prepared him for a first-year anatomy exam in Professor Premachandran's class. On the other side, in Tamil: *Dear Neelo Maami and Appa, my future is with the movement.* The Tamil word is iyak-kam. *I have gone with Dayalan and Seelan to join. Please don't look for me.*

Tear-blind, I returned the slip to her. But she must have guessed or known how I felt.

"They didn't leave you anything. You can keep it," she said quietly.

"Thank you," I muttered. I slipped it into the pocket of my house-dress. I took my letter to Appa out of the same pocket and handed it to Aran. "Thaambi, can you see if you can still catch the night mail? I wrote to Appa."

He took the envelope and glanced at me. "I'm going to cycle," he said.

I nodded. He wouldn't make it in time if he walked or took the bus. The only bicycle that remained was mine. They had taken his and See-lan's.

"Be careful," Amma said.

Please don't look for me. I looked for them everywhere. Of course I did. My brothers. And also K.

PART II
MOVEMENT

5.

What the Women Said

JAFFNA, JULY 1984

Y OU MUST UNDERSTAND: THERE IS NO SINGLE DAY ON WHICH a war begins. The conflict will collect around you gradually, the way carrion birds assemble around the vulnerable, until there are so many predators that the object of their hunger is not even visible. You will not even be able to see yourself in the gathering crowd of those who would kill you.

My father replied to the letter I had sent him with a brief note, saying that he didn't think it was a good time to visit our uncle, but seeing as they had already gone, he hoped my brothers would be happy and that our uncle would treat them well. A postscript: he did not blame me for their departure. When he next came home, he wandered around the house looking a little bit lost and a little bit angry, like he was waiting for Dayalan and Seelan to appear. Would he have scolded or loved them if they had? They did not, and woebegone, my father left again. I thought I knew how he felt. Even as the days filled up with work, they seemed empty. When the first anniversary of the riots and Niranjan's death came, I thought of the last rally my brothers had gone to without me, and did not even suggest to Aran that we support the party's daylong hunger strike to mark the year passing.

On the morning after the strike ended, Aran and Amma and I returned to the village temple for the first time since Niranjan's death. I washed my feet and met the eyes of the impish Pillaiyar near the entrance; I observed the priest performing the rituals of a one-year death anniversary. When he murmured his condolences to me, I accepted them. Then I walked out of the temple grounds, Amma on one side of me and Aran on the other, and left the striped walls behind. Niranjan had told me not to let others do my thinking. In this, if nothing else, I would keep my word. For the temple, that meant one thing only. Nothing I had seen in the year since Periannai's death had made me think that there was a god, and if there were a god, no god I was willing to worship would observe caste. Rajendran had tried to help us and had died alongside my brother. I could not go to a temple where he would have been treated differently than me. I swore to myself I would never go back.

DURING THE EARLY PART of that year, Sri Lankan Army soldiers still walked menacingly through the villages of the Jaffna peninsula. Some people may tell you that soldiers are not always menacing, but why should an unarmed civilian in their own village ever walk past a soldier with a gun? We did not consider the army protection, and never had. We wished to be protected from them. I heard from my school friends of the military detaining their brothers, cousins, sons, and neighbours on suspicion of being militants. They came to Tamil houses and kicked down Tamil doors. I looked at Aran and quivered. One remaining brother, not a militant—not yet. One remaining brother, not detained—not yet. But if the army came to our house, what would they do to Aran? If they asked where Dayalan and Seelan were, what would we say?

"They went to visit our uncle in Anuradhapura," Aran said practically.

I looked at Amma.

"My brother in Anuradhapura is extremely strict and demanded that I send them out of Jaffna," Amma said.

I threw up my hands. "I had better tell Appa how well their visit is going, that they're still there," I said, and went to post another letter to my father, who by then was in Trincomalee.

The next day, Aran was reading on the veranda when I found him. "I wish we did have an uncle in Anuradhapura and could send you there," I said.

He looked up from his book. "He and I have never gotten along," he said, and smiled. "He is so terribly strict, and I am such a badly behaved boy."

I laughed and then felt as though I had violated some unknown rule. "Cheeky thaambi. You are a badly behaved boy! How can you manage to joke? Tharini said her brother was stopped and searched by soldiers yesterday. They beat him just because they wanted to."

"Is he all right?" Aran asked.

"His mother went and got him from the camp where they had taken him," I said. "At first they denied having him at all. I don't want anything to happen to you. I wish they would come back."

I didn't have to tell him who I was talking about. "They could come back, Sashi," Aran said. "But that wouldn't keep us safe." But he put a bookmark in his book—*Ponniyin Selvan,* taken from Dayalan's shelf—closed it, and looked thoughtful.

That same month, the army began a new protocol of cordoning off villages with heavy weaponry and going house to house, searching for suspected militants. Their theory was that boys who had gone to India for training were coming back. In some places they detained all the Tamil men and boys over age fourteen. They did not come to our village, but when I crossed paths with my friends from other parts of Jaffna doing errands at the market, they wept as they spoke about what had happened to their brothers and the terror of armed vehicles closing in. Tharini's eyes were swollen with tears. Her brother had been rounded up again, and their mother had gone to have him released again. "Every morning Amma looks like she wants to scream," Tharini said, wiping her face. "I also want to scream. But if she goes to the army camp and screams, she won't get anything from them. We must not even cry out about what they have done." After weeks of such roundups and uproar among the civilian population of Jaffna, the army asked Tamil mothers to bring their sons for voluntary checking. Trucks passed through our lanes, blaring the instructions from megaphones. Bring your sons and your sons' identification, they said. They would check the boys and then be done, they promised. Our village was to be first. The designated day was the following week.

"Why should I go for such a request?" Aran asked when my mother brought it up. "What right do they have to be detaining people in such a fashion?"

"You told me this yourself," I pointed out. For some years the army had functioned under the umbrella of the Prevention of Terrorism Act. They could detain anyone for as long as they wanted, without charge. It was the passing of this act, back in the day, that had launched Aran into his brief phase of wanting to be a lawyer.

"I should have gone into law after all," he said. "What a lot of rubbish this is."

"If we go of our own accord, won't it be obvious that you're innocent?" Amma asked. "I wish there were time to ask your father." But, she said, she had gone down the road and rung him from Saras Aunty's house and been unable to reach him. "Even so," she said, "I don't know what choice we have. What would we do? Have you hide?"

At this, Aran looked troubled. "I don't know. I don't want to go," he said. "But if you want me to, Amma, I will."

I wanted to go with them, but they both refused; your presence, they said, is not required, and no one should go if it is not necessary. On the designated day I stayed at home alone while Amma took Aran to the checkpoint for our village, a makeshift camp where army trucks waited. I spent the day rereading the end of *Kanal,* since Aran had taken *Ponniyin Selvan* with him. When I finished at dusk, they still had not returned. Finally, around ten o'clock, I heard Amma's key in the front door and her voice bidding someone goodbye.

She stumbled in crying and alone. "But where is he?" I asked, gripping her arm. "What happened?"

"They kept him," she said, and sobbed.

"What?" I wanted to shake her. "Sit, Amma. Tell me—what happened? Where is he?"

"They kept him," she said again. "They kept him. He was right—we should never have gone there. I should have listened to him. He was right. Every mother who took her son to the army left her son with the army."

I couldn't grasp what she was saying. "What do you mean? Every mother?"

"Sashi." She swallowed and looked straight at me. "They detained all of them. Every boy from our village. Every single one."

AFTER SHE CALMED DOWN, I made her a cup of tea and gave her a tumbler of water and assembled a late meal for her. Despite my urging, she wouldn't touch it, but she sipped the tea as she told me how it had gone at the checkpoint.

A long queue of women and their sons had snaked from the gated entrance to the camp all the way down the road. Amma and Aran saw others they knew—boys from his school and acquaintances from the neighbourhood, all of them anxiously thumbing through their documents. Some had just brought their ID cards. Others carried multiple forms of proof: report cards, photographs, offers of university admission, exam results, character references from prominent people. Soldiers walked up and down, asking everyone to prepare what was needed. Some of the soldiers yelled in English; others repeated the same Tamil phrases over and over, probably because those were the only Tamil phrases they knew. Summoning the Sinhala of her Colombo childhood, Amma assured the nearest soldier that she had the necessary documents. She meant speaking to him in his language to be a friendly gesture, but it attracted unwanted attention. A couple of the soldiers looked Aran up and down; he looked them back in the eye, not disrespectfully, but not deferentially either. They did not like this. They had been training all of Jaffna to be deferential to the army. They looked Amma up and down also. Amma wished Aran had been more careful. She wished she had been more careful too. But how unfair this was, the asking with no reason, the scorn and the suspicion. She had come with her son, as she had been asked to come. They had told Tamils to speak their language, and she had spoken their language. Now the soldiers asked Aran where he went to school, what he was studying, and what he thought of the government. He answered only the first two questions as the line shifted forward; Amma staved off the third by explaining how she knew Sinhala.

Inside the entrance, there was yet another line. A short colonel with a thick moustache asked my brother for his name and identification. A soldier standing beside him recorded the answers on a clipboard. Then the colonel looked my brother over. "Show me your hands," he said. Aran did. The colonel turned his hands palm side down, then up again. He squeezed Aran's shoulders experimentally. Then: "Come this way," he said. It was on the tip of Aran's tongue to ask why, my mother could tell, but he did not do it.

"Shall I come with him?" Amma offered quickly, trying to keep her voice at a normal volume. "Just wait a moment, I'll also come." "No," they said, blocking her path, "sorry, madam, you are not allowed." Aran was vanishing in front of the soldier, who was pushing him forward into the crowd, into a third queue that she could not quite see. She craned her neck to make out what was happening. She had been too slow to notice this new, long snake of bodies: a group of boys standing without their mothers, without anyone but each other. The line was strangely colourless because there were no women in it. For the most part the boys wore plain school clothes or simple button-down shirts and trousers; they were a sober parade of grey and white and navy and black. How lost they looked, some obedient and some merely confused, each boy alone, each boy likely a stranger to the one behind him and the one in front of him, except in their common Tamilness. They were standing near the trucks, she realised. She had thought that the vehicles were to bring the soldiers to check the boys, but there were too many of them, and they were too empty. The trucks had come, she saw, to take the boys away. She could not let Aran be one of those boys. "You can't take him away from me!" she shouted after him. "I'm his mother!" In the crowd ahead of her, as they pushed and piled the boys onto the trucks, their voices and their bodies blurred together, until she could no longer make out which of them belonged to my brother.

WHEN THEY SHOVED HER outside the checkpoint still shouting and screaming for him she realised she had no proof of what had occurred. She had not thought to ask for a receipt for her own son, but if she reported him missing later, she would have no way to prove her story. She got back in the first line, but the soldiers there recognised her and saw that she was without her boy.

"You have to go home," they told her. This time they did not bother to speak in English or Tamil because they knew she understood. She hated that they recognised her. She wanted to curse them and their families and the government that had sent them here.

"I left something inside," she said. "I just need to get it."

"What was it?" one soldier said.

Another soldier laughed a little, cruelly. "That's too bad," he said, leering. "Was it your son that you lost? A kottiya? Come inside with me, and we can find him together."

Even now I do not wish to translate that word, kottiya. Must we explain each humiliation to be believed? My mother pretended he had said nothing. "If you are going to take my son from me you have to give me a piece of paper saying that you did it," she said. "You have to write down what you have done."

"We don't have to give you anything," the first soldier said. "You're finished here. You can go home."

This unbearable conversation might have continued, but another woman intervened. Telling the soldiers to leave my mother alone, she pulled Amma out of the line. Mrs. Antonipillai, a lawyer, had been one of my father's batchmates and recognised Amma. The army had detained her son also, she said to Amma, even with her informing them that she was a lawyer and that her son had done nothing wrong. Mrs. Antonipillai was upset but also determined. She counselled Amma to wait until the next day, when they would be able to join forces with others in the same situation.

"They seem to have some sort of plan," Amma said to me over her uneaten meal. "Aran didn't say anything suspicious before they took him. They took him just because they wanted to and because they could. I think I did not really believe it could happen. I should have known."

"You couldn't have," I said. "How could you have known, Amma? They made it sound like they would send everyone home." In those early days, you see, we were still bad readers of the army.

By the next morning word was everywhere: they had detained three hundred and sixty boys. The detainees had been removed to an unknown army camp. Everyone in our village knew a boy who had been detained, it seemed. Everyone had a son or a brother or had gone to school with a boy who had come under suspicion through no fault of his own.

Very early, before the Antonipillais were to come and get her, Amma and I went to Saras Aunty's to call Appa and tell him what had happened. This time she did reach him. With the luck of a good connection, his voice rumbled loudly through the receiver so that I could hear it too. To my surprise, I realised he was telling her just to wait. "No," she said bluntly. I had never heard them argue so baldly. Anything could be done to Aran while he was in detention, Amma said, and it would be too late. It was already too late and she had to do something. What, she asked again, should they do?

"They will release him after checking, when they see he hasn't done anything," Appa said.

To Amma and me this sounded impossibly naive. The military already knew that he hadn't done anything, I said to my mother. They had come to check everyone as a form of harassment. She covered the mouthpiece with her hand and mouthed, "I know." She let my father talk for a minute longer and then hung up.

"He thinks I should just wait," she said in disbelief.

"Can I come with you, Amma?" I asked.

"Hurry," she said, already halfway out the door.

MY MOTHER, SO LOST in the wake of her eldest son's death, seemed herself again as she worked to find her youngest. The group of women who had assembled themselves in the community centre where the Antonipillais brought us called themselves the Mothers' Front. Most of them had sons who had been taken; others had come because they were experienced activists. Still others had joined out of sympathy for their friends or students or neighbours, who were among the detained. "My son is a sportsman," said one short, plump woman with a plain, sweet face and a grey braid. "He would never give up his cricket to join one of these groups." "My boy is only thirteen," said another mother, who must have been almost six feet tall. "But he is so big that they think he is seventeen, and so strong that they think he looks like he has been training with one of these groups. But he is only a small child." "My son just likes to read and draw," said a third mother, "but they never asked anything about him at all. They just put him in the truck and drove away." The oldest among the detained was thirty; the youngest had just turned twelve. I remembered my own brother at twelve and thought about how terrified he would have been in an army camp. How terrified he might be now at seventeen.

My own mother spoke then. I was surprised to see that she could easily command the attention of the entire room. "When I called my husband, to tell him what had happened to our son, he said that there was nothing we could do. He said that I should wait," she said. I had never seen her look so resolute. "Even if they will not give me my son back, I won't let them hide this," she said. "My eldest boy already died in the riots. Did they think none of us would say anything? If the men will not do something, the women should." At this the other women murmured in agreement, and Mrs. Antonipillai nodded approvingly at Amma. As the meeting went on, we heard other women tell stories about their husbands. My father was not the only man who had failed to understand the urgency of the situation. And beyond those sorts of responses, other husbands and fathers had admitted that they were afraid. They were more vulnerable even than women, they claimed; women who confronted the army were less likely to be taken away.

"What will we do when the men are speechless?" Mrs. Antonipillai said. "We will put out a call for all the mothers of Jaffna to support the release of our sons. These boys must be released immediately. They are children, and they have done nothing wrong. All they did was comply with the army's request. We also complied, and this is our thanks?"

Her call to action prompted the large crowd of women to work together swiftly. First, we made ourselves into small groups; feeling nervous and new, I stayed by my mother. Mrs. Antonipillai assigned each group a village; organisers would have to go and visit each one to get women to attend the rally because so few people had telephones. Our group began drafting a memorandum with demands, while the people beside us talked about numbers and debated what the banners should say. Everyone discussed the route on which we would march. We would begin at the central bus stand. The terminus: the kachcheri building, the seat of government, where the mothers would deliver their demands for the boys' release.

One girl in the corner, who must have been my age, did not wait to be given a task but busied herself compiling a list of the names of the detained boys. As each woman approached her to recite her child's name, the girl wrote it down carefully and repeated the spelling back. I had first come to appreciate precision as a form of love during my time as a zoology student, under Sir's tutelage, but since those days I had found it in other, unexpected places. I saw it in that room, in that girl. Her attention to each devastated mother was total, her eyes huge and focused. She asked questions methodically, but somehow she also made the exchanges very gentle. "Tell me his age," she said, and then:

"Tell me where he goes to school. What is the name of your village? Since when has he been in the army camp?" Some of them told her things she did not need to know and she listened, letting them spill their grief out. Oh, he is on the cricket team? He has a hard time sleeping? He is very fond of his dog? He is the youngest of seven? Each detail did matter, even the ones she did not write down, I would realise later. She was documenting that which the government would have preferred we leave unrecorded; her patience and sympathy for their sorrow made them feel heard. I thought that if I began talking to her I might not be able to stop myself. My worry for my brother rose hot inside me.

Because my mother was occupied with other things I stood in the queue to talk to this girl, to make sure that my brother's name was also included. When it was my turn, she looked up at me quizzically. Most of the women she had spoken to had been my mother's age.

"What is the name of your relative?"

"Aravinthan Kulenthiren. He goes as Aran."

"How old is he?"

"Seventeen."

"Where does he go to school?" He went to the same school where all of us had gone, the school where I had finished my own Advanced Levels. I gave her the name and she wrote it down.

"What is your relationship to him?"

"His sister, Sashikala Kulenthiren. Sashi. I'm older than him."

She wrote that down, too, then frowned slightly. "So your mother is also here?" I indicated Amma. "Oh," the girl said. "She is talking to my mother."

I looked over at Amma, who was speaking to a woman with a streak of white in otherwise grey hair. The woman's face, in contrast, appeared curiously young. She and the girl had the same big, film-star eyes. She wore a royal blue sari. "Is your brother also detained?" I asked.

"No," she said. "My brother died at the Jaffna railway station during the riots."

As others had offered their stories to her, she offered hers to me. She told it matter-of-factly, as though she could see her own pain in its entirety, the way you might see a distant mountain from a moving train. Her only brother, who had been the same age as Seelan, had been at the railway station when a fight had broken out between arriving soldiers and some townspeople. He had been one of the first casualties. The girl's name was Chelvi, and she, too, was waiting to accept a place at the University of Jaffna, but in the arts stream. Her mother, Mrs. Balakrishnan, was in charge of the Mothers' Front, along with Mrs. Antonipillai and another woman, a Mrs. Premachandran, who was the president, and, I realised, Sir's cousin, Anjali's mother. They had been careful not to publicise their names, and I should not either, she warned me. None of the men of Jaffna knew what they were doing, and if army intelligence found out their plans, no doubt they would be taken away for questioning, and we would not see them again. Unlike men, they were not interested in credit, only success, and laid their plans accordingly.

The organisers scheduled the rally for five days later, which was as soon as they could manage given the work that had to be done. To succeed, they would need thousands of women to show up; if only fifty or even a few hundred appeared, the government would not take them seriously. On the other hand, if they left the boys with the army for any longer than that, who knew what might happen? During those four terrible days I spent every minute with my mother. We rose before dawn to work; I helped her to make placards and signs, and to organise women in different areas. Every day, it seemed, we were finding a ride to a place I had never visited before, and Amma was striding confidently into a stranger's house. Occasionally I crossed paths with Chelvi, who was doing the same tasks with her mother. The Balakrishnans worked as frantically as anyone with a son in the camps, a level of solidarity for which I felt grateful.

On the morning of the rally, the weather was clear and sunny. The Pillaiyar chess piece lay heavy in the pocket sewn into my sari petticoat, where I had put it for luck and safety. Amma and I boarded a bus to the central Jaffna bus stand. Ours was one of the first to arrive, and as we got down we saw Mrs. Premachandran, Mrs. Balakrishnan, and Mrs. Antonipillai waiting. They greeted us with considerable relief. They had asked everyone to arrive before nine so that we could deliver the demands to the government agent as soon as he opened his office. The three leaders paced back and forth with nervousness. But as the minutes ticked by, more and more buses full of women came, and we saw no sign of the army. They marvelled at their luck—no, Mrs. Balakrishnan corrected herself: not just luck, but also hard work, which meant that vehicle after vehicle deposited angry and supportive women passengers into our midst. Of course they had come for these boys and their mothers; if they had not, they said, the next children to be abducted would be their own. They hoisted banners and placards. Twenty women, thirty women, another twenty, more—among these, another bus from our village, filled with women who wept as they disembarked. My mother rushed to them; they were new allies of hers whose sons had been detained with Aran. By half past nine more women than we could count filled not only the grounds of the bus stand but also the neighbouring streets. The next day, the biggest Indian newspaper, *The Hindu,* would report that at least ten thousand had been in attendance. Amma surveyed the crowd with vengeful satisfaction. "You see?" she said, and left it at that. She was talking not to me but to my father.

The army was not the organisers' only worry. Now the leaders and their deputies moved up and down and among the restless crowd, looking for signs for other causes. When they found such material, they intervened, telling those who carried it that only Mothers' Front posters were permitted. Members of different Tamil militant groups had infiltrated the protest, but most of the women—and especially the mothers whose sons were detained—had agreed that this march was to return the children to their families and for nothing else. No militant group should be able to claim credit for it or to use it to promote their own slogans or causes. One woman who had come with a sign for Tamil Eelam argued with Mrs. Premachandran for a while and then left. Another yielded her Tamil Liberation sign and took a Mothers' Front banner so that she could remain.

At last the disciplined crowd of protesters stood shoulder to shoulder across the full breadth of the road, in so many even rows that I could no longer tell how far they stretched. I had never seen so many women take up so much room. Like the organisers, many had their children with them. Men trailed the periphery of the crowd, trying to hide their astonishment at the numbers, and looking sceptically at the mothers of Jaffna. "Why don't you bang your pots and pans?" one man called from his bicycle. His voice must not have carried very far over the chorus of women crying about their detained children because no one paid him any heed.

Amma pulled me with her towards the front of the crowd, where the women of our village had claimed the foremost places as the mothers of the detained children. A nearly physical sensation of pain and exhilaration lifted me. Around me the swarm of mothers was sweaty and noisy, but also ready and prepared. I did not know where my brother was—oh, how weary I was of that feeling, of not knowing where my brothers were—but I was surrounded by women who would not leave their sons in any dark corners. My mother, I finally saw, had a ferocity that my father lacked, a power amplified exponentially by the other women around her. They cried out and I heard Amma's voice among them. I raised my voice to match theirs and felt it submerged in and underlined by the other sounds. Someone moved to the head of the crowd to begin our walk. It was Chelvi's mother, with her young face and her grey hair and its crowning streak of white. She wore a blazing red sari.

"Will she make a speech?" I asked my mother.

"She doesn't need one," Amma said. "Wait."

I could see Mrs. Balakrishnan's huge eyes. They swept over all of us, taking the whole scene in. As she raised her hand to bid us forward, ten thousand women roared.

———

WE WALKED TWO OR three kilometres to the government agent's office at the kachcheri, and with every step our chants grew in volume and certainty. The sound swept over all of Jaffna proper. The route took the better part of an hour, and as we walked we passed houses where people had set up tables with food and drink for women who had come from far away to be part of the protest. The show of support made my mother weep. "We didn't think to organise that," she said. "We didn't have time. These people just thought to help us." The people in these neighbourhoods were cheering for us—waving and calling to us and urging us on. Some had made and hung their own banners. I waved back as though they were long-lost relatives. At one house where we accepted tumblers of water, a keen-eyed old woman grasped my mother's hands tightly. "Your son has a good mother," she told Amma, whose tears streamed openly down her face. The achchi could not have known how such a sentence would sound to my mother, who had been separated from every man in her family. Or perhaps she guessed. "Don't cry," she said sternly to Amma, and handed her a handkerchief. "Go and get your son back." Then she looked me up and down. "Good girl," she said. "Your thaambi, is it? They cannot be permitted to just take children. You go with your mother and tell them."

Ultimately, the train of mothers arrived at the kachcheri, the building that housed the government agent's office. But the gate was locked, and extra security awaited us. One security guard told us he had been instructed not to let us in. He would enquire nonetheless, he promised. The mothers waited, crying all the while, shouting the names of their sons upward at the bureaucrat in his office. The names drifted upward into the air and into his open windows. He must have heard them. With our numbers, we had given him no choice. When the security guard came back down again he said that the agent was willing to meet with five or so of our leaders. Mrs. Premachandran swiftly agreed to these terms.

But the women of our village did not. As the guard unbarred the gate and opened it slightly, they rushed forward. They flowed right past him and through him, around him and over him, into the grounds of the kachcheri building. I was swept up with them, this crowd of perhaps three hundred mothers, which included my own. Once inside the entrance, they looked at each other—which way?—and then one of them pointed. Up the stairs they rushed, to the office where the government agent waited, afraid of their righteous anger.

The women filled the room and spilled out into the hall. The ones heading the charge greeted him ferociously and formally and handed him the memorandum. He stared at it for a minute, dazed. "Release the children," Mrs. Antonipillai said to him, too impatient to let him read slowly. "You can arrange this. You should arrange it now, right now, or we will sleep here until they come."

"Please calm down," the bureaucrat said, reaching for the red telephone that connected him directly to the minister of defence. "I will call the minister and see what he says." The women, who saw no need to be calm, waited only because he was doing this. The minister of defence, a man who three years earlier had watched the Jaffna library burn, offered to send a helicopter for some of them to meet him in Colombo. "No," said Mrs. Premachandran. "We do not need to go to Colombo. There is nothing to talk about. This is not a negotiation. We will stay here until you release the children."

When the bureaucrat conveyed this, the minister reconsidered. The children, we learned, had been put on a ship at the Kankesanthurai harbour and sent to the famous Boosa prison, near Galle. It would take at least a day to bring them back, they explained. "A day?" said Mrs. Premachandran. A day they could do. The mothers had won, she realised. She tried not to show it. She would smile when she saw the women of our village reunited with their children.

TRUE TO THE WORD the Mothers' Front had forced from them, a day later the army let the boys go. The trucks came back to our village like overfull teacups. Some of the other boys and young men ran to their families, but Aran walked steadily towards me and Amma, his face clear and almost completely neutral. The way he carried himself reminded me of Periannai. One would have thought, looking at him, that nothing had happened. Only later would I recognise this as an expression he had taught himself to wear in front of people he did not trust. He was out of the soldiers' grasp but still within their sight, and although he had been forced to give them his time and his freedom, he refused to give them his feelings. At seventeen, the youngest of my brothers was already the smartest, already the bravest. Some people would have called him the luckiest, too, but I knew better; my mother, waiting with her arms open for him, was all the luck he had.

6.

Supporters

WHEN ARAN CAME BACK FROM DETENTION, HE REFUSED TO speak about what had occurred there. I tried a few times before I stopped asking. "What happened in *Ponniyin Selvan*?" "I don't know," he said curtly. "I didn't finish." That was as far as I got. Perhaps it was easier for him to bear whatever it was if he never recounted it to anyone who loved him.

My father finally came home from his posting a full fortnight after my brother's return. My mother did not even come to the door to greet him; she left that task to me. "Where is she?" Appa asked, and I pointed to their bedroom, where the door was closed. He knocked and entered. Through the walls I could discern that he was asking for her forgiveness, saying that because he hadn't been here, he hadn't understood what was happening. And then at last I could hear her. "When they take my child with no cause, why should I wait to find out what they will do to him?" she shouted. "You go to these postings, and when you are not here I do everything myself. And when I wanted to get him back I had to do that also myself!"

"I should have come," Appa said. "I'm sorry." I had never heard my father apologise to my mother.

"Go and apologise to your son," Amma said, and with that she stalked out and slammed the door behind her. She caught me waiting in the hall, staring at her. She strode in the direction of the kitchen and a second later the door opened again and my father came out, looking exhausted.

"I suppose you're angry also," he said.

I was angry, and more than that, I was confused. I remembered what his face had looked like when Ibrahim Uncle had informed him of how Niranjan had died. How, I asked him, could he not have worried about Aran in the hands of the army?

"I was worried," Appa said. "But I was not here." He threw a hand up. "In the riots there were mobs. But this checking is the government doing what I expect them to do. They were detaining boys, officially, and I hoped they would be returned, officially. And I also didn't want to make them angry. I didn't know what to do."

I realised then that he was thinking of Dayalan and Seelan, gone. If they had been home, they would have been detained too. But if they had been home, if there was no movement, would anyone have been detained? If no one was detained, would the movement be able to keep recruiting people? I saw the infinite loop of questions stretching out ahead of me, and only my mother standing in its center. "If Amma and the other mothers hadn't done anything—" I swallowed. "I don't know. I don't know where Aran would be. I thought you would come."

"I should have come," Appa said. He cleared his throat. "Where's your thaambi?" he asked.

Aran was lying in a cot in the courtyard, not reading but just staring up, which, since he had returned from detention, was a frequent pastime of his. Appa vanished through the courtyard entrance and reappeared only a minute later, looking surprised. When I asked Aran that night what words they had exchanged, he said only that he saw no need for Appa's apology. "I don't know how anyone who is not here could believe or understand what is going on," he said. "I have no reason to be angry at Appa."

We had other targets for our anger. Not long after Appa went back to work, Dayalan and Seelan were seen in town proper. Offended that she had not been the one to catch a glimpse of them, Amma stalked around the house; sometimes she stood under the picture of Niranjan and glared at it and talked to it. I wrote my father, who was still stationed in Trincomalee, another coded letter: Dayalan and Seelan had returned after their months in Anuradhapura. Appa called Saras Aunty and asked to talk to me, but when I went over there and took the receiver, we could not figure out what to say to each other. Like my mother, some part of me was still furious with my father for what he had said when Aran was detained. Beyond that, was it safe to talk? We did not know. If it was safe to talk, what should we do? We did not know.

Something beyond anger possessed me; eventually, ashamed, I discovered it was envy. While I had some sympathy for the Tamil nationalism taking hold in Jaffna, I did not know what it meant to feel an obligation greater than the one I felt to my family. I wished that I did. Dayalan and Seelan were in Jaffna, and they had not come to see me or Amma or Aran, and what kind of brothers were they, to be in our town without being with us? That was what Aran said over breakfast when I told him. Breakfast in those days seemed a lonely affair: Amma no longer ate, so it was just me and Aran, a sad pile of string hoppers or pittu left over from the night before.

At last, one morning, in the very early almost-dawn, when it was still dark, Dayalan and Seelan were at the front gate. I would have expected them to slip in at the side, or to come in from the back garden—a more furtive entrance, more appropriate to who I thought the Tigers were. But they waited at the front like penitent schoolboys, Henry barking plaintively at them from the other side. They waited as though they did not live here, and in this, although my mother did not want to see it, they were correct. I was astonished to realise they had become guests. I let them in wordlessly, and they came up the front steps and slipped inside, twin shadows.

The months away—in India, I assumed—had changed my brothers. They wore lungis—brighter than the ones in fashion here. Indian, perhaps. Both of them, already dark-skinned, were even darker. Their training must have taken place over long days in the sun, I thought. Dayalan, who had always been big and solid, looked leaner and more muscular. He also seemed sadder, even as he smiled slightly at me. Seelan appeared the same, but his expression had lost its liveliness; he looked angry. He did not smile. I resisted the urge to embrace them; I tried not to feel hurt that they did not even try to embrace me. My family had torn down the middle like an old newspaper.

"Are you allowed to be here?" I asked.

"How are you?" Dayalan asked at the same time, and I warmed at his familiar sweetness.

"Where is Amma?" Seelan asked coolly.

"Asleep, of course," I said.

"How is she?" Seelan said.

"How do you think she is?" I said.

"Shall I wake her?" Aran said. He had been standing behind me, watching us. I nodded at him and he disappeared down the hall.

"Tea?" I asked, and Seelan nodded reluctantly. The last cup of tea I had made them had gone to waste.

"Thank you," Dayalan said awkwardly.

I almost quoted Ammammah to him: You don't thank your family, I wanted to say. Instead, I said, "You must be hungry?"

"Yes," Dayalan said softly. "Yes, very."

Seelan frowned at Dayalan, but I softened even more. "What are you hungry for? I can make something. Pittu?"

A small, crushed sound came from the hallway. My mother stood there in her nightgown, her braid coming apart and her eyes bloodshot. Unlike me, she went to them straightaway and put her arms around them. Dayalan submitted meekly to her joy and exclamations; even Seelan could not stop himself from closing his eyes with his cheek against hers. Aran, waiting, stood still and furious. They had left us to inform and take care of Amma, and to apologise to her for what they had done. Still, she was nearly transparent with love for Dayalan and Seelan.

I fried them vadai and murukku, made them fresh pittu and fish curry, and peeled them two ripe mangoes. As they ate, my mother questioned them: Why did you leave us? Where did you go? Who took you there? Were you safe? How did you come back here? How long will you stay? Why won't you answer me? Dayalan, his mouth full of food, said almost nothing, while Seelan replied only tersely and with partial answers: to India, for training, by boat. When Amma asked them about K, and pressed them on what she should tell Neelo Aunty, Seelan said only that he was fine. My mother threw up her hands at this response. "He's fine?" she asked. "I saw him when he was born, and this is all you will tell me? Do you think this answer will suffice for someone who raised him? What will I say to her?"

At last, Seelan told her that K had ascended in the Tigers as he had at school, and that his aunt and father would be proud of him. Even Amma's continued hectoring could not move him to further details. I could see how powerless she felt at my brother's disobedience and, worse, his total obedience to someone else. We had been taught to think that Tamil children should only be that obedient to their parents, and it was strange to see another loyalty. And were the two of them perhaps loyal to people who treated them poorly? Did the movement give them enough to eat? Where did they sleep? Amma asked and asked, with a mother's persistence, but they would not say. Nor, to my increasing dismay, did they ask very much about us. Instead, Dayalan ate steadily, and Seelan wolfed what I put before him—Seelan, who in his earlier, student incarnation had been vain and elegant about his manners. When they were done, and had exchanged as little information as possible with us, Seelan looked at Dayalan and nodded. He stood up.

"No," my mother wailed. Aran went and put his arm around her.

"It's all right, Amma," he said. "You have to go already?" he asked Dayalan and Seelan, his fury barely hidden.

"We do have to go," Seelan said. "But don't worry, Amma, we'll come back."

"Where are you staying? Why won't you stay here?" she asked. "When will you be back?"

"Are you really going to go without—without telling us where you were and what it was like?" I asked. They had hardly acknowledged the reason for their absence. Had I dreamed the whole thing? The town emptying of boys, the sense of menace and excitement growing on the streets? I had thought of them daily, imagined them daily, but perhaps my imaginings were wrong. I wanted to know. And I needed to say things to them: You should not have left like that, why didn't you take me with you, you should have seen what Amma did to get Aran back, tell me where K is and if he remembers me. But I said none of these things. How seamlessly we had moved into the space of censoring ourselves around those we loved the most.

At my question, Dayalan looked unhappy. "It was—" Dayalan stopped. "We got up at dawn every morning. I got up every morning and thought of you three."

"It's good for us to be part of this," Seelan said. "It's good for our family to support this." I noticed that he did not say anything about thinking of us.

"Your family doesn't support this," Aran said. I wished he would tell them about being detained, and knew he would not.

Seelan ignored him. "If other groups come here asking for money you shouldn't give them anything," he warned us, looking at Amma. "They might come. Asking for money or even looking for us."

"Why should they do that?" Aran asked.

"Some of these fellows have no discipline," Seelan said. "They think they can go wherever they like. They haven't thought about the politics of anything at all."

"And you? Have you thought about the politics of anything at all?" Amma asked. "You studied your whole lives for the chance to go to school. And you gave it up without thinking." I had never heard her say something so direct to them. Usually, it was Appa who reminded us of the importance of education.

"I know you wanted me to go to university, Amma," Dayalan said. "But there isn't anything else I can do right now."

"When will you come back?" she asked.

"We'll have to wait and see," Dayalan said.

"Wait for what?" I asked. Waiting was my true career, I sometimes thought; I waited for my brothers, for governments, for politicians, and for examiners. I waited for K, I waited for my father. I waited for war to start.

"Just wait, thanggachi," Dayalan said, and put his hand on my shoulder. "Just wait."

I had heard that instruction before. I refused to follow it any longer.

I DID NOT WAIT. Neither did the war. It was with us now. Since Dayalan and Seelan would not tell us, I went out and asked my friends what they had heard or knew, and in that way began to collect information about the new lives people were choosing. Were they responding to the war or were they making it? Boys joined in droves; the ranks of the militant groups swelled. Almost every week now one of our neighbours told Amma about those they knew who were going. People spoke about it more and more freely. Some of the parents were proud. "What did we expect them to do, after all," said Jega Uncle, Saras Aunty's husband. His nephew had joined. "After what they did in Colombo, how did they expect us to react?"

As the militant groups seized control of Jaffna, a curious thing happened: Jaffna became worse and stranger in some ways, and safer in others. We no longer saw as many soldiers; the military stayed in Jaffna Fort. I got used to the sight of Tamil militants on the street, walking around with guns. For the most part, they did not wear uniforms. The girls I knew, who had been walking around with batons in their school bags to feel secure, began to move about town more easily. The Tigers were known for their discipline at least in this regard; eve-teasing almost entirely ceased. I wondered what Periannai would have thought of the Tigers' avowed anti-caste practises; rumour had it that when caste got in the way of some marriages, they could be counted upon to finalise the unions.

The Tigers kept their eye on other things as well. My brothers had promised to return, but the next militant visitors to our lane were other Tigers who came demanding money from our neighbours. They spoke like everyone owed them. A stranger, a scrawny teenage boy holding a Tiger ID card, went to Saras Aunty's gate. "I am here to collect," he announced. "Collect what," she said. He looked to be my age, she told us later, and she had no interest in deferring to him. "Every family must pay the Tigers," he said. "My nephew is in the movement," she responded. With two sons in the Tigers, we were considered a movement family, and so were not expected to contribute financially, but a nephew was not enough for that elevated status. "Then you understand why you must support," he said importantly.

He came back. They came again and again, and our neighbours could not refuse them. Five thousand rupees, they said; then ten. If you didn't have cash, they wanted gold sovereigns; if you didn't have sovereigns, they would accept jewellery. We'll give you two or three days to get it ready, they said generously. The Tamil people I knew kept cash, not because they were wealthy, but because it was tradition and also one way to stay safe. Everyone wanted any insurance they could have; the Tigers came and demanded what people had saved. "It's for us, they're fighting for us," Seelan would have said, but he was not there.

They developed a habit of coming to Saras Aunty's house on Mondays to ask for food. When I tried to explain to Aran, he figured out the situation immediately. "Ask," Aran said bitterly. "How generous of you to say 'ask' when she has no choice." They came at ten o'clock in the morning; after the first time it happened, I made a point of being home at that hour so that Amma and I could help her. "We can't leave her to do that all by herself," Amma said. Aran tried to stay home from school to help also, but Amma admonished him. "If you don't go to school, then what are we doing all this for? You're going to miss school once a week when you are preparing for Advanced Levels?" For that question he had no answer—just a resentful face.

Saras Aunty and Amma and I faced down the task together, then, just the three of us. "We need sixty parcels of food," the boy who came would say. Aran was right; it was not a request. It was usually the same scrawny boy. "Don't try to cheat by putting a lot of rice and few curries," he warned her. "We want good nutrition, less rice and more curries, and these are the curries we want." He would hand her a list of vegetables: snake gourd, bitter gourd, eggplant, murungakkai, cabbage, yuca root, potato, whatever it was that the boys were hungry for that day. "I'll come for you and then we'll bring it to this place at noon sharp," he said, and as soon as he was gone, we would scramble. "Go to the market and get these things, quick quick quick," Amma would say to me, and after I returned with the assigned shopping, I would begin to cut the onions and garlic for them. Then all of us would chop vegetables. Finally, we would assemble the parcels, laying out squares of newspaper to wrap them. When the boy returned, he and I walked towards the delivery point, each of us loaded down with food parcels. "You are a good family," the boy said to Saras Aunty the first time. "You support."

When I went back home on Mondays after dropping off the food, I would always find Amma fast asleep. Saras Aunty must have been doing the same after the frantic labour of cooking for sixty boys in two hours. During this period of time it was like she almost single-handedly ran a sizable restaurant once a week. They never paid her anything, and she never asked for money. I complained in front of her once, and she slapped me lightly on the hand. "Don't begrudge this," she said. "Do you think some other Amma is not feeding your brothers somewhere?" She was probably right; I desisted, and worried that if she was wrong, they were hungry. Come home again, my brothers, I thought. Come home to me, K. But they did not.

7.

Possible Militant

JAFFNA, LATE 1984–EARLY 1985

AT THE END OF OCTOBER, SOME SIX MONTHS AFTER MY BROTHERS
had gone, the Indian prime minister died or, more precisely, was killed.
I had not realised I could feel such sorrow about someone I did not
know. I did not like Indira Gandhi, and I did not trust her, but she had
spoken out against Sri Lankan government violence against Tamils.
She had stood as a dam between us and certain disaster. My mother cut
Gandhi's picture from the newspaper and garlanded it and put it in our
family shrine, next to a photograph of Periannai.

After Gandhi's death, the soldiers emerged from the refuge of the
Jaffna Fort to gloat. "Where is your mother?" they asked a passerby
gleefully, in their terrible Tamil. Since they largely did not speak our
language, they must have had to ask someone how to taunt us. "Where
is your mother now, has she left you?" they jeered. I almost shouted
back at them: Do you even have mothers? The grief of Jaffna was pal-
pable; we mourned her and we mourned what might have been possible for us, for the suggestion of rescue we had heard in her words.

We had spent the three months before her death in a bloody tear of
violence involving the military, militants, and civilians, during which
she had been one of the only people to raise an opposing voice. It was
a daily brutality roulette. The Tigers attacked the navy; the Tigers at-

tacked the police; the Tigers pilfered ammunition. The Tigers ambushed an army convoy, and the defence ministry put Jaffna under curfew. At night, when we took comfort in reading, Amma and Aran and I drew the heavy curtains tight, fearful that passing planes would see the light in our windows and shoot.

In mid-August, when Gandhi had addressed her country, she had promised that India would not ignore the bloodbath in Jaffna. I had let myself feel a ripple of thankfulness at the idea that someone was on our side. "She is also a mother, see," Amma said. But in Colombo, officials cried foul. Although they denied it publicly, India had offered support to the various Tamil groups jostling for favour and resources. I thought of my own brothers' training and where it had likely taken place. As the military and the militants exchanged blows, the main Tamil political party, weak as it was, exited and re-entered negotiations in Colombo. Reading about them, Aran threw his hands up in disgust. This was a reasonable reaction, and also what the Tigers wanted.

The newspapers, when we could get them, were full of such political whiplash. If I could have laid two days next to each other like puzzle pieces, they would not have fit. I longed to put the news down and also could not bear to do so. I scoured the stories for signs of where Dayalan and Seelan and K might be. The Tigers had declared that they were shifting their strategy to ongoing guerrilla warfare. Perhaps they meant for this to intimidate the military, which struggled to contain them, but it had the effect of frightening me as well. Not all of what occurred appeared in the newspapers, and much of it came to me by word of mouth.

K's aunt Neelo told me perhaps the worst story I heard, of soldiers stopping a bus of Tamil passengers on a break at a tea kade outside of Vavuniya. The soldiers commandeered the bus and redirected it to a remote location away from the road, where more than a third of the Jaffna-bound Tamil passengers were shot. Neelo Aunty had had a friend on the bus. The friend had survived, but partway through the story, partway through a sentence, Neelo Aunty went incoherent and then silent, like a radio without signal. Finally I made her a cup of tea and we went on like nothing had happened. But my school friends, too, heard the story, and whispered about what had happened to the women on the bus. Now we knew that the government was willing to do more than just detain us; they would kill us and say that we were with the movement. People who had at first been sceptical of the groups began, slowly, to speak of them with more sympathy. I was one of these people, even as I feared what the movement could do.

I had expected that the violence would remain in our part of the country, but in late September there was a bloody day in Colombo. When we heard about the series of bombs on the radio, I went down the lane to use Saras Aunty's telephone. In Wellawatte, Ammammah's telephone rang, and she did not answer. My mother was pale and drawn with fear, and I realised for the first time how my grandmother must have felt reading the news from Jaffna.

A week later we received proof of that: a letter from Ammammah asking us to shift to Colombo. It was the first letter she had sent in a year. "I never thought I would say this, but you would be safer here," she wrote, "even with what has just happened." Amma allowed herself to luxuriate in the knowledge that her mother was fine for a day before replying. "We cannot shift while the children are studying," my mother wrote back, although only Aran was still in school. She did not tell my grandmother that two of her grandsons were with the movement, but Ammammah must have suspected.

Then two of Indira Gandhi's bodyguards killed her on the last day of October. My father was home from his most recent posting that weekend and the four of us listened to the radio broadcast of the funeral. The sound of Indira Gandhi being mourned echoed out of every house on our street. That day, something in Jaffna exploded every half an hour: the militants, having their say.

WHEN A BLAST WENT off less than a week after the Indian leader's death, soldiers responded by firing near the Jaffna market. The market gunfire killed three boys my age, and state television described them as militants. Turn a dead boy into a militant and his death is excusable, you see. Every Tamil boy born in the year I was born was acceptable collateral damage.

At last, the same minister who had watched the library burn and who had offered to send a helicopter for the Mothers' Front asked the Tamils of Jaffna to leave their homes. Go on a holiday, he said. Go visit your family elsewhere. If you leave, we will know for sure whose side you are on.

I stared at my brother, who was telling me what he had read. "No, he couldn't possibly have said that," I said.

Aran shoved a newspaper at me. "He said it."

I took it and, spotting K's name and response, issued on behalf of the Tigers, flinched. Internally shaking off my surprise, I skimmed it and passed it to Amma. "What are we going to do?" I asked.

"Nobody will leave," Amma said. "The nerve of that man, to assume that everyone can afford to leave, that he gets to run our lives. We live here, this is where we are from, and it is their job to protect us. They seem to have forgotten."

"You'll never guess what else!" Aran said. "They have got rid of all the transport except state buses. No cars or minibuses or trucks or even motorbikes. And bicycles are not allowed!"

Finally, even I, the good sister, the good girl, could not ride a bicycle. Mine had lain unused and solitary by the gate for some months, as I had been too cautious to use it. Now that it was forbidden, I wanted nothing more than to swing my leg over the seat and ride away.

IN MID-DECEMBER, AFTER THE militants massacred almost 150 Sinhalese settlers who had been brought to the area by the government, there was once again a mass roundup of young men. A thousand, including Aran once more. This time Appa came home as fast as he could, but it was no use: they kept Aran for two weeks before he returned to us with a broken arm and a weariness I had never seen before. "How did you break your arm?" I asked him. "Oh, do you think I am the one who broke my arm?" he asked. Every time he came back, another piece of him was missing. Every minute, I learned a new way in which we could be hurt. In Colombo, the government said that they would begin to use rockets, bombs, and artillery against the militants. They meant: against us. As the peace talks crumbled, the army moved up and down the streets in convoys. By that time, I no longer needed the government to declare a curfew; I drew the curtains all on my own.

BY JUNE 1985, ALMOST two years after Black July, that dark and curtained state had become internal for me. I thought nothing could awaken me from that feeling. But that month, our house received an unexpected visitor. I was sitting on the veranda and he came to the gate, like it was nothing out of the ordinary, as though it were just another day. At first, he looked like a dream, some sweet breeze from the past. In a moment I would go inside to retrieve my brother and the three of us would walk to the library.

As he drew closer, I saw that I was wrong: K had changed. Like my brothers, since he had left our lane more than a year before, he had become thinner and darker. His body reminded me of nothing so much as a sharpened knife. His hair curled at the base of his neck and his moustache was thick; he wore a different pair of glasses. I was surprised—startled, even. Nothing had startled me, really, in months. I realised that he had come alone to our house, and not with my brothers.

"Here to visit your family?" I asked, keeping my voice light. But he had come from the direction of Neelo Aunty's house.

"No," he said from behind the gate, his face troubled.

"Aran isn't here," I said. My brother had gone on some errands. "Should I call Amma? She'll be glad to see you."

"I came here," he said, "to talk to you."

I gestured for him to come in. "Tea?" I asked.

He opened the gate. He came up the stairs to the top of the veranda and looked down at me with a gaze of such unsettling, hungry intensity that to break it I rose. "Can we go to the garden?" he said.

"Around the house, or through it, then?" I said.

"I'll come in," he said. He took his chappals off and held them in his hand and walked through with me. He had been in our house frequently over the years, but this time he moved leisurely, strolling through the cool hallway and lingering in the courtyard.

"It's a big place," he said, "without your brothers."

I supposed he was right. "Appa still comes. Not that big."

"Big enough," he said.

I stopped. "Big enough for what?" The Tigers sometimes seized homes for strategic reasons. With my brothers in their ranks, I had thought we were safe from that kind of danger.

K did not answer but kept walking, and was suddenly ahead of me. Because I was behind him, I could see him pause to look at each family picture on the wall. He stopped in front of the ones of Niranjan at school, and also his medical school graduation photo. Then K exited out the back and walked down the veranda steps into the garden. He slipped his shoes on.

"The garden looks all right," he said, almost to himself.

"Aran and I planted as much as we could manage," I said. "I'm no gardener, but even so, they grow." I came to stand beside him and pointed to the tallest coconut palm. "This is the strongest tree we've ever had."

"You know," he said, "years ago a coconut fell on my grandmother's head."

"But that's very dangerous! Did she die?"

"No," he said, walking around the trees and examining them. "But she almost completely lost her voice. None of the doctors had much of an explanation for it."

He walked around and around the garden, investigating. He was studying it in the same way he had looked at me, and the same way he had looked at the inside of the house: as though he had never really looked properly before. I followed at a distance. In one corner, by the front edge of the garden, he walked towards where the irrigation channels intersected. He stood there, contemplating something. I caught up to him again.

"This is quite well-built," he said. "Did Aran do it?"

"Seelan," I said.

"That maths brain," he said. Then, "Will you give me a glass of lime juice?"

"You don't want tea?"

"No. I missed your mother's lime juice, actually."

I snapped three small fruits from a branch and walked out to the kitchen to get a tumbler and some water. "Don't put any sugar," he called after me.

"It will be so bitter!" I called back.

"No sugar," he yelled again. When I came back and handed him the juice, he sipped it and then sighed and raised the glass to me. "It's as refreshing as I remember."

"Shall I get Amma? You can tell her yourself."

"This is when she usually naps," he said. "I wouldn't want to wake her."

He had timed it this way on purpose, I understood then. He had something to tell me, and he did not want to say it in the presence of anyone else.

"What is it?" I asked.

He sipped again, looking at me over his spectacles. "I wanted to let you know that I heard of the death of someone we both knew."

I put my hand over my mouth and then took it away again. My pulse quickened, a strange feeling after my long numbness. If he had come to tell me in this fashion, it was someone I loved.

"Tell me," I said.

"Sir was killed yesterday," he said.

For a moment it was like I could not hear him over the roar inside me. "But, who—"

He did not say anything more, and then I knew that not only was

Sir dead but that the movement had done it. I wanted to rush at K but whether I wanted to hit him or something else I didn't know. My eyes filled and in anger and embarrassment and grief I turned away.

He put his hand on my shoulder and turned me back towards him. It was the first time he had touched me in years, the first time since I had told him Niranjan was missing. "Sir had organised a cricket match between the boys of the school and the army team," K said quietly. "But the army is an occupying force, and so he was considered a traitor."

"Did you know he was going to be—"

"No," K said. "I didn't know." But, I noticed, he did not say what he would or could have done had he known. I had imagined the Tigers as a movement that might save us, but my wanting that had not made it so. I had understood the Tigers as a movement that had arisen from us, and that was true, and now, terrifying. What line would they not cross? I thought of Sir's giant glasses, his diagrams, his telling me to slow down before cutting, his urging me to try again when I failed. In recent years, he had taken a promotion from teacher to school principal. Uselessly, gracelessly, I tried to catch my tears in my own hands. They slipped between my fingers.

"I know how you feel," K said. "He was my teacher too."

"I don't think you know how I feel," I said. "How did you do it?"

He flinched. "It wasn't—" He stopped. I could hear the end of the sentence: it wasn't me. But wasn't it? "He was riding his motorbike," K said at last. "He was shot."

"When did it happen?"

"Yesterday," he said, and I realised I was making him repeat himself, as he had once asked me to tell the story of my brother's disappearance again.

"And you came back to tell me this," I said.

"I thought you would want to know," K said. "I'm sorry. I tried to get here before you heard it from someone else."

"So your movement will kill someone, but deliver the news kindly?"

He flinched again. "I didn't know," he repeated. And then, lower: "I wanted to come home."

"Your home is the movement—that's what you chose," I said cruelly. "Your home is the place that did this."

Oh, I wanted to hurt him, and I think I did. What I said was true, and K's eyes, too, glittered with tears. Our teacher had cut doors in the body and opened them and invited us in. How delicately he had unfolded the first specimen he had shown me. Look how beautiful the living, Sashi, he had said. Look at how marvellous. And they had cut him down.

"Please, will you go," I said through my tears.

"Sashi—" K said. He reached out towards me again, but this time he let his hand fall before he touched me. "I'm sorry," he said again. "Change always costs us."

Us, he said, but who did that include? Who were the Tigers to decide who would pay?

"Go," I said. "Consider your news delivered."

"I don't want to leave you alone like this," he said.

"I am already alone," I said, and closed my eyes. When I opened them again, K was gone.

8.

The Doctor Begins

JAFFNA, LATE 1985–EARLY 1986

NOT LONG AFTER SIR'S DEATH, I WAS INFORMED THAT I HAD A space at the medical school. I wished I could have told him. When I said this to Amma and Appa, my father wept. "Why did they," he said, unable to complete the sentence. "For a cricket game. After all he had done." In my own loss, I had forgotten Appa's; he and Sir had been batchmates and cricket teammates, and had known each other from their earliest school days. Appa had entrusted the education of his own children to his friend, and now I would continue without my teacher watching over me—without Sir knowing that I had lived up to his encouragement.

Matriculation at the university, like everything else, was messier than it appeared from a distance. With the onset of violence, the University of Jaffna was given to stops and starts; it was a hard time to begin. But after waiting the two mandated years, I did not want to put it off. I had turned twenty; if my studies were interrupted at all by what was happening, how old would I be by the time I graduated? To begin was best, I determined. My parents and I debated whether I should remain at home and commute to school, or do what K had done and take a space in a hostel. In the end, we decided that it would be safer for me to shift; if I had to do the full trip to and from home every

day, I would be more exposed to all the dangers we now associated
with being outside, the worst being shelling. As when I had gone to
Colombo with Periannai, all my good clothes fit in one suitcase; I had,
in the time since the riots, reassembled a modest wardrobe. I kept my
brother's stethoscope in my schoolbag; although a beginning medical
school student had no need of one, I was superstitious enough to want
it with me. I also took a few novels from Dayalan's room. Because
some had burned in the riots, and *Ponniyin Selvan* had vanished when
Aran had been detained, there were now only a few volumes left. The
shelf looked emptier and emptier.

It was unclear, in any case, whether I would have any time for reading outside of school. Our studies would commence with the three
basic subjects: anatomy, physiology, and biochemistry. For the first,
our professor was Anjali Premachandran. After years of hearing about
her from Sir, I could hardly believe I was about to step into her classroom. She was still the only woman on the medical faculty, and had
just returned from a year's sabbatical in England. Although I did not
realise it then, she was also the youngest of our professors, and the only
teacher of anatomy. As a result, every student at the medical school
was her student. This was true of no one else.

She had an unusually direct gaze and manner. In those violent days
people had fallen out of the habit of sustained eye contact. But if she
spoke to you, it was with a relentless concentration that was nearly
blinding. Her default expression was a smile. Almost thirty, she was
known to hold sway not with the authoritarian tactics of older aca-
demics, but through an intense moral engagement. Our other professors discussed politics in blunt, angry terms; Professor Premachandran
listened to us and asked questions. Later, speaking to Amma about my
early days on campus, I realised that it was a pattern they had in common. In other words, these were the qualities of a woman. I felt foolish
for not having understood sooner the advantages of being a person
who asked questions, and decided I would try to cultivate these habits
in myself.

Among the faculty, these tendencies marked Professor Premachan-

dran as an oddity and, to the dismay of older, more established men, a
leader. She respected but did not defer to them, an approach they
found confusing. She was known—some would say infamous—as a
critic of Tamil militancy generally and the Tigers in particular, but
when she heard that one of her students had been detained on suspicion of working with the movement, she went herself to argue for his
release, and succeeded, even though or perhaps because she spoke so
fearlessly to the army officers who had detained him. She was fair: she
was also vocally critical of the state and the military. She had departed
Jaffna for England promising to return and apparently no one had believed her. Who came back under such conditions? She did.

Her return might have marked her with a kind of glamour. Most of
us had never been overseas; the England I knew was contained in Enid
Blyton's children's books. But if she was glamorous, she was also approachable. Even so, I did not approach her; I felt shy. I remembered
that her mother was Mrs. Premachandran of the Jaffna Mothers' Front,
and that K's departure note had been written on the back of one of her
exams. I wondered what K and Professor Premachandran had thought
of each other, whether she had heard that the only student who might
have equalled her had left the university for the movement.

Her love of medicine did not preclude her enjoyment of the arts.
She liked, for example, to play Nina Simone and Aretha Franklin in
her office—quietly—and because we all loved the music and none of
us heard it at home, we would take study breaks by walking down the
hall where she worked. After hearing their albums, another student
and I researched them and were moved to realise the revolutionary
quality of the music. Seelan would have liked her taste in such songs.
This was one of the things that she and I had in common: parents who
would play the music of other countries for their children. Jaffna as a
place could be very insular, very proud of itself. We don't need the
opinions of outsiders, people would say. She was different; she loved
Jaffna, but she wanted to bring everything in the world there, and she
also wanted her students to leave Jaffna and come back to it with everything they had learned.

Once it was permitted again, she rode her bicycle alone and everywhere, unlike some of the other women faculty in other parts of the university, who were too fearful or dignified for that. This made her free, but also vulnerable. I, too, adopted this habit of cycling, out of admiration for her, and also in tribute to my brothers, who had had to let their cycles go. To see a young woman going around by herself like that in Jaffna at that time was a serious thing. We were so afraid of the men around us. Our mothers had trained us to look away from the soldiers on our streets, to be home by curfew, to walk with our brothers or each other, and only when there was still light, and on the most public of roads so that no one could take us away. She was different: she refused to rely on anyone else, even Varathan, to get around.

Everyone knew that she was seeing Varathan, who was a professor of geography. They had gone to university together years ago. The students who loved her, that is to say, most of us, never referred to their relationship, because it was clear that that was how she wanted it. But when he married her in March of my first year, we knew that too. Their religion was Marxism, so someone on the law faculty just took care of registering the marriage, and that was that. That day it felt like the air had become electric. We had learned the habit of keeping our politics and fears to ourselves, and this was a powerful, happy secret, a new language entirely. They would cross each other's paths on the campus and smile and their smiles had a sweetness no one's guns could touch. I watched them and saw what was possible and thought of vanished K.

When the war escalated in Jaffna, and things in general and the university in particular got so much worse, she began, at last, to talk about her family. "Come to my house," she would say to a student who went up to her desk after lecture. "My husband has a book that explains your question." I found this almost disturbing at first—very much against my own instinct to hide everything I loved—but then I realised that she thought that the more she announced her loves, the harder it would be for anyone to take them away from her. And she was reminding herself and all of us of what we had that was worth defending: the ordinary things. Our daily lives, our parents, our siblings. She would tell us that she had to go to take care of her sister, and she would ask us if we knew where our own siblings were. Her youngest sister, Kumudini, was almost twenty years younger than her, young enough really to be her daughter. Kumi—as we called her—came around the anatomy block too, after she was done with her classes at the nearby girls' school. We petted her and brought her around with us and joked that she was like the smallest medical student.

I have told you all this about Dr. Premachandran, Professor Premachandran, but I have not even told you what we called her. We did not call her Professor or even Doctor. She invited us to call her by her first name: Anjali. To address her as we would a beloved older sister: Acca.

IN THE FIRST YEAR of medical school, in Anjali Acca's anatomy block, we divided the body into five parts: head and neck, chest, abdomen, lower limbs, and upper limbs. For the first five terms of medical school we studied these five sections of the body, one section per term, and we worked in pairs called body partners. We were assigned cadavers. We knew nothing about these people, except that no one had claimed them. Some of us worked on men; others were given women. At some point you would be permitted a brief switch, to make sure that your knowledge was thorough.

Like the sharks of my A Level days, the bodies were preserved in formalin, which by this time did not trouble me; like most of the medical students, I wandered in and out of the large room where they were kept on tables, using the practical example to answer questions that arose from studying theory. We dissected and dissected again. Every two weeks, we participated in signature, a test during which an examiner, usually an aspiring surgeon on the lowest rungs of the faculty, would ask us questions. At the end of each term, Anjali Acca gave us a cumulative oral exam. This was called rehearsal. The language of our world was formal, elaborate, and oblique, and yet somehow also intimate in that it created a community where before there had been none. If I had described to my parents what I was doing, using the terms that had been given to me, very little of it would have been intelligible to them. The language of medicine was only beginning to become intelligible to me, but I swung the words around like I already understood them. This was bravado, which was necessary in medical school.

I had been assigned a body partner I did not know particularly well. Over the course of the time that we knew each other this never changed. Her name was Josephine, but she was called Josie. She kept to herself, perhaps because she was the sweetheart of a prominent Tiger. She was extremely beautiful and soft-spoken, and also helpfully reliable as a co-conspirator in preparing for exams, willing to spend whatever time was necessary for us to excel. We never spoke about anything other than our work, which made things lonely, at least for me; we spent many hours bent over the body, not talking. When I saw her around campus she was never in the company of any other medical students, always hurrying along with her head down and her books held tight to her chest, like a shield. Perhaps everyone was just giving her a wide berth, knowing who she was.

The Tigers' foothold in Jaffna was strengthening around that time. Not long before I matriculated, the Indian government had organised peace talks in Thimpu, Bhutan. The talks, which included not only the main Tamil political party but also representatives from each of the Tamil militant groups, began in July and collapsed by mid-August. The Tamil negotiators came up with four points; the government rejected all of them but one on the grounds that they violated the country's sovereignty. The idea was that Sri Lankan Tamils were a nation with a homeland, and had a right to self-determination, and that every Tamil had the right to citizenship, along with other basic rights. But the government agreed with only the final part of that formulation. The young people I knew, many of them other medical students, spoke openly about how there was no other choice than to fight.

As I listened to them talk, I thought of my absent brothers, and the brothers of so many of my friends and classmates, who had also gone to the movement. Perhaps it was true—perhaps we had no choice. But I also thought of Sir, whose encouragement had brought me this far. Did we have to fight each other as we fought the army? We were giving up so much for these ideas, these leaders who—like the leaders before them—I no longer trusted. Our families had fractured. Seelan and Dayalan should have been beginning their engineering studies in Colombo. K had abandoned not only our small lane but also his longed-for future as a doctor. So many of the people I loved had walked away from their lives—for what cause? I was no longer sure what they believed or who they would become. Sir's assassination had lit an ember of dread inside me.

In early 1985, when the Tigers massacred one hundred and fifty Sinhalese civilians in a town that was also home to a historic Buddhist site, it attracted the whole nation's attention. People wondered why the government could not stop such incidents. Reprisal killings by security forces and militant shows of strength punctuated the next several months. Tamil passengers on a glass boat called the *Kumudini* had their vessel seized, and passengers were taken to the fore of the boat one at a time to meet grisly fates. About fifty people died in this way; even the Sri Lankan government could not ignore it and launched an investigation. I was already too jaded to believe in this show of due diligence. No one else I knew believed in it either.

THE POLITICAL CONVERSATIONS I heard at the medical school made me uneasy. The world made me uneasy. I wished I could walk across the hall to talk to Aran. Homesick, I wanted to retreat inward, to curl into my bed and my books. Instead, I forced myself outward, hoping that if I spread my social wings further I would find better companionship. Gamely, I joined the Student Union, both the medical faculty union and the general union for students across the university. When I went to the first meeting of the latter I walked into the room and a familiar voice exclaimed, "Sashi!" Chelvi Balakrishnan's film-star eyes brightened when she saw me; she lit up the whole room. When she pulled a chair over for me and explained to the other students who I was, I felt bashful. "We know each other from working on the Jaffna Mothers' Front March," she said. I felt that this gave me credit I had not properly earned, but I had no way to correct her. What should I say, that I also had brothers who were militants? "We were just about to elect the officers," she said. "Would you like to run?" I demurred. She campaigned for treasurer and won. It was our first year, and she was already popular.

The medical students union was a different matter, more conservative, by which I mean more nationalist. In that space, I felt surveilled all the time. During the meetings, people would sometimes complain about Anjali Acca. "Did you hear what she was saying about the movement?" several people would say. Inevitably, one voice would offer a counter about her disagreements with the government, or remind us of her generosity with all of us, and the room would fall silent again, full of an inarticulable restlessness and danger. I always left that room wanting to run to hers.

"WHAT VILLAGE ARE YOU FROM?" she asked me during a day in my first term. I had been slow to pack up my books after class and was the last student remaining in the room. Perhaps I had done that on purpose, to have a chance to talk to her. I named our village. "I thought so," she said. "Someone else had mentioned that you came from there." Her face looked as bright and alert as a bird's. "I wonder if you knew K," she said.

I was not sure whether I should lie to her. Did knowing K implicate me? By that time, he had risen to a position of some prominence with the Tigers; he was in charge of much of their political wing, and the Tamil newspapers quoted him almost daily, which made sense given the depth of his intelligence and how well-spoken he was. I knew that when he was in Jaffna, he sometimes gave speeches. My long pause must have given away my uncertainty, because she said, "You can tell me."

"I grew up down the road from him," I said impulsively, and then immediately wished I had not told her even that much.

"So he is your friend," she said warmly. That I did not answer because I did not know if it was true. "He was a first-class student," she said. "He would have made an excellent physician. I was sorry not to see his name on the third-year roster. Do you think there's any chance he'll come back?"

So no one had told her. "He left right before the fifth-term exams," I said. "I don't know if there is a way for him to come back."

"And what is he doing?"

I wondered, then, if she was putting me on. How could she not know? His face had been on the front page of at least one newspaper that morning. She might have been testing me to see if I would admit knowing it too.

"He joined the movement, Professor," I said.

"Ah," she said. "Please, call me Anjali Acca. I see. Then I must have failed. He seemed to be thinking of that after the riots, and I asked him to reconsider. I left for England without knowing what he would decide."

"He has been with them a little bit more than a year," I said. I still measured everything in relation to the moment I had learned that the three of them were gone.

"And what does he do for them? Is he working on some kind of medical service?" She looked like she might find that interesting and even defensible.

"No," I said. "Although I am not in touch with him and don't really know. He is sometimes quoted in the newspaper, talking about politics. That is all I know about him now."

"I think it's very difficult for people who get involved in the movement to say what they think," she said. "You know, I was involved in the early days of the movement, talking to people in London, and they are unhappy with me because now I criticise them. They don't like that I changed my mind. They don't want debates or arguments. But we have to continue to debate and argue. We can only get through these ideas by talking about them openly. To move forward we have to question ourselves."

I didn't say anything to that. I didn't know of a space where I could speak openly. I thought of Seelan in the garden, warning me, and of the water he had poured into the earth travelling from tree to tree.

"Do you think K is happy?" she asked me. "Do you think he's glad he joined the movement?"

When K had told me about Sir being killed, he had said it as though the death were required. But the look in his eyes was grief. If I could have summoned him back to the garden to listen to me, I would have said, "You were going to be a doctor. And now you are describing a murder to me."

First do no harm, K.

"I don't know," I said truthfully. "When he went to join the movement he went with two of my brothers. I don't know how they are either."

"You must miss them," she said. She had done me the favour of making the sentence so that it could have included K, or not.

"I do," I said.

"Some people do leave the movement," she said. "I can say this because I was one such person."

"Now they would never permit it," I said. "I've never heard such a story."

But as she had said, it was already her story, already true. "If someone wants to, there's always a way," she said seriously.

I could not quite believe her, but I loved the optimism. I loved the idea that K could walk back into a classroom and we could still become doctors together. And already she seemed like someone to whom I could say almost anything. She would not let me get away with carelessness, but she would take me seriously and also give me the room to move. She had described a way in which I could engage with K and my brothers, even though I was angry with them, and I felt a part of my mind that had closed off and shut down open up again.

DESPITE MY DESIRE TO become a person who asked questions, in the wake of Sir's death, and now that I was at the University of Jaffna, more and more I found myself in the company of people with whom I could not speak freely. One senior, Thambirajah, dominated the medical student union conversations with fiery pro-Tiger speeches, and other students seemed to fall in line behind him without hesitation. Perhaps this was a way of defending themselves against the charge that they were insufficiently patriotic, since they had not joined the movement themselves. They trumpeted their admiration for the Tigers: the movement was so strong, so disciplined, so organised, so indisputably clever and honourable. Some of these students had, like me, prepared for medical school in Sir's classroom, and listening to their remarks about the Tigers' might was nearly unbearable. But Thambirajah mercilessly shut down the few people who dared to posit other ideas, and in my first year I was not yet brave enough to be one of them, especially when I thought of Seelan and Dayalan.

They spoke in quieter corners about Sir's death specifically. When did we begin to speak about such important things in corners? Only by looking back can I see: we began to silence ourselves when the Tigers killed Sir. Jaffna had loved him as a teacher and revered him as a principal. He criticised the government publicly when others would not; although—or perhaps because—he was against violence, he engaged with the militants when others would not. When the army increased security and a British reporter needed a safe space to interview militant leaders, Sir volunteered the principal's bungalow. But when the militants came to recruit students inside his school, he personally stopped them—a story I knew because Aran had been a student there then. Generations of students Sir had protected and nurtured lived all over the peninsula, and still, ordinary people I had thought of as unafraid talked as if he had died in his sleep, the manner of murder entirely erased. Carefully, deliberately, word by unchecked word, these conversations cut the threads of sanity and trust that tied us together. A coward, I said nothing; if I had spoken I would have wept.

Chelvi's company made those days more tolerable. When I told her confidentially how isolated I felt, she explained to me that she had joined the general student union because they were the one organisation that had issued a mild protest of Sir's death. When I asked her what they had done, she laughed bitterly. "They asked the Tigers to 'show cause,'" she said. "To explain it, as though such a thing can be explained. Can you believe I have to give them credit for only that? Rajan Master taught my brother also, and now they are both dead." She shook her head disbelievingly. "My mother told me that the Jaffna Citizens' Committee planned to call for a day of mourning, and then some of them received visits from the Tigers. Are we so cowardly that we cannot even talk? The student union did more than anyone else— not nearly enough, but I have to begin somewhere."

Even the Jaffna University Council had done nothing more than send a condolence note to his wife—and Sir had been a member of the council himself. One day that first September, early to Anjali Acca's office for an appointment, I caught the tail end of an argument about this. The other person—a tall, thin man I didn't recognise—leaned forward over her desk, speaking softly and persuasively. Unconvinced, Anjali Acca did not bother to keep her voice down. "The council should be ashamed," she said forcefully, and then looked up to greet me. "Ah, my student's come. We'll talk about it later, then, Jeya."

The man nodded at me as he headed out, and I inclined my head halfway, undecided as to whether I wanted to be polite to a person with whom my teacher would argue. Awkwardly, I sat and busied myself with my books and notes. "So many terrible things have happened here while I was gone," she said. "All, it seems, at the hands of men. I was in London when Rajan Master was killed. He was my mother's cousin, and also my teacher, and it—" She shaded her eyes with a hand for a moment. "I did hear about it, but I had no idea people had failed

to even hold a funeral for him. He was your teacher also, no? Sometimes I just want to be in a room full of women." She propped her
cheek up with her hand and her curly hair tumbled over her arm.
"What's that?" she asked, looking at my books with interest. "Oh, I
love *Mother*. Brecht did a play of it, did you know?"

The copy Dayalan had given me had burned in Colombo, of course,
and I had only recently come into another; Hasna had persuaded a
friend of hers bound from Colombo to Jaffna to bring me the English
version as a gift. Before the riots, Hasna and I had planned to read
Mother together. The steady stream of things she managed to send me
was a reminder that she knew what I had lost. As I looked down at the
book, I wished, not for the first time, that I had gone to the University
of Colombo with her. We were not from the same place or the same
community, but she understood me so well that with her, I had neither
to explain nor conceal myself. Since the riots, I had had no such friend
in Jaffna; no one, not even my brothers or parents, had endured what
had happened in Colombo, and Chelvi, Tharini, and my other friends
could not reach across the gap of that history. My eyes were wet. Before I even lifted my head, a handkerchief appeared before me. Reluctantly, I took it.

"Is it so hard for you to be here?" Anjali Acca asked gently.

"My brother gave me this book," I said.

She looked at me keenly. "Which one?" she asked.

"Dayalan, who is with the movement," I said.

"May I see it?" she asked. I handed it to her and she opened it to the
title page, looking at the ornate, old-fashioned frontispiece. The book
was a rare edition, from America. Ibrahim Uncle ran a bookshop, and
I suspected it was he who had found it among his imports. "This is an
unusually beautiful copy. Your brother has very good taste."

"He does," I said. "He loves to read. But he got the Tamil translation from the Poobalasingham Book Depot, I'm sure. A friend whose
father owns a bookstore sent me this one. The copy Dayalan gave me
burned in my grandmother's house in Colombo, two years ago."

"Do you want to tell me what happened?" I didn't, and yet I had already begun. She had that effect on people. "It won't unhappen just because you don't say it, Sashikala," she said sympathetically.

And because that was true, I told her. It was the first time since speaking to K after my return to Jaffna that I had told anyone the whole story in order. Perhaps I had been waiting especially for her, a merciful, attentive listener. With those intense eyes on me, I lifted each part of the story from inside myself like I was raising heavy buckets from a well that had been closed for too long. When I reached the part about Hasna and her father, Anjali Acca sat back with a look of recognition.

"I'm glad that your friend and her father were able to find out what happened to your brother. I'm so sorry for your loss," she said quietly. "And you must miss not only your elder brothers but also your friend."

I nodded. "I do," I said.

"Did you ever write down the story of what happened to you?" she asked.

"I never did," I admitted.

"You might think about it," she said. "I find that when I write things down, I can think about them more clearly."

I THOUGHT ABOUT WHAT she had said, but I wrote nothing down. I wrote nothing down, but I thought about it in class; I wrote nothing down, but I thought about it as I sat for exams; I wrote nothing down, but I thought about it as I read my textbooks at night. I thought about Niranjan, who had been a doctor; and K, who had left medicine for something else.

And before I was ready to see K again he sought me out. I was alone in the room where the first-year medical students kept their cadavers. I was reading, and occasionally cross-checking what I read on the body in front of me.

He knocked. "Sashikala," he said urgently. "It's me, it's K. Let me in."

I looked up from my book, unsure if I had really heard him. "K? No, I can't. I have to go to class."

"It's a Saturday."

"No," I said, and turned the page of my textbook.

"I have to ask you a favour."

"How did you know I was here? Amma is expecting me for lunch. I'll be late, K."

"You're always here. Let me in. I need you to treat someone," he said.

I cracked the door and peered out. He was holding someone up. The person was unconscious, clearly. K had his arm under one of theirs, and their weight braced on his hip. He struggled to keep them aloft.

"Oh no! What happened? Are you—"

"Let me in," he said, "and I'll tell you."

I hesitated. Almost certainly no one else was there. But—

"Sashi!" K said. "Hurry! There's no time for this."

I opened the door all the way and he stumbled in, the other body draped over his. He slung the person down on an empty table. I stared, seeing the blood but not its source.

"I need you to help me," K said quietly. "I don't have anything, do you understand? I don't have anything to treat this person—none of the supplies I would need. I don't have a way to do it safely. Can you help me?"

I bent down next to our patient.

"His name is Niroshan," K said. "He has a gunshot wound on the right side, middle of the abdomen. It passed right through him. I don't think it hit any organs. He's very lucky. But he lost a lot of blood. About an hour ago."

"Where were you?"

He just looked at me.

"Later." I moved to scrub my hands. I had never treated such a wound before. I had never had a patient before. I paused, thinking. "What did you pack it with?"

"What I had."

Running my hands over the man's right side, I located the wound under his clothes and unwrapped the rag around it. It was filthy, and also soaked with blood, although it was quite thick. Under the circumstances, K had done a good job.

"It'll get infected," K said despairingly.

"It won't," I said.

"You'll have to clean it."

"I know," I said impatiently. What he still wanted, what he could not have now, was medicine. Medicine was mine. "Are you going to let me do it? Here." I went to the cabinet and found a basin of supplies. "I hope he doesn't wake up. He might, though, so you have to hold him." I loaded a syringe with saline.

I lifted the cloth again and the wound gushed like a small, bloody fountain. I irrigated it, pushing saline inside, and the man stirred, moaned, and shook. I put my palm on his forehead. He had a sharp widow's peak. "I'm sorry, I'm sorry," I murmured. "I know this is painful. Just a minute. I'm almost done." I caught the excess, running pink, in a small dish. K gripped him tightly. "Now put pressure," I said. "Here." I shoved a wad of gauze at him. "Pack it."

"You pack it," he said. "My hands are—" He waved one, smeared with grime.

"I need your hands," I said. "Hold them up." I cleaned the fingers of K's left hand with a wet cloth and then with alcohol. He switched automatically to brace the patient, and I washed his right hand. Then I washed my own hands again. Hurry, I told myself. A small mountain of gauze went firmly against the wound. "Hold it," I said. "I'll have to plaster over it."

When we were done, he had gone limp again in K's arms. "I have to take him back," K said.

"If that dressing tears, all this will have been for nothing. Why can't he stay here?" I looked around. All the cadavers, save the one I had been studying, were covered with sheets. "He'll just be a body in a row of bodies, at least until Monday. I can take care of him."

"I can't leave him here," K said. "It's not safe for him if anyone finds him. It's not safe for you."

"If you cared about what was safe for me, you wouldn't have brought him here!" I exclaimed.

"If you cared about what was safe for you, you wouldn't have let me in," K said.

I raised my hands in protest. "It's not safe to let you in, it's not safe to turn you away—it's not right to let a man die in the hall of the medical school when there are supplies to help him just a few metres away. What would you have me do?"

He took a small, measured breath. "I wish you would leave," K said.

I stepped back, stunned. "What?" I asked.

His gaze was piercing. "Go abroad," he said, deliberately. "Leave. Some people are emigrating. I wish you were one of them."

He meant it. How dare he suggest such a path, one I knew he would never take himself? "You don't want me here?" I said, my voice rising in fury.

But K reached across the patient then, so that his bloody fingers touched mine. "I want you to be safe," he said. "I wish I could protect you."

The heat running through me was anger, but also suddenly, sweetly, and painfully something else. What use was such a wish made too late? When would anyone tell me the truth at the moment I needed to hear it? "I don't need anyone to protect me. You're not my brother."

"No," he said. "I'm not." I let my hand fall away from his. We were both silent. "Still, I'll take him with me. Will you give me some gauze and plasters? Next time I'll ask someone else to help."

Emptying my schoolbag, I upended the basin of supplies into it. "I have no plans to go abroad," I said, without looking at him.

"But you don't believe in the movement," he said, putting his arm under the man's shoulder and lifting.

I handed him the bag. "Here. Go, but keep his wound clean. If you come back with him, or someone else, you can look for me."

I meant what I said too. I saw then how in our world, time itself was at war, how anything I longed for might happen only at an hour long past its usefulness.

FOR DAYS AFTER, I worried about the patient—Niroshan. It had been satisfying, even exhilarating to treat him, but how would he fare, and how would I know? I wished I could find out without speaking to K. I wished I were already through medical school and could have treated him in a hospital, and followed up. I wanted to see him awake and talk to him and hear how he felt. I dared not tell the story to anyone. Had I done right by him? My own lack of knowledge and resources troubled me, along with an odd new sense of responsibility.

A steady stream of updates from other quarters distracted me from my fretting. Hasna continued to send me things: more books; new blouses and barrettes; news from the University of Colombo, where she was in the same batch as some of the other students from our old tuition class. ("They haven't grown any kinder," she wrote.) She stopped in to visit my grandmother and described the older version of Ammammah frankly, and with sadness. I was grateful for the glimpse of Colombo and her life there, but none of this replaced Hasna herself. Home, too, seemed distant—and with only Amma and Aran there most of the time, it was not quite the home I missed. I was lonely, and so I was selfishly glad when Tharini reported that the food in her boarding house was terrible. To save money, she would shift to my hostel, and, like me, buy her own meals.

We were already friends, but now proximity drew us even closer together. She could have chosen other company, but she was loyal; she wouldn't leave me behind. Later, I realised that she understood how Rajan Sir's death had affected me, and was trying to move me not out of my sorrow, but into the world. Knocking on doors to meet other residents of our hostel, she brought me along and introduced me too. Slowly my circle of acquaintances and friends enlarged. While I was inclined to stay in and study, she insisted on tea breaks and walks. She was particular about food and her standards lifted mine slightly. "Poor students deserve small joys," she said. "The right mutton roll helps me study." I couldn't help but laugh. She had a host of favourite shops near the university already, and took me around to each one in turn. Eventually we agreed that one shop run by a mother-and-daughter pair was the best.

This became our regular haunt. And to my surprise, Tharini, unlike most of the people from the university, was not condescending to the women who made their living selling us food. She knew their names and introduced them the same way she would have another university student. So I met cheerful Parvathy Aunty and her daughter, Bhavani, who was as tall as me and always reading. After buying their crisp, fresh mutton rolls and maalu paan for a month, we learned, to our considerable joy, that they made soththu parcels also. We began taking all our meals there, and when I undid the banana leaf wrapped around my lunch packet, I always found my preferred curries, made by people who knew me. Although the world of the campus remained oppressive and unfriendly, by the end of my first term, the hostel and my off-campus life began gradually to feel smaller and more like a kind of home.

ON A WEEKEND WHEN I had caught up on my schoolwork, I went to see Amma, as I often did. To my surprise, my brothers did too. The intersection was unexpected, lovely, and also fraught; it was only the second time I had seen them since they had left. This time, they brought K. He approached tentatively—unsure, I think, of how I would receive him after our exchange at the university a few weeks earlier.

When I saw K, I greeted my brothers and hurried to the kitchen, ostensibly to help my mother, so she could have as much time as possible with Dayalan and Seelan. In this way I was also able to buy a moment to gather myself. "How long will you stay?" I heard my mother ask. Seelan said they would leave in the evening. It was the late morning, and she sounded delighted at the prospect of almost a whole day with them. I had not seen her delighted in a long time, and that made me happy. Aran came and joined me in the kitchen, and I realised he did not want to speak to them or did not know what to say.

But we could overhear them from where we were working. This time, they were more open with her, telling her about the different things they were doing and places they had been. Cross-referencing what I had read and heard with what they were saying, I could tell that they were carefully excluding moments of danger. K's voice emerged from the conversation only occasionally. I wondered once more why he was there, when his own family was just down the street and presumably eager to spend time with him. Then I had a bad feeling. If he was in our house, he was not here to visit or to speak to Aran; once more, I feared, he had something to say to me. Perhaps he would tell me of yet another death or loss, some horror I had not yet imagined. When we were young, I had looked forward to our conversations, and it astonished me to feel dread when I saw him now.

When I went into the back garden to go to the outdoor portion of our kitchen, he followed me and no one commented on it, which I thought probably meant that he had already told my brothers about whatever it was. I was carrying a large pan towards the outdoor fire and partway there he took it from me without a word. I was tired and permitted him to do it. As I let the weight go, a strange relief and pleasure flooded me. I longed for the version of my life in which this was an ordinary walk. We went the rest of the way in silence.

The outdoor kitchen was hot. Perspiration ran down the back of my neck and dampened my hairline. I felt self-conscious. Every time K returned to me, I tried to see how he had changed, but I had not once thought about how I appeared to him. He was studying me again, this time with a more personal kind of looking.

"How is our patient?" I asked.

"Healing," K said. "You did well."

I closed my eyes briefly with relief. "Thank goodness."

"Sashi," he said. "The last time I was here, you asked me to go."

I put rice flour into the pan, which we had set up on the largest fire.

I was roasting it slightly to make pittu, since the last batch was finished and Dayalan had said that this was the dish he craved.

"I did," I said. "And the last time I saw you, you said you wished I would emigrate."

He waited for me to go on. I set the spoon down to hide my trembling. I had never been afraid of him before.

"I think the movement was wrong to kill Sir," I said. "That is not how we should be treating our own people. You wanted to be a doctor, and now you're with a movement that will kill people for disagreeing."

"I'm with a movement fighting for the liberation of our people," he said. "Do you know how often I think of seeing you come back to Jaffna after the riots? How often I think of Periannai?" Niranjan's pet name sounded warm in his voice. K had lost no one dearer to him than my brother.

I stirred the rice flour gently again. "You know, Sir was also asked to go abroad, and he said he would live and die in Jaffna. I have no plans to leave."

"Why do you want to be a doctor?" he said.

"Why did you stop wanting to be a doctor?" I asked.

"Who said that that was the case?"

I took a deep breath. "I want to be a doctor to help as many people as possible," I said. "Like my grandfather did, in Colombo. I think everyone deserves medicine. It's a kind of safety, and if I can make anyone feel safer, that's the kind of work I want to do."

No one had ever asked me that question before. Medicine in Jaffna was taken for granted as a worthy aspiration. I was glad to find that I had an answer I believed in.

"I asked your brothers what they thought—" he said. Once again he was having a hard time beginning.

"What they thought about what?"

"Sometimes, we have people with us who need treatment. Like the person I brought to you at the university. I wondered if you would be interested in helping. We have a small set of medics, some of whom were trained in the usual way and some of whom we have trained. To have someone with your talents join would be helpful."

"My talents? I'm only in the first year," I said, surprised.

"Your talents," he said. "I saw you. You move quickly—you'll learn quickly. And Dayalan and Seelan are in the movement, so we can trust you. You want to be a doctor for the right reasons. You would help anyone who was hurt, correct? Regardless of who they were?"

"First do no harm," I said, just as I had dreamed of saying it to him in this very place. Steam rose out of the pan.

"If I was to take you to a small field hospital where you could treat people, would you be willing to help?"

I blinked. Such a possibility had not occurred to me. I had thought he was coming to tell me about someone else we had lost. He had come, instead, to tell me about a way to avoid losing people.

"You mean cadres," I said.

"Cadres, yes, but civilians also come to us."

"If someone is hurt, I want to help," I said.

"You would help anyone?" he asked.

"Anyone," I said.

Unbidden, the image of the boy Tharini and I had seen tied to the lamppost came to me. K and I were quiet for a while.

"Your brothers didn't want me to ask you," he said. "They said that your family, your mother, had given enough. They thought your father would not want you to do this."

"I'm sure he wouldn't," I said. "They would prefer for me to keep my head down."

"You may remember my old tuition instructor, T—," he said. "He is with the movement now, and when I told him about you treating Niroshan, he thought you might be interested in this work."

I remembered hearing of T—, the tutor who had come to defend K when the police were interrogating him. Startled at the idea that K would speak about me with someone else, I bent my head over the pan. I hoped he would think any flush was the heat.

"Your family would prefer for you to keep your head down," K said quietly. "And as I said before, I would prefer that you be safe. But what would you prefer?"

How often did what I want even enter into the calculus of my choices? In Tamil, we talked about doing the needful. I had grown up with that phrase. It was the women who did the needful, I realised. And I wanted to treat patients.

"A doctor doesn't choose when to treat people," I said. "A doctor doesn't choose among her patients."

"The people who come to us for help are among the neediest people in Jaffna," he said. "Some of them have survived attacks by the security forces, and for one reason or another they cannot go to a government hospital."

"Do I have to keep it a secret?" I said.

"You will have to be discreet," he said. "Do you think you can do that?"

I wanted to say yes. But—"Promise me you won't tell me about another death like our teacher's," I said.

Through his now-fogged spectacles, his eyes were sad. "I would like to promise that," he said. "But I can't pretend to be in control of everything that happens. I have done things I would never have imagined. I can't pretend I'm asking you to do a completely safe thing, and I will understand if you refuse. I'm not sure I am right to ask. But we need you."

We, he said. Nothing was completely safe, nobody entirely trustworthy. But Niranjan had admonished me not to let others tell me what the world looked like; he had encouraged me to see it on my own. And I wanted more than just to see the world—I wanted to act. This offered me a way to put my hand in K's and try again.

"You will be able to help people, Sashi," he said. "This is what you wanted."

It was what I wanted. I hoped I wanted it for the right reasons. "Yes," I said. "Yes. I can do it. How do we begin?"

PART III
THE HALF-DOCTOR

PART III

THE HALF-DOCTOR

9.

Refusal

JAFFNA, 1986

I TOLD NO ONE—NOT THARINI, NOT CHELVI, NOT MY PARENTS or Aran—about the other kind of medical school I began attending, in the spare time that none of us had.

On my first day, a Saturday, K took me to the field hospital himself. I met him at the clock tower and we walked in the direction of the kachcheri, the Jaffna government headquarters where I had once gone with my mother and the Mothers' Front to deliver demands to the government agent. To my surprise, halfway there Seelan emerged from a side road and joined us. K grinned at my surprise. "Our destination is different," K said, "but I thought the occasion was worth a reunion of the Jaffna Public Library study group."

Seelan did not embrace me but nodded congenially and—I hoped—approvingly. "Does Amma know where you are?" I shook my head. "Better that way," he said, and stared straight ahead so seriously that part of me wanted to laugh. I hummed Bob Marley at him instead, which earned me a smile.

Our route took us past the Jaffna General Hospital, where some thoughtful person had installed a series of bunkers around the building for the convenience of civilians moving through town who might otherwise be caught out during shelling. I felt both grateful and sad that the place had altered to accommodate the war. Perhaps someday I would work at the hospital too.

The clinic was not far from the kachcheri. When we reached the entrance, I thought I would need to show a pass, but K and Seelan were well known enough; the sentry, after briefly asking who I was, waved us through.

Inside, a man was waiting for us. He was tall and solidly built and had thick eyebrows and thick-framed spectacles that seemed somewhat at odds with his face.

"T—," K said, "this is Sashikala Kulenthiren."

T— inclined his head. "Welcome," he said smoothly. "I've heard a great deal about your skills. We are indebted to you for the help you have already given K."

"I was glad to do it," I said.

He turned to Seelan. "And this is your sister, Seelan? Your family has done a great deal for the movement. Your parents must be proud."

"Thanggachi is clever," Seelan said. "She will do well here." I flushed at the compliment; had he ever praised me so before?

"Let's show her where she will work," K said quickly, and T— ushered us on.

The interior of the facility was larger than I had expected, and as ramshackle. A series of dingy cots stretched out before me. Over-whelmed, I tried to count capacity but kept losing track, my eyes distracted by people moving to and fro, hurrying between patients, calling requests to each other, and passing supplies from hand to hand. Most of the cots were occupied. What range of troubles brought people here? Shelling killed many people and cost others limbs, and by then I had several shell-shocked friends, too. Would the psychologically affected be among the patients? How long would it be before that included most of us? "We can keep only a hundred people here at once," T— said, noticing that I was scanning the rows. I was surprised; I would have guessed more. But of course what we had was not enough. Who had provided the beds? Where did the supplies come from? I brimmed with questions but knew I was not being invited to ask any.

"We'll assign you to a senior medic to begin with, and then you'll have some of your own cases," T— continued.

They walked me over to a young man who was bending over a little girl, cleaning a wound on her forehead. She was perhaps four or five years old and submitted meekly to his ministrations. T— waited for him to stand straight again before greeting him. When he turned around, I saw that it was Thambirajah, from the medical student union. Close up, he was extremely handsome and also quite tall, with a clean-shaven face and strong jaw. He raised his eyebrows at me, shook K's hand, and then offered a hand to my brother. They all knew each other, I realised. "Periannai," he said to T—, nodding his head. So they were brothers. I could see the resemblance.

"This is my sister, Sashikala," Seelan said.

"You're in the first year, no?" Thambirajah said.

"She is," K said, a note of defensiveness in his voice. "But she has already treated someone, and is eager to be useful."

"I thought she could start by observing you," T— said.

"Of course," Thambirajah said cordially, looking down at me from his impressive height. "I'm going to stitch the little girl. Come and see."

"We are glad to have you with us, Miss Kulenthiren," T— said gruffly.

"Good luck, Sashi," said K, smiling encouragingly at me. I smiled back without thinking about who was observing. Remembering, I turned self-consciously to say goodbye to my brother, but he was already gone. T— and K, too, strode away before I had a chance to say anything in return. Where were they going? I squared my shoulders and turned back to Thambirajah. I did not know and could not ask, so I would begin by being attentive to where I was.

I spent the day handing him what he needed and listening to his explanations of what he was doing with each patient. After a while, I ventured a few questions, and he answered them with increasing levels of detail. I hoped my enquiries did not make me seem foolish, but if they did, he gave no sign. I did not like how he conducted himself so imperiously in the union, but I had to concede that he was excellent here: sharp, attentive, and quick, but without acting at all rushed, despite the patients waiting for him. Likewise, his explanations and demonstrations of technique were clear and easy to grasp. He moved swiftly from the child to a young cadre with a dislocated shoulder. From their conversation I gathered that they were former batchmates. After that, he tended to a distrustful and pleasingly cranky old achchi who had been nearby when a shell landed in her garden. She had shrapnel festering in a calf. When he asked her if she had been walking on the leg, she begrudgingly admitted it. "How to rest in these times?" she asked plaintively. He cleaned the wound and extracted the shrapnel with a dexterity I coveted. When he asked her to stop walking until she healed, her daughter, who had brought her, came to the verge of grateful tears.

As K had said, this field clinic was open not only to cadres but also to civilians who could not go to the hospital, and many of the patients were women and children from the surrounding villages. Sometimes they were people who had been involved in altercations they did not want to discuss in an official hospital. Sometimes they were people who were afraid of doctors and who had been talked into treatment by relatives like the daughter.

The next time I came to the clinic, I came alone, and Thambirajah handed me off to another medical student, a skinny young man who gave the impression of nervousness but let me do several things on my own. The time after that, I had another person to shadow, and so it went until after a fortnight of being there for a few hours almost every day, I was given my own space. At first I felt anxious about actually treating people, but slowly, patient by patient, I realised how much I already knew. I began with just simple cases, and someone always lurking around to supervise: extract the shrapnel, put a plaster on this broken wrist, stitch this person's wound, give this person penicillin, give this person morphine. We had very little to work with in terms of supplies and so I quickly became inventive and resourceful in the way that is particular to those who practise field medicine. What do you need? What do you have available that you can make into what you need? Some of the other medical students were also doing this work, but I was the only one in my first year, and I realised that this was because of K, because he trusted me, and also because he thought that I would appreciate the chance to help people and learn as much as I could. He was right. I loved working there. When I did not know how to do something I asked, and then one of the older medical students would explain as quickly as possible, and in this way I advanced swiftly. Under different circumstances there was no way that I should have had any patients as a first-year medical student. But we were not under different circumstances.

Still, bedside manner was important, the older students impressed upon me. We tried to be as warm and kind as we could, given the time we had. The cadres in particular were often impatient, ready to be better and back in the action, but the senior students advised me not to rush treating them. I began to understand the calculus of Thambirajah's manner, which I had admired so much that first day. Some of the cadres had never had a day off since joining, I was told, and any spare moment I spent with them might offer relief beyond what was visible. I wished I could spend this time with my own brothers, or with K, and I was also glad not to see them. When I permitted myself to think about it, I was terrified of one of them entering the hospital not on his own two feet, but carried by his comrades.

THERE WAS MUCH ABOUT my new duties that I failed to anticipate. Although I was smart, intelligence could not make me ready for the toll of taking care of other people caught in the crossfire of the war. The work was exhilarating and exhausting; a heightened level of attention possessed me while I was at the clinic, and when I exited I was often entirely drained. On some days, I went back to my hostel and lay down without eating because I was too tired. Tharini knocked to no avail and when she heard nothing faithfully left dinner parcels at my door. One evening, after a union meeting, Chelvi invited me to dinner at her boarding house. But when the time came, a couple of days later, I had just completed a clinic shift and forgot to go. The next day when I happened to meet her on campus, she looked at me curiously.

"Did you forget about our plan?" she asked.

"Oh!" I exclaimed. The idea of being rude to her made me feel ashamed. "I am so sorry. I was studying and I must have fallen asleep."

She looked at me carefully with her big eyes that missed nothing. "You do look tired," she said. "But is studying what's tiring you? I had heard that medical school was the most exhausting, of course, but I don't know anyone else at the medical school, and certainly not anyone in the first year, who looks as tired as you."

I wanted to tell her, but I did not, and she knew I had been less than honest with her. K had asked me to keep the work to myself. While there were plenty of people at the university who would have applauded what I was doing, it was safer, he said, to tell only the people who needed to know. Which, he pointed out, was hardly anyone. He was teaching me the habits and secrecy of the movement; I was turning into someone who never said anything she did not strictly have to say, and it came with a cost. After I missed the appointment with Chelvi, she did not invite me to dinner again, and a small but noticeable distance entered our friendship. When I abbreviated a campus lunch or a coffee, or excused myself from a union meeting early, she no longer asked me where I was headed. I felt hurt by her seeming lack of interest, even though that was unfair. The price of doing what was necessary, I told myself.

A RENEWED BUT ALTERED loneliness borne of the need for secrecy led me to spend more and more of my time at the field hospital. I developed a knack for treating children; the other medics, mostly men, often brought me young women patients. I could not talk to Chelvi or Tharini about this space, so to this space I retreated. Here I was useful; here I was needed and could see the difference I made. I started to bring my textbooks to the hospital and studied there at odd hours, even when I was not scheduled. In this way, I came to know almost everyone who worked there.

One day at the end of the second term, very early in the morning before school, I was at the field hospital when it was almost deserted. I was studying for an exam when a short cadre rushed in. "Patient coming," he advised, and in the distance, I could see K running towards me. "Sashi!" he called, and behind him I could see two other men bearing a third. "Who else is here?" he cried, and I looked around to realise there were only three medics present: Thambirajah, a field-trained medic, and me. As the cadres drew closer, I saw who they were carrying: Seelan.

I put my hand over my mouth to keep from screaming. My brother was conscious, or looked it, his eyes huge and shocked, his head bloody. A wound gaped above his left eye. "A mine explosion," K said rapidly, pointing the cadres to my area, which was nearest. Thambirajah hurried over from where he had been organising supplies. When he saw who it was, he blanched visibly.

"She won't be able to treat him," Thambirajah said to K.

"What?" I said stupidly.

"If you help her, she can," K said. He turned to me. "You do it. Or I'll have to."

I couldn't. I would. There was no time for fear. The cadres lay Seelan on a cot and automatically I bent over him. The other medic came to my elbow and handed me a wad of wet gauze. I wiped at the blood and Seelan muttered and groaned. Thambirajah went behind his head and held it still with one hand. With the other, he ran his fingertips over Seelan's face and through Seelan's hair. I realised he was hunting for shrapnel. "I hope it's not that deep," he said. "The head's—"

"Yes," I said, "I know, the scalp bleeds." Quickly I took another wad of gauze. The first one was already soaked through. "Seelan Anna," I said. "Can you hear me?" He focused on me almost obediently. "Do you know who I am?"

"Amma?" he said, and I gasped.

"Sashi," K said from where he stood at Seelan's feet.

"Thanggachi," Seelan muttered. He lifted his hand as though to touch his wound, and Thambirajah pushed it down.

"We need to keep him awake," he said. "He may have a concussion."

"Machan, it's all right," K said to him. "It's going to be fine. Can you stay still? In a moment it will hurt a lot less." K's voice reminded me of the day he had treated me. Crack an egg, I thought, looking down at the blood on my hands. Crack one egg, and another.

"Put more pressure," Thambirajah said. "That's it. If he needs stitches, I can do them." The bloody gauze piled up until finally I reached the wound itself. Relief rushed through me. Seelan's eyebrow was completely gone, but beyond that, the gash was shallow.

Abruptly I sat down. The other medic seized the clean gauze from me and took over. Thambirajah checked Seelan's eyes.

"Is he all right?" K asked.

"I don't see any debris in his eyes. They must have been closed," Thambirajah said. "And his pupils are not dilated. I don't think he's concussed."

Seelan muttered.

"The wound is shallow," I said.

K exhaled. "Good." Behind him I heard the cadres murmuring to each other.

"He asked for Amma," I said.

"He thought you were your Amma," K corrected me.

"He should be fine," Thambirajah said reassuringly.

I wiped the back of my hand on my forehead. "Are you sure?" I checked Seelan's face again. He was sleeping, and the expression of pain had settled into peace. At rest, I saw, he resembled Niranjan.

"We'll take care of him," K said. "Weren't you about to go to your exam?"

I had entirely forgotten. The medical campus seemed a world away from what I had just done.

From where he sat slumped in a chair, Thambirajah lifted his head. "You did well," he said.

—

ALTHOUGH I HAD SEEN Seelan sleeping, it was his pain that stayed with me as I cycled to campus. When I tried to summon his peaceful face, only Niranjan emerged. Around and around my pedals went; around and around my brain whirred. It was a quarter of an hour's journey, short enough for me to make it in time and long enough to push me past exhaustion. He was all right, I told myself, but my body was caught in the long minutes—seconds?—of hunting for the wound, of not knowing how serious it might be. My eyes went from my wrist-watch to the road and back again. The time and the distance both felt wrong. I felt wrong, as though I were vibrating inside myself, moving without going anywhere. Despite going nowhere, to my confusion, I arrived. Mechanically, I dismounted. Before me, the buildings of the medical campus were enormous, disproportionate and strange.

It was the end of my second term, and my body partner Josie and I had eagerly anticipated our second rehearsal. That term we had studied the head, neck, and face. When Anjali Acca entered and found us pre-paring, she looked at me with an expression of some concern.

"Are you well?" she asked.

"I'm fine," I said. Josie, too, watched me with dismay. She was de-cent enough to be genuinely worried, but it was also true that if I con-ducted myself poorly it would reflect on her, and vice versa. Our fates were tied together. I resolved to perform with my usual energy, as though I had not spent the morning treating my own brother at the field clinic instead of studying. We approached the table. My head rang. In the wake of ebbing adrenalin a terrible fatigue swept over me. Josie lifted the cloth covering the body and laid it aside.

"You may begin," Anjali Acca said.

Josie started with the left half of the face, peeling back where we had cut to reveal the architecture of bones and nerves and muscle. The face! What a miracle, Sir would have said. "Stop," Anjali said. "De-scribe the nasal cavity." Josie swallowed nervously and then spoke. I tried to listen but could not focus. My mouth was dry and my palms were damp. I linked my hands behind my back to prevent myself from fidgeting. "Very well done, Josie," Anjali said, and Josie blushed slightly, as she always did for even the smallest bit of praise. Would Anjali Acca's words be repeated to the Tiger sweetheart later? She had never given any sign that she knew who Josie was. I would be just as detached and professional.

"Your turn, Sashi. Tell me about the facial nerve. There are twelve pairs of cranial nerves, of which the facial nerve is the seventh," Anjali said, prompting me.

"Like the vestibulocochlear nerve, the facial nerve enters the auditory canal via the temporal bone," I said. Seelan's face presented itself distractingly in my mind's eye once again, and I paused, hunting for the words that applied to this case instead of that one.

"Very good," she said. "And then?"

After conceding the loss of Seelan's eyebrow, I had worried about the supraorbital nerve underneath. He was fine, I reminded myself. I did not want this head, peeled apart, to turn into his.

"Exiting the stylomastoid foramen, the nerve branches to control the expressions of the face," I said. This meant that the nerve moved through an opening in the head and spread out like the branches of a fragile tree. In my first pass at studying this, I had found it fascinating and spent a long time moving my own expression around in front of the mirror.

"And as the nerve branches through the face, what lies laterally along its path?"

I stopped. "I—" The answer to this question had parts. But I could not muster the components. Someone had dropped a scalpel on the floor. That kind of carelessness was dangerous. I would have to remember to retrieve it later, I thought. "If a person who experiences blunt trauma has nerve damage, it is most likely to be in this nerve," I said finally.

"That was not my question," Anjali Acca said. "I'll repeat. As the facial nerve splits and goes through the head, what is lateral? That is, what is adjacent to the path of the nerve?"

I looked at her then. She was the kindest examiner we had, although she was also the most important. The sunlight of her gaze, I saw, excluded everything but me. She was measuring me in some way that had nothing to do with the exam. Josie glanced at me with rising alarm.

At last Anjali looked away from me. "Josie?" she asked. "Would you like to answer the question?"

Josie stepped forward and answered it at considerable length, with impressive detail. What a commendable person I had let down. I sighed, awaiting Anjali's verdict, although I knew what it had to be.

"As you both know, this isn't a passing mark," Anjali said. At this, prepared and responsible Josie appeared nearly ill. "Generally, we ask you to take a fortnight and then attempt the exam again. Then, if you fail, you have to repeat the body part during your holidays. But," and here she paused, "I could make an exception and give you the exam again in two days if you think you would be ready. And in that case I would not record this mark at all. It would be like today never occurred."

It was not yet noon, and oh, how I wished today had never occurred. Such generosity was unheard of. Josie turned to me. She could reasonably have looked furious, but instead her mouth trembled. "Sashi?" she said.

Dizziness swayed me. I could just hear Josie saying, "Two days from now should be fine," and then the dim, uncertain light of the examination room went completely out.

WHEN I CAME TO, they insisted that I lie down on an exam table, and when Anjali Acca determined that I was well enough, Josie took me back to the hostel. When I awoke again, I found Josie and Tharini by my bedside, each of them nursing me in her own way.

"Drink some water," Tharini said at once, seeing me awake. "I'll make tea."

"Professor Premachandran wanted to take you to her house, but I thought you would want to just come home," Josie said. It took me a few seconds to realise she meant Anjali Acca. "I hope that was right," she added timidly.

"Sashi, what happened?" Tharini asked. "Are you sick?"

"We have to take the exam again tomorrow!" I exclaimed, sitting up.

The two of them exchanged glances, and I wondered how much they had spoken to each other while I slept. "She said two days after you were better would be fine," Josie said. "She did want to see you when you felt able, either at her house or at her office. She left her address."

Tharini did not leave my side until I fell asleep, and so very early the next morning, which was a Saturday, I hurried to the field clinic to check on my brother. He was gone, but Thambirajah was there. He had given Seelan several stitches in the brow after I left; after several hours more, my brother had insisted on leaving. "When will he be back?" I asked, and Thambirajah's face was not without sympathy when he told me that he didn't know. "Go home and take rest," he suggested. Mercifully, he did not enquire about the exam. I stumbled out of the field hospital full of anxiety and fury. Couldn't Seelan have waited for me? And there was nothing I could do about it.

No matter how I felt, I knew, I still had to go to Anjali Acca's. I dreaded it, but such a summons could not be ignored. I fished in my bag for the address Josie had given me. Fortunately, it was just outside town proper—close enough to cycle. At Anjali's house, I found Mrs. Premachandran sitting on the veranda. Kumi stood beside her mother, eating a banana. Inside, someone was playing the piano. "Why, Sashi!" Mrs. Premachandran said. I had hoped she would not remember me, given the circumstances. "How are you?" she asked kindly.

"Fine, thank you," I said, shamefaced. "How are you?"

"Very busy these days," she said, and winked. She and Anjali had the same curly hair and wide smile. "In times like these mothers are the busiest." She was speaking to me in code. Sitting there in her beautiful teak rocking chair, she was not only good-humoured but also formidable. So she was still working with the Mothers' Front.

"I didn't think you would recognise me," I said.

"We don't forget young women like you," she said. I blushed. Surely I did not deserve this. "I was delighted when my daughter told me you were among her students."

"Acca has been waiting for you," Kumi said, eating the last bite of banana and balling up the peel. "Come."

Kumi led me inside, where Anjali sat at a piano, a small blond wood upright with sheet music in the stand. A violin lay on the mantel. A man about her age, his hair mussed, occupied a wicker rocker in the corner. He was reading a book and eating a bowlful of cut pineapple. Anjali wore a housedress and he was in a saram and checked shirt. If they had been my neighbours, I would have thought nothing of it, but because they were professors I felt like I was intruding.

"Sashi!" she said, closing the sheet music. "Do you play?"

"Oh, I'm afraid not," I said.

"This is Varathan," she said, gesturing in his direction.

Although I had seen him around campus, we had never formally met. He lifted his head and smiled pleasantly. "How are you feeling?" he asked.

So everyone in this house knew exactly how I had embarrassed myself. "Much better, thank you. I am so sorry about the exam," I said to Anjali Acca.

"As long as you're all right," she said. "Would you like a cup of tea? Come."

We left Varathan and Kumi, and I followed her to their kitchen, where water was already on the stove. She added a small piece of wood to the fire. "I'm so glad to be drinking Sri Lankan tea again," she said. She tipped some tea dust into a pot. "The British are known for their tea, but honestly, it was awful. Strange, considering they get the export quality. Do sit down."

Obediently, I sat at the small table, which was covered with a white cloth. I supposed she had brought it back from overseas. It was a style of ornate lace I had never seen before. "On the other hand," she said, "the British drink their tea with a civilised amount of sugar, so you can actually taste it. How many sugars for you?"

"Just two or three spoons," I said.

"That way diabetes lies," she advised cheerfully, but she put the requested amount into my cup before she handed it to me. "Hungry?"

"No, thank you," I said politely.

"Now," she said. "Did you have something to tell me?"

I hesitated. K's instructions had been very clear.

"My dear," she said, concern in her voice, "what had you so exhausted? Is there something I can do to help you? That's all I want to know. You aren't in trouble with me, but are you in trouble? Tell me."

Her question made me want to cry. You must understand: I was very young, and the world had rarely shown me such unconditional sympathy outside of my family. I thought of Periannai, who had always placed himself squarely on my side. Everything since his death had seemed both impossible and necessary. It was an impossible time, of course, but being young in that world underlined it.

"I want to tell you," I said.

"Please do," she said seriously.

I gave in. Slowly, haltingly, I explained my place at the Tiger field clinic, omitting only the work's connection to K and the identity of my most recent patient. When I was done, she sat back, her eyes wide. "I know about that clinic. So you're the only first-year medical student working there?" she said.

I nodded.

"Extraordinary that they would ask you and that you would be up for the task," she said. Had she discerned what I had not shared, that K was behind it? "You know," she said, "before I went to England the Tigers would sometimes bring me patients to treat."

I wondered under what conditions she had worked. Had the injured come to the doorstep of this house, to the office where she played her music, to her precious specimen lab? "What was it like?" I asked.

"I was helping people," she said simply.

So, I thought, she understood. "I don't agree with everything they do," I said. "But my brothers are in the movement, and if I'm able to help people who are hurt, how can I not? And some of the patients are civilians."

"All well and good," she said. "But when they brought me patients, I was already a full-fledged doctor. You're a student. These are your first cases. It's a great deal to ask."

My eyes filled. How desperately I wanted to be up to the challenge K had set.

"I know that the Tigers do all the training for some medics," she continued. "But you're at a medical school—a good one, if I say so myself. It's a better standard of training, and you've committed to that. So you have to pass medical school first." She pushed a hand into her curly hair. "Who would you disappoint if you gave up the clinic?"

I couldn't bring myself to say K's name, or Seelan's. "Myself," I said finally. "They don't have enough hands. I learn a lot there. And now I know how they work. I'm good at it—I'm useful."

"You'll be no good to them or anyone else if you don't get a proper medical education," she said. "And some proper sleep. How many hours a week do you spend there?"

I had been going every day for at least a couple of hours, and very often more; either I arrived early in the morning and stayed until I had to go to class, or I went immediately after class and stayed until someone sent me home. On days when I had no class, I spent the day. Thirty or forty hours a week, I guessed, and that might be a conservative number. Reluctantly, I told her. She sighed. "Would you be satisfied working there for half that?" she asked. "You have to study, and also to eat and sleep. And you have to make sure you have time away from medicine also. You can't run from the cadaver to your clinic patients. There has to be something in between."

"I suppose I could cut my hours," I said cautiously.

"Halve them," she said. "Do you have even a moment for yourself?"

Another question no one had asked me in a long time, if ever. "I haven't opened *Mother*," I admitted.

"Here, come and have a look at my bookshelves. It's fine, bring the tea."

We returned to the front parlor, where Varathan was reading the *Saturday Evening Review*. Kumi was sprawled on the floor, unselfconsciously strewing crumbs on some Asterix comics.

"What do you like to read?" Anjali asked.

"My brother Dayalan worked at the library, and he always gave me novels," I said. "Now sometimes I read the newspaper."

"Do you ever read political theory?"

"Oh, that's a low-key suggestion," Varathan said without looking up.

She ignored him. "Marx? Engels?"

At that Varathan stood up. "Haven't you just told her to do something that isn't work?" He turned around and stared at the shelves. Then he yanked a book to his left, another from his right, and one above his head. "Here," he said, handing the stack to me, and sat back down. I flipped the spines up: Kafka's *The Castle,* Achebe's *Things Fall Apart,* and Daniel's *Thanneer.*

"Oh, those are low-key suggestions," Anjali said, imitating him.

"I already have that one," I said, handing back *Thanneer.* Daniel, a Marxist, was from the Panchamar community. I had unearthed the volume, which bore an inscription from Malathy, among Niranjan's books after his death.

"How about taking this, then?" Anjali reached up to pluck another book from behind him and passed it to me: Kumari Jayawardena's *Feminism and Nationalism in the Third World.*

Varathan laughed. "Very relaxing," he said. "Don't lose them, bring them back."

AFTER I LEFT THEIR HOUSE, I returned to my own. Frequent visits home were another thing I had given up in assuming a position at the clinic; I spent most weekends treating patients. I missed Amma and Aran, although so subconsciously that it had not even occurred to me until Anjali asked if I ever had a moment to myself. My younger brother, who had finished his A Levels, was now at loose ends waiting for his own seat at university. I wanted to see him, and to get the kind of sleep I could only have in my own bed. I arrived home, however, to find not one brother but three.

When I entered, Dayalan, Seelan, and Aran were already sitting around the table, eating lunch, in the middle of a lively conversation. I struggled to hide my shock at seeing Seelan there. As they welcomed me with exclamations of joy, I examined him furtively; his forehead was clean, with only seven black sutures where his eyebrow had been. Its absence was uncanny; so often on the edge of anger, he now gave the impression of a menacing near-blankness. I trembled with the memory of his body on the cot in the field hospital. But in his manner, and in greeting me, he gave no indication that the events of the previous day had occurred. Reflexively, I mirrored him. Amma handed me a plate, and as I served myself, I listened.

"You should come back with us, thaambi," Seelan said to Aran. "You're old enough."

"No," Aran said shortly. He glanced at Amma. I knew that Aran, like me, was surprised at Seelan's audacity in trying to recruit him in front of her. I wondered if Seelan was also trying to distract everyone from those seven black stitches. What had they all discussed before I arrived? What did my mother think had happened?

Seelan leaned forward. "Why?" he asked Aran, his expression transforming into one I recognised as a dangerous, false neutrality.

Dayalan slid his plate over and Amma silently put a heaping serving of pittu on it.

"I don't believe——" Aran began.

Seelan cut him off. "If you don't care about the movement, what do you care about?"

"You were going to be engineers," Aran said.

"We still are," said Dayalan.

"No," said Aran, "you won't." He tore a chunk of bread from the soft, spongy loaf in the middle of the table. "Look, I understand why you joined. But you would have been of much more use—even to the movement—if you had degrees. And you would be of more use to yourselves. More use to Amma. What good are you doing now, when you haven't learned anything? This is just violence." While he talked, he spread margarine and then wood apple jam thickly on the slice. When he was done, he handed it to me. Dumbly, I took it. I had not realised he held such strong opinions and, more alarmingly, I was not sure he was wrong. In the field hospital, I saw a great deal of damage. But even in the spaces where one might have expected it—the student unions, or even more casual conversations—I heard very little political discussion.

"I can't make you stay," Amma said to Dayalan and Seelan. "But Aran isn't going." She turned to Seelan, frowning. She pointed to his forehead. "You won't even tell me what happened to you. Why should I let him go? I should lock the two of you in the house and forbid you to go back!"

"Nothing happened," Seelan said evenly, without even a glance in my direction. "I'm fine."

"Like anyone believes that," Aran scoffed. "Don't worry, Amma. I don't want to go. I'm going to study."

"We're learning things all the time," Seelan said. "I couldn't have imagined all the things I would learn as part of the movement." Thinking of the field hospital, I realised I couldn't argue with that either. "And what are we to do, wait until the right time to fight? It will never be the right time."

"It's your future, thaambi, that we're fighting for," Dayalan said.

"I didn't ask you to," Aran said. "You chose to go!"

"I wouldn't have thought you would be so ungrateful, thaambi," Seelan said. "You should be careful no one hears you."

At this Aran rose in a rage, and Seelan got up too. Seelan drew his arm back, ready to hit Aran, and Amma yelled at him to stop, but then Aran stepped forward, and the two of them were equal: the same height, the same power. I gaped. My youngest brother grinned viciously.

"You got stronger, did you, Seelan," Aran said. "With your special training. So did I, all by myself." He was right, I saw; in the time Seelan and Dayalan had been gone, he had solidified, like a sketch coloured in.

Seelan didn't say anything, but he rocked backwards slightly on his heels and glanced at Amma as if he were ashamed. Perhaps he was.

"Seelan Anna," he said, his mouth heavy on the second word. I had noticed it too, our youngest failing to defer to his elders, as he had done since he was small.

"Do you think I should be afraid of you? Do you want me to be? I'm not," Aran said. Then, slower, "The Annas I loved never hit me. They never hurt anyone." We all heard what he did not say: that the one he had loved the most was no longer there.

"You don't think Periannai would have joined us?" Dayalan asked. "He would have."

"He might have," Aran said. "We can't know. He might have. But if he did, when he saw what you all do to your own people, your own friends—he would have left. He would have tried to stop you. He would have put himself between me and a movement like that, not tried to recruit me to it. And he"—Aran stopped—"he isn't here to stand up for me. So I'll do it myself, I'll say what I think. And any movement that expects me to fall in line, to be obedient? He would have known better. And so should you."

Dayalan looked thoughtful rather than angry.

"Let your movement try to come for me. I won't go," Aran continued. "And none of them—none of you—can make me. I know what you all did. Massacring people from other groups, even your own batchmates and friends. Periannai died. But do you think those boys the movement killed were not other people's brothers?"

He had been speaking in English, but he switched to Tamil.

"Your movement killed a friend of mine," Aran said. "Should we find out if the people in your movement are willing to have you kill your own brother when he does not agree with you? Should we find out"—and here Aran smiled again, that smile that terrified me with its irrational fearlessness—"if you are the kind of brothers who are willing to do it?"

I did not know the story Aran was telling, but even if he was not afraid, I was, because, suddenly, I knew Seelan's answer, and understood how precious my little brother had become to me. Niranjan was dead; Appa was rarely at home. Dayalan and Seelan had gone, and Amma and Aran and I had withstood everything that came after without them. To threaten or touch Aran, Seelan would have to go through me.

I stood. "Stop!" I said. "Just stop. It's enough." I looked at Seelan directly. "He said no. Amma said no. Leave him alone."

Seelan stared back at me, and his face was a different face than the one I knew and loved, and had been a different face for longer than I had dared to admit, long before his comrades carried him into the field hospital. The events of the previous day swung between us like a silent pendulum.

"So, Periannai was killed while you were with him, and now you are pretending to take his place?" he said.

I don't know what would have happened then had my mother not been there. "What kind of children are you to speak like this to each other," Amma shouted, "when your brother is already gone? Always a fight with you," she said to Aran. "So much of politics, so much of arguing when you could be studying. And you!" She whirled on Dayalan and Seelan. "You wanted to go," she said, "so go. But don't come here and try to take him also. You come when you please and expect me to feed you, expect me to help you and hide you, and I do it, because I am your mother, and what choice do I have in all of this? What have you left me?"

All four of us fell silent.

"Nothing at all," she said bitterly. "I am supposed to be proud that my sons fight with the Tigers. But it doesn't make my life easier. What did I do to deserve this? To deserve such children? Nothing at all."

AFTER SEELAN AND DAYALAN had gone and Amma had taken to her bed, Aran and I sat in the courtyard, and its cup of sky poured moonlight over us. In the corner, Henry made swift work of the bones left over from some chicken curry and sporadically rolled around with pleasure. Aran held a book open idly.

I indicated the book with a tip of my chin. "What are you reading?"

"It's called *Puthiyathor Ulagam*," Aran said. "The Tigers have been handing out free copies of it, but I'm not sure any of them read it properly. It's about a character who joins PLOTE and then becomes disillusioned."

I remembered hearing about this book, which was by someone who had belonged to the People's Liberation Organisation of Tamil Eelam. The title meant *A New World*. "Perhaps I can read it after you," I said.

"I'm finished," he said. "I was rereading. Or, rather, not reading." He closed it and set it down. "The character becomes disillusioned because he joins thinking there will be a socialist revolution. But then he learns that PLOTE is torturing people, and he suspects that some of them are his comrades. The Tigers give it out because it's critical of PLOTE. They don't realise they aren't that different."

I picked up the slim volume from where it lay between us and flipped the pages. "Was it someone you knew well?" I asked. "The boy who died?"

He glanced over at me. "The boy the Tigers killed?" he said. "I knew him well enough. Does he only matter if we know him? He was one of my classmates, a fellow just one year senior to me. He was in one of the other groups. TELO." His lip trembled. "I tried to talk him out of it."

I had thought Aran was sad, and that was partly right, he was sad to have fought with our brothers, whom he loved, but oh, that mouth was also as furious as any I had seen. Aran had become as angry as Seelan or Dayalan or K. I quivered myself, perceiving it for the first time. Aran was my littlest brother, and I had underestimated him.

"The Tigers, the boys, they are trying to make everyone join their group only, and if someone goes to one of the other groups, then that person is a traitor. I mean, Acca, a Tamil person, a person from Jaffna. One of us," he said.

I realised I was clutching Aran's book and put it down. "What did they do?" I asked.

"They attacked houses where some of the TELO members lived," Aran said. "To find them."

"And?"

"The TELO boys were outnumbered, so some of them came out of their houses and surrendered. They put their hands on their heads."

Aran demonstrated this, and, appalled at how clearly I could imagine the scene, I pulled his arms down.

"And then the Tigers who were there," he said, "they went up to those other boys, close, like this. In front of their own houses, in front of their families."

Aran laid his finger against his own forehead.

"That is the distance from which the Tigers shoot their own people," Aran said. "People who had already surrendered."

"What was your friend's name?" I asked.

"You remember Sivan," Aran said. His eyes shone. "It was him."

And I did, you know. I did remember Sivan. I wish that you did too, but you will never know him. I said, "He was the one with—"

"Yes," Aran said. "The gap in his smile."

He put his own thumb between his front teeth to remind me where the space had been.

"When I was small," Aran said, "he used to cycle over and play cricket on our lane with me. That was how I learned. Before Dayalan or Seelan or even Niranjan would play with me."

I leaned over and put my arms around Aran. He cried for a minute but then pushed me away.

"We have to get out of here," he said. "This is going to get worse. These people will come for me. Worse, they will come for you."

"No," I said. "How could they? Why would they? With brothers in the movement?"

"We thought the government was bad," Aran said. "And they are. But these are our own people. They know where we live, and how we move, and they are in our temples and at our classes. They are watching us. Soon someone will know what I said to my own brothers, in my own house. Probably my brothers will be the ones to tell them. Perhaps my brothers will be the ones sent to kill me, or worse, collect me."

Aran took a breath. "I won't be recruited like what I think doesn't count," he said.

I put my hand on his arm. "I care about what you think," I said.

He hesitated. "Acca, I have to tell you—someone told me that Dayalan was at the TELO massacre."

I flinched. I could believe that such an event had occurred, but that Dayalan had participated in murdering boys who had already surrendered? I shook my head. "No, no, no, that's not possible!" I exclaimed. "Who told you that?"

He laughed bitterly. "You say it's not possible, but Sivan is dead. So you will believe that the Tigers do some wrong things, but you think Seelan and Dayalan must be blameless? The person said Dayalan was one of the people in charge, Acca—that he didn't just do it, he gloried in it. Evil is not limited by what you personally can imagine." He put his head in his hands. "And I ate a meal with him," he muttered. "Amma's food, in this house. He barely said anything. Did you notice that? If you are quiet, like Dayalan, no one asks you to be accountable for much."

I was guilty of that kind of quiet too. In my throat a choking terror expanded, that I did not know Dayalan or what he might do. But I knew what I had done, and that I could tell Aran. I had not planned to inform him about my work at the field hospital, and now I saw that by omitting aspects of my life from my exchanges with him, I was making a choice. I could lie to him; I could leave things out. Or I could openly do things with which I suspected he would disagree.

"I've been working for them too," I said.

He glanced over at me. "What do you mean?"

Without mentioning the day at the university when K had brought me that first patient, I explained the invitation to work at the field hospital.

"And you said yes?" he asked incredulously.

"I'm not the only medical student there," I protested. "Plenty of senior students are doing the same thing. With so many injured, and some who can't or won't go to hospital—I'm trained to help, and no one but the movement will let me do it."

"What sorts of people have you been treating?" he wanted to know.

"People who can't go to hospital," I said indignantly.

"They're using you," he said. "You're treating cadres."

"Don't they deserve treatment too?" Even as I was glad that Aran had not seen what I had seen yesterday, I wondered what he would have done in my place. I could not ask. It was Seelan's injury, and although I was angry at him, although I had treated him, it was not my story to tell. "Your own brothers are cadres!" I said.

Aran remained unmoved. "They shot my friend and left him to die," he said. "And he had already surrendered. Do you think he ended up at the field hospital?"

I had nothing to say to that. "I can do more good there than I can do anywhere else," I said. "They gave me a place to be."

"A place to be," Aran repeated, and got up. "Here," he said, and handed me the book. "*Puthiyathor Ulagam*. You should read it.

"They killed the man who taught you first," he said. "Don't forget that, either. If that is worth the place they have given you, then my brothers are not the only ones who have left me."

10.

Lights Out

———

JAFFNA, 1986

JOSIE AND I PASSED THE SECOND TERM REHEARSAL ON OUR second try. Relieved, I resolved to ask if I could reduce my time at the clinic after the term holiday. I could not forget what Aran had said about Dayalan and the TELO massacre; Aran's anger and Anjali's admonishment to make space for myself were both on my mind as I made my way to the field hospital. The person who needed to clear my request was Thambirajah, who since the incident with Seelan had been noticeably warmer to me. K was not there, and I was glad he would not hear my question. He would have seen in my face that I had more than one reason for wanting to step back.

"You wanted to talk to me?" Thambirajah said. He was wrapping a cadre's swollen fingers.

"Yes," I said, embarrassed.

He tucked the end of the wrapping in. "Done," he said to the cadre, who thanked him, flexed his hand experimentally, and got up. Now Thambirajah's full attention was on me. "How's the work here?"

"That's what I need to speak to you about," I said, and hesitated. "I need to cut my hours when classes start again."

He laughed and rubbed his chin. "I was wondering how long it would take you to ask, or if you ever would," he said. "You've been working at quite a pace."

"I had some problems with my exams recently," I said.

"Not the day you treated your brother?"

"No," I said, hoping to save some small dignity.

"Yes," he said. "That day. I heard you. And I remember those exams. I wouldn't have passed them, working like you do. What were you even doing here at that hour?" He studied me. He was very handsome, I noticed again. Disarmingly so. "It's good that Seelan healed so well and quickly," he said. "That wound could have been far worse. It's all right. Study first, and then come here to work."

BUT WE HAD SEVERAL weeks of term holiday still, and with the war intensifying, I ended up spending most of it at the clinic after all. They needed me, and with the promise of scaled-down hours ahead of me, I could and did tell myself it was temporary, a sprint instead of a marathon.

I allowed Amma the impression that I was continuing to study intensely and hoped Aran would not disabuse her of that idea. But a month into that stint, I came home late one night to find my father unexpectedly home and smoking at the table on the back veranda. I had lost track of time, not just the hour but also the day, including his schedule. I longed for my mother's food, but seeing Appa, I regretted not going back to the hostel. Although I had missed him, I had no stomach for a difficult conversation, and his characteristic smile was absent.

"Where have you been?" he asked, flicking ash towards the garden. "I got home this morning and expected to see you."

I pushed the ashtray towards him. "Studying," I said. My mother had left some food out, and I moved to make myself a plate, but he lifted a hand.

"I'm still talking to you," he said.

"It's late," I said. "I'm hungry."

"It is, and I'm sure you are." He took a drag from his cigarette, knocking the ash into the ashtray this time. "Do you think your mother and I are so stupid that we don't know it's term holiday?"

I shifted my weight from one foot to the other. My legs ached after a day of standing. There was an empty chair across from my father, but I did not dare to take it. "Of course it's term holiday. But I want to do better in my third term exams."

His cigarette was down to a nub, and he stubbed it out. "I don't believe you," he said quietly. "And I didn't raise you to lie to me. So I'll ask you again. Where have you been?"

I exhaled. When Aran had been detained, when Amma had called Appa and he had not come, my idea of him had collapsed into itself. I had grown up thinking of him as reliable. If he did not come when we needed him, what did I owe him? I had believed in him as a person who knew what to do and could be counted upon to do it, and with that falsehood stripped away, my love for him was at sea. But even if he had not lived up to my idea of who he was, he was right: I did not want to lie. And why should I? I had done nothing to be ashamed of. K had asked for my discretion regarding the field hospital, but surely he would not blame me for telling my parents, who after all had two sons in the movement. I looked at the clock.

"I'll tell you," I said. "But—"

He waved his hands impatiently. "Eat while you tell me," he said.

I ate eggplant poriyal and rice and parippu, and between mouthfuls the story spilled out of me. I was too tired, really, to care how I told it. Although he was the one sitting there, I addressed myself not to my father but to everyone else I wished I could tell: Sir, Niranjan, my grandmother, Hasna, Chelvi. With each bite, each sentence, I breathed easier. When I was done, my plate empty, I sat back and stared at him.

Appa's expression registered neither pride nor anger, only a neutrality that reminded me of Seelan's face at this table a month ago, before his altercation with Aran. Appa lit another cigarette. "Seelan asked you to do this? Your brothers permitted this?"

I had wanted Appa's approval without knowing it, and realising it was not forthcoming crushed me. "Seelan didn't ask me," I said. "Day-alan and Seelan couldn't have stopped me if they tried." I had no inten-tion of mentioning K, or Aran's criticisms.

"Your mother said Seelan had an injury," Appa said. "She said he came home but he wouldn't tell her how it happened. Do you know?"

"Yes," I said, growing more furious by the minute. He could have embraced me, he could have told me I was smart and strong and re-sourceful, and instead he was asking me questions to which he should have known the answers himself. If Appa had been home, I would have told my parents the truth about the field hospital when I joined. If Appa had been home, Seelan would have shared the story of his wound. If Appa had been home, perhaps they never would have joined—perhaps I would never have asked myself whether I still trusted them. The anger I had held back flashed out of me like lightning. "Yes, I know. I know how all of my brothers are. Do you?"

He gaped and then looked furious. "Who do you think you are, to talk to me like that? What bloody cheek!" He stood and braced his hands against the table.

I no longer cared what happened. I leaned forward. "I marched for Aran's release when you were not there," I said, biting off each word. "That's who I am. I was with Amma, I was here. She got him back by herself when you wouldn't come. And I treated Seelan in the field hos-pital. He's fine."

"What happened to him?" Appa roared.

"I won't tell you!" I shouted back. "You're never here! I took care of him! Amma and I took care of everything without you."

Suddenly, everything rocked, and a spiderweb of pain wove itself across my cheek. It had not occurred to me that he might hit me, be-cause he never had before. My right eye stung and teared. I pressed my hand to where his hand had been. In the corner of my vision, I saw a spark that I realised was his fallen cigarette.

Appa sat down again. He looked suddenly older. I put my hand to my mouth, appalled at him and at myself. It was one thing to miss him during peacetime, and another during war. We had been his fixed point, the place to which he could always return, and now, we were unstable. I wanted him to be steady, to be in one place, but none of us were. We moved and the world moved around us and an ache opened inside of me, and that ache was the only fixed point I had. I was angry with him for being absent. But my being present was not enough either. I saw my brothers, I tried to care for my brothers, but despite what I had said to Appa, I did not know how all of my brothers were.

I thought of Dayalan. If he had been at the TELO massacre, where had Seelan been? Where had K gone without telling me? I did not have the details, but could I really claim that I did not understand?

Amma's slippers shuffled down the hall, a familiar, homely sound. Her dimly lit, sleep-confused face appeared at the entry to the veranda, her arms wrapped tightly around herself, as though she was cold.

"What's all this noise?" she said. "What time is it? You should go to bed, both of you."

Appa and I could hardly look at each other.

"You could have said you were proud of me for working at the field hospital," I said softly as we followed her down the hallway, him one step ahead of me.

He disappeared into their room behind her. It was too late, I thought; I had broken something between us, perhaps irreparably. But before the door swung shut behind them, I heard him say, "You should have known, Sashi, that I am."

MY FATHER DID NOT APOLOGISE, which did not surprise me; indeed, I could not think of the Jaffna father who would. I did not apologise either, which did surprise me slightly; it turned out I could survive being out of his good graces. Other than the cold between us, we might have pretended that nothing had happened. The world was such that nobody troubled to ask after the faint mark on my face, which—for everyone's convenience—faded quickly. Amma and Appa did not attempt to prevent me from going to the field hospital, but after that, I spent most of my nights at the hostel, or left the house too early to see my father. This would have been justifiable anyway; the cases at the clinic were growing in number, and I was sure we were sometimes exceeding our original limit of a hundred patients.

The dearest mercies of those exhausting days: the books that reminded me of Niranjan, of Hasna, and—with pained confusion—of Dayalan. I had promised to write Hasna a letter with my thoughts about *Mother*. And I had the other volumes Anjali and Varathan had loaned me: Kafka, Achebe, and Jayawardena. When I returned from the clinic, I flung myself not into bed or back into my studies, but into those volumes. Their words drained the nights of terror. In the Colombo refugee camp, I had longed for a book to remove me from reality. With every chapter I read now, I felt not removed but partially returned to a safety I had thought entirely lost. I tethered my interior life to the pages, which the people I loved had turned in different times and places.

I began with the Achebe, and when I finished it, I went to Anjali's office to return it. She was writing by longhand in a notebook. She pushed it away when she saw me.

"What are you writing?"

"I'm just trying to document something I think happened," she said. "To record it for myself. Did you enjoy the book?" she asked me.

I slid it across the desk to her. "The ending was brilliant," I said.

"Had you read any African writers before?"

I hadn't. "Would you recommend any others?"

"Oh, I can suggest several. It's a bit of a cliché to have given you that first, although I do like it," she said, leaning back in her chair and threading a hand through her curly hair. "Do you know, I've been thinking, it would be nice to have a reading group. I had a women's study circle in England."

"I would love to discuss these books with someone," I said, sitting down in the chair across from her desk. I did still miss Hasna, the company of her mind. For all the time I spent with Tharini, I had no idea if she read novels, or even some other kind of writing. Chelvi, I knew, loved to read—but we were always reading different things, not together.

"We can be in a room full of women, even here, can't we?" Anjali said. "Why shouldn't we have a feminist reading group here? We can begin with *Feminism and Nationalism in the Third World*."

"I don't have time—"

"I know what it's like to be in medical school and have no spare time," she said. "In fact, it's supposed to be my job to make sure you have no spare time. But you love to read, and so do I. So we should do it. We can invite just a few people—we'll be very informal."

With the library gone and the difficulty of getting things into and out of Jaffna, even a few people reading the same thing would be a feat. My own schedule was daunting, and yet I could not bring myself to refuse her. "How will we manage to get enough copies?" I asked.

"We'll have to share, I suppose," she said cheerfully. She smiled. "Fortunately for women that isn't hard."

AFTER THE INCIDENT WITH SEELAN, K stayed away from the field hospital for some time, and so I did not see him. Piecing together newspaper articles and campus chatter, I discerned that he was travelling; other parts of the peninsula were seeing fighting. How were he and my brothers involved? What information was not making it into the news? I nursed my worry like another patient.

To distract myself, when I was not working, I prepared for the women's study circle Anjali Acca and I had planned. We were cobbling together a small group and a book list; our first two selections were *Feminism and Nationalism in the Third World* and Gorky's *Mother*. Some people were reading the latter in English, and others had elected the Tamil. A couple of the people we had invited were excited about both books, but in most cases, we coaxed people to read one book with the incentive of the other. I had expected to prefer *Mother* myself; although

I prided myself on my ability to dive into any medical text, I was not accustomed to reading dense political or historical writing.

I opened *Feminism and Nationalism* with the same feeling I used to bring to subjects I studied out of duty instead of love. Jayawardena's interests crossed countries, class, religion, and caste. I read the chapters about Turkey, Egypt, Iran, and Afghanistan, and when I reached the sections on India and Sri Lanka I carried the book everywhere with me. Her writing gave me a sense of urgency, recognition, and discovery. When I reached the parts about caste and its critics, and critiques of Hinduism more broadly, I thought of Niranjan. Jayawardena's views on Mahatma Gandhi's limitations as a feminist startled me; his religious and patriarchal lenses, she said, prevented him from understanding women as men's equals. I had grown up idolizing Gandhi, because Appa did, and now I resisted the impulse to quote sections of this book to him. Women were especially suited to nonviolence as a strategy, Gandhi opined, because of their ability to withstand suffering. I don't want to withstand suffering, I wanted to shout back at the page, and I don't want my mother to withstand it either. I made a margin note and planned to bring it up at our first meeting.

Another section on doctors also interested me especially. Jayawardena mentioned several Indian women who had gone overseas to study because they could not attend medical school at home. I was the first woman in my family to go to medical school, and somehow I had never thought about it. On the day that he brought me my first patient, K had told me he wished I would go abroad, because it was safer. My heart sank when I remembered that, because there was nothing I wanted less. Even now, I felt lucky to study and work in the town that was my home. If I travelled abroad, I wanted to do so like Anjali Acca, who had left only to return.

I saved this up to tell to K, and at last, in the middle of the third term, in mid-June, I saw him striding through the field clinic, between the rows of patients. Everything in me hummed, as though my own personal current had been cut and come back on again. I did not have class that day, but I did have the first official meeting of the women's study circle, and so I was not supposed to work for long; I was scheduled to go to campus in only another hour, and I had a great deal to get done first. But I stopped sorting medical supplies and watched, hungry for the chance to observe him without being observed. His hair had grown, and he was leaner. He did not see me; he was looking for someone. He stopped and conferred with a man who looked familiar. When that man turned slightly, I saw that it was T—. At last, K caught my eye and I ducked briefly, embarrassed. He inclined his head, acknowledging me without pausing his conversation. A moment later he took his leave of the other man and walked towards me.

"I have to tell you something," he said, without greeting or preamble. My hand tightened around the bandage I had been holding. "Come with me," he said, and I followed him, fist still clenched.

We took a circuitous route around the clinic, detouring to investigate various spots, before we finally halted in a corner that had been set aside as a temporary mess or canteen, with upended buckets functioning as seats and old wooden crates as tables. No one else was there. He had been hunting for a private place, I realised, and this was the best we could muster. Whatever he had to say was unpleasant. I wanted him to hurry up and tell me so that I did not have to live with this sick feeling of not knowing for too long—and I wished he wouldn't say another word. Could I not just see him, and never hear this terrible news?

"Sit down," he said. And then, "Please."

Again I obeyed. He perched on a bucket across from me and took off his glasses. His eyes looked a familiar kind of sad, and dread rose in me. I had seen him look this way before, when I told him what had happened in Colombo.

"I am so sorry to tell you this, Sashi," he said, "but Dayalan has been killed."

I gasped. I shut my eyes for a long moment in which I let every terrible void inside me open. My life yawned big and wide and bleak and another brother emptier. I had asked myself who Dayalan was. I had

been too cowardly to ask him directly. Now he was gone, and I understood: no matter the answer, he was mine. I had worked as hard as I
could for as long as I could, filling every minute with other people and
other thoughts and near-ceaseless work so that I had no room to linger
in my fear for Dayalan and Seelan, and Aran too. Now the terror I had
suppressed overtook me. I had been operating as if I could shield them,
as if I could bargain for their safety by filling every crevice of my time
with usefulness and study. They would not die, I had thought in the
deepest parts of myself, because our family deserved more, and because
Niranjan was already gone. Because I worked hard, and we had already
paid so dearly. But when had any of that ever mattered? My brothers
were still boys like any other boys; they could be killed like any other
boys. I had no way to protect them, and I mourned Dayalan no matter
what he had done.

When I opened my eyes, I forced myself to look around, and to
look at K. Everything in that makeshift place was the same as before. I
was sitting on an overturned bucket in the clinic and my brother was
dead. I met K's gaze steadily, but my voice choked.

"Does Amma know?"

"No," he said. "Seelan stopped them from notifying her. He wanted
you to tell her, or decide how she should be told."

He had left me by myself to do it. "Tell me what happened," I said.

"Shelling," K said. He did not elaborate. Bombings in Jaffna were
by this point so regular that most newspapers no longer even carried
obituaries. I felt as if I were in a vise and could not get out.

The reading group was set to meet for lunch and discussion. I
needed to go home to tell my mother the news, but I stopped by the
meeting first, so that no one there would wonder where I was. When I
arrived, they were gathering in Anjali Acca's office. She wasn't there
yet. I stood in the doorway, looking at the happy scene. Chelvi had
arranged chairs in a ring, and someone knocked at the door behind me:
Bhavani, bearing food parcels. Tharini had ordered from her shop, and
also asked her to join us. "You can't have a reading group without
eats," said Tharini, and then saw my face. She stopped where she stood,

halfway to taking Bhavani's burden. "Sashi, what is it? What's happened?"

I blurted it out and then they were embracing and consoling me, Tharini and Chelvi weeping, although I did not. Perhaps they were thinking of their brothers. I could not cry. Tharini and Chelvi were explaining to Bhavani that my brother had been in the movement. A blank spread inside me. I had to tell Amma. We would have to telephone Appa, who as usual was at an outstation post. "You're going home, of course," Bhavani said. "Why don't you take the parcels to your family? I'll ride with you."

"We'll clean up," Chelvi said.

They were so kind. I wondered what they had heard about him, if anything. Guilt tinted my grief. I could not stop my own sorrow, but it did not deserve their support. "Oh, please have the discussion," I said. "Everyone has prepared."

"It can wait," Anjali Acca said. She was crying too.

"I finished reading," I said dully. "Someone else can use this until we meet again." I handed over the book, thinking of Dayalan, who—like Anjali—had been so easy about loaning out his beloved personal shelf.

Bhavani rode all the way to my house with me, her basket stacked with food parcels, her eye on me as I wobbled, my bicycle dipping unsteadily across the road. When we got there, she walked me to the front veranda. Laying the parcels down, she put her arms around me, and although we were not exactly friends, I thought one day we might be. "You have to tell her," she said to me, softly but firmly, and then I went in alone.

I CAN'T TELL YOU when I last saw my brother.

In those days, books were not the only things that were hard to obtain. Because Tamil militant groups ran Jaffna, the military came out much less frequently, although the bombing seemed constant. The Tigers and the other groups collected taxes, manufactured some of their own goods for sale, and even ran courts. We were expected to treat all this as ordinary. But tasks that had once been mindless turned arduous, and items that had once been easy to obtain grew increasingly dear.

As I returned in earnest to studying in my third term, despite reducing my hours at the clinic, medical school became harder: unpredictable power cuts forced students to construct improvised lanterns. The university had generators for lectures and lab work, but at home or the hostel, where we were often without current, I timed my work carefully to daylight. When that was not possible, I squinted as long as I could through the dusk. As the power cuts grew more frequent, kerosene was in short supply. Then Amma's old hurricane lantern broke. I despaired, but one weekend at the end of May, Dayalan appeared at our house by himself. Aran had gone out to see a friend, and Amma was sleeping, as she often did in the hot afternoons.

What Aran had told me the last time we had all been home lay heavy on my mind. I did not want to speak to Dayalan alone, but when I went to wake Amma he said, "No, don't bother her." He grinned conspiratorially. "I have something for you, and you mustn't tell anyone I brought it." He proffered a bottle of kerosene. Even ensconced as he was with the movement, somehow Dayalan must have imagined my difficulty, or perhaps someone else told him of the problems students faced. At that time to get such an amount one would have had to stand in a queue and pay a significant sum. I held the bottle incredulously. "I thought perhaps you were having a hard time studying," he said. He had surprised me, which pleased him. "Do you have half a coconut shell?" he asked. We did, leftover from lunch. "You can use this," he said, and mimed pouring the oil in. "Or do you have a jam jar?" I found one. "Give me the salt," he said. He filled the jar with crystals and twisted a wick from a scrap of cloth. He wedged the wick down. "See? In this way you can keep the wick short and use less oil, but still have light. Make it last."

"Dayalan Anna," I said. I hadn't called him that in a long time. "Do you miss reading?"

"I miss it all the time," he said, and blinked. I thought of all the detailed work he had done, his meticulous tinkering on his bicycle, the diagrams he had made when he was planning out an idea. His sketch of our family, which had burned in the riots, crammed between the pages of Niranjan's medical textbook.

"When I read, you're the person I remember," I said.

"I used to read you to sleep when we were small," he said. "You wouldn't go to sleep without me." I remembered this too. I had insisted on singing him a nursery rhyme about mangoes. "When I was a student I always read before bed," he said. "Do you know where I sleep now?" He laughed genially. "You mustn't tell anyone this either. The safest place for us to sleep is the cemetery. Nobody will look for us there, and it's warm, even at night. The most peaceful place."

I was astonished. "You sleep in the cemetery?"

He nodded. "Good company," he said wryly. "But I don't have anything to read there. Or sometimes we are given the official material of the movement."

I remembered the book Aran had given me. "Did you ever read a book called *Puthiyathor Ulagam*?" I asked. "Aran said the movement was handing it out."

"I heard some fellows talking about it, but I haven't read it yet," he said.

It was then that I should have asked him about what Aran had said, but I did not. I was afraid. No; I was selfish. I did not want to hear that story. I wanted a simpler one in which we were all good.

He straightened up. "I have to go, thanggachi, but I wanted to make sure you would be able to read. At least for a little bit. Try using the salt lamp. That way the kerosene will last. I don't know when I can bring you more." Before he left he peered around Amma's door to see her sleeping. "Give her a kiss for me," he said. "Tell her Seelan is all right. I'll be back to see her."

I would have given him my copy of *Puthiyathor Ulagam* then, but I was still in the middle myself. I would have liked that, the idea of him reading something I had given him in one place while I read by the light he had given me in another. I used the kerosene until it ran out and never told anyone where I got it. The salt lamp he had taught me to make gave only enough light for a paragraph, so I moved it block by block down the pages with painstaking care. From the mantel, the Pillaiyar chess piece my grandmother had left behind presided over my work.

By the time I drained the bottle's precious dregs, the medical school students had figured out a new habit: we stood under the streetlamps outside the Jaffna Teaching Hospital to study. The area around there had been designated a safety zone to preserve it from aerial attack, and the lamps had tube bulbs that faced the sky and emanated a precious and unnatural brightness. Every night, a hundred or so people would cycle with their books to crowd under those lamps until they went out. Those jostling for space ranged from year five children aiming for scholarships to my batchmates.

One night I stayed particularly late, preparing for another signature exam. As I packed up my belongings, I saw across the street a tall and solid and recognisable silhouette reminiscent of Appa's. Was it—? I lifted a tentative hand; my brother raised one back. Inwardly, I cheered. He had guessed or known that I would be there. An idea seized me: I had just finished *Puthiyathor Ulagam,* which I could pass to him, as he had handed so many books to me. What would we say to each other when he had read it? Swinging my bag onto my shoulder and hurrying onto my bicycle, I passed across the light's threshold into the dark. I could see him in the shadows just ahead. "Dayalan Anna," I called out. "Wait!" But the figure I had thought was him began to bleed into the night, its edges becoming less and less discernible. Before I could reach him, he was gone. There was no proof that anyone had seen me or that I had seen anyone. I was left with only the echo of togetherness, my own sure feeling that he had come.

11.

Liberation

JAFFNA, 1986–1987

BEFORE THE WAR, WE HAD NO FREQUENT CAUSE TO MOURN the young. Hindu Saivite rituals for the dead are for the old. Those who passed away had generally lived full lives. When the war began, and the young began to die, we had no words for it. Our customs did not give us a way to say their names. You must understand: our children light their parents' funeral pyres. What, then, for those who have no children? What, then, for the parents who outlive their sons?

Since Niranjan's death, his photograph had presided over my mother's front parlour. After Dayalan's death, she moved her first son's frame over to make room for the portrait of her second. Grief-stricken and angrier than before, Aran helped her silently. I stood back and told them when the pictures were level. My father came home, but it was too late for me to forgive him.

THE LAST MONTH OF the third term loomed ahead of me. The year had already been brutal, and in the wake of Dayalan's death I was even more exhausted. In some abstract way I had supported what the militants were fighting for, or at least what they said they were fighting against; we all knew the cruelty of the state. But that year, when the militants turned on each other and when I heard where my brother had stood in that fight, I no longer knew what to believe.

The way out of this fighting was less and less clear, as the Tigers and many of their rivals behaved with extraordinary, unabashed cruelty. Since Dayalan's death, Chelvi spoke warmly to me again, and as one of her confidantes, I heard important, unofficial news without much delay. If one of the groups harmed someone she knew, she told me about it. Through her mother, among others, she was well connected, and unlike almost anyone else, she did not soften the details of what she said. She reported hearing, for example, about Tiger cadres walking into another faction's camp, where unarmed men lay recovering from a virus. The patients still had their eyes closed, Chelvi told me, and the Tigers shot them.

As we hurried to and from our hostels, our classrooms, our homes and errands, we inevitably passed the sites of other atrocities. Daily we were haunted, not by ghosts but by the malevolent, unavoidable present. On Temple Road, the Tigers had established a prison where they tortured people from other Tamil militant groups. The location of this prison, called Kanthan Karunai, was well known. When Tharini and I walked on the road and neared that spot, we always chose a route that would put as much distance as possible between ourselves and that place. But how much distance was really possible? The war offered us only tight quarters. Anjali Acca compared Kanthan Karunai to the fourth floor of a well-known government building in Colombo, where the state detained, interrogated, and tortured people. One day, half a kilometre past where the prison was, I found her slowly walking her bicycle instead of riding. I knew immediately the route she had taken. She was weeping, her curly hair a tangle around her tear-blotched face. "I don't know what will become of us," she said, "if we can be no better than them. I don't know how we can survive this."

Still, I worked in the field hospital. I could not decide what to do, and out of habit and indecision I continued to go. I repeated to myself the arguments I had offered to Aran, and to Anjali: taking action, caring for civilians. When I went to work, I saw Thambirajah and others with issues of *Porkural,* the movement's magazine. When I brought one to Chelvi, she frowned and told me what had happened to the editors of *Kaatru* and *Teechudar,* who had tried to publish critiques of the Tigers. They had disappeared. She thought they were someplace like Kanthan Karunai, and she subsequently destroyed her own back issues of the subversive publications. We cannot allow traitors to remain among us, Tiger leaders said in interviews designed to celebrate the purity of the movement and to scare those who did not fall in line. K was one of those quoted. Even as someone working with them, I was duly terrified.

In every space we were watched, and worse, they taught us to watch ourselves. Even the most mundane errand at a corner shop was perilous. One day early that spring, I went to the bakery near Jaffna Hindu College, which had the bread that Amma preferred. As I stood in the queue, the customer to my left tapped my arm, pointed to a man ahead of us, and murmured the name of a well-known Tiger leader. The man carried a monkey on his shoulder and addressed it affectionately as Mani. The name meant bell.

When the man departed with a large parcel of maalu paan, the monkey leapt from his shoulder to the shop floor and surveyed us authoritatively, tiny monkey paws on tiny monkey hips. After the animal, too, left, with a censorious backwards glance, the customer who had pointed them out joked quietly that he dared not say anything in front of the beast, since surely Mani would deliver a report to his master. A small, piercing siren, signalling disobedience.

BECAUSE OF DAYALAN'S DEATH, the women's study circle missed its first meeting; after that, we rescheduled again and again. "It seems rather typical that we can't book the time," Anjali Acca said ruefully. "We shouldn't shove our own priorities to the back." At last, we reserved a room and put our discussion on the calendar for late July,

practically the end of the term. It would be a party of sorts, Anjali suggested. Everyone who had attended the first meeting swore to come.
Chelvi, who had my copy of *Feminism and Nationalism,* promised to
bring it. "You had better," I joked. "I'll need it. Did you see all my
angry margin notes?"

When the day came, I entered the room eager for our discussion—
and stopped in dismay. There, in the ring of chairs, was an unwelcome
guest: Josie. Of course, the conversation was on university grounds
and technically should have been open to anyone, but how had she,
with her Tiger sweetheart, come to know about it? I had taken care not
to mention it widely, and the others had also been discreet, I thought.
How could we have a frank discussion unless it was with people we
trusted? No matter how it had happened, she was here, and we could
not ask her to leave; that would be too much of a scene. I looked at
Anjali Acca in alarm, but her back was to me as she set out biscuits in a
corner. She and I had never discussed Josie, but I was sure she knew my
body partner's affiliations. Chelvi and Tharini came up to me, smiling
too brightly, and as they greeted me, Chelvi pressed my book into my
hands. Taking it, I put my schoolbag down next to the chair with Anjali's things. When I sat and opened the book, I found a note: ???
WHAT DO WE DO? I folded it up and tucked it away. We could cen-
sor ourselves, or we could talk as we had planned. I had no idea which
was the better route.

"Sashi, were you going to begin?" Anjali asked, taking her seat.

"Perhaps we should do introductions," I said pointedly, and just
then, Bhavani showed up at the door, out of breath.

"Bhavani!" Tharini exclaimed. "Excellent. I was afraid we were
only having biscuits." Bhavani laid out the armful of parcels she was
carrying. Then she smiled at Josie, her usual friendly smile, and I realised she didn't know who the new person was.

"I don't think we've met," she said cheerfully. "I'm Bhavani."

"This is Josie," Chelvi said. "She's at the medical faculty with
Sashi."

"Sashi and I were paired for anatomy this year," Josie said. "I hope you will all forgive my intruding. I heard there was a feminist group meeting, and I was excited to come. I'm afraid I haven't even got the book."

"That's all right," Anjali Acca said. "I know Sashi has read and re-read this one, so we can start with her questions, and if we move to more general conversations, that's fine."

I spent every rehearsal exam in a room with Josie and Anjali. Then, as now, I realised, I had prepared. I opened to the pages about India and Sri Lanka. If we were now about to cross a conversational minefield, well—all I could do was to keep an eye out for where I wanted to arrive and what on the way there might be dangerous.

"I was interested in how Jayawardena wrote about Gandhi," I said.

"Oh, I've always admired Gandhi," Josie said. "It seems like that kind of support—satyagraha, nonviolence—is one thing women can do for the struggle."

None of us asked which struggle she meant. It seemed that not having read the book was not going to prevent her from participating.

"I grew up idolising him, because my father did," I said. "But I didn't know the nuances of some of his views. Jayawardena's critiques of Gandhi seem very persuasive. I hate the idea that women are better suited for nonviolent action because they are better at withstanding suffering. I don't want to suffer. Why should that be my role?"

I had opened a door; now it was up to someone else to walk through.

"Yes," Anjali Acca said. "And better at suffering for what? Under whose direction do women suffer? What is the right way to suffer? I really appreciated the inclusion of Subramaniya Bharathi's critiques of how conservative Tamil society oppresses women. Isn't that happening even here? What kind of struggle expects women to support a cause but does not address our concerns?"

This was rather more direct than I had expected.

"I wish Sri Lanka had had a leader like Nehru around its independence," Bhavani said. "What if our independence had been different, rather than both that and women's rights coming so gradually? We have the vote, and we can study, as the book says, but," and here she opened it to quote,

> The processes of education for women also contributed to the socializing of women into roles that were only superficially different from those of traditional society. Sri Lanka is thus an interesting example of a society in which women were not subjected to harsh and overt forms of oppression, and therefore did not develop a movement for women's emancipation that went beyond the existing social parameters. It is precisely this background that has enabled Sri Lanka to produce a woman prime minister, as well as many women in the professions, but without disturbing the general patterns of subordination.

As I listened to Bhavani read, I realised that this idea of gradual improvement was how I had heard my parents, who considered themselves progressive, speak about caste when Aran brought it up: yes, it's very unfortunate—as though such a system had simply happened naturally. Things have to develop, it takes time, you can't expect change overnight, they have to educate themselves, we are sympathetic, but—! This was, I suddenly understood, a very patient, middle-class way to talk about change.

"The general patterns of subordination," Bhavani repeated, dragging out each word. "That's very accurate. I also appreciated what she said about how the gradual approach is a limitation. So many things are in the hands of bourgeois women, and where does that get anyone?" She looked around. "Present company excluded," she said.

"We don't deserve to be excluded, probably," Tharini said around a mouthful of lunch parcel. "If you only work to improve things within the existing framework, then you can't question the existing framework. That seems obvious enough."

"That's why the movement is so important," Josie said. "It questions the existing framework."

At the mention of the movement, Tharini filled her mouth with rice and stopped talking. She had become even more cautious since her brother had joined PLOTE.

"Does it?" Chelvi asked. "The movement does expect women to support the cause in all the proper ways."

"But as Jayawardena writes, isn't that within the existing patriarchal structures?" Anjali said. I remembered the meals Saras Aunty and Amma and I had cooked at the Tigers' demand.

"The Tigers promise to liberate women, to lift us up," Josie said. "What about the women's wing?"

I had heard of this; the Tigers had started a section for women in 1983, but I did not know anyone involved in it and had never treated any women fighters. I did know that like other Tigers, the women cadres wore cyanide capsules around their necks in case of capture. This was not my idea of liberation, but I was not sure that in this room I should say so.

"The women's wing is very interesting," Anjali Acca said. "But what is the role of dissent for feminism? Can an organisation that does not allow dissent be a feminist organisation?"

And there it was. The classroom clock ticked loudly in the echo of her question, which none of us answered, although each of us certainly had an opinion.

"That's a very complicated question," Chelvi said. "We should think about it and take a tea break."

"Of course," Anjali said, smiling a little bit.

"Yes," said Tharini, getting up. It was not that complicated of a question, but with that, we scattered to serve and replenish food, talking loudly about casual matters. Josie delicately took a biscuit and excused herself quietly. When it became clear that she would not return, the rest of us stared at each other, speechless. Eventually Chelvi suggested that when we met in the next school year, after the term holiday, we could read a novel by one of the Ilankai Tamil women writers Jayawardena mentioned, in addition to discussing *Mother*.

"You have great ambitions for us," Anjali Acca said lightly. "I appreciate that."

THIS TIME, DURING THE term holiday, I slept at home. I wanted distance from campus, and some separation from the tiring feeling of constant watchfulness. I should have known that even at my parents' house, no such refuge could be guaranteed. One evening in August, I heard shots. They sounded quite close to the house. I tried to go back to sleep, but my heart repeated the irregular, violent sounds as I heard them.

The next morning, when I went out to go to the market, I saw the children headed to the nearby nursery school staring at a body on the road. The body was wearing a bright white shirt and dark brown trousers; the body lay on its belly. He had fallen and been shot, in which order I didn't know. While I chased the children away from the sight, some men came by on bicycles. They thanked me; they also didn't want the children to see the body. I could not reply to them; I could not swallow. They thanked me again and then bicycled away, leaving me alone with him.

I knew I could do nothing for that body. I could not care for it; too late. I could not remove it from the road; too dangerous. I could only know about it and remember it. I couldn't even speak openly about what I had seen, but when I returned home I wrote a small note about it to myself. I addressed it to Niranjan and slipped it into a book I was reading. That boy's mother would not know he was there. How had we felt when we didn't know where Niranjan was?

For three days, Amma and Aran and I walked by him—the boy, the body, the corpse—and had to pretend not to see him. For three nights, something cried in the tree outside my window, down the road from where the body lay. On the fourth morning, the boys, by which I mean the Tigers, came and took him away.

———

AFTER THAT, I WROTE more and more, with the hope that it would help me understand. When I had told Anjali Acca about Niranjan's death and my experience in the riots, she had said, "I find that when I write things down, I can think about them more clearly." I could not yet write my way past confusion, but still I tried. Almost every time, I felt my words a failure and threw them away.

With every day that passed, home became a different place. Its very landscape changed. When I came back from the clinic one day, no one was inside. Then I heard, distinctly, a scraping sound. I could not tell where it was coming from. I called for Aran, and then, realising that the person in the house might be a thief, stopped. I crept around the side of the house, where we used to lock the bicycles, so that I could see into the back garden. Aran was there with another man, who was striking something against the ground. I hurried towards them, and as I drew closer I could see them digging.

Aran looked up and saw me. "I thought I would have this taken care of," he said.

"Thank you," I said. I had known we needed a bunker at home. These days, the army launched cannon bombs from the Fort in all directions. We also knew about fighter planes dropping aerial bombs, and gunfire coming from helicopters. I had promised to hire someone to build a bunker. But I had put off making the arrangements. Once I had seen other people's bunkers, I did not want to get inside one. I did not want one in the back garden, which I had once tended with four brothers instead of one.

"How long will it take?" Aran asked.

"We have to be done quickly as others are also waiting," the man said. "We give the houses with children priority."

"Quick is good," Aran said. "They might not wait until tomorrow to shell us." He laughed grimly. "Some people on this lane have been envying our house." He meant its traditional four-sided design, with the beloved central courtyard. "If we didn't already have such a house,"

Aran joked, "perhaps we could have gotten one now. Just let the shell fall in the right place, and you, too, can have a home with a courtyard."

When Amma came home and heard us in the garden, she came back to see what was going on. In the heat of the day, the man digging the bunker was as wet as if he were fresh from a monsoon puddle, and as dishevelled. "Did it rain?" Amma whispered to Aran, looking at him. "Yes," Aran said with a straight face. "The gods decided to pour a storm on all the fools who did not have bunkers yet."

"Don't you want to stop for the day?" Amma asked the man.

He wiped his face on his shoulder. "I have to finish up to a certain point, or we won't be able to start at the next house tomorrow."

"Stop and eat," Amma said to him. She went inside and brought him a full plate of rice, parippu, fish, eggplant poriyal. He accepted it gratefully. Then he drank four tumblers of water and poured another directly onto his head.

In the days before the bunkers, in early 1986, when the shelling was farther away, we sometimes ran down the road to shelter with K's aunt and father because their house had a concrete roof. It had taken a war to bring me into K's house. I wished he were with us. I wished that my father, Dayalan, and Seelan were with us. When the bombing seemed especially distant we would dare to sit on the roof or on the top floor of their house and watch. Bombed Jaffna spread out before us like a heap of scattered cigarette ends in the dark. We could see the planes take off and then dive and then lift again. As they began the second ascent, they would drop the explosives. Decades later, when I was long gone from there, someone told me about the Indian Ocean tsunami and its second wave, and I remembered those planes: the deceptive moment before they rose again, when everything seemed like it could still be safe. When the bombs fell, we could hear the little children of the neighbourhood screaming and their mothers comforting and scolding them. Sometimes the mothers, too, screamed, and a tuneful chorus of fear rose from the town. At this point my own mother was beyond screaming, a fact for which I was grateful.

We learned how to anticipate the bombs. First, Henry would begin to cry. Even now, I find the weeping of animals worse than the weeping of people because the grief of animals is nearly inconsolable. One can talk to a person, even lie to a person, and tell them everything will be all right. My mother, Aran, and I did that with each other every day, as though such lies were a form of blessing. But you cannot lie to a weeping dog; an animal's body knows the truth. Eventually we figured out that poor, terrorised Henry could hear what we could not: tanks or planes on the move in the distance, the whine of their engines too high or far for people's hearing to find.

On the roof of K's house, we put our hands in Henry's fur and soothed him and ourselves while we watched the sky. With his eyes trained up, Aran folded loving hands around Henry's ears, murmuring about what a good boy he was. Don't listen, Henry, we said, but oh, in our arms he shook.

At first I had not understood why the army would attack Jaffna with planes. My brother explained to me that the army could no longer use the roads because the Tamil militant groups had mined the likeliest routes. After he said that, I thought: Of course. How many victims of mine explosions had I treated, my own brother included? In my head, Dayalan and Seelan carefully mined a road, as deliberately as they had once planted seeds in our garden. Such seeds bear ugly fruit: one of my school friends from my Ordinary Levels lost her foot in an accidental mine explosion that year. I had my own scares, too. One night, I went to pluck curry leaves from the plant in the front garden so that Amma and I could cook. A passing helicopter caught the flicker of my torch and began shooting. Aran and Amma could see me from inside but could do nothing to help me. I wrapped my arms around one corner of our house, under our veranda roof, and held the embrace until the thrum of the propellers moved on. The next morning the sun shone through several bullet holes in the tall coconut tree I had so proudly shown K. When Appa came home the following weekend, he was ready to take an ax to it, and Aran and I had to stop him, to point to its stubborn growth, despite everything.

By the time we used our own bunker, in September, I wished the worker we had hired had dug it twice as deep. But that wasn't practical: it was unlit, and the deeper you went, the darker it got. The bunker could comfortably fit me, Amma, Aran, and Henry, who had to be dragged in every time. He hated the bunker as much as I did, but he was free to express it, and did, barking furiously. Our other animals stayed in the back garden shed, if we could get them there. Sometimes we could hear them—a cow, goats, chickens, whatever we had at that moment—screaming during the shelling, which was twice as uncanny as any sounds we made. Three or four more people could easily join us, and sometimes they did: neighbours; Appa, if he had come home, as he now did more often; visiting friends; once, the postman, who was twice as big as Dayalan. When we ran to the bunker we tried to remember to carry our torches so that we could check for snakes. Sometimes there were cobras in the bunker; sometimes after a storm foul-smelling water filled it, and we rose from it dank and cold.

One night in October, just after my second year of medical school had started, I was home. I had not yet shifted back to the hostel, greedy for a few more nights with my mother. When the shelling began, Aran and Amma raced to the bunker, but I refused to go. "I have to study," I shouted. "Will you hurry?" my brother yelled back. "I don't want to lie down in the dark with the snakes. Let me just die out here!" I wailed. The sound of the shelling was coming closer, the arc of the nearest ones whistling in our ears. Then Aran was beside me. "Sashi," he said. "Acca, don't be stupid. Come on." He pulled me by the arm until I went with him, crying, and then I squatted down in the bunker next to my mother, who for the first time in my life slapped me full in the face. "Don't ever say that again," she said. "That you'd rather die. I had five children, and only two of you are with me, and God knows where your father is, so when I tell you to do it, Sashikala, you had better get in."

A WEEK LATER, I was home once more when T— came to our lane on Saturday morning and called a greeting from the gate. When I came out and saw who it was, I quailed. No one in the movement had ever turned up to bring me good news.

"Sashi," he said. I eyed him sceptically. "How are you? You're doing good work at the field hospital, I hear."

I nodded. "I'm glad to be there," I said cautiously. He was high in the movement's ranks these days, I had been given to understand, and he was not prone to compliments.

He put his hand to his chest. "I was sorry to hear of your brother's passing," he said. "I am late, of course, but I came to offer my condolences. I knew Dayalan slightly. He was an excellent cadre."

Surely our measures of excellence differed. "He was a good brother," I said.

"To honour all that your family has given, we thought we would move you to a better house," he said. He looked past me. "This place is very big, and now that two of your brothers are gone you might wish to shift."

So he wanted the house. I did not wish to shift, and he knew it. "I should go and get Amma," I said, and hurried inside.

The previous year, K had come to tell me of Sir's murder. I had forgotten that before delivering the news, he had noted how big our house was, how convenient, how—minus three of my brothers—it had more room than we needed. He must have passed these observations on; Seelan must have agreed to all this. I bit my lip, feeling foolish and betrayed. T— took his time dressing up the request, but it seemed that our house was located at a strategic point, where it would now be convenient for the Tigers to house some members. Because we were a movement family, they conveyed their request for us to shift by offering what he called a small recognition of our contribution: a house that was empty, just as convenient and nicely furnished for civilians, but smaller. It was actually quite grand in some ways, he promised, with furniture and dishes from England. "I think you'll find yourselves very comfortable there," he said. "Perhaps even more comfortable than you are here." I wondered who had been uncomfortable there, who had left or been kicked out.

"For how long do you think you will need the house?" Amma asked nervously.

He gestured extravagantly, arms sweeping wide. "Who thought the war would go on in this way for this long?" he said. "We can promise that you will return. After all, we are fighting to defend your ancestral home. Until we attain liberation, we will provide housing for you. And we will help you to go."

Because it was not a request—"We will help you to go?" Aran repeated witheringly when I told him—we consented. We packed our own things, declining the help of the cadres who showed up on moving day. Aran sorted through Niranjan's remaining possessions, and Amma packed Seelan's things; I organised Dayalan's too-quiet room into a single, large suitcase because Amma could not bear to do it. The kerosene bottle that he had given me was dry, but I put it in my school bag anyway; I swept the books off of his shelf and into the suitcase. I wished I could pack the green of the trees, the gate he had unlatched, the bicycle he had lost so long ago. I felt myself emptying along with the house.

We yielded what we had collected to the cadres, who loaded our worldly goods into a lorry. We went behind them in a hired auto, so that we could follow them to a place and a house we had never seen before. Even as we pulled away from the small, dear lane, I could see more cadres walking up the veranda steps; I could imagine them exploring the garden and exclaiming at the beauty of the small courtyard. They would strip the house, certainly, and if they did not, others would. They would walk across the veranda where Niranjan had shared his medical textbooks; the courtyard where Aran had read the newspaper; the dirt patch by the gate where Seelan and Dayalan and K had wielded their cricket bats. I tried to remember if I had taken Niranjan's medical school graduation photo down, if I had put his portrait and Dayalan's portrait among our things. Or were they still on the wall in our house, which was now theirs? In my lap, Henry cried openly as only dogs can.

———

THE NEW HOUSE WAS easy to hate and easier to leave because it was not ours. I wanted memories of the seven of us together, and that house was not big enough for them. Amma performed the work of setting up absentmindedly; Appa returned to Jaffna and bemoaned our displacement; Aran grumbled and harvested fruit from the previous occupants' sad trees. Seelan did not come; we had not seen him since Dayalan's death. I spent as little time as possible there, and kept my room at the hostel, even though the new place was much closer to town and to the university. And all was well, or well enough, or as well as could be expected under the circumstances, when everything suddenly got worse because a university student one year senior to me went missing.

None of us had ever taken Ravikumar too seriously: he was a good-looking, fun-loving, drinking, joking fellow who could take a ribbing and also give one. He studied political science and lived at home with his parents, and one day he simply did not come back from campus. His mother was beside herself, and I remembered how Amma had been when she knew her sons were in danger. "You know what happened to that boy," Chelvi said to me over lunch the day after we heard that he was missing. Our friendship was continuing to restore itself. "The Tigers took him."

I looked automatically to see who was nearby. "Tell me what you think happened," I said.

Chelvi leaned forward. "He ragged Josie when he saw her in the student union room the other day," she said. Everyone had come to see a film, Chelvi explained, and Josie was also there. Everyone was being very quiet and careful, except Ravikumar, who didn't seem to care who she was, because he was giving her grief about being the girlfriend of—

"Oh, no," I said in horror. "And she told him? She told her boyfriend what he said?"

Josie's boyfriend was famous for his short fuse.

Chelvi nodded. "That's what James guessed," she said. "Have you seen Josie recently?" James was another Arts student who was part of the university-wide student union, an even-keeled and pleasant boy besotted with Chelvi. If this account came from him, I thought, it was reliable. And he was right: Josie had been uncharacteristically absent from our dissections for the past few days. I had assumed she was ill.

"How long has Ravikumar been missing?" I asked.

"A few days already," Chelvi said. "A few days too long."

We both knew that every day he stayed missing increased the odds that he would be killed. By the end of the first week of November, Josie was still nowhere to be seen on campus. "We have to say something," Chelvi said. "If they took him and we do nothing, the next time it could be any of us."

She was talking to a meeting of the general student union. There were very few medical students there; I looked around and saw no one but myself and Tharini. As a rule, our faculty was more supportive of the movement. "What can we do?" asked a boy in the back. "Any suggestions?" the president asked. "We should boycott classes," Chelvi said. I took a deep breath. Skipping would mean something because it would cost us something. Given how the war interrupted the goings-on of the university, we would already finish our degrees late. I had never taken such a public stance against something the movement was probably responsible for—not even Sir's death. But Ravikumar was one of us. How could I fight for lives in the field hospital and let disappearances pass unremarked on campus? I hesitated, but in the end I raised my hand along with those in favor of the boycott. When I looked over, I saw that Tharini had lifted hers too. Most of us had never done anything like this. With each one of us who voted yes, we were safer.

The Tigers, of course, denied any involvement in Ravikumar's absence, which no one believed. Terrified and empowered, I joined in daily protests at the campus entrance, and because my involvement at the field clinic was not generally known, because almost no medical students participated in this strike, no one suggested that I was being inconsistent. Indeed, there were so many of us that my participation did not even stand out. At the fringes of the crowd, Anjali Acca looked on approvingly. I knew she was glad to see me joining in after the four and a half months of listless depression that had followed Dayalan's death. Chelvi had made me a placard that said, simply, WHERE IS RAVI-KUMAR. I held it as high as I could until my arms ached. The Mothers' Front had organised the last protest I had attended. In comparison, we were a smaller group, and so had to persist for many days. But eventually, we did attract attention; traffic near the university could not move for the crowds. As more and more people saw us, we bumped shoulders and held hands to reassure each other. I had worried that the Tigers would do something to us. Were we a big enough number to be safe? Too few to trouble them? We held our breath to find out. Would they return him?

It was not enough; he did not surface. A week later, when there was still no sign of him, some of the students began to fast in protest; by the end of the month, when he still hadn't been found, a peace march was organised. I did not march because I was assigned to work at the clinic that day. I told Chelvi that I didn't feel well. Later, she came by the hostel to tell me what had transpired, how at several points along the way Tiger supporters had hurled abuse at the marchers, and even attacked them. "Where is Josie?" she asked. Tharini and Anjali had asked me the same thing, and I did not know. My body partner did not reappear until a full fortnight later. As the general fighting of the war had worsened, the students had had little choice but to let the matter of Ravikumar fade. We were frustrated, and by unspoken and collective agreement, most of us did not address Josie beyond what was absolutely necessary. She moved around the campus nervously. She was no longer one of us, if she ever had been. When she entered her first class after her long absence, she took the empty chair next to mine and greeted me quietly. I thought about all the hours we had spent together and wondered if she would casually endanger me, too, if she knew of my qualms about the movement. Across campus, in another class, Ravikumar's seat sat empty. The answer was already obvious, and recklessly, I did not greet her back.

In the days after we gave up the boycott, we returned to our student routines feeling resentful. Only one sign of resistance remained: an unsigned pamphlet that said at the top *A Report of What Has Occurred in Our Community Regarding the Disappearance of the Student Ravikumar.* The document contained a record of everything that had happened concerning Ravikumar, some things I had known and others I had not, in words that surprised me with their candor and fairness. The writer had managed to sort out the timeline of his vanishing, beginning with the morning of the day he had last been seen. The pamphlet also included a description of him that impressed me with its accuracy. The writer did not make him out to be a saint, but eloquently lamented Ravikumar as one of many young people missing in Jaffna. Bravely, whoever it was named the Tigers as responsible for his disappearance.

Because we saw no accountability for our classmate's abduction, this was all the satisfaction we had. Those in power seemed to think that if one of us went missing, the rest should pretend that we did not notice, that such an absence was just a pebble slipping into the ocean. We all knew the Tigers had done it, and now someone had named them. The students handed the pamphlet silently to each other, down the rows of the lecture halls, in the Student Union, as they crossed the streets of Jaffna. We speculated quietly and admired the author. Perhaps it was one of us.

AS 1986 WOUND DOWN, the Tigers briefly negotiated directly with the Sri Lankan government, minus any Indian mediation, but the talks ended in confusion. The New Year brought what the Tigers called their Secretariat; they wished to demonstrate that they could run a state, and set up some of the bureaucracy to do so. In response, an enraged Sri Lankan government cut off all fuel coming into Jaffna. No buses; no boats. Anything that could have been of use to the Tigers was stripped from Jaffna routes. Unfortunately, many of these things would have been useful to civilians as well. Certain vegetables went missing from the market. As we could not talk about missing people, we could not talk about missing food; although potato curry was Aran's favourite food, my mother no longer offered to make it, and as if by contract, my brother no longer asked. Fuel and food were not coming in, but soldiers did, pouring in from multiple directions. The Tigers fought back. I thought of going past our old house to see how it was faring but suspected I would not be able to bear the sight of our home if it was damaged.

The parties traded civilian massacres, and the Tigers set fire to prominent buildings, saying that the army had planned to take them over. The fire at Veerasingham Hall was so big that—as we realised later—Amma, Aran, and I could all see the smoke, although all three of us were well away, in different directions. I began coming to the house more frequently to check on my mother and brother. "Don't worry," Amma said reassuringly. "The Indians will come. The Indians will not let us starve."

But the Indians did not come, and we were very hungry.

AROUND THIS SAME TIME, both the medical school and the field hospital were electric with worry. The Sri Lankan government wanted to shut down the Jaffna General Hospital. Technically, it was a public hospital under their control, and a civilian site that they could not attack—but the Tigers regularly fired on the military from its vicinity. Although I could not abide that the Tigers used a civilian hospital for their own protection, if it were to close, the ill and injured would have fewer places to go. Many civilians would leave Jaffna. And that would give the military a clear route to seize control.

As we waited to find out what would happen, a terrible suspense propelled our days. How would the field clinic survive if the hospital were not nearby? It was unbombable, but we were not. Would we abandon the place, along with the civilians who would surely flee, or would we be forced to stay with the Tigers?

When classes ground to a halt and the hospital began discharging patients, I fought down my panic. Some of these patients came to the field clinic, both to find out what we knew and to receive further treatment. I was checking one such case, an elderly man with a broken left arm in plaster, when I heard a cheery voice behind me.

"Mr. Casipillai! How much longer in the cast?"

Mr. Casipillai beamed, and I turned. I hadn't seen K since he had come to tell me of Dayalan's death, and judging by the look on his face, he had not planned to talk to me today either. He was, again, thinner and shaggier. There were so many things I wanted to say to him: Where have you been? What about my house? What about the hospital? Where have you been and what have you done?

Stunned as I was, I let Mr. Casipillai question him first.

"K! How are you, thaambi? Do you know anything about this hospital business? Should I be packing to leave?"

"I don't think so, Mr. Casipillai," K said casually.

I knew he must have come to discuss the situation with someone. "Mr. Casipillai," I said calmly, "do you mind if I speak with K for a moment?"

He clearly did not want to talk to me, but I drew him away from the cot. People hurried around us, carrying supplies, and we stood closer together to make room for them.

"What will happen to us if the hospital closes?" My voice cracked.

"You'll be safe," he said. "I promise."

"Where?" I demanded. Did he mean that I would be safely away? Safe with the Tigers? Safe with him?

"I don't have time, Sashi," he said regretfully, and with a quick nod, he was gone again, leaving me and my fury behind.

Things were so hectic that day that I did not see Thambirajah there; I don't know if he heard the same story that I did. Unusually, I did see him a few days later at the medical student union, where he stood, his handsome face sanctimonious, to announce that he had had the Tigers arrest the editor of the *Saturday Evening Review*. The likable Sinhalese gentleman, who travelled back and forth between Colombo and Jaffna, was reportedly part of a group that wanted the Tigers to participate in peace talks. The Tigers would fight for what our people deserved, Thambirajah said, and when he added that the Tigers had the offender in custody, his handsome face shone with a pleasure that made me feel sick. I realised the source of his power with the Tigers: his brother, T—. I had never been able to shake the sense I had of being watched at the university, even more than the field hospital, and what I was hearing now bore that out. When the closure order came a few days later, it was announced that the student union would gather to discuss our response. I was not sure what would happen and felt jittery with anxiety.

Finishing my work at the clinic ahead of schedule that evening, I decided to head to campus early. Classes had concluded for the day and I found the grounds unusually empty and peaceful. The breeze was warm and sweet as dusk approached, and I wandered alone across the green, appreciating the rare opportunity to take my time. When had I last been unhurried? I could not remember. Passing the familiar places where I studied, I remembered how the medical faculty had looked to me the day I had arrived for exams after treating my brother: huge and strange and terrifying. Tonight it seemed like home, and I wished that someone from home were with me.

As I rounded a corner past the building where K had brought me my first patient, I heard an odd click somewhere close to my body. I looked down to see that I had ridden all the way to campus with Periannai's stethoscope still around my neck. I had not even registered its smooth weight. Bemused, I reached up to unclip it and twisted slightly to drop it over my shoulder and into my satchel. It was then, half turned back, that I noticed that someone in the nearby shadows was following me.

I swallowed and continued, trying to keep an even pace. The path that would lead me to the meeting hall was still some distance away.

The person stayed several steps behind me at first, but gradually length-ened their stride, drawing steadily nearer. My pulse quickened. I tried to walk faster. If it was someone I knew, why didn't they call out? I didn't dare turn my head. I was too far from the hall for anyone to hear me scream. I was shaking. Closer and closer the figure came, until fi-nally we were abreast.

"Sashi," K said quietly. "Aren't you going to look at me?"

I came to a halt and turned at last. His voice was low and my pulse was still thrumming. At the sight of those Jaffna eyes, so dark and cer-tain behind his spectacles, I felt a rush of relief—and then past that, a familiar and frightening sweetness.

It took me a moment to trust myself to speak. "Did you have to scare me?" I asked.

He smiled and then gazed around the green, which in the partly moonlit dusk looked like a still from a film. "I was looking for you," he said.

"Why?" I asked.

"Just because," he said. If you speak Tamil, you will know the sin-gle word he said, its ease and simplicity, and perhaps you can imagine how it made me feel. I had so often dreaded his unexpected appear-ances, which came with painful news, but I could see it in his face: to-night there was none, not yet.

"You know," he said wistfully, "I've never been back here since I left."

"Really? But aren't there movement people here all the time?"

"Yes," he admitted. He took the glasses off and polished them and I studied his slim, sensitive face hungrily. "But not me."

"You told me the hospital wouldn't close," I said.

"They haven't complied yet," he pointed out. "They told me to come to the medical student union meeting, to hear the discussion." He replaced his spectacles.

I laughed. "Like you're a student." We started walking again.

"Well, by all rights you and I should have been in medical school at the same time," he said. "I would have been your senior. I loved medical school. My favourite class in the first year was anatomy."

"It was my favourite class too," I said, and hesitated. "Of course, Anjali Acca is a critic of the movement."

My remark failed to fluster him. "I know," he said. "It's legend. In the early days she was a supporter. She's brilliant."

His admiration for her confused and pleased me. "She is," I said. "When she came back from England she was sorry to hear you'd left school."

"I thought she would be," he said. "We have different ideas about the way society can move. I think if she had been here when I decided, she would have tried to talk me out of it."

I cleared my throat. "If I had been there when you decided, I would have tried to talk you out of it too," I said.

He was silent for a moment. "Would you?" he asked.

I had sounded too personal, I realised. "She told me how she left the movement," I said quickly. "You could too. You could come back to medical school."

He laughed, and I thought I had not seen him in such a mood for years. "Is she trying to get you to talk me out of it now?" he asked. "I can't. Don't you ever think about what it would have been like if I were still here? We would go to these meetings together." He sounded regretful.

There wasn't a place on campus I hadn't imagined him. "Your father and your aunt are proud," I said, "but I'm sure they wish you had stayed."

He was undeterred, his eyes fixed on mine. "Don't you ever think about the other life we might have had?" he said.

There was no mistaking what he meant. I had never put it so plainly, even to myself. I looked away. "What does it matter if I do?" I said.

He reached out and wrapped his fingers around mine, so that we were walking and holding hands, and I wondered if anyone could see us, if I wanted that, if it would matter if someone saw, and then I knew that no one could, because if anyone could, he would never have done it. This stolen, safe hour could not last.

"Did you think I never thought about it?" he said quietly.

"What do you think about?" I said, my eyes still on the darkening sky.

Then his other hand touched my cheek, and my whole body curved towards him. Somehow we were beside a tree, one leafy branch a wing over us. "Aren't you going to look at me?" he said again. "I was waiting for you to look at me, Sashi."

I had wanted someone from home with me, and here he was, the person I could not have, telling me that he knew it. Had he known all along?

"I can't," I said, but I already was. Everything in me blazed, and I thought again of him bringing me my first patient, I thought of him asking me to work in the field hospital, I thought of coming home to him off of the ship from Colombo, and I realised that every time I saw him it was like coming home. A strange, heady rightness held me still before him, like my whole self had fallen into place.

"I would have spent the other life with you," he said.

I closed my eyes and opened them again. Everything was perfect and unbearable because it would end.

"Then why did you choose not to?" I asked.

"There was never any choice," he said.

I knew I would never agree with him. "Do you ever think about home?" I asked.

He met my eyes squarely. "Every day," he said.

A light came on ahead of us as the hall lit up, and he shaded his eyes with his hand briefly. We were walking again. In the distance, I could discern silhouettes, and next to me, I could feel his fingers slipping from mine.

"I miss my family. I miss your brothers," he said, and it was already past, the moment when he would have included me in the list and said it aloud.

Suddenly, I was angry at him, and I missed them too. Didn't K owe me more than this? Niranjan and Dayalan gone; Aran isolated at twenty, ducking the militant groups and waiting to enroll or leave; Seelan all but lost to me. "Don't you talk to Seelan? Where have you been?" I asked. "Did you have anything to do with the movement taking our house?"

We were nearing the entrance, where I saw groups clustering, and he scanned the faces before us, assessing something. He turned to me. "I wanted to see you here," he said. "But I can't stay with you." Then, as the doors opened, I was swept into the moving crowd. When I emerged inside the hall, only my classmates were beside me.

ALMOST EVERY STUDENT IN the school had turned up. I looked around the crowded room and saw Tharini and Josie and, of course, at the front of the room, Thambirajah. He declared that we had the Tigers' support for the medical students to demonstrate to keep the hospital open. That made me worry; I wanted the hospital open, but was that the Tigers' only goal? I looked around the edges of the room, hunting for K, but as he had intended, although he was watching, I could not find him.

I was not sure what to do. Should I join the demonstration? Did I want to? Thambirajah and I wanted the same thing, but for different reasons. The next day, I rose with trepidation. Tharini, similarly resigned, arrived at my door with homemade placards. "My brother has fled to India," she said. "And now the movement has me demonstrating for them."

At the hospital, we paced back and forth in front of the entrance, shouting that the staff should ignore the closure order and stay. If I had not shown up among the protestors, Thambirajah would surely have noticed. Indeed, virtually every medical student was there. Across the crowd, I saw Josie chanting enthusiastically. Later, at the hostel, I could not sleep, hoping that we had been successful and wondering if I had made it easy for others to manipulate me.

We finally caught wind of the news: the hospital's doctors had

agreed to the suggestion that there be a safe zone around the building—
meaning they had promised no attacks would originate there. The
Tiger leadership—and their acolytes, like Thambirajah—were furious. The doctors had no authority to negotiate, they declared. They
put out the word that the government had tried to shut down the hospital, and news outlets picked up the story. The publicity battle lost,
the government gave up: the hospital could stay open, no conditions.

At the field hospital, on campus, Thambirajah was visibly gleeful. But
a strange ominous feeling stayed with me, even when he announced—
rather magnanimously—that the editor of the *Saturday Evening Review*
had been released. Shortly afterward, someone handed me an unsigned
pamphlet entitled *A Report on the Attempted Closing of the Jaffna General
Hospital*. It had the whole story right, including the Tigers' motivations,
and—audaciously referencing Thambirajah's involvement—mentioned
the editor's case also. This time I wondered whether the editor himself
was behind it, but the level of detail seemed far beyond anything even
his quite reputable publication had ever managed.

THOUGH THE HOSPITAL STAYED OPEN, the fighting went on—
not only in Jaffna. A bomb in Colombo killed a hundred people and
seriously injured three hundred more. After the blast, the furious Sri
Lankan president dismissed the idea of a political solution, and the
military intensified its bombings of Jaffna. People hurried to dig more
bunkers, but palmyra and coconut leaves and gunnysacks of sand did
not protect us. Staying in the bunkers for hours did not protect us.

In May 1987, at what should have been the middle of my second
year of medical school, the military launched Operation Liberation,
and eight thousand troops advanced on the Jaffna peninsula. The government air-dropped pamphlets telling us to shelter in churches and
temples. I went to check on my parents and Aran. Appa had come
home desperate to see us and now was stuck in Jaffna. "Who is going
to come to save us?" I asked. "I don't think anyone is," Aran replied.

Between the four of us, we packed in haste and badly and fled the house. It was our first time being displaced together and on such short notice. For ten days we struggled from place to place. First—despite my old promise to myself—we sought refuge in a nearby temple, as we had been told to do. But following directions did not protect us: the military bombed the temples too. They did not have good bombs— What is a good bomb? Like you, I do not know—and so they improvised roughly and cruelly. Once, horribly, they bombed Jaffna with barrels of human shit.

No words can conjure the stink of those days. Even the holiest temple, crowded with refugees, became the foulest dump, smeared with waste. As others died in shelling, by some miracle, we did not; we gathered our dwindling things and moved, and moved again. I wondered where K and Seelan were, and how they were surviving. We went from kovil to church to kovil, hunting for one with room, one that hadn't been bombed. We could not believe it—to begin to believe all of this, we had to write it down. You must understand: I have to tell myself again, because even though I was there it seems impossible.

"SURELY THE INDIANS WILL not let us starve," Amma kept saying. "Oh, you think they won't?" Appa said, exasperated. The army seized some places where the militants had been in control; when the Tigers left civilians to fend for themselves, boys of the wrong age were slain or imprisoned. "Do you think the Indians are on the way?" Amma asked hopefully, and then, my God, they were trying, nineteen boatfuls of Indian supplies sailing across the Palk Strait, emblazoned with the Red Cross. The navy stopped them. But now, finally, India had had enough: the next day, the tenth day, when we were staying in our third temple, Indian planes air-dropped twenty-five tonnes of relief supplies. By that time we had not eaten for three days. What fell from the sky? I remember milk powder, I remember rice. The Sri Lankan military backed off, and after another fortnight, we were able to move to a refugee camp. I felt unendingly grateful. I remember thinking that perhaps I should reconsider my atheism, and wondering how the field hospital, which I had not been able to reach, had fared in all this mess.

By the end of June, we were thinking of going home, and two more Indian ships brought us more rice, sugar, oil, pulses, matches, medicine. We were beginning to feel human again. But even with a big Indian packet of sugar I could not bring myself to put my usual two to three spoonfuls in my tea. Who knew when we might next run out of food? Amma saw me hesitate. "Go ahead," she said happily. "You can have as much sugar as you want, my darling. Everything will be all right now that the Indians are here."

I wish there had been a way to keep hold of Amma's glad feeling. But Mother India had come to save us, as everyone had hoped and feared she would.

12.

Saviours

JAFFNA, MID-1987

NOT LONG AFTER THE INDIAN SOLDIERS ARRIVED AND WE returned home, a third Report began to circulate: *A Report of What Our Community Has Experienced During Recent Displacement*. It was the longest document yet. I had written down my own experience, but my work didn't compare to the scale and detail of theirs. The Report contained dozens of personal stories, as well as broad political analysis, and a comprehensive discussion of the harm people had suffered in the recent attacks. The writer—or writers, I had begun to speculate—had gone to the trouble of chronicling several families' stints in different places of refuge, for example. Where exactly had the government bombed temples? Who said so? Was it true that they had bombed Jaffna with human shit? What food and messages had India and Sri Lanka dropped from the sky? The Report authors said yes, everything we had gone through had actually occurred. They gathered information and verified it and wrote it down.

What was the ending to this story? At least for now, the Indo-Lanka Accord. Signed at the end of July by the Indian and Sri Lankan governments, it said that Sri Lanka would decentralise and give more power to its provinces and therefore, local communities; that Sri Lankan troops would remain confined to their barracks in the north rather than engaging in active, unrestricted combat; and the Tamil Tigers and other Tamil militant groups would relinquish their arms. "Fat chance," Aran said to me, even though the Indian Peace Keeping Force's charge was to ensure that it happened. Appa, for his part, heaved a sigh of relief. "Finally, this will end," he said. "Perhaps Seelan will come home."

Aran raised an eyebrow. "I wouldn't count on that," he said. We had not seen Seelan since his fight with Aran the previous year, and had had no word from him about Dayalan's death either. I wondered what he thought of our transforming world. I did not yet know what I thought of it myself. The shift was thrilling in some ways—we could move and eat and even talk a bit, and I allowed myself a cautious happiness. But in other ways, the Indian newcomers were confusing and surprising. We were not what they expected either. When they came to enforce the accord—and especially the Tigers' disarmament—many soldiers from the IPKF found that we Tamils did not exactly match their idea of people who needed saving. Some of the soldiers came from difficult circumstances. Here, the land was fertile and the schools good; What did we need peacekeepers for? they asked. When I heard this I wanted to crawl back into our bunker. Instead, I returned to the field hospital, and my work.

It would have been better, certainly, if we could have talked to the Indians. But it was hard. With some exceptions, they could not say very much to us. They communicated in English, when possible, or hired interpreters to smooth their passage through town. Some of them did end up being well-liked; when two died de-mining a major road, we all mourned. But while some Indian officers were truly there to help, others were considered useless, cowardly, or even evil. They entered into the fray of Jaffna politics with perhaps less information than they should have had, and almost immediately made enemies. The people observed the fecklessness of some soldiers who stood by while Tamil militants fought each other, as they continued to do despite claiming to have laid down their weapons. Tamil people, who had expected more of the Indians, began to be disappointed.

Around this time, a very short fourth pamphlet circulated: *A Report*

on the Status of Disarming Tamil Militancy. In brief, in case anyone was
wondering: disarmament was a farce, and the militants still had weapons. They had given up some arms for the sake of publicity but were
hoarding many more. The Sri Lankan government was displeased, and
in this environment of disapproval, the Indians grew restive. The
Tamil civilians, who had originally welcomed their arrival, quickly realised that rather than finding relief from the Tamil militants and the
Sri Lankan forces, they had invited yet another antagonist into the room.
How long would it take before everyone—including the Indians—
admitted that they wanted the Indians out?

IN LATE AUGUST, K came to find me at the field hospital. Once again,
I noticed, T— was there. This time he was observing us. I was finishing up with a patient, a little girl who was about four years old. As her
mother bid me goodbye, K appeared next to me.

"I have something to ask you," he said. "I need your help."

"What is it," I said, keeping my eyes on the page I was filling out.

"It's important," he said. "Our Leader has asked for volunteers to
go on a hunger strike."

"What?" I looked up.

"A fast," he said.

"And who is going to fast?" I asked, already fearful of the answer.

"I am, Sashi," he said gently.

"You're going to fast? And who else will do it?"

"Only me," he said.

"Why are you the one doing it?"

"Well," he said, "I volunteered. And I was chosen."

I understood: Prabhakaran, the Tiger leader, had chosen him.

"Why would you volunteer? What will you be fasting for?" I asked.

"You were so angry with me about the violence," he said. "You
were angry with your brothers and you were angry with me. And this
isn't violent. We are saying what we want, for the Indians to leave, and
we will be doing it peacefully. I thought you would support me."

Of course the Tigers wanted the Indians to leave. They had never intended to disarm or to abide by the terms of an agreement they had not negotiated directly. But why a hunger fast? Why K?

"But you'll die," I said bluntly. I said it to shock him, to get him to deny it. I wanted him to tell me I was wrong.

"It will be announced as a fast unto death," K said evenly. "People will come, and it will be a chance to talk to them about the movement, what it means, what it stands for. It will be an event. They will listen."

I wanted the idea to sound outlandish, but as the Tigers' political leader in Jaffna, K was well known and popular. Although I spoke to K one on one, others saw him from a distance, in a crowd, giving speeches. As a hunger striker he would certainly draw an audience. "What does this have to do with me?" I asked.

He sat down across from me, as if he were a patient. His eyes were plaintive. "I wanted to ask you if you would stay with me during the fast. The Tigers have a doctor who will be there, but I thought you would also be helpful. It would be good to have a friend from home with me."

"What would I have to do?" I asked.

"You would help the movement physician," he said. "You would monitor my vital signs. You would chart the progress of the fast. Small, simple things."

"I don't know," I said slowly.

"You owe me a debt," he said, trying to sound light, although clearly none of this was casual.

"What debt?"

"You were my first patient, of course," he said.

I THOUGHT ABOUT THE question alone for three days and finally when I could no longer bear the solitude of my own uncertain, sick feeling, I told three people.

"If you go up on that stage with him everyone will know who you are," Amma said.

"To help them quietly is one thing, Sashi," Aran said. "And at the field hospital you are at least treating some ordinary people. I wish you were not working with the Tigers, but some of the patients are just those caught up in things. After all, perhaps I shouldn't have faulted you for that."

"But," I said.

"But Amma is right," he said. "This is something else. If you go up on the stage next to K, all of Jaffna will see you. The government will see you. The Indians will see you. And the movement will have succeeded in putting you where they want you."

"I wouldn't be doing it for the movement," I said. "I would be doing it for K." There it was, out in the open, the thread of the past connecting us—not the history of countries but the history of home.

"Why don't you do something for yourself and walk away?" Aran said.

That reminded me of Anjali Acca's old advice. I went to see her last. I found her alone in her office, reading. Seeing me in her doorway, she invited me in. "Sit," she said, looking at me over her spectacles. "You have something to ask me?"

"I need advice," I said.

"Is someone in danger?" she asked. "Tell me."

"The Tigers are going to stage a hunger strike to demand that the Indians leave," I said.

"What does that have to do with you?" she said, just as I had said to K. "Interesting that they would adopt the theatre of the satyagraha for their purposes. I remember—Gandhi said women are better at suffering. So you are to be a satyagrahi?"

I hesitated. "The hunger striker is K," I said.

"Oh," she said. "I see." She took her spectacles off and set them down on her desk. Her face appeared curiously bare and defenceless without them. Quiet stretched between us.

"He volunteered," I said simply.

"And what does that have to do with you, Sashi?" she said again.

"He has asked me to sit on the stage with him as one of the Tiger medics," I said. "I think the Tigers have asked a few of the medical students. But he personally has asked me."

"And what are you going to do?"

"What do you think I should do?"

"What will your presence on that stage accomplish?"

"If he is going to do this," I said, and swallowed, "I don't want him to be alone."

"He would be surrounded by people from the movement," she said.

"I don't know what will happen, but he should be with someone from home," I said. From before there was a movement, I thought. Before there was a movement, there were six children on a lane. Shouldn't I go with him as far as I could, even if I did not agree with him?

"Don't you know what will happen?" she said. "It will be a spectacle. And you will be part of it. Is there no way you can talk him out of this?"

"I think it's too late," I said.

"So you think if you can't talk him out of fasting you might as well be there," she said. I nodded miserably. "Who is the organiser of this hunger strike?"

"A man named T—," I said. "I'm not sure I can describe his position. But he's fairly high up, and he recruited K, and so I suppose he is responsible for my brothers joining as well."

"I know who that is," Anjali said, sitting back. She had an odd look on her face. I guessed she knew something about him that she wasn't telling me. "He was my batchmate once upon a time. We used to be friends, actually. But if he were going to die on a stage and asked me to be there, I would not do it." She sighed. "K might not mean to use you, Sashi, but make no mistake, you will be used. You will look like a dutiful Tamil girl attending a hero. Will people even know you are a doctor? Will people know you are his doctor?"

"He will know," I said. "And I'm not a doctor yet. But I want to be a doctor so that I can treat anyone."

"You know I agree with you," she said. "And it doesn't mean that you're one of them, to treat them. I've treated them. It's the right thing to do, to help someone who's hurt. But that isn't the only thing that will happen on that stage. Who is K to you? He isn't just anyone. And even if he is someone from home, well"—she hesitated—"there may be things about K that you don't know."

Again I wondered what she knew that I did not. As for her question—Who is K to you?—I couldn't answer. I looked down at my hands. "Have you seen those anonymous Reports?" I said. "Perhaps there will be one called *A Report of a Decision Badly Made*."

She laughed but then looked sober. "It sounds like you have already decided, Sashi," she said. "It sounds like you already know what you want to do."

As usual, she was right: I did know. I had known for years, perhaps, from the moment I had called out for help and he had come.

PART IV
THE END OF HUNGER

13.

K Becomes K

K BEGAN HIS HUNGER STRIKE ON A STAGE THAT THE TAMIL
Tigers had built especially for him to do so. It was outside one of the
temples of my childhood, and his childhood—one of our holiest and
most loved places. Again I stood where I had promised not to go.

The first day began with a press conference at Jaffna Fort: K would
protest the Indo-Lanka Accord by committing himself to a fast.
Through the Tigers, he made his demands for the Tamils of Sri Lanka,
which included: an immediate halt to Sinhalese colonization of traditionally Tamil lands; release of all young Tamil men held under the
Prevention of Terrorism Act; formation of an interim government for
the Tamil homeland; and the departure of Sri Lankan security—
including both the army and the police—from the Northeast Tamil
areas, where the army occupied villages, schools, and religious buildings. He held up a finger for each point. T— stood behind him, his face
impassive. I stood aside, making sure I did not appear in any pictures.

"Those who oppose us," K said, lifting his hand, "have brought the
Indo-Lanka Accord to subdue us, because they fear the strength of
the love we feel for our people and our nation. Because they fear the
strength of our unity. But their victory is impossible." He turned to
point his finger at Jaffna Fort. "See how others have come to enslave us!

The Dutch, the Portuguese, the British, the Sinhalese, the Indians—their accords and promises cannot stop our liberation. The banner of Tamil freedom will fly over this fort. The Indians must go.

"Our future and our rights depend on our will at this moment. This is our fight—no others will come to save us. Count yourselves with us! If we come together, together we may triumph to create the country we deserve. The Tigers are willing to sacrifice themselves for this Tamil cause! Tomorrow is ours!"

The press took pictures steadily. K tilted his face towards them. He smiled.

"Any and all among us who volunteer to battle for this country, this home—I swear to you, we are the ones who belong to this place, as it belongs to us."

ON THE SECOND DAY, when I arrived at the temple in the early dawn, the priests were already awake. One of them gave me two glasses of water. I drank one myself and then walked outside with the other. The morning was sweet and cool and my bare feet made a soft brushing noise against the concrete. I climbed the stairs to the stage quietly, so that I did not wake dozing cadres or aides. K was, of course, already awake.

"Good morning," he whispered.

"Good morning," I whispered back, and leaned down to hand him the glass of water.

He put it aside.

"K, even Gandhi drank water when he fasted," I protested.

"Exactly," he said.

ON THE THIRD DAY, two Indian journalists came to take K's picture and interview him. They never made it to the stage. The small crowd gathered before the stage recognised them as foreigners and prevented them from moving. A few particularly rowdy men chased them away, yelling and brandishing bottles and other haphazard weapons. "Indians! Indians!" they screamed, waving their fists. The journalists ran. K smiled.

ON THE FOURTH DAY, Prabhakaran came, escorted by T— and, to my surprise, Seelan, who spared me just one glance of approval.

No one, not even the Tiger physician or me, was allowed to sit near the four of them as they conferred in low tones. I watched them with jealous eyes and listened with a careful ear. K, it seemed, was doing most of the talking, and he was speaking very fast and eagerly. Seelan and T— said nothing, though T— seemed to be taking notes. The Leader interjected what sounded like questions and comments here and there, but mostly he seemed to be avoiding eye contact with K, as though it hurt to look at him. With the Leader seated on his pallet and K propping himself up on one elbow, I could see clearly that K's face was beginning to have a pronounced bird-like quality. His nose had sharpened, his forehead showed his veins, and there was a strange pleading look about those lovely clear brown eyes.

I must have looked concerned, because one of the cadres leaned forward to reassure me.

"Don't worry, miss," he said. "It won't go on much longer."

"Do you think?" another cadre asked, sitting up. "I guess the Leader could call it off. I wish he would."

PEOPLE FROM ALL OVER the Jaffna peninsula started marching towards us on the fifth day. They marched towards Nallur, declaring that they wanted to join K in his fast for their people. Supporters poured towards the temple. From the air it must have looked like the annual feast day, when thousands fought for places to watch and participate in the honoring of the gods. They walked from just as far now to honour K. They were accompanied by vans filled with men who blared out their support for the Tigers and for K through megaphones.

"Prabhakaran is our true Leader!"

"If K dies, Tamil Eelam will become an exploding volcano!"

When the first mob arrived I turned to K, unable to keep the surprise from my face. Of course the Tigers' political leader in Jaffna attracted a crowd, but for some reason I had not expected one this large. He grinned at me with half his face, so that the crowd could not see it.

"What did you expect?" he asked me out of the corner of his mouth, not bothering to hide his amusement.

In the distance another crowd arrived from a different direction, with several more cars. Behind the vehicles, cameramen positioned themselves and local men set up speakers and microphones. Close to the stage, K's father and Neelo Aunty murmured to each other anxiously. The cadres glanced over and hoisted their guns on their shoulders, eyes straight ahead. Women were tugging children by the hands, carrying others on their backs, and passing around silver dippers of water. Elderly men with canes, many of them prominent Jaffna politicians, watched with grave faces. Throughout the crowd, I saw remnants of my life: Jega Uncle and Saras Aunty, distant relatives, old batchmates from Sir's school, neighbourhood gossips, former teachers. My fellow medical students, including some of the other field clinic medics, positioned themselves near the front. Not far from Thambirajah's spot sat Josie, wearing a perfectly pleated white sari and looking ostentatiously beautiful and saintly. Chelvi remained off to the side in the back. She was wearing a bright blue salwar, so that I could spot her. James, Tharini, and Bhavani were next to her, and adjacent to them, my parents and Aran, with worried looks. Across the way, Anjali Acca and Varathan had come to remain informed, and also to support me. Around them were scores of people I had forgotten or purposefully stopped contacting. Some people knew where I was, but the others I had no intention of informing. Unlike K, I had no desire to call attention to myself.

I stood up and tried to move back, to hide behind the curtains around the stage, so that no one could see me, but I stumbled, and one of the cadres caught me.

"Sorry, miss," he said.

ON THE SIXTH DAY his tireless body began to tire. It acted with its own economy, producing almost no waste because he could afford none. I tried to ignore my alarm. The body must rid itself of certain poisons every day. When it stops doing this, death cannot wait very long.

Nevertheless, K entertained a stream of visitors with no visible sign of fatigue: the Leader's chief political advisor and his Australian wife; a number of Indian army officers with whom he traded brief greetings; two Indian politicians, Nedumaran and Ramachandran. Despite the thrill of hope they inspired in the crowd, they inspired none in K, who was unmoved by their showy pleas that he eat. A sunburnt white diplomat, mopping his brow with a handkerchief, observed that the scene looked as though it were out of the film *Gandhi*.

Only when all the dignitaries were gone and what remained of the crowd was asleep did K begin to show small signs of weakness. When I went to give him a bath—or as much of one as we could manage on that stage—he let me do it, too weary to resist. He lifted each arm at my prompting and let me dab at the layer of sweaty film on his skin. I did this very cautiously and without actually touching him myself. It had to look like I was there to do the work and not just to be near him. I felt very self-conscious. I dipped and patted gently. If I rubbed too vigorously he might fall apart.

To distract him—to distract both of us—from the unpleasant, intimate task, I told him the news of town. "There are work and transportation stoppages," I said. "Not even regular train service."

I could see the cogs of his brain moving. "Jaffna has stopped," he said slowly. Although his face had lost its usual vivacity, I could tell he was pleased; this was even better than he had expected. They had orchestrated the appearance of chaos around him, but everything was planned. They had done nothing without a calculation of its effect. Was I part of the equation? I remembered what Anjali had said to me about being used.

"What I wouldn't give for a chessboard," K said, and I remembered that as a schoolboy, he had played.

ON THE EVENING OF the seventh day, we listened to the radio together, K and I. Seelan brought it to us in the morning. I would have talked to my brother but the moment was not right; K lay there, looking up at the sky, and I sat cross-legged near him. The All India Radio broadcast played some diplomatic announcement as I swatted at mosquitoes buzzing around both of us—mostly him. Probably he knew who the speaker was, but I was not familiar with the name. He lay on the pallet with his head cocked, his ears pricked up as the radio turned to talk of him.

"In our days," the unknown voice said, "Mahatma Gandhi used to himself undertake fasts and not ask his followers to do so."

This jab at the Leader sounded accurate to me, but I held my peace. K shut his eyes. He kept his hands crossed behind his head and stayed as still as though he had fallen asleep, but I knew he had not. His eyes being closed meant that I could study him without fear or self-consciousness. His flesh was hanging more loosely off his bones—he was losing muscle mass. This was the third and final stage of starvation—the stage in which the body consumes itself.

That was the first night I did not leave the temple. Instead I unrolled my bamboo mat beside him and fell asleep.

ON THE EIGHTH DAY, Mr. Dixit, the Indian High Commissioner with whom the Tigers had been dealing, came to Jaffna to meet with the Leader. We heard from others about how the Leader had tried to manipulate Mr. Dixit to come to the temple to talk to K.

The Leader and one of his closest aides met Mr. Dixit at the Palaly airport. There might have been pleasantries although there was very little that was pleasant between these men. They were supposed to go to an undisclosed location and commence discussions about the Tigers' problems with the Indian Peace Keeping Force. But before the discussions began, the Leader had another topic to broach: K. He crossed his arms over his chest and addressed the diplomat with an earnest face.

"Before we talk, let's go together to the hunger strike site and offer him fruit juice," the Leader said to Mr. Dixit.

Mr. Dixit considered this.

"I'll come with you to the hunger strike site, this Nallur Temple, if you'll guarantee that when I offer him a drink he will agree to break his fast."

The Leader shook his head. "The fast was not the Tigers' decision, and it's not being maintained by the Tigers," he said. "I can't give you such an assurance. To break the fast or not to break the fast is K's decision and not mine."

Mr. Dixit shrugged disbelievingly. "Come now—you are supporting him, aren't you? This fast has nothing to do with India. What can I do? If I go there and offer him juice and he doesn't take it, it will be adding fuel to this fire you have built. I won't do that. I can't do that."

The Leader looked at him. "These are very simple demands, Mr. Dixit. Surely you can go and save this man's life."

"This fast is nothing more than an act of instigation!" Mr. Dixit said. "You are trying to get the Tamils of Sri Lanka to rise up against those who were sent to protect them. You want me to put on a show before these people and humiliate the government of India! I won't."

"He can barely sit up. Go to him and offer him some food—tell him that your government will honour his requests. Surely you can do this," the Leader persisted.

"I didn't come here to pacify this man!" Mr. Dixit said. "This wasn't part of my mission. I have nothing to do with this fast. This fast is an act of provocation. A gimmick, nothing more. Not a true satyagraha. I didn't ask him to do this. Unless you guarantee that he'll break the fast, I won't go."

———

BY THE NINTH DAY, I had pushed through my wish for him to live and had come out on the other side. I just wanted it to be over. Let the Leader call off the fast and say he was deferring to the wishes of the people, who loved K although they did not know him. Let the jawans, the Indian soldiers, destroy the temple with us inside it. Let me lie down again, next to him, and go to sleep, not with him, not condoning him, but still beside him. We had grown up together. Say goodbye to someone every day for a week and you will know what I mean. Do it in public when you cannot help but weep half in humiliation and you will know what I mean. Do it without saying what you really want to say, and you will know what I mean.

The thrum of music and the shrill voices of women singing rose to a higher pitch as though he had turned the knob on his stereo clockwise. He cleared his throat, and Seelan moved the microphone closer to him. The doctor helped him to sit up, and static brushed our ears. The hint of sound from the stage immediately silenced the restless crowd. K gathered all of his breath and strength to speak above the whisper he had been using for the past several days. He did not manage to do it, but the microphone caught the rasp of his voice anyway.

"I am going to die," he said, and I saw that he had not reached the point of believing that. He cleared his throat again and—with what I could see was truly an effort for him—raised his voice even more.

"Beloved people! It is time to rebel against the Indians who occupy our homeland! We must rise against the government of Sri Lanka! For generations they have oppressed us!"

The crowd roared with approval and with grief and with excitement.

"When I die," he said, and I could hear the sound of women weeping from the audience. The sound grew, but it did not swallow the sound of his voice, which was amplified by the microphone. He spoke beautifully, as he always had. "When I die—I will join six hundred and fifty Tamil martyrs. So many have given their lives for freedom! I want to look down on Eelam with these martyrs and see our flag flying."

He paused again for effect.

"Let the Tamil people's war erupt," he said.

The crowd shouted its approval.

He ignored them and moved to lie down again. The doctor went quickly to his side to help him. Around them the wails rose again to a high and calculated din. The doctor beckoned to me, and I went over to join them. K looked at the doctor, who excused himself.

I leaned over K. "You don't have to do this," I said.

"Sashi," he said, his voice just louder than a breath. I bent my head to hear. "I know you don't agree with everything the movement has done. How we work." His glance flickered to the crowd. "It was selfish of me to ask you to do this. So much was out of my control, but your being here, your being at the field hospital"—he took a breath—"you said yes because I asked you. I should have kept you far away. When this is over, you should leave."

"I can't," I said, crying at last. I covered my face so no one would see me. Why wouldn't he ask for water?

But he closed his eyes.

ON THE TENTH DAY, I spent a long time writing everything down. I had the sense that it would be important.

I sat cross-legged near K as he turned slowly to paper. And I overheard a conversation. Mr. Nagalingam, a community leader and a prominent member of the temple, asked to see the movement's second-in-command. He was ushered onto the stage and behind a draped curtain to talk to the Leader's deputy, but still I could hear and understand them.

"I am wondering, sir—shouldn't we revive him? We ought to be able to do it," Mr. Nagalingam said. "It might not be too late."

I felt rather than heard the Leader's deputy shake his head. "A decision has already been taken," he said. "Thank you for your support."

Feet shuffled across the floor and the doctor knelt next to me. He offered me his handkerchief.

"I know it's difficult," he said. "You can go home if you need, or take rest. No one expects you to be here the whole time."

"He does," I said. It was true; he would have wanted and expected me to be there, and I resented it. I was so angry. A final decision has already been taken, I thought. What kind of friend would leave? But what kind of friend would have asked me to stay?

SOMETIME DURING THE TENTH NIGHT, he slipped into unconsciousness, and on the eleventh morning, we discovered him that way. This was like a first death. K silent was not K. K sleeping was not K. He had never slept very much. Nor had he kept silent. It was not his nature.

He should have died days earlier. Death by fasting should not have taken him longer than a week. I had a suspicion that they had somehow stretched it out on purpose. For show. He went to sleep, but no one else could. Around the crowd, televisions had been set up. They were broadcasting only one channel, the channel of the Tigers, which was called Nidarshanam. I remember looking up to the screen, where the twin heads of K and Gandhi shone. As I watched, the two heads moved closer together, merged, and blended into one. I could hear a group of women beginning a set of thevaram, devotional songs. Air rose from deep inside me, and I breathed heavily to expel it. I started to laugh. I could not help it. K's moustache on Gandhi's face did not fit at all. Gandhi's protruding ears instead of K's obedient ones made no sense. It was funny—it was funny. I laughed as quietly as I could, which was not very quietly, and wiped my face, which was not wet, with the backs of my hands.

When it was five o'clock exactly, we could hear the priests beginning to sing inside the temple, doing the daily prayers. The cadres brought me a plate of rice and curried vegetables but, for the first time, I was unable to eat it. The smell of the food made my stomach turn.

"Aren't you going to eat, miss?" asked the cadre who was offering me the plate. They were always solicitous and careful with me, because they knew I was Seelan's sister and that I worked at the field hospital.

I pushed it away. "No," I said. "I'm not hungry."

"Miss," he said, "you're not the one on a fast."

"I know," I said. "I would never be able to do it."

IT WAS THE MORNING of the twelfth day of what was being called his satyagraha. When I tell people here this story now, they don't believe me. They ask me who could live for so long under such conditions, but what they mean is: Who could die so slowly? Still, like so much else about our war that I wish were implausible, it remains true, regardless of who believes it or not.

Thousands and thousands of people crowded around us. I felt both alone and the desire to be alone. People swarmed, clinging to each other and to the stage's edge. There might have been as many as a hundred thousand. When they came too close to me, I fought down an unreasonable alarm. I did not want them to see me—and perhaps they didn't. They were so hungry for him, even as his body consumed itself. Many had been fasting in solidarity. Like him, some of them were also performers and opportunists. Our leaders had scattered speakers and microphones through the crowd, and for days people had taken turns crying out their grievances. Now the temple was finally silent. The speakers hummed only with wind. No one knew what would happen at a moment of death. There had been rumours of rioting and calls for blood. For the moment, we felt only terrible anticipation.

I stood on the stage with K's doctor. It was hot, and I had been standing there since sunrise. K lay on the floor of the stage, surrounded by the flags of the Tigers. I had known and watched the rhythm of his breathing for years in private. To do the same in public felt like a violation, but now habit and duty compelled me: his chest rose, his chest fell, his chest rose, his chest fell. His glasses slid askew, more askew with each slow breath, his eyes closed under them as though he were just nodding off on his veranda at home. His chest rose; his chest stilled, and once more I anticipated its descent. I waited, and the space of that wait grew infinite.

The doctor put his hand on my elbow, which was wet with perspiration.

"Sashi," he said. "Sashi."

And then I breathed again, and K did not. It was the first moment in which such a thing was possible, and the sharp quickening pain of it stunned me. How swiftly the world reshaped itself! Perhaps someone you know has died and you have a sense of what I mean: the horror of knowing that everything is going to continue very nearly as it did before.

Death has its order: it has to be announced, the hour marked and recorded. The doctor had told me he would do it, and I was glad to be spared this. It was a moment for the spotlight, which suited the doctor and did not suit me. I watched him play to the tense and waiting theatre of people, as T— wanted, and as I could not have done. He leaned down and, with an exaggerated motion, put two fingers to the curve of K's dry neck, and then to the inside of his dry wrist. K looked as though, were he to be cut open, he would not even bleed. The doctor looked up at me, and at K's father next to me, and drew his fingers down his face, tracing the path of tears.

K DIED AT 8:37 A.M., at the age of twenty-three, with a rebel's name that was different from the one with which he had been born and with which I had loved him. It was a Saturday. Today Tiger supporters around the world mark this time as a holy hour, but I can tell you that at the moment of his death K was still an ordinary man—a grown-up version of the boy who had lived down the road from me in our village. His dying made him no more saintly than he had been in life, which is to say not very. This made it worse to mourn him. And while in many ways he did resemble the boy who had been my friend, in its hunger and thirst his body had travelled a great distance from its previous self. No act of violence we had committed had ever attracted as much support for a homeland as the act of violence K had committed on his own body.

As if he had been waiting for a cue, K's father began to cry. The doctor turned to the crowd and, seeing his face, they began to weep in unison, keening and wailing and mourning. In the distance, at the far end of the temple grounds, the cadres began to move out. They had been instructed to occupy and protect property that otherwise would be at risk for destruction. Voices echoed through distant megaphones, spreading the news and asking for calm. But no one threw a stone, fired a gun, or lit a match. Above the weeping audience, three beautiful crows circled. They, too, had been waiting for days, but now they swooped away from us, higher and higher, their paths looping upward like incense smoke.

Seelan joined three other cadres in lifting K from the dais. His sarong fell around his limp legs, and they looked even thinner. Behind his plain checked shirt, the red flag of the Tigers was the brightest spot in the crowd, which had arrived wearing white in a pre-emptive strike at lamentation. I wanted to step down off the platform and tell them that I had loved K, that we had come from the same place and learned the same things and grown up together. I wanted them to know that we had believed in the same causes and means, until one day we didn't. I wanted the people beside the stage to be with me, and I wanted to be with them, but the difference in our grief separated us. They looked like me and spoke my language and had grown up in the same places, but they were mourning someone else.

If you had asked me immediately afterward what I did as K died, I would have told you that I bent down to touch my forehead to his, that his skin felt warm and dry, that he still smelled faintly of iluppai flowers and other growing, living things. I would have told you that I went with him into the endless country of that trapped breath, a place where neither of us could cry out or make any human sound. I would have told you that although I had known that he would die—known it, perhaps, from the first time I had chosen to help him—that although this was the seed that had been planted, and watered, and planned for, in the face of its bloom, the air stopped in my throat too, and I could not believe what we had done.

Later, other people told me that when he died, I did not touch him: I stood apart on the stand and moved my hand to my mouth as if to silence myself.

THE TEMPLE WAS THE most beautiful of all the Hindu temples in Jaffna, and arguably, of all the Hindu temples in Sri Lanka: a good place for K to die, to make his last gesture, not least because it was dedicated to Murugan, the god of war, to whom he had always shown particular devotion. When K's body was carried away, the doctor and I followed, and even as we moved across the stage and away from the temple, we met the smell of jasmine and incense, and the burnt, clean odor I had associated with holiness from childhood. As though the temple itself also walked behind us.

The cadres bore his body down the steps of the stage to the sandy corridor by the side of the building. Before the passage, which was both wide and long, the crowd parted for K. Behind and above me, the bells of the clock in the main tower sounded. Encircling the clock, carved figures of temple guardians and gods watched over us. He could not have chosen a grander theatre.

At the other end, the priests, too, cried with great ostentation and decorum. One of them came forward to usher the cadres inside the small makeshift building where we had kept what we needed to care for him. And then the door closed behind them. I was his friend, but I was an unmarried woman, and they shut me out.

You must understand: still, his body was mine. There was no distance at which I would not know it. I had touched the desert tenderness of his eyelids and the long, brittle brush of his lashes. If they had allowed me in, I could have pushed a finger between his teeth and pulled it out again, still dry from his sandpaper tongue. I was not K's wife, or his sister, or his mother, but I would have touched my stethoscope to the crater of his shallow chest. I was not K's doctor, and I was not his lover, but I could have put my thumbs into his elbows and cupped my hands around their edges, which were sharper than his bones as I had previously known them. I could have drawn the last outline of his body. I had always suspected that my head would fit into a perfect place his joints made for me. If they had let me, I would have laid my temple against his shoulder and matched each of my living parts against his dead ones so that my whole self was pressed against him. Tall as I was, there was almost no difference between us.

No matter what was done to K's body, the crowd had already seen things as the Tigers wished them to be seen. He would be anointed with oil and garlanded. He would be marked with sweet ash and saffron paste and kungumum, the red powder. His body would move through the streets and villages of Jaffna like the statue of a god. They would say that he was greater than Gandhi, and he was not.

WHEN THE DOCTOR AND priests finished their work, they dressed K in a new uniform T— had provided. K had received a promotion upon his death, just as though he had died in battle. They buttoned up his dear body in its brown shirt, latched his belt around his waist, pulled up the zipper of his trousers, and straightened his medals. They draped the Tiger sash around K's shoulders.

The cadres laid him in an open casket. Already, despite the doctor's care, K's hands were beginning to curl and freeze. His back stiffened, and already he was a stranger. Already he belonged to people who did not know him. The cadres put K's coffin into the back of a black Jeep, and the crowd, wailing, followed on foot, forming a gruesome train of white. I lingered at the end, along with the doctor. As we passed into the town, we saw house after house already festooned with the plaits of coconut leaves, a symbol of grief. From other temples and schools we could hear funeral music blasting with obscene volume and pompousness. In front of all the houses, we saw pictures of K, garlanded and lit by oil lamps. People came out to join the mourners. Bare feet kicked up dust, and from far away, villages could see us coming by the cloud we brought with us. For hours, the weeping rang so loud that it carried across farms and across paddy fields, to beaches and lagoons, over the entire northern province. Sorrow took up residence in every street of every borough.

"I GO ONLY TO RETURN," K had said to me before closing his eyes: the traditional farewell. "Go and come back," I answered: the traditional answer. And although I have told you this story in English, you must remember, we were in Tamil. A private language for me now, here, and I remember him saying that as though it were private.

In a time of peace, as a Hindu, K would have been cremated. He would have burst and sparked on a funeral pyre like tinder. He would have risen into the air as smoke. If he had had a son, the boy would have carried the torch to light the flame. Since he had no son, his father would have done the deed. Since he had no wife, only his friends would have borne witness.

Only his friends. I could say that he was only a friend, but that would not be true; that would not be right. K is more, always; he is with me still. Here in the West, people think women of my country leap into fire with the bodies of men we have loved. But he was only a friend—only—and I let him go. They took his body from me, but it did not matter. Do you see now? Do you understand? In K, I had and lost such a friend that I became the place where his body burned.

I HAVE BEEN WAITING for you to ask me K's real name. But there is no point in telling you. No point in keeping it from you either, you say, but he's already gone. Some people tell the story one way, and some people tell it another. Don't make the mistake of thinking the different versions are the same; don't make the mistake of thinking the different tellers have the same kinds of freedom. Some people say that early on in the fast, he said, If I ask for food, no matter what happens, don't give it to me. Remember, he said, that I volunteered, that I promised to see it through.

But I'm also told that during the last night when he could talk, while I slept, he begged for food. Why didn't I hear him? Others said he didn't truly think he would die, that he thought the fast would be called off before it went that far, that everyone was waiting for the Leader to come and say he could stop. That everyone was praying for it. I haven't prayed for anything in years myself. But if this version of the story is true, he was murdered, on a stage, and slowly, with me beside him. Was I helping him, or the people who killed him?

You must understand: if I could stop imagining it, I would.

AFTER HE DIED, AFTER his body was taken around the town, Anjali Acca—not the Tiger physician—performed his autopsy. This was what he had requested, and she agreed, I think, for me. I witnessed it; they wanted two signatures to certify the death. "You don't have to," she said, but I did not want to be saved from it. He had donated his body to science, or that was what they said.

Sometimes I am in the room still, the specimen lab at the medical school. I have been there for years, perhaps. I am still a girl, my belly bright with burn. Those eggs, cracking and sliding across me where he broke them. The hands that held mine are under glass now.

14.

The Authors

———

JAFFNA, LATE 1987

ONE WEEK AFTER K'S DEATH, MRS. PREMACHANDRAN SAT ON the veranda of Anjali Acca's house, sewing something. When she saw me with my bicycle at the gate, she looked sad. "Oh, Sashi," she said. "How are you doing?" How much did she know? Perhaps she had seen me on the stage, or Anjali had told her. I felt myself the object of a curious kind of recognition in some quarters of Jaffna these days. While I had been mostly successful in staying out of the media coverage of the event, I had also been beside K on the stage while hundreds of thousands of people watched. Now many people thought that they knew me from somewhere—and they did, but I wasn't about to explain. As for Mrs. Premachandran, perhaps she considered me a saint, or a fool. I did not want to know. When K had joined the Tigers, I had lost him privately. When he died, everyone in my life heard about it, but with a few exceptions, nobody had much to say.

"I'm fine, Aunty," I said. "Is Acca here?"

"Yes," she said. "I'm sure she'll be happy to see you."

Inside, Anjali was sitting at the piano again, even though I hadn't heard any music. She turned and smiled at me. "I hate this music," she said, waving at the music stand, "and I'm determined to learn how to play it anyway."

"What is it?" I asked.

"Bach," she said, "and do you know what is so difficult about Bach? Most pieces of music can be broken into sections, but Bach is like a stream of consciousness. He doesn't stop, and so you have to choose where to take your own breath. It's beautiful to listen to and terrible to memorise."

"Admirable to try," Varathan said dryly over his newspaper. He rubbed an ear and gave a dramatic wince.

"She is very admirable!" Kumi said loyally from the floor, where she was constructing a small fort of pillows and sheets.

"Well, I'm going to very admirably stop for now," Anjali said. "I'm sure my terrible rendition of this will still be available later." She pulled a small cloth over the keyboard and closed the piano. "Shall we have a cup of tea?"

I followed her to the kitchen. "How are you doing?" she asked me as she busied herself heating the water.

"You mean because K is dead," I said bluntly.

"Yes," she said evenly. "Because K is dead. How do you feel?"

"How I feel doesn't matter," I said. "It only matters what I do."

"Of course how you feel matters," she said. Now she sounded shocked. "Of course it does."

"I came to ask you something," I said abruptly. "I was thinking about what you said in my first year, about writing things down. I want to work with you."

"On what?" she asked. She put clean cups out.

"I know about the Reports," I said. If I had counted correctly, in the time since Ravikumar's disappearance, there had been six other cyclostyled pamphlets containing meticulously verified narratives about the conduct of the war and its effects on civilians. In the last Report I had seen, the nameless authors went back to an earlier period in the war and wrote about the fighting between different Tamil groups. They captured what had happened with a precision I admired. Reading the pamphlets had surprised me. I had thought that I couldn't keep track of the violence in which we lived, but in fact it was possible;

the authors of the Reports had done it. I wondered what it had cost them.

Anjali Acca's expression shifted slightly.

"What do you know about the Reports?" she asked. Her voice was carefully neutral.

It was the most recent document, *A Report of What Has Occurred in Our Community Regarding Sexual Violence and the Status of Women,* that had given it away. It had had an idea, a sentence, that I recognised from the feminist reading group: the intellectual echo of the afternoon we had spent discussing Kumari Jayawardena's book in Josie's presence. The writer, like Subramaniya Bharathi, called Tamil society to account for its conservative posture towards women, especially those who had survived sexual violence over the course of the war. Such violence, especially at the hands of the Indian Peace Keeping Force, was increasing at a terrifying rate. The Report also identified civilian women— like the Mothers' Front—as an important source of dissent and resistance to militarization and violence in Jaffna. The writing was full of words I had heard in Anjali's voice: community, civilians, women, children, justice, dignity. The fingerprints of her beliefs were all over the sentences.

" 'In standing up for others we also stand up for ourselves. This course requires courage, and no other is open to us,' " I said to her, quoting the Report. "You wrote that. No one else would have said that."

She sighed and studied me, considering something. "Wait a second, will you? I'm going to call Varathan." She hollered for him.

He came grumbling down the hall, folding his newspaper. "Did you make me a cup of tea?"

She handed him hers. "Sit down and listen for a moment," Anjali said.

I took a breath and began again. "I know you're writing the Reports. I want to help you. I work for the Tigers in the field clinic. And everything I've seen, everything I've done since the war started—I'll tell you what I know from there and from the university. I want it to be written down, the way it was in the Report I saw. I want it to be written down as I know it happened. Not the government's version and not the Tigers' version. Not the Indian version. Ours."

Varathan looked at Anjali, who raised an eyebrow at him as if to say, Well?

He sighed. "All right, Sashi. Yes, we are the ones documenting and writing Reports," he said. "And we have been collecting information about how the army, the Tigers, and the other militant groups have treated ordinary people. Human rights violations. We have begun to compile a book, which I think people will want to read."

"Now," Anjali said, "we will need to document the presence of the Indians. We have focused on civilians, women, children. Nobody else is doing that. We thought there should be a record."

"It's slow work," Varathan said. "It's extremely slow and hard. Sometimes I travel in disguise to see someone to check a story. Sometimes I go back four or five times to interview them, to make sure that I have heard and understood properly. In some cases we can't figure out what happened and we have to write that down. Then we include all the different versions and our limitations."

"That's the worst part," Anjali said. "Your feelings are important. I meant that, Sashi. But in this case, we first have to record the facts and check them, again and again. And then we have to take them as far as we can." She looked troubled. "It's not only slow but also dangerous. And sometimes what we learn is very disturbing."

"I understand. But please," I said. "K is dead. I can't go back to the Tigers as though nothing happened. I can't tell the story they want me to tell. And I also can't leave them. But now that I've been on that stage, they think I'm an obedient girl. Let me help you. They can think what they want. Perhaps that will even be useful. No one will ever suspect me."

"What you are proposing is very dangerous," Anjali said again.

So many people wanted to protect me from what was dangerous, and none of them could. If I wanted to escape the trap this war had set for me, I would have to do it on my own.

"I'm a good writer," I said. "I'm thorough. I'm careful."

"I know you are," she said. "I read your exams. That's not the point."

Varathan took off his spectacles and polished them on his shirt. "We should say yes," Varathan said to her.

Anjali frowned. "It's my job to talk her out of it," she replied. "I'm her professor."

"It's not your choice," Varathan said. "If she says she'll do it, she will. Sashi finishes what she starts—you said so yourself." He glanced at me. "Let her do it. We need the help. How will we ever get everything done without help?"

She was silent. Then at last, she said, "He's right, it's not my choice. It's yours. I can't tell people to be responsible for their choices and then make yours for you."

"And I can't promise you anything but work," Varathan said seriously. "But you will be able to help people."

"Which is what you said you wanted," Anjali said.

I heard K in their words. How could I not? "Yes," I said. "Yes. I can do it. Will you teach me? How do we begin?"

15.

Innocent People

____

JAFFNA, LATE 1987–1989

O BEGIN, YOU MUST PUT ONE FOOT IN FRONT OF THE OTHER, one word after another word, one story after another story. Have you ever tried to record this kind of history? No sooner would we write something down than the Tigers or the Indians or the Sri Lankan Army would follow in our wake, trying to erase it. I had asked Anjali and Varathan to teach me how to collect the truth. They showed me that this was something I could learn only by talking to ordinary people, by asking them questions, by waiting and listening.

In the early days, I went on interviews with them to distant villages around the peninsula and took notes as they asked witnesses to various atrocities to recount the devastating details. I observed their gentleness and kindness and also their determination as they encouraged people to tell us what had happened to them. At the time I did not recognise their form of questioning as an extraordinary act of love, but that was what it was. They did not hesitate to be exacting. I once observed Anjali take an old woman through the reconstruction of her nephews' assassination, which had happened on her front steps. "And where were the soldiers standing?" Anjali asked. "And were you standing between your nephews, or were they both standing to your right? Can you show me? And what did the soldiers say to you? And did they speak in English? Were they carrying weapons? What did the weapons look like? Can you describe the gun?" On some nights, when our note-taking trailed into the dawn, I slept in their house and could hear Anjali sobbing quietly through the walls, trying and failing to contain all that she had heard.

When people reached the limits of what they knew or could bear to remember, Varathan and Anjali treated them with such grace. They took care in every way I had imagined they would, and in several others that had not occurred to me. They redacted names when they thought anonymity safer, even when their interviewees did not think to ask. They verified stories with multiple sources, which also made anonymity easier to maintain. When those they spoke to became distraught, they always stopped the interview. They also persisted, re-interviewing people over discrepancies I might initially have thought small. No one minded; they appreciated the attention and precision.

We also sought to protect them by protecting ourselves. When Varathan travelled by bus and took me with him, we boarded at different stops and took seats apart from each other. Once he wore the garb of a priest; once he dressed as a farmer. In both guises he was believable. They trained me to be like them: to be keenly attentive while evading attention, simultaneously approachable, trustworthy, and unremarkable. I acquired a pair of spectacles with glass lenses that changed the shape of my face in a subtle manner. On these assignments, I regularly altered the style of my hair and clothing. These were small details, I understood, but they accumulated in a way that would cause someone seeing me casually to remember me differently from the way I actually was.

Much of my life continued as it had before, but as I now wore the false spectacles to become a different person, my way of seeing also changed. I returned to the field hospital. There, between patients, I read over everything I had written for myself since the war's beginning. What had I done and who had I become? So much of what I had written made no sense. In those pages my memories were rotten with pain. How much of the riots could I remember with precision? What did I recall of the Sri Lankan government's shelling and my days of displacement? Trying to answer those questions stopped me cold. It was easier to sort out others' blurriness than my own, easier to probe their wounds than mine. Where had I treated a patient who had recounted a story of violence between militant groups? What had my brothers and K told me about the movement in unguarded moments? What did people say about the brutality of the Sri Lankan Army and the presence of the newly arrived Indian peacekeepers? Those were questions I could approach. We were trying to return our history to its place, to call it by its name, to see the mistakes of others, and to reckon with our own.

As I cross-referenced different versions of the same stories, I began to see even more clearly the gaps between the narratives of ordinary people and the sanctioned ones belonging to the government, the Tigers, and the Indians. One of those official stories was everywhere. All over Jaffna, photographs of K appeared, plastered on walls and fastened to lampposts. No matter where I turned, I faced him. At the end of a long day, when I permitted myself to think about him, I opened the notebook I had saved for myself, took out my pen, and tried again to take my own history, as I had taken the histories of others. Have you ever been haunted by propaganda? It can be a kind of ghost. I longed for the real and imperfect person I had known. But when it came to K, what I desired was not history: I wanted the life on the other side of the war's looking-glass, the future we might have had, and which no longer existed.

ONCE, I SAW JOSIE in the field hospital. It was then that I realised that her sweetheart was in a patient cot a few rows across from where I was working. It was obvious that she was trying to avoid looking at me and that he was in rather serious condition—I could hear the talk of amputation from where I was working. Eventually, when he was moved, presumably for surgery, she raised a tentative hand to me as she followed him. This time, surrounded by movement people, I nodded back at her.

Later that week Thambirajah came and said that a patient was looking for me. When I went to the row and cot where he pointed me, the woman waiting for me was Bhavani. She was a tall girl, but lying down in the cot, she looked tiny and hurt, curled into herself. Parvathy sat in a chair near her, holding her hand.

"How did you know I was here?" I asked.

She told me the beginning of a story I had heard before, but never from the mouth of someone I knew personally. She and Parvathy Aunty had been at home, cooking, when two Indian soldiers came in, yelling, "Checking—checking!" They did not speak Tamil; one was short and stout and the other taller and imposing. When the taller one tried to separate her from her mother, Bhavani said, she shouted, hoping the neighbours would hear and intervene. We had all heard the stories of young women parted from their parents and assaulted in the next room. But at this moment, the story changed: Bhavani said that it was not the neighbours who came to her aid but the other soldier, who, suddenly understanding and repulsed by his partner's intentions, tried to stop him. But the larger man did not listen, Bhavani said, and as the shorter one pleaded with him, a gun went off. The taller soldier had fled, leaving the smaller man bleeding and sobbing on the floor of their house.

"But where did you take him?" I asked her.

"The professor," she said. Of course. She could not have brought an Indian soldier here. She had taken him to Anjali, who would have treated him with mercy. And Anjali had sent her to me.

I checked her quickly: she would have heavy bruises and her shoulder had been brutally wrenched, almost dislocated. "I'm so sorry," I said to her, and she shrugged lightly and then gave a small cry of pain. "They didn't rape me," she said. "Others haven't been so lucky."

The others she was talking about were largely middle-class girls, girls who were raped by the Indian Peace Keeping Force and then regarded as ruined by their families, which subscribed to conventional ideas about virginity and purity. I had never treated one of these survivors myself, but the stories were familiar; I had heard third-hand accounts of women being sent to Colombo on short notice, which was, I realised, a way of excising the need to deal with what had happened. Don't talk about it; cover it up; send her away. Bhavani had not been raped, and she was not middle-class, and she was fatherless; beyond that, she was brave. She did not try to hide the incident; to the contrary, she spoke about it openly and told all of us in the feminist reading group what had happened in considerable detail. On the day of that meeting, we did not read the scheduled book; we listened to her talk. When she was done, Anjali asked her to stay for a minute. "You, too, Sashi," she said. And then she went behind her desk and withdrew from her drawer the notebook I had seen months earlier. "Now, Bhavani," she said. "The day this happened, you brought me the wounded man, and I took care of him, but I didn't have time to ask you carefully about the details. Can you start once more from the beginning, and may I write it down?"

Anjali took notes as Bhavani related the story again. When she was done, she said, "I want to file a complaint."

Anjali and I exchanged glances. Hardly anyone took such action. But Anjali did not try to dissuade her. Instead she said, "I'll go with you." I thought of the carefully wrapped lunch parcels, Parvathy Aunty's dimmed cheer, the bicycle ride from the university to my parents' house after Dayalan's death. "I'll go too," I said.

We went with her to the IPKF camp, where the commander knew Anjali from earlier visits and other complaints. The Indians dutifully wrote down everything she said and promised to investigate, smiling politely all the while. After this happened, gossip spread around the university; Bhavani sat defiantly in the shop, which all the girls insistently patronised, even as others whispered about what had happened to her and whether she had been, as they called it, "spoilt." When she came back to the feminist reading group on the day we were finishing up the discussion of *Mother* and told us that she had seen the taller soldier walking down the street near her house, we were not surprised. The smaller man, of course, was nowhere to be found. Anjali wrote that down in her notebook too, and we edited it into a longer manuscript we were writing, which included a section on the sexual violence Tamil women were experiencing at the hands of the Indian Peace Keeping Force. "A working-class girl who narrowly escaped assault filed a complaint," Anjali wrote. "For her bravery and honesty, much of Jaffna thanked her with rumour."

MY TIME IN THE field hospital, too, transferred to my notes. At night, after I worked and studied, I wrote in my own notebook about not only the patients I treated and how they had been hurt, but also the events of past years: the burned library; the riots and Niranjan's death; my brothers joining the movement; Aran's detention and my mother's intervention. I wrote about Dayalan's death and treating Bhavani; I wrote about standing over a cadaver with Josie at the medical school. Once a week I gave these notes to Anjali, who read them and gave them back to me with questions. "Who can verify this?" she would scrawl in the margin. Once I included a meeting of the medical student union, and she asked to meet with me in her office. What was said about the Tigers? she wanted to know. Who spoke, and did anyone dare to disagree? Would Tharini tell her about the same meeting? I thought so. Carefully, she shored up the dams of my stories with proof: witnesses, newspapers, even caveats about rumour. Adding each individual incident to our book manuscript was like doing a set of painful sums, knowing that the total would be terrible. She and Varathan were very interested in the field hospital, both because of individual stories and the possibility of aggregating data, and I told them about my experiences there.

I would have forgotten to include the first patient K brought me in the manuscript, but for an incident at the clinic. In the months after the fast, many people at the field hospital looked at me strangely. I was the girl who had sat on the stage. So one day when a patient stared at me oddly, as though he recognised me, I thought nothing of it.

"You have treated me before," he said.

I was wrapping a wound on his leg, the left thigh, a gash that was getting infected. "Oh?" I said. I was concentrating on the motion instead of listening. The injury was old and whoever had treated it in the first place had not been able to do a good job.

"Your friend brought me to the university, and you treated me there," he said.

That made me look up. "My friend," I said. His face looked familiar.

"I saw you on the stage," he said. "But you saw me before that. K brought me to you when I had a gunshot wound."

I stood up. Now I could see that he had a widow's peak. K had told me that the man's name was Niroshan.

"K told me later that you would be sitting on the stage with him," he said. "He told me that you were the one who helped him to save me. He thought you were very impressive, a very good physician." He stopped, perhaps unused to being so voluble. I was just as unused to the praise. "I didn't think I would ever meet you, but when this was getting worse, someone said that you worked here, so I came to find you.

"I remember your voice," he said. "I couldn't picture your face until I saw you on television. Then I knew it was you."

Had he heard me talking to him as I cleaned his bullet wound years before? I shivered. "Is there something I can do for you?" I asked.

"No," he said. "I came because I wanted to thank you." He gestured at his leg. "Thank you for helping me to take care of this also. But really I came to say that if you ever need anything—"

Patients did not come back to the field hospital to say thank you.

"I mean it," he said. "This is my address." He pressed a piece of paper into my hand and clasped it briefly between both of his. Then, leaving me stunned, he hurried away.

———

ON THE STAGE WHERE I had tended K's body, he had been visited by
Indian officials who had offered him food and drink, which he had
declined, or which had been declined on his behalf. Now his death
brought a certain anger and also word that the Tigers' strategy would
change. Although the publicity and gambit of the fast had secured
them a certain power with India and the status of the premier Tamil
militant group, these concessions did not appease them. The Tigers
jostled with the Sri Lankan government, demanding last-minute
changes and more and more power in the new council planned to gov-
ern the north and east. The Indians could not broker a deal that would
satisfy everyone. Violent incidents began to rupture what little peace
the accord had brought. In the east a mysterious sniper picked off an
Indian jawan. In Jaffna, another group of Indian soldiers took fire from
a passing vehicle. Giving chase, they found themselves at the entrance
of a Sri Lankan Army camp, where the resident commander would not
even admit that the car existed. Yet another Indian soldier embarked
on a random shooting spree in a downtown crowd, catching three
civilians—Sinhalese, Tamil, and Muslim—in his line of fire. Nobody
was happy with the Indian presence. The Indians did not want to be
there and found our conflict inexplicable; the Sri Lankan government
blamed the Indians for the deaths of Sinhalese civilians; the Tigers and
their counterparts ran amok.

Early in October, the Sri Lankan Navy captured a boat with seventeen Tigers. Reading the news, I shuddered; I had met some of these
men during the hunger strike when they had visited K. They wore
cyanide capsules around their necks in case of capture. I worried that
they would bite and imagined their dying. As they waited, Tiger leadership and the government argued over whether the weapons found on
the imprisoned Tigers or their arrests were in violation of the peace
accord. The government wanted to bring their captives to Colombo;
the Indians begged them, for the sake of peace, not to do it. The cyanide had been confiscated, but on a secret visit authorised by the Indi-

ans, one of the Tigers' superiors passed out new ones. When it became clear that there was no way out of being paraded through the capital, all of them swallowed. Of the seventeen, a dozen died. I knew that there was no way to maintain the peace now. The Tigers would take their revenge.

They did, slaughtering combatants and noncombatants. They moved from the Sinhalese, soldiers and civilians, to the Indian soldiers. Indian officials came to meet the Tigers in Jaffna and pleaded once more, but the Tigers declared that they were ready for any battle. A short while later the Tigers ambushed and necklaced five Indian soldiers, placing rubber tyres around their necks and setting them alight. This gruesome act was the last straw. The Indians raided all the Tamil militant groups, coming away with a small haul of weaponry. The Sri Lankan president declared the Tigers beyond the bounds of the law and put a bounty on Prabhakaran's head. At last, the Indians attacked the Tigers' printing press and other media outlets. Among the casualties was the Tiger television station, the same one that had broadcast K's death.

After only a few months, we were back at war, or back in war, as the Indians attempted to seize control of Jaffna from the Tigers. From the first the Indians were outstripped: the militants outnumbered them, knew the terrain, and fought in unpredictable ways. They had supporters everywhere, and during this period the cadres did not wear uniforms. Even in the field hospital, treating patients, I sometimes could not tell who was a cadre and who was a civilian. The Indians would not have known Seelan from Aran, and perhaps would not have cared. The Tigers shot at the Indians from behind civilians, from temples, from the leafy heights of trees. The militant sharpshooters were so successful in assassinating higher-ranked Indian officers that those who remained hid their insignia. When the Sri Lankan government had tried to starve us, the Indians had fed us; now the Tigers cut off the Indian supply chains. In response, the Indian Peace Keeping Force shelled Jaffna. We ran back to our bunkers.

Again we gathered at temples. Again we were afraid to stay at home, again we were afraid to go out. Again we assessed what we should carry with us when we fled. We had thought the Indians would save us, but in fact their brutality was greater than that of the Sri Lankan government. As atrocities mounted, the Indian Peace Keeping Force gained a different nickname: the Innocent People Killing Force. I dared not return to our lane, where our former house now lay empty. It was probably rigged. Houses like ours, which had been occupied by the Tigers, were abandoned and wired with explosives. If an Indian soldier wandered in and flipped a switch, the whole place might explode. Our home, turned trap, had in it the room in which I had slept as a child, the celestial courtyard, the walls where the pictures of my brothers had hung, the study where my father's music had played, the altar at which my mother had prayed when she did not know where my brothers were. My house was not the only place I loved and could not protect. The campus, which had been a site of fighting, was closed. My beloved Jaffna General Hospital, despite its status as a declared safe zone, had been damaged. It was barely running. I stopped going home and for some days did not manage to contact Anjali or Varathan. At the field hospital people waited to be treated in long queues; they clustered close together, and I could not keep up.

ONE DAY, GOING FROM the hospital to the field hospital to the hostel, I managed to detour to Anjali and Varathan's house. Unusually, I found Anjali at home. "My colleagues are saying that they will keep the campus closed for six months, as a protest against the staff shortage," she said. She had her head in her hands. "How can they do it?" she asked. "After all that people have been through, after all the students have been through, they should at least have the campus. This should be a place for us to talk about what has happened, and the Tigers and the Indians have taken it, and it is not theirs, and we cannot permit this. It is a university."

Although her colleagues insisted that the campus remain closed, she went daily to work on reopening it. She was the only faculty member who did this. The work was exhausting, but also sustaining. What else were we doing that was looking to the future? The others who went were far lower in rank than her: medical students, lab assistants, and others who were concerned with making space for the habits of living rather than the habits of killing. Chelvi came to my part of campus and helped me clean up a lab; I went to her part of campus and helped her clear out a stage. During this period of time, when Anjali crossed the path of Indian officers, she would dismount her cycle and talk to them sternly. They never knew what to say to her, this woman who spoke to them of the terror of the Tigers in the same breath that she spoke of the terror of the IPKF.

In early 1988 I helped Anjali and Varathan to write a letter to the Indian army, setting expectations for how they should deal with the students and other civilians. The letter resulted in an offer of a meeting. We would go to the kachcheri and talk to them. I was the only student there, present in the guise of a notetaker, but in fact I wrote nothing down. Still, it is one of the few moments in the war that I remember perfectly: Anjali, in a white sari, in a white-hot rage, speaking with unflinching clarity. She spoke about what had happened to ordinary people, her anger at the Indian army, her horror at the plight of women surrounded by soldiers for so many years. The Indian army had raped and slain so many civilians. In her speech she did not spare the Tigers. In this she perhaps surprised and impressed them. But the Indian response was cowardly and bureaucratic: the soldiers, so far from home, were under a great strain, they said. This only angered her further. That is no excuse, she said to them, without fear.

TIME SEIZED AND CONTRACTED. Did the clocks themselves shudder? In 1988 we wrote by candlelight.

ONE NIGHT, AT THE field hospital, I watched a figure approach. From far away, I thought that he resembled Niranjan, or Dayalan. But that was impossible. Then I thought it was Seelan. At last, I understood that it was Aran. He was as tall as any of my lost brothers. He stood in front of me with his hands stretched out. "Will you come home?" he said.

"What are you doing here?" I asked.

"Please come home," he said. "I haven't talked to you in so long."

I realised he was right—I couldn't remember the last time I had seen him, and I had no idea how he was spending his time. "Let me just finish with this patient," I said. The person before me was a child, a shy girl of about thirteen. She had a small wound in her leg from some rubble that had hit her after a shelling. I was the only person in the field hospital she would permit to touch her. "Stay still," I said to her. I turned to my brother. "I am almost done. Please go away for just a moment. Let me finish."

He waited for me outside, at the edge of where the field hospital began. When I came out of the exit, wiping my hands clean with a rag, he stood there with his arms crossed, watching me. "It's a Saturday," he said. "I know," I said. "Can you come with me to see Amma and Appa?" he said. "It's Amma's birthday." I had completely forgotten.

On the bus to Amma and Appa's place, we sat together as though this were all usual, as though we were just a brother and a sister going to visit our parents under normal circumstances. We did not speak of Seelan, who in a time without a war might have accompanied us. In fact, we did not talk at all. Around us others spoke rapidly, murmuring about what had happened where they lived and where they worked, what had happened to their houses and their children and their parents and their jobs and their studies. They talked about waiting in temples to see if they could return home, and they talked about how women walked around town waiting to be attacked by soldiers. Indian soldiers, Sri Lankan soldiers—either way, the women were afraid. As we listened to them, I started shaking, and Aran's hand crept into mine as though he were still a little boy.

When we reached my parents' place, I could smell my mother's cooking wafting through the windows. My eyes widened. "What is she making?" I asked. Aran laughed. "She's been waiting for you. I got her a visit from you for her birthday present. You haven't been to see her in a month. What kind of daughter are you?" I couldn't tell whether he was joking. We walked up the steps into the house that was not our house. My mother was washing dishes and did not see me come in. I went up behind her and put my arms around her waist and pressed my face into her back, between her shoulder blades. She laughed a little and put the dishes down and turned around and kissed me on the forehead and then on the cheek. She put her arms around me. She looked so much older than the last time I had seen her. "Happy birthday, Amma," I said.

"Where have you been, kunju?" she said.

"Working," I said.

"You're not a doctor yet," my father said, coming in. Unusually, he embraced me also, which made me feel small. He had not put his arms around me in years—not since the night he had struck me.

When we sat down at last it appeared to be a feast. From what unlikely sources my mother had assembled such a banquet I do not know. She had managed to make pittu and fish curry and eggplant poriyal. She served me murungakkai curry, and also bitter gourd cooked the way she knew I liked best. I had been spending all my time in a wider world where people did not really know me, and to be remembered here with such quiet love filled me with a warmth I had not known I needed.

We ate in silence for several moments before my brother spoke. "What are you working on, Sashi?" he asked.

"I'm still working at the field hospital," I said. "And also I spend some time at the general hospital."

"Is that all you're working on?" he asked. I blinked. "I found something that you left the last time you were here," he said, and produced from his pocket a piece of paper. Instantly I recognised it as the set of notes I had taken when I was reconstructing the Jaffna Hospital massacre, which had occurred in October 1987. I had been in the building myself, which I had never told my family. The paper contained the notes from my conversation with some of the other doctors who had been there. Instinctively, I reached out for the scrap, but my brother held it away from me. "Sashi," Aran said. "Are you one of the writers of the Reports?"

I did not want to lie to my family, not explicitly, but I also needed to keep my promise to Anjali and Varathan. "No," I said at last, but as I said it I knew that he did not and would not believe me. But I could lie to him, and he would understand why. "No," I said to him, "I am not one of the writers of the Reports."

"Sashi," Amma said, "we are very proud of you, you know? You work so hard. Look at how many people you have treated and helped. We did not want you to sit on that stage, but even when you did that we were proud of you."

This was not a celebration of my mother's birthday, then. My mother was making her birthday into some other kind of occasion. My whole family had an agenda.

"Sashi, if this is what happened to you"—Aran held up the piece of paper with the massacre notes—"you have taken such good care of other people. What about you? I was angry when you told me you were working with the Tigers," he continued. "And I tried to understand, I did, because you're treating patients. But working on the Reports is far more dangerous. If they find out what you're doing—"

"Everything is dangerous," I said.

"If they find out what you are doing they will kill you."

"Then they mustn't find out," I said.

"No," Appa said. "They can't find out. I am proud of you, too. But you have done enough. We've saved some money."

"It's enough to pay someone to get the two of us out of this country," Aran said.

"Sashi," Amma said, "I would do anything to have the two of you safe. I can't have your brothers back. But you don't have to stay here. I don't want you to stay here."

"I don't want to leave," I said. "I'm not done."

"Sashi," Appa said, "we are asking you to be done." I wondered if he had come home especially for this conversation.

"I have never asked you for anything," Amma said. "Please do this."

I looked from my parents to my brother. Aran stretched out his hands once more, palms up. "I will go if you will go," he said.

"I don't want to send only one of you and wonder later if I should have sent the other. I want you both to go abroad," Appa said. "You would be safer together."

Years ago, my mother had taken comfort in the fact that Dayalan and Seelan had joined the Tigers at the same time. I also remembered my father's apology to us after Aran's first detention. That night, I promised to think about what they had asked of me. My parents had always believed that none of us should be alone for too long, and that we were safer together.

16.

Hospital Notes

———

JAFFNA, OCTOBER 1987

N HIS POCKET, ON THE DAY MY PARENTS ASKED ME TO LEAVE, my brother held a story I would prefer to have forgotten. Instead, I had documented it meticulously, and from every angle. I can tell you what happened at the Jaffna Hospital Massacre in October 1987 because I was there.

First, I must tell you the story as you might have heard it overseas, from those who support the Tigers and those who criticise the Indians. The Indian peacekeepers burst into the hospital, which had been declared a safe zone, and shot at doctors, nurses, patients in their beds. They massacred people who were caring for others, people who held up their hands in surrender, people who identified themselves as part of the medical profession. Eighty-seven people died.

The story is already unbearable, but now you must shift how you see. Widen your lens, stand farther away, and see who the Tigers have left out of the picture, see who profits from the deaths of ordinary people. Do you remember when the hospital almost closed? The Tigers stand on the roof, shooting outwards. The Tigers remove their own people from the hospital, cadres we are treating, and leave everyone else to the mercy of the vengeful Indian soldiers, who slaughter with no care for who is civilian and who is combatant.

You must understand: I hate this version of the story. To tell it I have to tell you how the Tigers abandoned the doctors who had helped them, and made them targets for the guns of others. I was one of the doctors. I happened to survive. I lay among my colleagues, some of them breathing and others not, and when I emerged from the building I could not speak for some hours.

PART V
THE PALACE OF HISTORY

I ask you, could you write straight
When people die in lots?

—RAJANI THIRANAGAMA
IN THE *TAMIL TIMES*, 1988

17.

Hippocrates

COLOMBO/JAFFNA, 1989

I RETURNED TO THE FIELD HOSPITAL THE DAY AFTER MY MOTHER'S birthday, wondering what I wanted and what I was able to do. What was the distance between those two things? T— walked by me and I knew the answer. How could he say no to me? My family had lost two sons: one in the riots and one in the war. He had seen me sit on the stage at the fast and attend to one of the movement's most famous martyrs. I had spent years working in the field hospital, and had treated my own brother, one of their most valued members. By their unimaginable and ever-changing calculus, at this moment I had lost and given enough to be let go. I only needed to decide if I wanted to leave.

I FELT THE CLOCK stretching and contracting, no matter what I did. I had agreed to tip the hourglass of my own life here. With my habits as a medical student more firmly established and my clandestine interest in gathering information rising, by early 1989 I had gone back to working more hours at the clinic. I tried to pace myself; I rested, and ate, and remembered to drink water, but I went back to a schedule of near-unceasing work. I carried my novels around but more as talismans than reading material. Thambirajah had graduated from medical school and now worked at the Jaffna General Hospital, but also doubled at the clinic. He gave me more and more complex cases, and, wanting both more information and more medical experience, I never protested. One day in February, he pointed me to a side entrance to the clinic. Beyond that, a patient was waiting in a small tent I hadn't realised was there.

"I wanted a woman," she said calmly, although her nose was obviously broken and one of her ears was torn. She was about my age. She had wound her long skirt between her legs and around her waist, and gripped it tightly, as though it were all that was holding her together. I had seen some older women in the village do this; people whispered that they had had so many children that their wombs were falling out. But I knew that this was not her situation. She did not tell me what had happened to her; the sentry who had brought her in did that, presumably so that she did not have to repeat herself. He had known her from his village, he said, from before the Indian soldiers had come to keep peace and to rape women, and he spoke more professionally about what had happened to her than I could have managed myself, if I had already known her. One of her dead brothers, I later learned, had been his classmate.

She was the first rape victim I had ever treated, and so I remember it clearly, especially because now, as an emergency room physician here, oceans away from those medical tents, I perform rape kits all the time. Back then, in Tiger territory, treating girls from the villages, I did not have rape kits. I did not know that there was an order, a procedure, to the cataloguing of a body that has suffered this most particular trauma; I did not know that there is a script of things that are proper to say and to do. This was what our mothers had warned us about: men and their desires, men and their wills, men and their bodies encroaching on ours. In whispers we had been warned of the ruin of rape, how it was something from which we could not recover.

I wondered if her mother had told her that—if she believed it. It was wrong, of course; she had not lost her value. But we were not in a world that knew that. Even I, the medic, the half-doctor, did not think in that moment to say that. I was too young and stunned, unrolling gauze and tapping alcohol gently onto it to clean her face. This was the fate Bhavani had escaped. Not yet a doctor, I already knew bones; I could appreciate this face, or what this face had been until very recently. I could see in the wreckage of its topography where its lines had fallen before: the high, shattered cheekbone, the formerly slender nose, the bloodied row of teeth, the small, red tongue, which she had bitten deeply. She had long eyes with very fine lashes, eyes that stared at me almost without blinking.

After giving her brief history and her name, which was Priya, the sentry left us. The tent was big enough for only a few patients, and we were alone. I took her to the far end, where I had her lie down on a sheet on the ground. I knelt beside her.

"I am sorry there is not anything better," I said.

She did not answer, but I heard her moan quietly as she lowered herself down. I gave her some painkillers. A morphine injection. Mercifully, we had some left, and it was easy to find a vein. I cleaned her surface cuts and abrasions, but I did not bother to save and bag the evidence, as I would have done today. I left the blood under her fingernails; I untangled a long black hair from her clenched right fist and threw it away. It would not have done any good to keep it.

Then I lifted her knees so that her ankles were flat on the ground and unwound the skirt, exposing her.

"All right," I said, but this was just as much to reassure myself as her.

I had hoped that the morphine would help her to go to sleep, to forget that I was retracing the path of violation, but she stared dry-eyed up at the ceiling of the tent as I examined her. The men had torn her; her body had ripped as though it had undergone a hellish labour. I wondered if I could stand to sew this most private wound together, and then, with a sudden rush of something that was not quite terror, I knew that I could. The knowledge was terrible, and to keep my grief for her—for us—to myself, I folded my lips together.

"This is going to hurt you more," I said.

"It doesn't matter now," she said.

I offered her more morphine, but she only looked away. There was nothing to wait for. I lit the match to sterilise the first needle. I wished then, as I do now, that I could have held her hand, but I needed both of mine for this.

AFTERWARDS, I LET HER lie there for an hour, but I did not see her sleep. When I returned with another suture kit for her ear, and the plaster for her nose, I had her sit up. When I tilted her head away from me so I could see the ear in the waning light, she opened her mouth and started talking.

"I had four brothers," she said.

I hesitated before I spoke. But then: "I had four brothers too," I said, swabbing her ear with cotton.

"What did they do to yours?" she asked me.

I dipped the needle in alcohol and lit a match to sterilise it. By then, I had fallen out of the habit of talking about myself.

"One of my brothers was killed in the riots," I said. "The others—"

"The soldiers killed all four of my brothers," she said.

"I know," I said. "I am very sorry."

I inserted the needle. She had made no noise before, but now she hissed at the pain.

"Do you want the morphine?" I asked.

"No," she said. "I am feeling something, you know? I want to know what is happening and if the pain goes away, then that might be worse."

I held the pieces of her earlobe together and tried to make the stitches small. She was right. Doctors resolve to relieve pain, but pain is information, and to lose it can mean losing something valuable. Pain draws a map. And if your body hurts, then your mind is occupied and cannot think too deeply about what has happened to you. I was trying not only to ease her pain but also to make her scar as small as possible. It should have been obvious to me that she no longer cared about the evidence of damage. But perhaps that was part of my job: to care on her behalf.

"Am I bleeding inside?" she asked.

"No, just outside," I said. Her bruises were beginning to colour, the dappled plums of swelling standing out on her forehead and cheeks.

"It hurts when I breathe," she said.

Her ribs were probably fractured. I picked up the morphine syringe again.

"I am afraid of falling asleep," she said.

"Talk to me," I offered, and readied the injection.

She talked about her brothers and I did not listen to her. I thought, instead, about my own, how Dayalan and Seelan had played cricket with Aran in front of our house while Niranjan studied on the veranda. He had handed each medical textbook to me when he was done, because I liked to leaf through them. I was almost a decade younger than him, but he had given me each one seriously, like medicine was an important responsibility he believed I could bear. Had he been wrong? Priya was starting to speak slower, her voice slurring from the morphine, and I wished that I could share it, that I could lean over, exchange the syringe, and pump my own arm full of sleep, that I could lie down next to her on the sheet, that we could both close our eyes and not worry. We were not so different: two girls, from villages in Jaffna, each of us with brothers we loved.

"What about their bodies?" she said. "What will happen to their bodies? What will my parents do?"

"Go to sleep for now," I said.

She sobbed suddenly and finally—a dry, sharp sob that sounded almost like a cough. She closed her eyes, but I stayed awake by her for a long time, writing in my notebook.

I TOLD VARATHAN AND Anjali what my parents were asking on the day I handed them an anonymised account of what had happened to Priya. By then she was pregnant and had come for a second visit, and a

third; she had met several people in the field hospital and in the movement. I saw her talking with T—, and with Thambirajah, and with the
sentry who had originally brought her in. When I described to Varathan and Anjali the outlines of what had occurred, they took the document and looked at each other and then me.

"You have helped so much," Varathan said. "You should go. And
the Tigers will let you."

"Your parents have already lost two children," Anjali Acca said. "If
this is what your family needs you to do, if this is what you need to
do—we'll keep on here."

"I don't need to leave," I said. "I don't want to leave."

"Go and come back," Anjali said. "We will still need you."

It was a simple, faithful sentence, but that was how she made it possible for me to go. I told my parents to give me six more months to
finish out the year of medical school. And then, I agreed, Aran and I
could go. Don't tell Seelan anything, I requested, until after I'm gone.

I want you to know, I can still see it, how radiant Anjali looked sitting there, sipping her cup of tea. What can I tell you about being in
the presence of such a warm person? No one looking at the sun thinks
about how swiftly it can be eclipsed.

FOR THE SAKE OF propriety, although it was far too late for propriety, on the last leg of my journey from Jaffna to Colombo, I rode the
train in the company of another girl. My parents had made this ar-
rangement, for us to travel together for safety, and she was the daughter of friends of theirs. Even so, we were only acquaintances, nearly
strangers, and when the train jostled us so that our sweaty wrists
touched, she jerked her body away from mine, and I thought I deserved it. Wasn't I leaving my real friends behind? I had asked Bhavani
to come with me, and she had refused. Infamous or not, she said, she
could not leave and did not want to. I thought of the other girls who
had been sent from Jaffna to Colombo and felt both glad that she had
said no and ashamed of my own departure. I wondered why my travel-

ling companion was going to Colombo, and knew I would not ask her, as I did not want to answer the question myself.

But none of the women I loved had faulted me for my choice. I had told Chelvi the whole story, my work at the field hospital and—with Varathan and Anjali's permission—my work on the Reports, and she had listened without saying anything until the end. "I guessed," she said. When I tried to apologise, she waved me off. "I understand," she said, and then, in Tamil, "What to do?" Tharini, on the other hand, had been completely surprised. "How did you manage to hide it?" she asked. "You're not that observant," I teased her. She laughed, and then said, "Anjali Acca will need more help now." I had never thought of Tharini as determined, but she was. "I'll do it," she promised, and bid me goodbye.

Before I had left, I had said farewell to my parents, wondering when I would see them again. "Soon," Amma had said, pressing her nose to my cheek. "Soon enough." I went back to our old house and our small lane one last time, too. I thought perhaps I would walk to K's house and take my leave of his father and Neelo Aunty. I thought I could thank Saras Aunty for all she had done for us over the years. But I could not bring myself to knock on their doors. Instead, I stopped at our former home and unlatched the gate. I went up the veranda steps, and a man walking down the street yelled a warning at me. "That used to be a Tiger house!" he called. I nodded my thanks to him. I had probably already gone too far. Opening the door would be ill-advised. I stayed on the veranda, looking out. No one else passing even acknowledged me. We had reached a moment at which living took so much effort that no one in my former neighbourhood could spare the breath to speak to me. I understood this and was not offended. I had been with the Tigers, and I was leaving. I could not stay in the village now, although it was still the place I knew and loved the best.

My uncle came to receive me at Colombo Fort Station. The other girl separated from me without saying goodbye. I watched her go towards the rows of three-wheelers, moving, like me, into a world of strangers. Even my uncle was a stranger. Still, I knew him immediately as I stepped off the train platform, because he held himself in the same way as my mother. He looked as though he never hurried, but he moved quickly through the crowd. His peculiarly large hands reached for my suitcase before he even said hello to me. His hands met mine before his eyes met mine, and this, too, was like my mother: his first instinct was motion.

"You look like your mother," he said to me in Tamil. If he had said this to me later, perhaps now, I might have replied: So do you. But I was only twenty-four, and he did not expect to have a conversation with me. He did not want my opinions, and I did not want to give them to him. He wanted to exchange facts. We were to be relatives only. This was the beginning of my exit from that life—he was to be one of the last people I met who looked like my mother, who knew what my mother looked like.

"Did you eat?" he asked.

"I had something on the train," I said.

"Amma will have some tea for you when we reach Wellawatte," he said. "You must be tired."

He did not wait for me to confirm this but turned and pushed his way into the crowd. I followed him through the train station and out the other side, to the street. I was no longer new here, but even so, I had never learned to navigate the crowds and foulness of the city. The people who moved for him pushed back at me, perhaps sensing my vulnerability and strangeness. By the time I caught up with him, he was waving to the driver of a big black car a few metres away.

My grandmother still lived in Wellawatte. We were going, I understood dimly, to her new house there. My uncle, recently returned from several years living overseas, must have found that shift jarring. He had grown up in the house I remembered, the one that had burned. But he said nothing to me about it, and nothing to the driver, who drove from Fort to Wellawatte with the windows open. Even if they had been closed, I would have remembered that Colombo was not as clean or quiet as Jaffna. It did not feel like home, and never had. Breathing felt hard, and my ears were tired from hearing so much. I felt dirty. I blew my nose and lifted my handkerchief blackened with soot and exhaust.

Through the open windows, everything passed by—the lights and architecture of the city—and I did not see it. My eyes were still full of Jaffna. Periannai had been with me the last time I had travelled from our village to Ammammah's house. I wished he were with me still. I wanted my brothers—my brothers, who were gone. And I wanted my mother and father, even though they did not presently want me. Who would know me now? This man, my uncle, looked like my family, but he did not know me, he did not want to know me, and the feeling of being surrounded by strangers made a pocket of pain inside my chest.

The car stopped, and the driver came round and opened the door for me. I got out, and my uncle was already up the path of the house, moving deftly around a small, barking dog. A hunched, wrinkled woman at the door took the bag from him and smiled at me, holding her hand out in a gesture of welcome.

"Come," she said in Tamil.

My uncle vanished into the back. I stood by the door, removing my shoes with unnecessary care. I listened for and then could hear the car pulling out of the driveway.

"Sit, sit," the woman said, smiling more, and then she, too, disappeared down a side hallway, pulling the suitcase along.

The chair I sat in was very old, with the wooden bones of the frame pushing through the upholstery on the arms. The floor was bare and warm, its boards smoother against my toes than the concrete of my family's house in Jaffna. The walls were crowded with photographs, and I noticed, finally seeing Colombo again, that some of them were of me. They were different than the ones my grandmother had kept in her old house. I was so small in some of the pictures that I did not remember being myself in them. In a more recent photograph, Niranjan and I posed with our arms around each other's shoulders in the old house's garden. That frame had fresh jasmine looped around it, and a fingerprint of ash on the glass over my brother's forehead.

"I couldn't find one of him alone," my grandmother said, and I stood up suddenly, so fast that I almost knocked the tea tray from her hands. She steadied herself and put the tray down on a table.

Ammammah looked much older than when she had come to Jaffna with me six years earlier. On this day I saw for the first time that I was taller than her. I was tall for a woman, and height ran in our family, but the intervening years had made her shorter, too. Her face, paler now, told me how I would look when the softness was stripped from my face. She regarded me soberly; I missed the sweet, bright torch of her old smile. Her hands were still unwrinkled, and when she reached up to pat me on the cheek, I remembered that she coated them with oil every day to keep them that way. We kissed each other once on each side of the face, the way we had always greeted each other.

She glanced up at the picture. "I had sent that picture abroad to one of our relatives and after the riots they sent a copy back," she said. "You were usually together," she added, her voice lower.

She talked to me while I had tea, and gave me supper: idiappam and fish curry, the same meal she had often given us as breakfast when we were younger. She did not mention Niranjan again. Neither did she mention in even the smallest way my upcoming journey. She spoke instead of the new house, and of the difficulty of being an old woman slowly filling a new house with new things. She was too old, she told me, to be surrounded by new things. Although she had been in the house for a few years already, the place still felt fresh to her: unfamiliar, dangerous, flammable. She listed for me the many ways in which she had been careful. I remembered the other house as marked by oil lamps, but here she had no kuththu vilakku. No new piano, she had decreed; she had chosen a new china pattern of green leaves, which was nothing like the old one. Like my uncle, my grandmother did not expect me to respond to what she said, but unlike my uncle, she loved me and I liked to listen to her. She talked and I ate my fill. When I finished, her arms shook as she lifted the tray again to take it away, and I glimpsed, like the flutter of a bird under her bending hand, the sharp scar at her wrist.

Afterwards, she put me to bed as though I were still a small child. The room in which I slept that night had nothing in it of my school days. But she stroked my forehead as I drifted off, and I let her; to be treated like a child for an hour comforted me, although even now, I am ashamed to admit that to myself.

WHEN I WOKE, I could hear the bells of a temple ringing in the distance. The temples of Colombo were not as big as ours in Jaffna, I recalled. The gods of Colombo were cramped and noisy, sweaty and smoky, elbow to elbow.

I could hear someone else moving around towards the back of the house, in the kitchen, and the noise of a kettle being settled onto a stove. It was not the sound of the servant woman; it was my uncle's quiet, quick step. I put a housecoat on over my nightdress and went out into the corridor and back towards the kitchen, very slowly so as to not disturb his routine. Halfway there, I heard him turn the radio on. The voice of a news announcer crackled out into the morning. I heard him very clearly. I heard what he said, and then I forgot to be quiet and ran, the pounding of my feet waking up the house.

The voice on the radio said what had happened was this: a pregnant woman had gone to a government office building in Colombo. She had ridden the elevator to the top floor of this building, which was an important building that I did not know. At the top floor, she got off and asked to see a man in charge. She told them that she had an appointment; the secretary checked the records and saw that this was true.

The voice on the radio did not say this, but I imagined it to be so: the woman was seated and offered tea, which she accepted, with milk and plenty of sugar. She was from Jaffna; she liked a lot of sugar in her tea. She waited for ten minutes, and then, when the secretary called her, she picked up her bag and rose from the chair to be escorted into the office. The man called her madam, respectfully, although she was not very old, perhaps no older than her mid-twenties. Her pregnancy was obvious, but this did not desexualise her in his eyes; she was a very beautiful woman, wearing a large green silk salwar kameez that brought out the fairness of her skin and the darkness of her hair. She was wearing a red pottu between her eyebrows, the mark of a married woman, although she was not actually married. She smiled back at him disarmingly.

The voice on the radio only said: She pressed a button to detonate the primary bomb she was carrying.

I suppose that was the part that mattered.

I want you to understand: I was not born to fight for a political cause. I did not feel chosen. And this woman was not born this way— she was not chosen. She was born in a village in Jaffna, and soldiers raided her house and raped her, and she watched the men who had raped her kill her four brothers. I want you to understand: this is not an excuse, or an explanation. It is a fact. She was not born to walk into an office building on an ordinary day, a day when the sun was shining and three-wheelers cluttered the streets, to try to detonate a bomb. And in fact, later, the forensics said that was what had happened. She tried to detonate a bomb. But she failed, because it had been built improperly. I want you to imagine this, as I did when I heard that: the bomb blew up, but not completely, not enough to kill them quickly as she had intended. The first small, potent blast caught her and the man together, and with her right arm gone and his left leg severed beneath the knee, they looked like one person, dancing. Her hair fell out of its pins into his open mouth. Two building security guards burst into the room after only a few moments, and she screamed, and they pointed their guns at her. She held up like a prize the other bomb, the auxiliary fuse and its detonator, and shouted in Tamil. The man reached out to wrestle with her, screaming also but in Sinhala, and the guards aimed for her. No one had trained them for this. If they shot the bomb, it would blow up; if they shot the woman, she would probably manage to detonate it anyway. They aimed for the woman; they fired; they missed. They aimed again, the man shouting again, trying to push her between himself and the guards, and this time one of them hit her in the shoulder. Blood bloomed on the green silk. The other one aimed and shot her again. The bullet pierced her neck, and as she reached up to hold the wound, she let go of the other detonator.

She died and she killed other people and she did not mind, and in this she was different from me forever.

MY GRANDMOTHER FOUND ME vomiting into the toilet. She came behind me and held my hair.

"What is it?" she asked me. "Are you sick? What happened?"

I wiped my mouth. I did not look up, and I did not answer. I vomited again, but there was nothing left in my stomach. I looked down at my stomach and thought of Priya's stomach, the rounded belly of pregnancy. Some female suicide bombers use pregnancy as a disguise, not only because it is easy to conceal explosives but also because it weakens the resolve of police officers to see a mother. A transgression against a mother is a universal transgression; when a man treats a mother kindly, he imagines that somewhere else, someone is getting up on a train to offer a seat to his own mother, or perhaps helping her to carry her shopping from the market. He is remembering what his wife looked like in her first trimester; he is thinking of his younger siblings or perhaps his own children. He is thinking of life, and of repetition, and of things happening again as they have happened to him. He is not thinking that anyone carrying a belly that size, that shape, would carry death.

This is why it is the best disguise. And that is why I was sick; I knew that the woman in the office building, who had ridden the elevator to the top floor, must be Priya. Because the voice on the radio had said that: they had been able to tell that the bomber's pregnancy was not a disguise but real. I knew how she had become pregnant; I had had to tell her that she was. And I knew the bomber had to be her. Anyone but Priya would have faked it.

———

AFTER THIS YOU MIGHT wonder: Was I still glad to have said yes to K that day when he asked me to treat patients at the field hospital? What can I tell you? I had gone to the Tigers because of my belief that everyone deserved medicine, because they would allow me to help. And I was grateful the day that I treated Priya. It felt like pure medicine, medicine the way I had dreamt of it as a child. Sitting with her in the tent, I thought that I had a patient whose treatment held no consequences, a civilian who could go back to her village and lead a life— a life made more bearable by what I had done. I thought, truly, that someday we might both be able to return to the places where we had been born.

IF I HAD PLANNED to go back to Jaffna, I would never have said a word to my grandmother. But I was leaving. I had promised to leave. So I told Ammammah the truth, or part of it: what I had been and done in Jaffna, that I had treated not only civilians but also Tigers, that I had become only half the doctor we had all dreamed I might be. That the woman on the top floor of the building had been my patient. I was going to say her name, but I couldn't finish. My grandmother put her hands around mine and held on to them.

"Why should any of this happen to a child?" she said.

"I'm not a child, Ammammah," I said. "I wish that I were."

"You're a child," she said again.

Whether I was a child or not, I was young still, uncertain and scared, wondering if I was wrong and unable to admit it. Then I saw the others around us, the world widening, the important man at his wooden desk, and time stretched back and back until I did not know where the fuse began.

"I'd like to see the building," I said.

"No, no, Sashi, you can't," my grandmother said. "You're to leave so soon."

"I can be quick about it. No one will notice me," I said. My grand-mother did not know I had such long practise in being the figure at the edge of the picture.

"It's your last day here with me," she said a little wistfully. Then, "Why should this be different? If you need to go, I'll go with you. And then it will be time to leave."

It was her first acknowledgement that Aran was waiting for me in England. He and I had travelled separately to avoid suspicion. It was my last day in Colombo. I would keep my promise to meet my brother overseas. But first I would see what they had done.

WE WENT OUT TO the street and called a driver my grandmother knew. As the three-wheeler jolted along, I realised that the man was the same as the one who had retrieved me at the station. He had the grace not to ask why I wanted to go to such a place, for which I was thankful. He took us as far as they would let us go by auto, and then I got down. Ammammah tried to get down too, to come with me. When I refused, she said, "It will be safer if you're with me." Because she was right, I took her arm and helped her out, and then we walked slowly to the top of the street, from where we could see what remained after the bombing.

They had made an impromptu checkpoint, because there were a few other offices on the same road and people who needed to go to them. We joined a small but disorderly queue of people yielding their bags and bodies for inspection. The face of each police officer we passed registered my grandmother's pottu and mukkuthi. A Tamil lady, her Tamil granddaughter. They searched us with diligence, but then we moved into the crowd unremarkably. The commuters milled and gawked at the wreckage and I stood among them in my office blouse and long, tidy skirt, my hair plaited and pinned up like I, too, was on the way to my desk.

As I had imagined, the lower floors stood almost untouched, but at the top, the walls were gone. The upper end of the frame's structure thrust into the air like pleading arms. Because the roof, too, had been blown off, between those bare architectural limbs we could see the blue sky. Shreds of what I thought was clothing clung to a few shards of remaining window. Out of one gap, I could see half a desk and the legs of a toppled chair. Perhaps the bodies had already been removed. When I lifted my face to the breeze, I could detect the faint smell that lingers in the wake of smoke. It reminded me of my father's stubbed-out cigarettes, but those had the sweet trace of Jaffna tobacco, and this air had a residue of stone. Police barriers blocked off certain sections of the street, and the explosion's dust sugared the ground and drifted through the air. At the entrance, near a group of police officers and soldiers, a very short woman screamed in Sinhala and sobbed. One of the soldiers was consoling her gently, and although I did not speak enough Sinhala, I understood her face blotted with tears, and his face twisted in sympathy.

"Have you seen what you needed to see?" my grandmother asked quietly.

I felt both alone and the desire to be alone. Everyone had witnessed what the bomber had done, but was I the only person other than the Tigers who knew who she was and what had happened to her? She had been a civilian, and they—the soldiers, the peacekeepers, and the Tigers—had made her into someone else. Although I knew the sequence of facts, I could not understand, and then I understood and could not bear to be outside this building and inside that knowing. I shivered like an animal trying to fling off water.

My grandmother laid her hand on my wrist and put her cold fingers at my racing pulse.

"Sashi," she said. "People are watching."

Have you had a moment like this, in which you had no choice but to gather yourself? I willed myself to be still. I had gone there for a reason, and so I made myself look at the building again: the ordinary entrance—the top floor's naked embrace—the indecent void within it—the sky above. It was unusual to bomb a building at its top, that much I knew. To destroy a whole building you should begin, properly, at the bottom. Sometimes bombers drove or were driven in lorries that rammed into first floors. You could have a bigger bomb that way, too—hundreds of kilos. Dayalan and Seelan would have explained it in terms of physics: each floor should sink into the one crushed below it. A person who executed that kind of attack was not alone.

But she had been alone, and she had done something different.

She had been after someone in particular.

"Wait a moment," I said.

I left my grandmother standing there and walked to a newsstand across the street, where I bought a copy of the *Ceylon Daily News* from the proprietor, a Muslim man with a genial look who was listening to the radio and doing his receipts. They were playing the same broadcast I had heard that morning, on a loop, but now I was only half-listening. I made a pretence of scanning the newspaper, which had been printed before the bombing and contained nothing I wanted.

"Who worked in that building?" I asked the shop owner. No one else was in the shop, so I spoke to him in Tamil. He looked up from his ledger, startled.

"I don't know," he said. "Some military fellows. Some ordinary office people also, I think. Very sad. A few lived," he added, almost as an afterthought.

Would these survivors, these few-lived-also, remake themselves, as Priya had? Across the street, my grandmother was talking to one of the police officers. I thanked the shop proprietor and hurried back to her.

"Terrible," she said to the police officer. They were speaking in English.

He shook his head. "The corporal was a good man," he said.

She took my arm and nodded at me. "Your office is closed after all, is it? Shall we go?"

As we got back into the auto she started to say something and I motioned for her to be quiet, seeing the driver's ears prick up. Once we were back in the house, she said, "That woman went to see someone who had been in the army, who had served in Jaffna as a liaison to the IPKF, and then come back here. He had left the army and was working on the top floor of that building. She was looking for him. What did you say had happened to her?"

"I didn't say, Ammammah."

"Tell me," she said.

I covered my eyes with my hands and told her. This time I did not leave anything out—the rape, Priya's four brothers, her parents—and when I was done, my grandmother's birthmark stood out darkly on her pale face. She was weeping, which I had never seen before, even when she herself had been displaced, even when my brothers had vanished. I knew she was thinking of my grandfather and his discreet Colombo clinic, of the women who had gone there for a thousand reasons, none of them yet war.

"It's good you are leaving," she said. "We should all leave. But oh, God, we belong to this place. How can we live anywhere else?"

Standing in front of that building full of emptiness where the bomb had been, I had asked myself the same question and found that I had no answer.

BECAUSE I WAS AT the end of the truth I could tell her, the next morning I got up and readied myself for the airport. They had booked me on a flight to London. In those days people dressed as well as they could for life-altering journeys on airplanes, and I followed suit, tying a sari my mother had given me. In my bag I carried a jumper; the flights were known to be cool, and beyond that, England would be colder still. My parents had given me a gold chain before I left Jaffna, and thinking of them, I fastened it around my neck. Much of my old clothing seemed like a costume now, but the necklace felt like it belonged to me.

With a student visa to study engineering, Aran had travelled under his own name, and had also acquired the papers I needed to travel. Unlike him, I could not emigrate as myself; my face had appeared in news photographs with the Tiger flag, and there was too great a risk of my being stopped in the Colombo airport. Something more complicated and dangerous was required. My grandmother handed me the folder Aran had prepared for me. He had gone to one of the Wellawatte agencies that handled such matters; he had paid to get someone else's passport. It had belonged to a Malaysian businessman. In those days, the pages were not laminated, and so, in the back of that same Colombo tea stall, forgery artists scraped the original picture away from the thick paper and then carefully replaced it with the one he had given them. I had sent the photograph from Jaffna via people we knew rather than by mail for fear of being caught. After affixing it, the agents had painted the appropriate government seal over it. It was a precise job; my new identity was convincing, at least to me. But buying it had required most of my brother's cherished savings, and he had gone to England with little in his pockets. The plane ticket had put my parents and me in debt, too. My father had waved me off gruffly when I tried to mention the cost: five lakhs, and more.

My trip had been planned as an echo of Aran's: my grandmother's driver would take me to Katunayake and to check in, and then I would walk through security and into the other life we had purchased. At that time, the Malaysian passport was one of the best in the world; I didn't even need a British visa. So I would get to London, and then, in Heathrow, I would return the passport to another agency contact. Then I would walk out and claim asylum. Like the bombed building, I would open my arms to the sky. And Aran would find me.

My grandmother said good luck to me with her forehead pressed tenderly to mine. I cupped her cheeks and thought of the lotus flowers at the thresholds of Buddhist stupas, their pale petals resting in the palms of the faithful. Once again I kissed each soft side of the old and perfect face I loved. "I go only to return," I said, because Tamil has no words for last goodbyes.

BACK THEN SUCH FLIGHTS took off in the evenings. When we arrived at Katunayake, many of the travellers around me were bidding tearful goodbyes to entire busloads of relatives. The driver escorted me in, brought my bag to the ticketing area, watched me receive my boarding pass, and then inclined his head, smiling slightly. "Good luck, madam," he said. A nearby Air Lanka official pointed me in the right direction, and I went to stand in the passport control queue. I had never left the country; I had never boarded a plane. I had never travelled without another person. When my turn arrived, I stepped forward, the Malaysian passport in my right hand, the nails of my left digging into my hot palm.

"And where are you going, madam?" the officer asked mechanically. He flipped through the passport pages. The agency had put a few stamps in it; an entirely blank document might have raised suspicion too.

"London," I said.

"For what reason? Business or pleasure?"

"To visit family," I said meekly.

"How long will you stay?"

"One month," I said.

"And then?"

"Home to Malaysia," I said.

"And what have you been doing here?" he asked.

"Visiting family," I said. This was plausible enough; many Sri Lankan Tamils had Malaysian Tamil relatives. The name in the passport was not mine, but it was still Tamil.

The officer flipped another page and then stamped it.

"Have a nice trip, madam," he said. "Next?"

The door of belief swung open. I could leave. I walked through it, through the duty-free, and down the corridor towards my flight. I had never been inside the airport before and I tried not to stare. When I found an empty seat near a tea shop, I paused to watch the other travellers: small children running disobedient circles around their families; clusters of friends; suited, sweating businessmen; vacationing Indians sipping tea; white Europeans wearing gauzy clothing with elephants and peacocks on it; sunburned Australians with backpacks. Among these people no other woman was alone. The chair across from me sat empty, and I imagined my brother Aran sitting there two weeks earlier, also alone, wearing his rectangular spectacles, his too-wide trousers, his suit jacket that had never quite fit him correctly.

At the gate, I looked at the clock. Aran was waiting for me. Priya had asked what her parents would do without her brothers. She had failed to ask what they would do without her. What would my parents do without their children? I sat apart from the other passengers, carefully, and spoke to no one. Solitude was both what I expected and what I thought I wanted. I was wrong. I was too scared to speak to anyone. Although I was desperate for anyone to meet my eyes or say my name, I kept my head down. The Air Lanka hostesses walking through the waiting area were saying ayubowan, ayubowan, the Sinhalese greeting. One of them smiled at me.

Eventually someone came and sat to my left. A kind and obviously wealthy and perhaps somewhat naive Sinhalese man from Cinnamon Gardens, he asked for my name.

"Anjali," I said, without thinking.

The second after I said it a clutching, choking feeling seized me. If you have ever told such a lie, you know that when dreaming of another self, you will reach first for the name of someone you love. I realised afresh that I would not see her again. Then, another horror: I did not know how to break the habits of secrecy. They were so ingrained, you understand. For years I had trained myself to be wary of unknown persons, and now I was going to a life that would have mostly unknown persons. For the next hour, as we waited, I fell further and further into the persona I had so hastily and needlessly invented. Yes, sir, I had a very pleasant journey. I was returning to university abroad after visiting my family in Colombo, I told him. I would have given anything to say something true. Ask what happened to me, sir, to anything I loved. He reminded me of my grandmother. But I had shed my former life, a life I knew better than to admit to a stranger. As I spoke to him about a place I did not know and a family that was not mine, I remembered the snake I had seen in the Jaffna garden of one of my teachers, its series of skins molted across the wet green.

"Did you have a good visit?" the gentleman asked.

"Yes, it was good to see my family," I said.

"When you are done studying abroad, will you come back here?"

"Oh, I hope so," I said. In saying it, I discovered that it was true.

"I do too," he said earnestly. "Our country cannot afford to lose people like you. It was nice to meet you," he said, and then it was his turn to board.

He headed down the corridor and away from me, his grey-suited back growing smaller. I watched him go. I could have another place and another name—even the one I had given him. I could get on the plane, too, and be Anjali, or whoever I wanted. I would be safe and free and never home. But he had reminded me that there were people who thought that Sri Lanka could not afford to lose me. I had never heard his question—Will you come back?—so plainly and sweetly; no one in my own life had asked, because they all understood how impossible it was to know the answer. If I ever returned to Jaffna, what would I find? I turned my face to the window to see the airplane and stared at my own reflection until it gave way to the machine, the clear stretch of runway, and the dark sky beyond it.

18.

Safe Passage

COLOMBO TO JAFFNA, LATE 1989

YOU MUST HAVE REALISED BY NOW: ALTHOUGH I HAD BEEN so afraid, in the end, nobody turned me around; nobody refused to let me go. But I went only as far as the boarding gate. I was the one who turned around. I was the one who refused to leave. I wanted to go back to Anjali and Varathan. I wanted to write with them until everything I knew was in our book. I had thought I had given them a full accounting of what had happened to Priya, when I had told them only half the story.

All this time later, and I have never asked my brother what it was like to wait for me at Heathrow Airport. If it had been the other way around, I would have stayed hours, wondering what had happened. These days, I remember every watch as a stilled face, but for him, the minutes must have ticked on dangerously. If I had told him I was not coming, I would have lost valuable time and my parents would have immediately looked for me. My mother lived the secretive life of a Tamil civilian woman in an occupied area and not the secretive life of a combatant, and it was she who taught me: Don't say unnecessary things. Share nothing of yourself beyond what is required. But by not telling him, I chose something else over Aran for the last time. Even as I did it, I knew that though I might see him again, he would never entirely trust me. He had lost Niranjan, and Dayalan, and Seelan, and then I broke my word. I see him still: my one remaining brother, checking his watch, rocking back and forth on his feet gently at airport arrivals, pushing an empty trolley.

I kept the passport. It was worth too much money to throw away. I put it in my pocket and walked out of the airport and found a taxicab. My suitcase had gone on the plane and perhaps been offloaded since I hadn't boarded; I had no hope of retrieving it. The things most dear to me I had kept with me or sewn into my sari petticoat. The taxicab driver took me to the address I gave him and then I knocked on the door of a friend.

The door opened.

Hasna's eyes went wide at the sight of me, and with a quick glance up and down the street, she reached out and pulled me inside.

AFTER A CUP OF TEA and a plate of mutton rolls, Hasna sat back in her chair and stared at me. I had told her most if not all of the story, and what I had not said she was probably able to guess. "Sashi, you can't be serious," she said. "You want to go back?"

"I have to go back," I said.

"But—your brother," she said.

"He's in England," I said. "He'll be fine in England. And he should leave the country. My mother deserves to have at least one son who she knows will live. But Varathan and Anjali need my help in Jaffna."

"So you're determined, then," she said. "There's no talking you out of it." She leaned back in the chair and studied my face. "What about your parents?"

"My parents think I'm going to London. By the day after tomorrow, they will think I'm missing or detained," I said. Hasna's expression changed subtly. These days she lived with one flatmate; her siblings had mostly immigrated or taken jobs in other parts of the country. Her parents lived in Galle with one of them. They were scattered, but I envied her the comparative wholeness of her family and her ability to be honest with them. "It's better if that's what they think, Hasna," I said.

"Aran will tell them you didn't come," she said.

"Better for them to wonder where I am than for them to know, which would not be safe," I said. "Don't you think? Considering?"

She looked sadder than I had ever seen her, sadder than she had looked after the riots when she had come to see me in the refugee camp, sadder than she had looked when she had learned we were going to different medical schools.

"All right," she said softly. "If you want to go back I'll help you."

She walked down the hall and went into her bedroom. She emerged a moment later carrying something under her arm. She came into the kitchen and sat again, her lips pursed thoughtfully. She unfolded the item into her lap, held it up, and shook it out: a burqa.

She looked me up and down, appraising. "This will fit you," she said.

DURING THE JOURNEY BACK to Jaffna, I wrote almost constantly. I wrote on buses and trains and in lorries and while waiting for transport. I wrote during rare meals, and I wrote when I could not sleep or bathe. And when I got back to Jaffna, I did not return to my parents. Instead, I went directly to Varathan and Anjali's house. When I got there around noon, four long, confused, and unpleasant days after leaving Colombo, no one was sitting on the veranda, which was unusual. I knocked on the door tentatively, holding my notebook. I did not want to call out; I did not want to call any attention to myself. I stood there at the doorstep in my burqa, waiting and sweating.

Kumi opened the door. She gaped at me for a second before letting me in. "I almost didn't recognise you, Sashi Acca," she said. "Why didn't you go? Did you hear something and turn back?"

"Hear something?" I said. "I was in Colombo for the bombing of that building, and then I just couldn't bear to get on the plane—"

"So you haven't heard what happened to Acca," she said. She was preternaturally calm for such a young person. "The Tigers have taken her."

SHORTLY AFTER I LEFT Jaffna, the Tigers arrested Anjali. One moment she was riding her bicycle down a path she always took on her way home from the university, and the next she had vanished. When they told him, Varathan screamed, beating his hands against the walls of his office, his secretary trying in vain to stop him.

The Tigers sent someone to their house later to tell him to come and get Anjali's personal items. The cadre who had come to inform him, a university dropout they had both known slightly, invited him to collect what had belonged to her with an impossible, cold face, as though neither Varathan nor Anjali had ever taught him. Varathan was able to control himself only for the minute that the boy stayed. The next morning he went to the camp where they had told him to come, and another young boy pushed Anjali's bicycle at him through a gate. He caught the handlebars, and the boy dropped the chain Anjali had worn around her neck into his cupped and lifted palm, like a priest dropping vibhuthi into the hand of a worshipper at temple. He'd turned away, pulling the bicycle, unable to get onto it himself, sure he would still be able to sense the warmth of her body curved around its skeleton.

"Dey," the boy called after him. He could not have been more than fifteen.

Varathan looked back, and the boy held out one more item: the wristwatch Anjali had always worn, even after accidentally breaking it, because he had given it to her as a wedding present.

"Doesn't work," he said, sneering, and Varathan understood that the boy had intended to keep it before realising it was of no use.

"Maybe she's still alive," Varathan said to me, pointlessly winding the wristwatch in one direction and then the other. It happened sometimes. They took prisoners and transported them in lorries up and down the island, telling a loved one outside that the person was dead because that was the eventual plan. It was a kind of efficiency, he supposed. They had heard about the pits in which the Tigers held some of their prisoners; in fact, it had been in the last Report the two of them had written, so Varathan knew the dimensions of the cells, the number of other prisoners there might be, and the kinds of torture the Tigers favoured using on Tamils who had criticised them. Even women. Even Anjali, who at the moment we were thinking of her was listening to a man she had been detained with scream.

"Maybe she's still alive," he said again.

"It's possible," I said gently. I was the only person who said this to Varathan, and I suspect that this is something for which he was grateful. Everyone else thought the other answer was best: tell him that she died swiftly so that he didn't think of her in pain. When, several days later, Varathan received a message by way of someone else who had managed to escape such a prison, he told me: Anjali was alive, and trying to be released. He was afraid it was a trap. What should he do?

"Do you want me to come with you?" I asked. "Even just so you don't have to go alone?"

"If the Tigers are waiting for me, I might as well go alone," Varathan said.

"I worked for them," I said. "Perhaps they will listen to me."

"But Sashi," Varathan said. "They let you go. They think you're overseas. If you walk in there with me, they will know you came back. They will know whose side you're on."

"Let them know," I said. "I can't leave her there without saying something."

So we went together. I did not have to show Varathan the way. He knew every step of the route to a place he had never gone—the local Tiger headquarters. And it turned out all of them knew who Varathan was. When we arrived, the sentry—one of Varathan's former students and neighbours—recognised him and looked curiously at me.

"Sir," he said.

On another day Varathan would have told him how his mother and sisters were doing, asked after him, pushed on the question of when he would return to school. Today he said, "I would like to speak to T—."

When we were shown in, Varathan did not even sit before he said:

"You have my wife. Give her back to me."

T— looked at him and then at me.

"Sashi," he said. "I did not expect to see you here. We went to a lot of trouble to help you leave. Back so soon?" He beckoned to the cadre standing outside the door. The boy obeyed, and T— whispered something brief in his ear. He hurried off.

"Well, then. Would you two like a cup of tea? Sashi, how was your journey, if you had one?"

"I'll do anything you want," Varathan said.

I put my hand on his wrist. He was shaking. "We came to demand Professor Premachandran's release," I said.

Behind me, I heard someone else enter. I turned around. Seelan's eyes met mine and then he moved to stand next to T—.

"Is she missing?" my brother said.

"You came to demand the release of a traitor," T— said.

"I'm a student," I said. "I'm here to demand the release of my teacher. Didn't I do enough for the Tigers?" I looked at Seelan. "Dr. Varathan, this is my brother, Seelan."

Seelan said nothing.

"Tell me what you want," Varathan said, his voice cracking.

T— stood up and pushed his chair back and walked around the desk so that they were face-to-face. They were of a height.

"We want you and Anjali to stop writing the book. We know it's yours."

"What?" Varathan said stupidly.

"The book of Reports the two of you have been writing and compiling," T— said. "Or should I say the three of you? We have a copy. We've been reading it. Very interesting. I'm surprised you weren't more careful."

We had dreamed of people reading it, but not him, not yet. During the evenings we had written it, we had spoken about the people we wanted to live in its pages. These were the same people we thought would find relief in knowing that their stories were both written down and collected together. How many of us had felt that we had suffered alone at the hands of the militants or the state or the Indians? But we were not alone; as I had placed one story next to another, Anjali over my shoulder, I could see how each small piece fit, until the whole war stretched out around us, its costs horrific and fathomable.

We had wanted to make the book meticulous, open, truthful, compassionate. Varathan would have used the same words to describe Anjali; to us, it was as much of her as could be contained by a document. How had they gotten a copy? How had they known who the authors were? I had thought I understood the danger of what I was doing, but I felt sick when I realised: if they knew about Varathan and Anjali, then—as T— had insinuated—a third author would not be difficult to guess. Were our fingerprints so obvious to others?

Later, Varathan told me that he had almost the feeling that Anjali was listening, that it was a test. He imagined her voice: What would you want me to say, love? What would you want me to do? He had thought he would have given anything to have her back, but in fact what he wanted then was to do what she thought was right, because she was the measure of rightness he had always used.

"I can't do that," Varathan said. In the moment, he was certain. It was the last moment in which he ever felt clear. For the rest of his life he would wonder what he could have said or done differently, even knowing that had he said yes, had they said they would release her, their word was not a word that could be believed. For the rest of his life he would get a look in his eye when he was back in this moment. I learned to put my hand on his and wait until he could breathe again.

"Yes, I am one of the writers," Varathan said. "But those stories don't belong to me. They belong to so many people."

"You can't do that?" T— said. "Then they'll kill her." He smiled a little. "And then they'll deal with you."

Across from me, Seelan's dear, known face with its single brow was immovable. I thought of walking to the library with him, his quick grin and temper. I loved him. He was not going to help us.

"They'll deal with me," Varathan said. "They. You say it as though you weren't one of them. You don't mean they. You mean you. Look at where we are. She was your classmate, T—. She's a teacher."

We had been taught to love and respect teachers. T— had been a teacher himself, but he said nothing, and Seelan stood beside him like the statue of a brother.

"Give her back to me," Varathan said.

"Now that you've said no, Varathan, that's impossible," T— said sadly. "It's impossible." On his desk a stack of pages lifted in the breeze.

YEARS LATER, WE LEARNED part of the story from another woman who had been imprisoned with her. Varathan cried soundlessly while she talked; I took notes.

Like so many others, Anjali rose one night when her number was called. She lifted her hands for her jailers to lead her into the woods, where she knew the odds of her being released were much lower than her odds of simply being shot. She had marked out a calendar on the wall of her cell and knew how long she had been inside, that the prison held about three thousand people, that it was getting crowded, and that there was one very obvious solution to overcrowding of this kind. After all, she had written the Reports. She knew what was in them: deaths like this. Some people wanted to forget that not only the state but also the Tigers killed Tamils. Anjali had refused, and now she would become one of them. She would become the book.

Calmly she held out her hand to the person who told us this story. "Tell my husband I—"

"Yes, Acca," the other prisoner said quickly. The cadre was already yanking at Anjali's arm.

The rest of it I make up. I'm sure Varathan does too. We never talk about it. I never tell him my version. Every time what happens is different, but what I want is the same: to walk into the woods with her, to hold her outstretched hand against what I know is coming. But even when I dream it, there is a point in my brain where the dark folds in, and in, and in on itself, and her fingers slip out of mine.

She was alone. She can't tell this story. So you will have to believe me.

I am not going to be released, she told herself, and I am never going to see Varathan again. She wished she could have died with his hand on her cheek, or moving in her hair, with the two of them at home together in their quiet house full of books and music, him reading to her. Her mother on the veranda and her sister playing. When the young cadre behind her trembled and lifted his Kalashnikov she deliberately turned around so that he would have to shoot her through the eyes instead of the back of the head, without facing her.

"If you kill me you'll never get over it," she said to him in Tamil. "I won't even have to curse you. The gods you believe in won't even curse you. You'll just live a long life and remember me always.

"I don't believe in God," she told him clearly. "But I believe that you can do something else."

But he didn't.

EVEN IN DEATH, EVEN in my dream, Anjali is right: he remembers her always, as we do, even after he runs away from the Tigers himself and emigrates to Europe, where he becomes a priest. In a small village in Germany or maybe Norway, he listens to BBC Tamil Osai via streaming Internet and thinks of his former comrades, thinks of the famous teacher he'd been assigned to kill in the jungle. He knew who she was; everyone in the camp knew who the women were because there were so few of them. And she had been so forthright, so direct in what she'd said. She had taught some of his friends, people both in the movement and beyond it, and had made him, too, one of her students in her final moments.

You'll just live a long life and remember me always.

Publicly, the Tigers denied that they had killed her. We returned her things to you because we found them, they said. A service to the people, a mid-ranking cadre at the camp claimed, practically daring Varathan to argue.

Varathan put it in the next Report: *The LTTE killed my wife,* he wrote in his dark, fine, precise hand. *My wife my wife my wife.* He gave it to the geography department secretary who had been typing the Reports, and she looked down at the paper and up at him.

"If you wouldn't mind typing one more," he said.

"Of course, sir," she said. "And then we'll copy it and make sure it's distributed."

He paused.

"Is there anything else, sir?"

"Put my name on it," he said.

"Sir," she said quietly.

"Put my name on it," he said.

19.

The Body

JAFFNA, 1989

For the third time in my life, I lost someone I loved and there was no body.

"I don't know if I want to have a funeral," Varathan said. "How can we have a funeral without the body?"

I thought of Tharini and Chelvi. "The students will want to have one," I said.

"Oh," he said listlessly. "Will they?"

"Of course they will. They loved her."

He looked at me for a second, thinking. "Yes," he said at last, "there should be a funeral, a grand commemoration of her life, and a march through the streets. The Tigers have denied killing her, but I wrote it down."

"What do you mean you wrote it down?" I said.

"I put it in a Report," he said.

"What?"

"Indra typed it and copied it. I think it's ready to be distributed."

I gaped at him. "Where were you thinking that we would distribute it?"

"At her memorial," he said.

"But what will happen after that? They'll kill us," I said.

"Well," he said. He blinked. "We'll have to run."

PEOPLE CAME FROM ALL over the country for her funeral. Former students, former colleagues, relatives distant and close, even people who knew her from her time overseas made the trip. It was difficult to organise because the Tigers tried to intimidate us out of holding anything to honour her. They did not want her life discussed in all its complexity; they did not want anyone to talk about how good she had been to the students, even the ones with whom she disagreed; they did not want pictures of her face plastered to the walls of Jaffna town or the university; they did not want people crying out her name. But people in Jaffna, especially students, wanted all of these things. Because the Tigers had denied killing her, they could not openly discourage the commemoration. I could not work in the open, as everyone thought I had already left. This made for a curious standoff. Others took on the task of planning in the face of administrative and militant obstacles. Varathan and Chelvi did most of it. One day, she told me Tiger leaders had paid a visit to them as they made placards. "Why not carry signs demanding that the Indians leave?" the men suggested. The students refused: this was Anjali's funeral, they said, not a political event. The Tiger leaders got angrier, and Chelvi and Tharini stood their ground.

On the day of the march, some people stayed away, among them prominent university leaders. As the walk began, Varathan was at the head of the crowd. Students moved through the mass of people, passing out the Report, which was signed and which had all of the evidence of what had happened to her. The crowd began to murmur as the copies went from hand to hand. Varathan held his head high. What would they do, kill him in front of the whole crowd? He took one step forward. He was so angry, nearly suicidally angry, almost daring them to do it.

As this was happening, in his house, the house where I had spent so

many happy hours with Varathan and Anjali and Kumi and Mrs. Premachandran, my family away from my family, I packed a bag. It was so
small that no one would even think I was leaving town for any significant amount of time—just the plain and simple bag that I had used for
school all these years. But I did not plan to come back this time. When
I thought of my mother, in a house that did not belong to her, without
any of her children, I nearly wept. And I wished I could have gone to
the funeral. I knew my friends were standing in the crowd in support
of Varathan. Chelvi was holding a sign that said EELAM IS OUR GRAVE-
YARD. I wondered how she would pay for that. I hoped Bhavani was
standing next to her. I took Hasna's burqa out of my bag and put it
back on. I braided my hair and put on my glasses.

HALFWAY THROUGH THE MARCH it began to rain softly. Some people lifted umbrellas but Varathan did nothing. When someone else
tried to shelter him he pushed that person away gently. He wanted
nothing between himself and the grey sky. You must understand: this
was the gift he was giving himself, listening to everyone talk about
how much they loved her, hearing about her life and her friends and
her scholarship and her activism. He wanted to hear everything he
knew repeated back to him and he wanted to hear everything he had
not known, the tiny corners of her life that she had kept private from
even him. She had been giving the anatomy examinations when she
had been abducted. Several medical students spoke of her thorough-
ness as a teacher. Among the crowd were students known to be affili-
ated with the Tigers; many of them were also weeping, while others
were watching carefully. Years later, Chelvi told me that even Josie
was there, and that she attempted, nervously, to embrace Varathan
and offer him condolences. Indian officers circled the mourners. Rumour had it that they had also seen a copy of the book and, like the
Tigers, had had it translated so that they could understand what the
book said about them. I do not doubt that Sri Lankan intelligence was
there, too.

At last, when everyone was ready to leave, Varathan looked at Mrs. Premachandran and Kumi and nodded slightly. Then he slipped into the edges of the crowd and away. He carried with him a precious copy of the book.

AS WE HAD AGREED and planned, Varathan went one direction and I went the other.

THEY MUST HAVE GIVEN him the length of the funeral, thinking that if they took him in beforehand it would be obvious that they had killed her. They did not want the blame for that. But an hour after the funeral ended, someone told them that his house was empty. The widowed of Jaffna stay at home to mourn. They knew something was wrong.

He arrived at the house of a friend who had helped with the writing of the book, a retired gentleman who had previously been a postmaster. The man gave him a cup of tea and a small meal. They waited for a third man to come and accompany Varathan on the next leg of his journey. Earlier than they expected, a knock came. When the friend went to see who it was, he found a cadre waiting on the other side. But in the unnecessarily long time the retired postmaster had taken to answer the door, Varathan had concealed himself. From where he was hidden he could see the kitchen fire burning merrily, fueled by the manuscript.

ANJALI HAD LEFT VARATHAN nothing written other than the Reports, nothing personal. She had not been a writer of love letters— after all, they had been together most of the time before she was abducted. They wrote together, not to each other. She was the only person with whom he had ever been able to write. When confirmation came to us through our informants that Anjali had been killed, I wrote a letter to her and left it for him to find.

When he fled Jaffna, it was this letter that he concealed most tenderly on his person. I had written it on a scrap of the *Saturday Evening Review,* in extremely small and meticulous Tamil script, in between the lines of one of his own old columns, and put it inside a blue aerogramme. After he left the retired postmaster's house, he had to wait until it was safe to leave. He smuggled himself out in a lorry full of red onions on a day when the Tigers lifted their pass system. The man who ran the pass system that day had the *nom de guerre* of Gandhi. Later Varathan joked that it was the scent of that many Jaffna onions, even unpeeled, that made him weep as he rode out past that man. But I think it was the note. He was leaving the place where he had discovered and lost the scent of Anjali's hair, the quick sound of her laugh, the feeling of the soft skin at her wrist, the taste of her mouth, her unflinching mind. He would never have these things again, and he had no picture of her. But he had my words. The words were something he could memorise and repeat, the way he had recited the proverbs of the *Thirukkural* as a child. A prayer. It would be impossible for someone to take such a thing from him, he thought, but still he clutched the scrap of paper tight in his fist.

WHO WOULD HELP ME NOW? I grew up knowing the answer to this question. Like Pillaiyar, I circled my parents, the world. By habit and heart I went back to where they lived. From outside the house that was not their house, I could see Amma doing something in the garden; I could see Appa sweeping the veranda steps. If I asked them for help, I would put them in danger. It was foolish to go there.

I was just about to cycle away when I heard a voice behind me.

"Can I help you?" Seelan said. Automatically I turned around. "Oh," he said. "I didn't recognise you." His eyes landed on the bag. "But I should have." It was true, I had carried just such a bag with me every time we had gone to the library together. If he upended this one now, he would know everything in it: the Pillaiyar chess piece, Anjali's lace tablecloth, the garnet earrings, the copy of Kafka's *The Castle,* the stethoscope that had belonged to Niranjan.

"You can still pretend you didn't," I said.

"What are you doing here? Isn't today your teacher's funeral?"

So he knew what was going on at the university. "The commemoration event. There's no proper funeral because we don't have her body. I just"—I hesitated—"I just wanted to see them."

"Ah," he said. "You're truly leaving this time. You've caused me a lot of trouble. I should take you back to T—."

"You were a brother before you were a Tiger," I said. "Will you really do that?" Aran had said our brothers might come to collect us.

"When they found out that you had worked on the Reports, I think they wanted to kill you," Seelan said. "But T— said that after all you did for the movement, after you sat on that stage and took care of K, we couldn't have that. What would people think of you betraying us?"

That was not the question. The question was what people would think of them, think of the Tigers.

"Do you have a copy of the book?" he asked.

"I don't have a copy of the book," I said.

As he was deciding whether to believe me, from the window came the sound of my parents talking to each other, my father joking and my mother telling him how to do something. Henry barked. Perhaps he was trying to tell them that I was out there. We had moved from house to house, but my parents were my home, just out of my reach.

Seelan tilted his head, thinking still. He touched his finger to where his eyebrow had been. "I think you should go," he said. "I can tell them I saw you."

"I suppose you think I should thank you," I said.

"No, I should thank you," he said. Then he said slowly: "I'm grateful for everything you've done for the movement."

I thought of all the patients I had treated, including him. Either he meant what he was saying, or it was a threat. I could not tell.

———

I HAD THROWN AWAY the piece of paper Niroshan had given me at the field hospital, but I had memorised the address. As I hurried there, I repeated the number and street quietly to myself. When I arrived, his wife opened the door before I could knock and said simply, "We've been waiting for you."

"I just need to get the book and then I'll go," I said. "Do you have it?"

"Of course," Niroshan said from behind her.

I tried to depart again immediately. There was no time to waste, I said. But they made me come inside and have a meal and a wash. I removed the pieces of my disguise one by one: braids, glass-lensed spectacles, burqa.

I WAS ABLE TO TRAVEL AWAY.

I got into a lorry, bought a train ticket, took a car, boarded an airplane, and said goodbye. But I could not leave such a country, or its war; it followed me and whispered in my ears, even when I clapped my hands over them and screamed for it to stop. Perhaps you know all of this already; perhaps I am telling you a story you already understand. What I wouldn't give for that to be true! But we both know it isn't. Because I am talking to you, because I'm sitting here and you're sitting there, you expect me to explain.

20.

The Next Report

WHEN I LEFT SRI LANKA YEARS AGO, WITH THE BOOK AND without Anjali, I never expected or wanted to see my only remaining older brother again. On the plane, I took out the notebook with the end of Priya's story in it and rewrote it into the full manuscript. My pen moving across the page described the intense horror of treating Priya, of telling her that she was pregnant, of seeing the remains of the blasted building in Colombo. Bracing myself against a rickety tray table, I waved off airplane meals and ignored turbulence, looking only at the words rising out of the page, each one a brick in the wall of a sentence, each wall leaning against another to assemble the city of facts, the palace of history.

It was only when the last words of that story were set in place that I let myself wander into questions. I wrote to Anjali, dear and gone, she who believed in the importance of the smallest details of every past, she who would have asked me how the wind smelled as it went singing through the cool bombed dark. She had cried out and said, I'm confused, I'm terrified, I don't know what's going to happen to us. *Anjali Acca, what could I have done differently? I feel responsible,* I wrote. If I could have turned to the seat beside me and seen her buckled in there, safe and loved, she could not have offered me absolution. And that was not what I wanted. What I wanted was the relief of her presence, to be with someone who understood how I felt—what I feared, everything I missed and regretted and loved—without my having to explain. I wanted to be known already. I did not want to explain. In this country of grief, the best kind of shelter is to be understood, to have someone stop next to me and, without asking anything, put their umbrella over us both, between us and the rain.

Without her, alone, I stood then with my bare face up to the sky. And at last, as page turned unto page and each sentence unwound itself, I told Anjali about imagining her death. I was still trying to follow her, you see. *There is so much about my own people that I cannot know,* I wrote to her. *So much even about you.* But I need you to understand: I did not want just to follow her. I wanted to take her place. The Tigers had persuaded me at last: I would have martyred myself. But my reasons—or wishes—were my own. I wanted to bring Niranjan back, to bring Dayalan back, to bring Sir and K back. To bring her back. To undo the war. There was nothing I would not have traded, nothing I would not have done. I want you to hear me: I loved my life, and I would have given it away. And although I realised then what I was willing to die for, there was no way to make that offer, which was also against everything we had fought for and believed.

The pages were true, and they did not belong in the book that we had written together. Had she been there, she would not have faulted me. She would have taken my hand in hers and held it, as she had so many times before. But the fingers on the armrest next to me belonged to a stranger. All I had were her words, the stories she had collected and that had been entrusted to me.

I tore out the pages I had written to her and put them at the beginning of a fresh, blank notebook. Then I added my name to the book the three of us had written.

Onward I went, to the strange new life that awaited me.

AT MY LONDON CONNECTION, I disembarked to find Aran waiting to receive me. I no longer felt that I deserved it. Although my brother

presented himself without fanfare, although his face was still young, I
was shocked: white threads had found their way into his hair. He held
his arms out distrustfully, as though I might walk not into but through
them. "At last," he said. And then: "They let you go." Whether he
meant Anjali and Varathan or the Tigers and Seelan I did not know.
First Aran had wanted me not to support the militants, and then he had
wanted me to protect myself, to be his sister before being an activist,
and in both parts of my life I had failed him. I could not apologise. Still
he came for me, and I understood that after all, he loved me.

As another measure of that, in his small Harrow flat, I spent days
drinking cups of tea beside people who had known Anjali when she
lived there. He had sought them out and brought them to me—
a steady stream of friends and colleagues of whom she had spoken with
great fondness. We had sometimes talked of how we would, in some
longed-for future, visit London together. She had promised to show
me her haunts: her libraries, her tea shops, the Tamil stores where she
liked to buy her short eats. Now I ate and sipped without her, nodding
at people spilling out stories of her student days. As they talked, I listened carefully. At night, before I slept, I wrote each day down in a
fresh notebook, as she had trained me to do for others. This time I did
it just for myself. And then after that I reread the book we had written,
from the beginning, with an eye I hoped was as exacting as hers and
Varathan's had been.

This was what I owed Varathan and Anjali. In those first days, I did
not know where Varathan was, and I stanched my worry with work, as
I always had. Mourning Niranjan, I had filled my nights with studying
for exams: reciting the lessons of biology and chemistry. Now I became a student of history. Every morning I scoured the British newspapers to see what was printed about our war. Every morning I held
our accounts up against theirs and saw what had been erased, and who.

When at the end of a fortnight it was time to leave my brother, I
promised him that I would return. "This time I believe you," he said.
"Good," I replied. "If you talk to Amma and Appa"—I stopped, and
he nodded. He would tell them that he had seen me, that I seemed safe

and well. In all the days I had spent with him we had not called them. Neither did we mention Seelan.

My next and last flight away took me to New York. I would never have come here, but I had promised to carry the book to those who were waiting for it, people who knew Anjali and Varathan. They worked at the United Nations, and after that, I saw Anjali's fingerprints, although not her name, in every sentence they wrote about Sri Lanka.

FOR TWENTY YEARS IT was like that. I delivered a stream of information to the United Nations, and they listened and wrote their own reports, even when they took no action. When the Indians left Sri Lanka, when my parents left Jaffna for London to live with Aran, when the tsunami hit, when the ceasefire briefly held, when the War on Terror came for the Tigers, I wrote. More honestly, I should say: we wrote. During the day—at last a doctor—I treated patients in an emergency room. At night, I picked up the phone to talk with Varathan. It was slower and more difficult now that we were farther apart, but we still followed the same meticulous processes of verification that Anjali and Varathan had developed before she died.

We wrote perhaps ten such Reports in two decades. Then, at last, in the spring of 2009, the end of the war drew near.

I HAD LIVED IN and studied and watched this war for as long as I could remember, and yet the final battles seemed different from any others. Never before had I seen such an avoidable catastrophe coming from so far away. After more than a quarter century of fighting, Sri Lankan security forces cornered the Tigers on a small strip of beach. The news from Mullivaikkal ranged wildly—300,000 Tamil civilians were trapped between the Tigers and the Sri Lankan Army; 40,000 civilians were trapped; certainly, tens of thousands of civilians were trapped. They counted; they didn't count; no one had counted them;

they were counted incorrectly. The Tigers said the civilians were with them by choice, which I knew enough not to believe. The government, for its part, directed civilians to a no-fire zone, but shelled the same areas—and denied it. The pro-Tiger protestors of the Tamil diaspora waved their flags in cities around the world and failed to acknowledge that the militants were complicit in civilian death. The government and its supporters alleged that any grief for Tamil civilians was only a ploy to stop them from defeating the terrorists. Calls for international intervention or a ceasefire yielded nothing.

To endure this horrific spring, Varathan and I recited facts, collecting them as a kind of armour. For weeks, we pored over the news and spoke to our contacts, patching together information to learn as much as we could about what was happening. His cell phone, like mine, became a ticking bomb that endlessly reset, each explosion a desperate voice telling him what it was like there, in the No-Fire Zone. Tell the U.N., tell the Red Cross, tell the newspapers that we are dying, they said. What was it like? Oh, they told us, we die on the beach. We die in the sea, swimming for rescue, and we die in the sand. We dig bunkers for shelter and they become graves. Our bodies bleed and shatter and burn. We are leaving our elders and children behind us. Always the people on the phone said we we we. Naangal. (Divided in our politics, but together in the dying, they noted bitterly.) In my head, the beach heated up like a thosai in a griddle, the batter poured onto a pan spitting hot explosives and gingelly oil. On a plate laid before hungry armies, the strip's edges were eaten away.

IN THOSE MONTHS, TIME moved like I was looking out of a subway car hurtling through the tunnels of New York—a jerky series of pictures giving the impression of real life just out of reach. The days were such that when Aran called me from London, I had not spoken to him in several weeks. I answered eager for some kind of relief, a voice from home.

"Have you seen Seelan yet, Acca?" Aran asked me.

I gasped before I could stop myself. "He's here?" I asked.

"You didn't know? Yes, he's there," Aran said, and hesitated. "When you do, give him my regards."

"I will," I said, and hung up, shaking.

I dialed Varathan, but as usual, I could tell him little that he did not already know. He had already spoken to someone who had spoken to someone who had spoken to someone. The chain confirmed that Seelan was in New York. I reeled. Why had my brother come, and where did he stand with the Tigers? What would he want of me? I knew, with a sharp and sudden intensity, what I wanted of him. English could not withstand this conversation; Varathan and I spoke in Tamil. What do you want to do? Varathan asked urgently, and then: What will you do?

There was a long silence.

Give me the address, I said at last.

Do you see now? Do you understand? I sent a letter to a terrorist I used to know.

SEELAN'S REPLY SAID *Dear Sashi, come and see me.* And although I was the one who had written to him, I did not want to go.

On the day that Seelan asked me to come, I changed my shift and left work early. I gave neither myself nor the hospital any clear reason, and as I turned my key in the door of my flat, I thought that I might just stay at home and read. I could drink a cup of tea and watch the birds at their nest on the ledge beyond my window, or go to the park and walk around the reservoir, where the flowers were opening.

The hospital smell had come home with me, so that even as I pulled my scrubs over my head I felt myself redolent with iodine and saline, the odour in each strand of my hair, the emergency room an almost unwashable stain. I remembered, as I often do, the shark in formalin. Even after many years in New York, I have kept my small Sri Lankan vanities: the bottle of Yardley English Lavender, the sandalwood soap I buy in Chinatown so that I have the safe fragrance of my mother always with me. The arsenal of home against the stink of medicine. I did not bathe again, but I washed my hands and face, plaited my hair, and patted each cheek with a puff of lavender powder. I wound my plait around my head, as I had done years ago in the field hospital. Then I looked at myself in the mirror and stopped cold. I had automatically straightened myself into the regimented, cautious bearing of another time.

And now I could not bear these small regressions. I unravelled my hair and slumped my shoulders. I searched in the drawer for lipstick, which I never wear, and traced it across my mouth. I put my doctor's coat back on. The clean armour of those white sleeves, which I had earned myself.

I went angry. But I asked to see him, after all. How rebellious was that?

SEELAN WAS STAYING IN Queens, in a shabby flat that was some distance from the subway stop, and it took me a quarter of an hour to locate it. Still, I arrived early. I stood on the stoop in the bright afternoon and waited for my watch to tick past our appointed hour before I pressed the buzzer with his new name on it. He was not called Seelan here, and he had not told me his alias, but among the listed names only one could have belonged to him. He had guessed that I would know which door was his, and that presumption and its accuracy made me furious.

He buzzed me upstairs without saying anything. I climbed the six flights of stairs swiftly.

When he opened the door, relief flooded me, along with anger. I breathed him in. The nearness of my entire past was heady. How many times in the years since we had last spoken in front of my parents' house had I wondered whether he lived? Almost against my will, I stepped forward; his arms opened. For a moment, we were once again in a dear house on a small lane in Jaffna, our Advanced Level exams ahead of us.

When he released me, I could see that even as a middle-aged man, he still bristled with barely contained energy. But his fox-clever face had become lean, its lines sharper and more severe. His once-thick hair had given way to a shaved head, the familiar disguise of bald men. His brown skin had the pallor of a book bleached in the sun. His arms, no longer muscled, hung slack and fleshy by his sides. And his single eyebrow had turned as white as my doctor's coat.

He looked embarrassed by his display of emotion. "Now you look like Amma," he said. "Come in." You must remember: I have to tell you this story in English, but we spoke in Tamil. And in Tamil that invitation sounded bittersweet—the words my family had used to welcome me home after long absences. But I no longer knew whether he was family; certainly, this was not home, though the place smelled warmly of rice and chicken curry and tea.

"Sit, sit," he said, and gestured to a sunken sofa. I sat down before a half-empty bottle of arrack on the coffee table, and when he saw me looking at it, he said, "Would you like a glass? Something to eat?" I have never liked the burning, fermented taste of that liquor, although our father drank it. I shook my head. "Where is Professor Varathan? I expected him to come with you." Seelan sat at the other end of the couch, facing me.

Next to the bottle was a stack of Tamil newspapers, some of them familiar nationalist publications. "How long have you been here?" I asked, picking one up.

"Three months. Surely you're in touch with him?"

He was inquiring about Varathan as though they were ordinary, friendly acquaintances. "Of course I am," I said pleasantly. "And you didn't call me? Did you come via London?"

"Paris. I didn't have much of a choice."

No matter what he had done, my parents would have wanted to see him. Had he called them in London? "You could have stayed in France," I said.

"I don't speak French. I was given permission to come here."

"Then the Americans don't know who you are."

At this he sat back slightly. "Are you going to tell them? Or perhaps the professor will."

"I'm not going to tell you where Varathan is. And I'm not going to tell the Americans who you are. I'd just like to tell you why I'm here," I said.

"Why are you here, then?" he asked evenly.

"Do you know how many people are in the No-Fire Zone?" I asked him. "The government is shelling although they know civilians are there, and the movement is holding people hostage."

He was stroking the place where his eyebrow had been. "The people are staying with the movement of their own free will—"

"*DON'T—LIE!*" I shouted. Each word hung in the air, and he flinched, shocked. I stopped myself, looked down, and took a deep breath. Count to ten when you're angry, Varathan says, so I did it first in Tamil and then in English and then in Tamil again. Finally I looked up.

"You have to call whoever you know," I said. "Someone who can convey a message."

"Sashikala," he said, "do you know how many of my comrades are in the No-Fire Zone? They think that someone is coming to save them from the government. The United Nations. Barack Obama." He laughed, and it was a dried-out sound. "They'll die in a church, in a hospital, in the lagoon. Do you think I didn't already call?"

"You called the Tigers," I repeated.

"I called the people I still know, yes," he said, and I realised he meant T—. "I asked for a message to be sent to them. I asked them to consider surrendering, or if they will not, at least releasing the civilians. They won't do it."

"But—"

"I know," he said. "And that was what they said, that the people are there of their own free will."

"You don't believe that," I said.

"I want you to go to the U.N. and ask if they will intervene," he said steadily.

So now my status as one of the writers of the Reports was useful to him. I stood up. "I won't do anything for you," I said. "Not anything. Ever."

"Please," he said. "I tried. Anything I can still give you," he pleaded, his thumb back at the blank space above his eye.

Something savage surged inside me: a violent current of joy in his desperation, even though it only reflected my own. "I want you to understand that nothing I'm doing is for you," I said. "That if I go it's because I choose to, and not because you asked. You—you can call them again."

"Sashi—" he said as I stood up to leave.

I was halfway to the door before I turned around. "When this is all over," I said, "when this is done, I want K's name off your buzzer. I don't want to see you again, or even think of you here. You have no right to any part of him now."

And on my way down the stairs I tore my dead friend's name from the door.

WHEN THE WRONG PERSON asks you to do the right thing, do you do it? I did.

Two days ago, the afternoon after I saw Seelan, I walked the thirty blocks from the emergency room to the United Nations. I had made the appointment with a man I knew from my first days in New York City but whom I had not seen in a number of years. Daniel had come downstairs from his office to meet me himself rather than sending his assistant, and when I had passed through security and collected my things from the conveyor belt, I could see his face through the rotating doors of the visitor's entrance. He seemed unguarded, even appealing, in his simple anxieties: he checked his watch, bending his head, which had turned white since I had last seen him, and then asked one of the attendants behind the desk a question I could not hear. I was a few minutes late, and I had hurried to be there. But I paused, and even as I did it I knew that I was trying to extend the period of time during which I could still lie to myself about what he was going to say.

I went inside.

When he had ushered me into the grey lobby, past the desk, he took both of my hands in both of his and kissed me on each cheek, like I was an old friend, even though the opposite is true. His lips and fingers were very cold, and I was glad when he released me. He handed me a visitor's badge to wear around my neck, and we went to a many-windowed room that I recognised as his office, although his name was not on the door. He invited me to sit in the chair across from his desk and offered me a coffee, which I accepted out of politeness. I held the cup lightly between my palms so that I would not cover my eyes against the sunshine. The light felt almost obscene in its uncurtained bright-ness. In the long history of our conversations, I had never trafficked in pleasantries, and this did not seem the moment to begin. Once I had asked my question and he had answered it, I would go, I decided, and we would distance ourselves again, slowly but steadily widening the fault between our two pieces of earth.

"What can I do for you?" he asked.

"I want to know if you—if the United Nations is going to do any-thing in Sri Lanka," I said. "If you're going to intervene."

He studied me, as Seelan had. He, too, knew what I meant. I wanted to cover my face with my hands.

"Do you think we should?" he asked.

"Yes," I said. "Yes. You should. There are so many civilians there." I could not stop myself from leaning forward and putting one hand on his desk, closing the space between us. He had grey eyes. He had the long, grey face a person gets from practicing a certain sort of official kindness in a long, grey building. "People I know are in there, in the No-Fire Zone. Do you know how many people?"

"I'm so sorry to hear that," he said gently, and reached out to put his hand on mine. His condolences, when they weren't even dead yet, when it was his job to stop such things. He did know how many people were in there. I knew what the U.N. counted.

"You can still do something," I said.

He sighed heavily. "They're hostages," he said. "It's going to be a massive humanitarian disaster. I know some parties are trying to reach the Tiger leadership to encourage them to surrender, or at least to let the civilians go." He paused. "You might consider some efforts in that direction yourself, if that is a route still available to you."

"I know they're being asked—and they should do it," I said. "But if they don't? It's the government's responsibility to protect them."

"And what do you think we should do?"

"Demand a humanitarian ceasefire, long enough to evacuate the civilians," I said. "A humanitarian pause."

"Yes," he said. "Well. We've asked for that. The government refused. They say it's ceding to the Tigers. That they'll just use the reprieve to rearm."

"That may not be wrong," I said. "But if they don't do it and the Tigers don't let those people go, they'll die. You know the government is shelling the No-Fire Zone. Daniel. Please, please. Is the U.N. really not going to do anything? They're acceptable collateral damage?"

He didn't say anything.

"It's supposed to be a safe zone. Why am I getting phone calls from people I know are there, telling me that that beach is being shelled? Those people are innocent. The people in there—there are children and old people, sick people. They don't have enough food! There's no shelter. Some of those people are conscripts! They didn't willingly—if you don't take them out, if you don't send—"

Chelvi had called me from the No-Fire Zone on a borrowed NGO satellite phone. She married someone from Mullaitivu years ago, and when she rang me, her voice was as calm as if she were teaching a child the Tamil alphabet. Aah-nah. Aah-venna. Good. Yes, shells are falling here. Eee-nah. Eee-yenna. It feels like we've been walking for days. Yesterday five people died next to me, in a trench, in the mud, and we did not have time to bury them. Varathan had given me a list of five questions to ask her, information he wanted to confirm, and we managed three before she lost the connection.

"Sashi," Daniel said. "How many people do you think are in the No-Fire Zone? What are the going estimates from your end?"

Some people we had spoken to had told us that there might be more than 300,000 people in Mullivaikkal, in the No-Fire Zone, the place the government had declared safe and was now targeting. Others had said 80,000.

I told him.

"And what is the U.N.'s official count?" I asked.

"I'm so sorry," he said softly. And now his face changed; he really did look sorry. Ashamed, almost. "Sashi, do you understand that for me to answer this question—we're not even having this conversation. This isn't an official meeting. You know that."

"I don't care if it's official or not," I said. "That doesn't matter. I just want you to do something."

"That's not enough, Sashi," he said, his voice almost a whisper now.

"What?"

"I'm sorry," he said. "It's not enough people. There's nothing more we can do. You know how we work. No one is going to push for this. It's already done. I really wish I could say something else. But you have to prepare yourself—if the government and the Tigers want to play this out, they can do it. No one is going to stop them."

He took his hand away.

I looked around the room, which was blank and undistinguished, and I thought for a moment that this was what hell might look like: blank. I tried to concentrate on all the things around me, so that what he had said would not get inside me, but he had a picture of his family on the desk, the little blond boy in the frame holding a red balloon, and before I could stop myself my body filled up with knowing and re-membering and imagining those I had already lost and what was to come. I had lived in New York for years, but so much of what mat-tered in my life was still there. I thought of Tharini and Chelvi and Kumi; I thought of Dayalan and Niranjan, Sir and Anjali. I thought of Seelan, lost to me, not on that beach but here in New York. I thought of Varathan, the precious secret of where he lived his life. His decision to stay in Sri Lanka had made continuing the Reports possible. And of course, I thought of K. His name on Seelan's buzzer, become anonymous, as though it no longer meant anything to anyone.

You have to understand: the most important part of Daniel's job, as he himself had said many times before, was to make sure that people lived. And because I am a doctor, this has been my work too. I have no affection for the dramatic, and so I describe it to you plainly, as it was: a man in a grey building, behind a desk, as ordinary-looking as so many other men and so many other desks in New York, telling me that tens, maybe hundreds of thousands of innocent people were going to be killed, and that there was nothing either of us could do, even though neither of us had any greater purpose than standing in the way of such a thing. I wish I could tell you that this day and this meeting were not ordinary for him, but I would not be able to believe it. And what I felt, hearing what Daniel said? Call it what it was: this, too, was terror.

Daniel said it once, and then, as though he was not sure I had heard him, he said it again, and as he reached the end of the sentence—I'm sorry, there is nothing more we can do—I knew that as many times as I had been told this, I had run out of the capacity to hear it. I had arrived expecting him to disappoint me, but I had not expected to disappoint myself, to feel a fresh rush of fury at my own powerlessness. I had come to this cold building, on this bright day, for nothing, expecting nothing. And there was nothing I could do. Although I had not covered my eyes against the sun, for a moment I was so consumed by heat that I could not even see.

WHAT WOULD YOU DO not to remember something like this? Not to know it? Not to walk around this ripe, living city every day, full of this irrational death? When I walk by Central Park all I see is how many bodies it might contain. It's the same size as the place where the civilians were trapped. Look around us—all the people moving, and eating, and talking. Laughing. Arguing. Catching taxis, entering subway stations. I thought I would burst. When Daniel got up to walk me out I pushed him away and stood up and walked down the hall, almost blind. I found my own way out, past the chapel, to the circular desk, where, shaking with the effort of ordinary motion, I dropped my visitor's card. Later I realised that I had failed to retrieve my regular identification. At another checkpoint, in another time, that would have meant my life. But I did not notice or care. I moved through the lobby to the revolving glass doors, and automatically, my body led me back towards the emergency room at the hospital. On those thirty blocks, I must have passed hot dog vendors, cars, buildings, but I saw only my own feet moving before me. I was nearly running. A part of me hoped a car would crash on Third Avenue, that pieces of people would be brought to me, that I could stitch them back together. Give me something I can heal, I thought—any solvable problem.

I said nothing to anyone as I re-entered the hospital. I was not on the schedule, but they were busy enough not to question my willingness to work. I had carried my white coat with me to the meeting, and now, in the hospital, I put it on. I put it on, and it failed to protect me; it failed to make me anyone good or powerful. Nurses handed me charts and I took them. Like you, I asked questions and wrote down histories. But my stethoscope, which my brother had given me so long ago, hung like a pendulum around my neck.

The last patient I treated before I left the hospital again yesterday was a man who had fallen into a mirror, or been pushed: an unremarkable patient. His tolerance for pain did not impress me; his forehead, with its high widow's peak, was like a thousand others I had seen. When that patient screamed because his face was full of glass, I did not really hear him. I recorded what had happened to him, and a minute later, when I put the chart down at reception, I could not recall behind which curtain he slept, although in all my years of treating people I had never before forgotten anyone.

I had become useless, finally. Doctors must work in the present tense. I should have been able to tolerate it—imagining all those trapped civilians. But I could not, cannot. When I realised that that patient had become unimportant to me, that I had become unable to keep track of both my own life and the one I remembered half a world away, I knew that I should leave.

VARATHAN CALLED ME FROM Sri Lanka to say we should write a Report on the end of the war. Don't let them lie to you about rescue, he said. "Some of the soldiers reached their hands across the water to catch the Tamil civilians, and some of the Tiger cadres fired over people's heads when their superiors weren't looking so that they could flee," he told me. But you can tell who shot the fallen people, he explained: the army shot them from the front as they tried to reach safety, and the Tigers shot them in the back as they fled.

As they died, they called overseas on borrowed phones, while the Tigers listened to make sure they said the right things. "Here, call your brother overseas. Call your classmate, call your mother, say goodbye," they were told. When the Tigers' ranks dwindled and they no longer had enough bodies to control everything, some cadres spoke freely about what was happening. One village had moved with the Tigers many times, and had its sons among the cadre ranks. When their superiors weren't watching, they spoke into the receivers: if we let any civilians go the Tigers will kill our families.

Varathan said that as the government shelled them in the places they had declared safe, the Tigers made them burn money. Huge piles of banknotes ripped from necks, torn from hands. A bonfire of everything they had worked for, torched as terrible bait for someone to come and save them. When they were hungry—so hungry, so hungry—the story travelled from one civilian to the next, to Varathan, to me: a man in the No-Fire Zone sold his auto for three coconuts.

When the security forces finally defeated the Tigers, tens of thousands of civilians poured out of their prison and into illegal internment camps. But in the days before that, tens of thousands of others surely died, their bodies fallen on the fields of those battles. I don't believe in God. I realise now I never did. But I am Anjali's student, always. I believe that we could have done something else.

———

YEARS LATER, WHEN I return to Sri Lanka, Varathan will be an old man who has never left his country.

When he sees me again his eyes brim. His shock of hair has gone white, and under my palms I can feel the bones of his shoulders. I press my cheek to his. I know, because he has told me, that Anjali's photograph is still, after all this time, not on the *in memoriam* wall for faculty at the University of Jaffna. But he has brought Kumi, and in her face, I recognise her sister's sunlit smile.

The three of us ride for some hours in a white van that brings us to a jungle beyond which there is a beach.

"This is it," Varathan says. "It's not marked."

But they would not mark the No-Fire Zone, would they.

"That's a hospital they shelled." The driver points out the window. "They're building on top of it," he says.

There is no sign of the structure that was destroyed. Armed sentries guard either side of the road. Houses that haven't been looted yet, the driver says bitterly: that's what he thinks the sentries are guarding. Monsoon season, so there is the muck and there is the red northern mire. Past that, fences, and past those, piles and piles of mud-smeared clothing. They stand twice as high as I am tall, and I am a tall woman. And in all this ocean of trash, a shining lighthouse of aluminium: a heap of plates and cups. Place settings for last suppers. At the next field, melted and twisted bicycles, the impressions of bodies almost visible on them. A horizon of blackened, empty buses. Iyakkam buses, he says. Movement buses, empty and burned.

They were set on fire with people in them, he says.

Kumi puts her hand to her mouth. "I've never read that anywhere," she says.

"You won't read about that anywhere," the driver says. "That doesn't mean it didn't happen."

Someone will have to hear all of the stories of the people who say it did. And you will read about it somewhere, I promise you, if I have to write it myself. When we reach our destination, Chelvi will be there waiting. How far must we go? There is flooding, but at each stop the driver sticks his head out the window and asks if we can pass and never does anyone say no. The thin bridge across the Nandikadal Lagoon is low and water streams over it. He drives on, undaunted, and we look out the window. Down, down, down into the water. And then beyond that, at the shoreline, the beach where the tide laps, and the sky above it.

There are no microphones, no stage, no crowds, no priests, no clear signs of what has taken place here, except for all the survivors who know it did. You must understand: this is not the book for which Anjali died. You can find that book in your library. This is the one next to it on the shelf. I can promise you there will be another, and another. Whose stories will you believe? For how long will you listen? Tell me why you think you are here, and that will be as true as anything I can say.

AUTHOR'S NOTES
AND ACKNOWLEDGMENTS

A S YOU MAY UNDERSTAND IF YOU HAVE READ THIS FAR, IN alignment with the narrator of this novel, I have a complicated relationship with explanations. Who is required to give them, and why?

THAT SAID, A FEW NOTES:

Given her age, Sashi would not have had to complete a practical exam to enter medical school during her Advanced Levels; she would only have had a theoretical exam. The sharks, frogs, and other specimens of earlier days were preserved in formalin.

In a wild coincidence, one of the last lines I wrote in this novel was the one about Anjali's portrait not appearing on the *in memoriam* wall for faculty at the University of Jaffna. That same day, I saw that Rajani Thiranagama's photograph had, at long last, been placed on the wall in the Senior Common Room at the university.

At the moment I write this, Sri Lanka has come to a crossroads. In the wake of disastrous economic mismanagement by the government, the country is running short on fuel. Low-income communities are bearing the brunt of current hardships, including massive price hikes on essential goods. In response to these conditions, the Aragalaya movement, which takes its name from the Sinhala word for struggle, has drawn many Sri Lankans from different communities and classes together in protest. For months, they demanded the departures of the president and prime minister, and earlier this summer, Gotabhaya and Mahinda Rajapaksa, who were once thought politically invincible, finally resigned.

But within his first twenty-four hours in office, the new president, Ranil Wickremesinghe—a career politician and recent Rajapaksa ally who was elected by Parliament against the people's wishes—authorised a brutal assault on journalists and peaceful civilians at the #GotaGoGama protests. It bears mentioning that during the anti-Tamil Black July riots of 1983, Wickremesinghe was an MP, and his uncle J. R. Jayewardene was president.

As the Aragalaya movement continues, and as people struggle to live in Sri Lanka, I write in solidarity from Minneapolis.

I AM IMMEASURABLY GRATEFUL to my kind and brilliant editor at Penguin Random House, Caitlin McKenna, without whose support and keen eye I could not have finished. I have also been fortunate to work with Emma Caruso and Noa Shapiro, and appreciate their care with my words. I also thank Andy Ward, publisher; Avideh Bashirrad and Rachel Rokicki, deputy publishers; Mark Birkey, production editor; Donna Cheng, cover designer; Barbara Bachman, interior designer; Muriel Jorgensen, copy editor; Vanessa DeJesus, publicist; Madison Dettlinger, marketer; and Matthew Martin, lawyer. The support of British editor Isabel Wall and everyone at Viking UK has been invaluable.

Rebecca Shapiro, my first editor at PRH and a friend of almost forty years, acquired this book, and her faith in it sustained me during its earliest days. I have been beyond lucky to have my wonderful agent, Stephanie Cabot, as an ally and advocate for almost two decades. I am grateful for the support of the teams at Susanna Lea, in London and Paris.

As a work in progress, this book received support from the National Endowment for the Arts, the American Academy in Berlin, the University of Minnesota's Institute for Advanced Study, the Radcliffe Institute for Advanced Study at Harvard University, the Corporation of Yaddo, MacDowell, the Hermitage, and the Bennett Fellowship at Phillips Exeter Academy. I thank the incredible staff at these institutions, as well as the artists and scholars I met there.

Earlier versions of some sections appeared in *Granta, Ploughshares,* and *The Best American Nonrequired Reading* as short stories. Ted Hodgkinson, then at *Granta,* worked with me on an essay called "The Politics of Grief," a portion of which also appears in these pages, somewhat transformed. Many thanks to these publications and their editors.

I began this novel some eighteen years ago, and during that time, I spoke with many people who were extraordinarily generous with their time and knowledge. Among them: beloved friends, family, and more distant connections, all of whom shared valuable perspectives and information. Several of these people hosted me in their homes. I am indebted to them. I also note that the politics of this novel (and any errors) are entirely my own.

I also drew heavily on writing by University Teachers for Human Rights (Jaffna), especially *The Broken Palmyra,* and books by Rajan Hoole, including *Palmyra Fallen* and *Sri Lanka: The Arrogance of Power: Myths, Decadence & Murder;* as well as *Tigers of Lanka: From Boys to Guerrillas* and *Inside an Elusive Mind: Prabhakaran* by M. R. Narayan Swamy were key sources. I also read official reports from the United Nations and the Panel of Experts it appointed to investigate the end of the Sri Lankan civil war, the Lessons Learnt and Reconciliation Commission, the International Crisis Group, the Centre for Policy Alternatives, Groundviews, and other organisations. Writing and reporting by D.B.S. Jeyaraj, Namini Wijedasa, Gordon Weiss, Frances Harrison, Rohini Mohan, Mahendran Thiruvarangan, Meena Nallainathan, Meera Srinivasan, and others informed me.

I am grateful to Sharika Thiranagama, Narmada Thiranagama, Nirmala Rajasingam, and Sumi Kailasapathy, who generously read drafts of this book and shared feedback. I am also thankful for conversations with Chinniah Rajeshkumar, Sivamohan Sumathy, and Sarvam Kailasapathy.

I also thank Ahilan Kadirgamar, Sanjana Hattotuwa, Hasanthika Sirisena, Mythri Jegathesan, Ashwini Vasanthakumar, Mathumai Sivasubramanian, Kitana Ananda, Vivek Bharathan, YaliniDream, Vasuki Nesiah, Suppiramaniam Nanthikesan, M. Niranjan, Sunila Galappatti, Amiththan Sebarajah, Romesh Gunesekera, Shreen Saroor, Srikumar Kanagaratnam, and Sashi Selvendran. I have appreciated exchanges with my colleagues in the American Institute for Sri Lankan Studies and Lanka Solidarity.

Danielle Crickman, my research assistant at Skidmore College, was cheerful, conscientious, and unfailingly helpful.

From 2009 to 2014 I taught in the University of Michigan's Helen Zell Writers' Program. My position and time there were made possible by the support of Helen Zell, to whom I owe a thousand thanks. Deepest appreciation for my colleagues, who made Ann Arbor feel like home. Farina Mir and Will Glover welcomed me to the Center for South Asian Studies. Geoffrey Martin, South Asia librarian, provided resources and ideas.

At Radcliffe, several people—including Patrick Keating, Tyrell Haberkorn, Meghan O'Rourke, ZZ Packer, Irmtrud Wojak, Ben Miller, and the human rights discussion group—provided invaluable feedback. Thank you also to Nick Fandos, who read a draft and gave me notes. Dear friends Juliet Schor and Prasannan Parthasarathi extended warmth and hospitality.

I thank my colleagues at the University of Minnesota, in the English department and the MFA program in creative writing. Special gratitude to Kathryn Nuernberger, Douglas Kearney, Kimberley Todd, Julie Schumacher, Charles Baxter, Josephine Lee, Andrew Elfenbein, and Holly Vanderhaar. Several affiliates of the Human Rights Program shared thoughts on an excerpt; thanks especially to Barbara Frey, and to Steve Meili and Leigh Payne, who hosted a memorable evening conversation.

In memory of my late colleague Qadri Ismail, who offered the warmth of his friendship, hospitality, argument, and encouragement. Gratitude for conversations with students past and present.

When I was physically unable to type, others did it for me. Thank you to Caroline Casey, Carolyn Byrne, Han Mallek, Hannah Karau, and Travis Workman. William Solboe, of the University of Minnesota's Disability Resource Center, made sure that I had what I needed.

Thanks to friends who provided feedback and encouragement: Tricia Khleif, Lacy Johnson, Natalie Bakopoulos, Beth Nguyen, Jeremiah Chamberlain, Catherine Shoichet, Jessica Benko, Prasanna Puwanarajah, Yiyun Li, Catherine Nichols, Megan Bernhard, Emily Halpern, Tracy Manaster, Catherine Cafferty, Jody Caldwell, Rebecca Lehmann, James Renfro, RO Kwon, Nawaaz Ahmed, Ken Chen, Mary Anne Mohanraj, Tahmima Anam, Leslie Jamison, Joanna Luloff, Sejal Shah, Nam Le, Mira Jacob, Bennett Sims, Padma Viswanathan, Vauhini Vara, Andrew Altschul, Greg Hrbek, Preeta Samarasan, Asali Solomon, Sarah Rogers, Rebecca Trissler, Michelle Falkoff, Megan Levad, Tung-Hui Hu, Keith Taylor, A. Van Jordan, Khaled Mattawa, Cody Walker, Polly Rosenwaike, Danielle Evans, Celeste Ng, Brit Bennett, Mara Hvistendahl, Jessica Nordell, Sally Franson, Lesley Arimah, Erin White, Curtis Sittenfeld, and Whitney Terrell, who is also an excellent person with whom to co-host a podcast. In memory of Erik Lemke and Matthew Power.

Thanks also to pals Natalie Tronson, Katherine Currie, Sarah Gollust, Ezra Golberstein, Jacob Kurlander, Dorothy Gotlib, Shobita Parthasarathy, Kira Thurman. Vivian Choi and Caroline Casey, for all kinds of sustenance. Maggie Hennefeld, Sonali Pahwa, Lorenzo Fabbri, Jennie Row, Joe Farag, Ainsley Boe, Suvadip Sinha, Siri Suh, Daniel and Hannah Baxter, Nima Paidipaty, Mandira Banerjee and Aswin Punathambekar, Shazia Iftkhar, Chamindika Wanduragala, Krishna and Ben Lewis, Marion Greene and Bart Cannon. Georgeanna and Katherine Lewis offered me a place to go when I really needed one. Tami, David, Georgia, and Olivia Federlein, the neighbors you want in a pinch. I am grateful for Small Twitter's big welcome.

Special thanks to Peter Ho Davies, Eileen Pollack, Elizabeth McCracken, and Lan Samantha Chang, for kindness, encouragement, wisdom, and friendship. Gratitude also to James Hynes, Marilynne Robinson, Margot Livesey, and Ethan Canin, as well as Connie Brothers, Deb West, and Jan Zenisek. In memory of James Alan McPherson and Frank Conroy, both of whom encouraged me when this project was in its earliest stages.

Many beloved people passed away during the years in which I wrote this. Two in particular had an influence on this book: in loving memory, Ganesh Uncle, and also Saro Maami, who handed me *The Broken Palmyra* twenty years ago.

Love to: Meera and Chirag, Kaavya and Kabir; Kanthan, Michelle, Ian and Nicole; Devan, Chrissy, Maya, and Asha. Philli and Immi. (I promise not to say "I'm finishing the book!" for a while, and I am sorry that it's possible to finish a book so many times.) Kunju. (Who knew I was a dog person?)

Amma and Appa, of course and always.

And Travis Workman, who was beside me in every way as I typed the last words.

—V. V. Ganeshananthan, July 2022